I0823384

LAST SEEN

ALSO BY CHRISTOPHER CASTELLANI

A Kiss from Maddalena

The Saint of Lost Things

All This Talk of Love

The Art of Perspective

Leading Men

LAST SEEN

A Novel

Christopher Castellani

VIKING

VIKING
An imprint of Penguin Random House LLC
1745 Broadway, New York, NY 10019
penguinrandomhouse.com

Grateful acknowledgment is made for permission to reprint "Short Talk on Walking Backwards" from *Short Talks*, which was first published by Brick Books, © 1992 by Anne Carson. Reprinted by permission of Anne Carson and Aragi Inc. All rights reserved.

Designed by Alexis Sulaimani

LIBRARY OF CONGRESS CATALOGING-IN-PUBLICATION DATA
Names: Castellani, Christopher, 1972– author
Title: Last seen : a novel / Christopher Castellani.
Description: New York, NY : Viking, 2026.
Identifiers: LCCN 2025020244 (print) | LCCN 2025020245 (ebook) | ISBN 9798217061037 hardcover | ISBN 9798217061044 ebook
Subjects: LCGFT: Fiction | Novels
Classification: LCC PS3603.A875 L37 2026 (print) | LCC PS3603.A875 (ebook) | DDC 813/.6—dc23/eng/20250626
LC record available at https://lccn.loc.gov/2025020244
LC ebook record available at https://lccn.loc.gov/2025020245

Printed in the United States of America
1st Printing

The authorized representative in the EU for product safety and compliance is Penguin Random House Ireland, Morrison Chambers, 32 Nassau Street, Dublin D02 YH68, Ireland, https://eu-contact.penguin.ie.

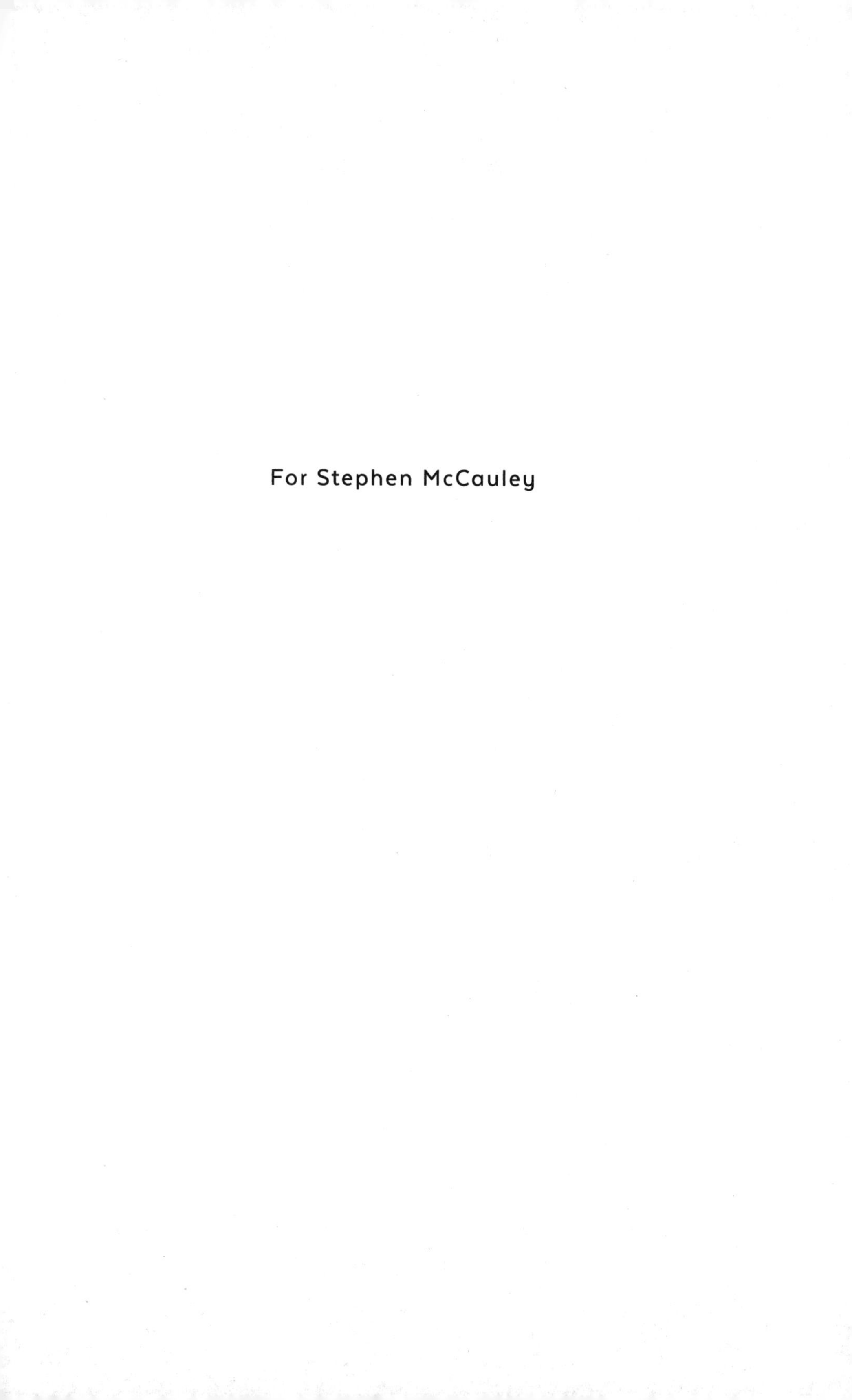

For Stephen McCauley

My mother forbad us to walk backwards. That is how the dead walk, she would say. Where did she get this idea? Perhaps from a bad translation. The dead, after all, do not walk backwards but they do walk behind us. They have no lungs and cannot call out but would love for us to turn around. They are victims of love, many of them.

ANNE CARSON,
"SHORT TALK ON WALKING BACKWARDS"

CONTENTS

LAST SEEN

CRIME SEEN

Late afternoon, Caleb driving south on a country road. Vermont, maybe, or he's already crossed into New York. It's the first week of winter and snow is falling fast. Now faster. Wind rattles the car doors. A major storm, the radio says. Avoid unnecessary travel. He turns up the heat, blasts his music. Nobody's around until the truck speeds up behind him and follows him so close that their bumpers nearly touch. Caleb squints into the rearview mirror. The old man at the wheel flicks his high beams on and off and ticks his head toward the shoulder, urging him onto it. Because no one has a guiltier conscience, Caleb immediately figures he's done something wrong: run over the old man's dog or blown through a stop sign or, worse—because no one has a bigger heart—that the guy's lost or in trouble. A flat tire, a stroke.

Safely on the shoulder, Caleb watches him step down from his truck, walk toward his car in his heavy boots, and knock on the driver's-side window. But it's only when the man is up close, his face framed by his furry hooded parka, that Caleb finally recognizes him. From where, though? Online? The Gaze? He can't quite place the man. Or maybe he knows him quite well. Either way, he seems kind enough. Jolly. *Avuncular.* A word Caleb always loved.

"You shouldn't be out in this mess," the man says, stepping back to survey Caleb's Toyota. "Your tires are as bald as I am. Ever heard of black ice? It's sneaky. I can drive you where you need to go."

"All the way to Poughkeepsie?" Caleb says, like the refrain of a folk song. "Don't worry, this baby's tougher than she looks." He pats the dashboard. His mom and dad are waiting for him back home, he explains to the man; he was supposed to be there yesterday, and today's Christmas Eve, so he can't be any later. "It's super kind of you, though," Caleb says, flashing that wide, flirty smile. "Really, I'll be fine."

The man's face falls. He looks about to cry.

Caleb turns his wipers back on. Ice has crusted the blades. The snow has already covered the tire tracks on the empty road ahead. *Okay*, he's about to suggest. *How about you follow me as far as the interstate.* Would that make you feel better? But by then the man's hands are already around his throat. He's stuck the needle in the boy's arm. Or he's held the sweet-smelling rag over his nose and mouth. However he does it, he must act quickly now. He ties Caleb's ankles and wrists, wraps him in a tarp, carries him to the trunk of the Toyota, and drops him in it.

James has imagined this day so many times, in so many variations, that the events have come to feel like his own memories. In one of these almost-memories, the man lays Caleb on his stomach in the back seat of the Toyota and tucks him in with a black-and-red blanket up to his shoulders, so that he appears to be sleeping. Once the boy is settled, the man speeds off with him, leaving his truck in the turnout for later. He swerves along the slippery roads, watching for black ice, one hand on the wheel and the other reaching back to run his fingers through Caleb's blond curls. It's a short distance to the house in the deep woods.

Because James can't bear to follow the man inside, he ends the scene at the door of the house. How can he even half-see what the man is doing through the dark windows, or the look on his face when he drags the body to the quarry?

Instead, James starts the day over in his mind. He wakes up not as himself, but as Caleb. It's that same morning more than twelve years ago, December 24, 2007. He throws on Caleb's gray cable sweater and his barn jacket with the green corduroy collar. He scrapes the ice from the front and back windshields of the Toyota, but he's too lazy to do the roof and the side windows even though James continually stresses their importance safety-wise. He has plenty of gas, having just filled the tank the night before at the Sunoco on State Street in Rutland, where, according to the police report, at 7:22 p.m. he handed a guy named Mo Blevins his Mastercard. At a stoplight, he texts James forty-three awful words he doesn't mean and instantly regrets, then tosses his BlackBerry onto the passenger seat, puts in one of his Belle and Sebastian CDs, sings along to the maudlin lyrics he knows by heart, panics about the forty-three words and the intensifying snow and the wind and the gunmetal sky. He takes what he hopes is a shortcut on the country road, almost turns back, almost calls James. Then he notices the truck in the rearview mirror, the high beams, and has the sense, immediately, that he's done something wrong, that someone's in trouble, so he pulls over, rolls down his window, feels relieved when he recognizes—or thinks he recognizes—the man's avuncular face . . .

A boy like him goes missing every day, and then a week, a month, a year later, he floats to the surface of some frozen river. Most of the boys get found, get solved, eventually, but in all this time no one has found Caleb Aldrich. Or his gray Toyota. Or the gifts James gave him the day before when, alone in their room at the Cactus Tree Motel, they stole six hours from the outside world and called it Christmas.

Once James learned how many lost and found young men there were, he looked for them everywhere. Alone in his upstairs office while Iris, his wife, slept in their bedroom below, he secretly read every article he could find, watched the documentaries and YouTube interviews about the so-called Smiley Face Killers, the network of murderers who targeted college-aged boys. He pored over the evidence two detectives named Duarte and Gannon displayed on charts and maps. He lurked on message boards and posted in Reddit groups under multiple usernames. He created fake Facebook profiles so he could join community search groups in cities he had no intention of traveling to: Pittsburgh, Des Moines, Bloomington. In his real life, whatever that is, James Hahn is no detective; he works in the Middlebury College Library as an archivist, a job well suited to his impulse to preserve and document and catalogue, which he does meticulously with—for?—the histories of these boys, their hometowns and ages and heights and weights and photos and last-known whereabouts and causes of death. Even at his most feverish, as he was in those first blinkered years after Caleb disappeared, James never truly believed he'd solve these cases, only that, in some magical way, his attention and devotion to them keeps the search alive—a search in which, given his connection to the boy, he could take no part.

Before they go cold, cases mostly solve themselves. After they do, James lets them go, leaves the boys in peace. He rarely reopens the files of the confirmed suicides and accidents, which most of the so-called Smiley Face drownings turn out to be. It's the unfound or unsolved boys who haunt him, the ones found floating on their backs in the water, arms crossed over their chests; the ones who, like Caleb, were last seen laughing, cheering, full of life.

Once in a while, usually after a new boy is discovered, he gets a message on the alias Gmail account he uses to communicate with Derrick and George, two other men who knew Caleb, and who are now, like James, hobbyists, dabblers in the same lurid genre. The message usually includes a link, or an attachment, or a cut-and-pasted obituary from the local newspaper of a Rust Belt city. What does James think of this one, they ask. What does James think of that one.

What James thinks is: *Where are you, Caleb? What really happened to you?*

What he writes back to Derrick and George is, *Hmm.* Or, *That poor kid.* Or, *Reminds me of the Leo Ridgeway case.*

To know a thing that has not happened to you, to even approach whatever truth there is to it, you have to imagine it from as many sides as possible. Which is why, sometimes, when James starts Christmas Eve 2007, over again in his mind, he forces himself to live in the skin of the old man in the truck. As an old man himself, pushing sixty, James feels a kinship of sorts with him. A boy of unspeakable beauty came into their lives. The boy shone his light on them for a while, teased them with his screen name and his holiday plans and his batting eyes and his deferential nature. The effortlessness of the boy's beauty, its extravagance, its easy generosity, dazzled them; it reminded them of something they'd lost or never had or would never have; it made their own uselessness visible; it made them snap.

By the grace of God, or so the saying went, this is where James's kinship with the man ends.

After this other man met Caleb, James imagines, he started following him everywhere. He slept in his truck outside the boy's dorm, in the parking lot of the Cactus Tree Motel, in the field down the road from Derrick's. He'd been ready to follow Caleb all the way to Poughkeepsie. The snowstorm wasn't just a stroke of luck; to him it was a sign, an excuse to talk to the boy again, to warn him about his tires, and the dangers of black ice, and texting while driving, and leading older guys on. Mostly he just wanted to see Caleb's eyes again up close, to dive into them as into a summer lake. That was it. In his life until then, this man, like James, had never hurt a soul.

He stepped on the gas, flashed his lights.

Afterward, it must have surprised the man what a taste and a talent he had for it: hurting someone, getting away with it. The satisfaction of punishment, the rush of escape. Maybe he woke in the middle of the night with blood in his mouth. Maybe he figured other men had the same taste, and once he started looking, with the help of the internet, he found them easily. Smiley Face? They move around the country, he and his friends, sometimes alone, sometimes together, targeting boys who look like Caleb, who command the attention nobody shows them anymore, slipping GHB into their drinks, tracking them down unlit streets, and then drowning them in the nearest river. The man relocates a few hundred miles every couple years or so, thinking maybe he'll lose the taste in Saint Paul, in Boston, in Green Bay, but there are so many of these boys, their beauty is everywhere. He can't escape them, and he doesn't want to. One day, of course, he'll be too old to catch them, to lift them. He'll need a new knee, a new hip. He'll grow forgetful. Eventually, finally, James believes, he'll slip up, and get caught, and the full extent of his depravity and pain will be revealed. Maybe then, somehow, Caleb will reappear. In the meantime, James has only his articles and files and almost-memories.

Sometimes it's Derrick behind the wheel of the truck. Sometimes it's George in the front doorway of the house in the woods. For years James distrusted these men, and others like them, and shut them out. The double lives they led, their irreconcilable desires, their infatuation with boys like Caleb, reminded James too much of his own. He's not so paranoid anymore. He considers the men comrades, if not friends. He wonders sometimes how much they even remember of Caleb, of whom they rarely speak.

Today he has a message from Derrick on one of his Gmail accounts. He hasn't checked this account since early March, just before the Middlebury campus shut down and people started working from home. *First and most importantly*, Derrick's message begins, *I hope you and your wife are healthy*. He's symptom-free so far, he says, and so are all the guys he's heard from. Fingers crossed. He closed the Gaze just in case, even locked his front and back doors for the first time since he moved to Vermont. He's scared, he admits, the way he hasn't been since the '80s. Anyway, he asks, did James see this latest missing boy, Matthew Cardullo? All-American, handsome, Smiley Face written all over him? He just came upon it himself, Derrick says, but from now on he'll be monitoring. Maybe they could talk on the phone, or try that Zoom thing? He's not great with the computer, but he figures it's time he learns. I'm scared, Derrick repeats. It feels like the end of the world all over again.

The name Matthew Cardullo links to a video story from February 27 on Detroit's WDIV News. James puts his earbuds in and presses Play. A two-minute report on a University of Michigan junior, last seen stumbling out of a bar in Ann Arbor, his car found a few blocks away. His mother at the kitchen table shoving his framed photo at the cameraman, angry at the cops for sitting on their asses. His mustached and roly-poly father silently beside her, rubbing her shoulder. A reporter on the front steps of a grand academic building of white stone columns, reading quotes from professors and teammates. A model student. A leader. Nicest guy you'll ever meet.

James has just started a reply to Derrick—*Well, here we go again . . .*—when he hears Iris on the stairs, calling him to dinner.

LAST SEEN

I am one of those boys they keep finding in the river. For now, I am floating at the surface of the Huron, somewhere in Ann Arbor, my arms hugging my chest like I'm trying to keep warm, watching the slow progress of clouds through a thick window of ice. I am waiting to be pulled onto shore, delivered into the arms of my mother, to see my name, Matthew Cardullo, in the papers one last time, not with the words STILL MISSING above my senior portrait, but with the dates of my life: December 18, 1999–February 23, 2020. I am waiting to be solved. I am waiting, like you, like everyone, for the end of the story. In the meantime: sunrise, moonrise, rain, helicopters, flashes of birds, the smudged *lacrimulae* of stars, all of it beautiful and horrible and wild and fucking tedious, same as it was in the Before.

Day and night as I float and let the current carry me to a place where I will be found, I am listening to the other boys, and when their voices get too loud and annoying, I practice my declensions.

Lacrimulārum. Lacrimulīs. I was loud, too, when I got here, kicking my feet as I plunged through the frigid water, screaming and thrashing in the mud at the bottom of the river, trying to wriggle off my heavy coat, calling out to the boys I could hear but not yet see in the blackness. Where was I? What was happening to me? Weeks ago. Months. A year? Time does still matter here, even if we have no way to measure it, even though it keeps leaping out of our hands and disappearing in the muck, like that pet frog I had for a single day when I was ten, Fritzie I called him. I chased that little fucker up and down Quail Creek one of those endless summer afternoons you get a million of when you're a kid and never again, and I swear Fritzie made a game out of it, winking back at me before hopping away, turning up behind me somehow, letting me hold him cupped in my chubby hands and then flying off to a rock in the middle of the creek. Anyway, I'm figuring out that's the slippery way time works for us here, now, like it's teasing us and tricking us and won't care one bit when it's finally done with us.

I'd been writing a paper on Catullus for my junior seminar. I'd been consistently repping two-fifty on my max bench set. I'd been showing up on time, more or less, to my job at the library circulations desk. I'd been at the Ravens Club reaping the rewards of my fake ID, hoping Tessa would show up and forgive me and invite me back to her apartment. And then, out of nowhere, I wasn't. I was walking on Packard, checking the side streets for her car, worrying it broke down again and she hadn't charged her phone, like always, and as a last resort I started to call her friend Chloe, who hated me, and then, like I said, I wasn't.

You'd think I'd mind my circumstances more than I do, but, for now, I don't. I feel nothing, or, at least, I feel even less than I used to, and nobody ever accused me of being a person of deep emotions, except in regard to Tessa. Mostly I'm curious what's going to happen next. So far it's not lonely, there are so many of us around, more than fifty now, and that's fifty lives, so there's a lot to talk about. Fifty guys times twenty-ish years of age, a whole millennium of history to cover. Some of the guys get really confessional. Some never stop crying. Some are just dickheads. Like I said, same as it was in the Before. Some are blurrier than others, their bodies almost indistinguishable from the water, and their voices are faint, like the volume on their mics have been turned down. We can't understand them, but we can tell they're shouting, that they know something. The guys like me who are still clear, still loud, have the most to say, even though we know the least. My mom would say that's typical of men in general.

The only times I really mind, or get big deep feelings like loneliness or fear or anger and start to cry, are when I look in on her, my mom. So I won't anymore. That's one lesson I've learned and the first lesson I try to teach other new guys like me: don't think too hard about the people you miss, and don't look in on the one you've been given, no matter how much you want to, not your mom or dad or kid brother or best friend or girlfriend. Definitely not your girlfriend. Most definitely not your ex-girlfriend. The guys who never stop crying are the ones who can't learn that simple lesson, who don't have the kind of self-control and discipline that I do. I'm the type of person who can set his mind to any task and stick to it. Anyway, the first time I did look in on my mom should have taught me never to look again. You'd think I'd have found her sitting on the edge of the bathtub with no clothes on or something, screaming and ripping her hair out and calling my name and cursing God or whatever, like they do in the movies when a kid goes missing, but no, she was just on our couch watching TV, some dumb rerun of *Three's Company*, and she was laughing her ass off with a half-eaten plate of nachos next to her right on the cushion. Caleb said not to analyze it, that was just her specific way of coping, that everyone grieves in a different language, that I caught her at the wrong time, but I know that's not how I'd be, ever, if the situation were reversed. I'd be out in the streets every minute of every day looking for her, knocking on every door, sending out fucking *bloodhounds*. I'd never give up and I know for sure I'd never laugh again.

Caleb's the guy I listen to most. I guess you could say he's my best friend here. He's in Dog River, over in Vermont, a state I never got to travel to, though the way he describes it, all green trees and wood cabins, it sounds a lot like Michigan with moose. He's one of the few smart ones like me, into languages and history and music. He was going to be a diplomat. I hate saying this, and of course I'd never say this to him, but no one's ever going to find Caleb. He's knotted up in so many vines on the floor of the Dog, his entire body trapped under what must be a giant boulder, stuck there since the very first night, his only view for weeks, months (years?), the silty dark swishing with bass and trout and catfish that nibble at him and move on, freer than he is and will ever be.

Sometimes I worry more about Caleb than I do myself, because he's a better person than I am, and I get to wondering who I'd choose if I could save just one of us. Like, who'd have been better for the world? Caleb's the kind of guy you'd have wanted to live a long life, to accomplish all the big plans he had in his head. We talk a lot about what we might have made of ourselves, and how we'd probably never have met if it weren't for this. We agree that, at most, one day we might have passed each other on the streets of Paris or something, me on vacation with my wife and kids, him on his way to some embassy. I'd have wanted my wife and kids to be cultured. He'd have wanted the leaders of major industrialized nations to adopt his policy on greenhouse gases. We'd have brushed shoulders or nodded at each other on the Rue de la BlahBlahBlah, or maybe I'd have tried to ask him in French where the nearest bathroom was, but that would have been it.

Instead, here's what happened to Caleb. He was on his way home to Poughkeepsie for Christmas, but he couldn't face his parents, so he stopped at this place called the Gaze. An old guy named Derrick lived there in the upstairs rooms; he'd found Caleb online and given him directions, said it would be a good place to meet people who understood him the way he did. The Gaze wasn't a real bar like Ravens, but a rambling white-shingled shack, a secret hangout that served drinks for cash only, no credit cards, nothing to trace, fifty miles northeast of Middlebury, where Caleb went to school. He figured it couldn't hurt to take a short detour to say hi in real life to Derrick, who was the friendliest and least creepy of the guys he'd been chatting with in the Vermontm4m AOL chat room. Derrick, who hadn't once even asked Caleb to send a pic or describe his genitals, who fixed poor people's teeth for free and lobbied his congressmen for better sustainable farming policy; Derrick, who, when Caleb showed up at his door, threw his arms around him and pulled him close like he was the Prodigal Son. They'd sat for a while on rocking chairs on the creaky covered porch watching the sunset over the Green Mountains and Derrick made some phone calls from the rotary phone on the table beside him and then, one by one, every half hour or so, men rolled up in pickups. With every man's arrival, Caleb and Derrick split another beer, and he made sure not to drink from any can or glass Derrick or one of the other guys wasn't drinking from, but he didn't have anything to worry about from these guys, he thought, and he liked talking to them; they had stories and human interests; they were mechanics and snowplow drivers and innkeepers, men like the ones he'd known in Poughkeepsie, nothing at all like the kids in his classes and the sailing club at Middlebury. Most were family men with children his age. They called their wives when it got late, and by then Caleb was too drunk to drive all the way to his mom's—he didn't know what he'd been thinking, going so far out of his way, the opposite direction in fact—so he crashed on the couch in Derrick's living room under an afghan in front of a fire, which is the last thing he remembers before waking up in Dog River.

That's Caleb. The next-smartest guy I'd say is Leo Ridgeway (Rum River, outside Minneapolis), followed by Steven Donovan (Charles River, Boston). Then, if I'm being honest, we go off a steep cliff, intelligence-wise. I don't want you to think I'm a snob. I don't typically go around ranking guys based on their IQ. But you lose your tolerance for bullshit when you're in a fucked-up situation such as ours. You find your people quick. It's obvious. Like in World War I, and I guess the other big wars, too, those guys in the trenches, I'm sure they didn't all love each other or get along equally, especially once they got out of their foxholes and started their lives proper and had families and wrote each other letters. My point is they had an unbreakable bond, which is why fifty sixty seventy years later they still put on their uniforms and meet up with each other at ceremonies and reenactments and banquets until there's only one super-old guy left standing up on the stage all shrunken and stooped under the weight of his medals. No matter how much of a dickhead some of them could be (like Ryan Sumter, who's in the Susquehanna, or Brian Price, not far from me in the Owl Kill, a guy I actually knew in high school and stayed far the fuck away from), those war guys recognized the fact that they were stuck with each other forever, and that, when they get the chance to stand next to any one of their buddies on a stage, they should take it.

The big difference between the soldiers and us, of course, is that we didn't do anything brave.

Imagine you're in the nuthouse and all you've got to entertain yourself is an old-fashioned radio, and the only thing you're able to do twenty-four hours a day, seven days a week is scan the stations, except the stations aren't music or sports or news but different guys broadcasting from their own nuthouses all over the country. Some will be more entertaining than others, right? Some will be boring as hell. So mostly I tune into the more interesting guys who've got something to say, Caleb and Leo and Steve, which I can accomplish by closing my eyes and concentrating on them and listening for them and kind of calling out to them with my mind. *Summoning* is the word Leo coined for it. When we summon, we see each other in our bodies floating, even Steve and Leo in their blurriness, and they can see me and Caleb clear as day, and their voices get louder and sharper and then come through perfectly clear. It's like I've knocked on a door and stepped into the dorm room where we're hanging out, and they're like, *hey*, and I'm like, *hey*, and we tell stories and talk about whatever—stupid stuff, heavy stuff, dirty stuff, school stuff, family stuff—and the other guys, a few dozen it seemed like at first but it's probably more, are always around somewhere, but we don't let them into that dorm-y space with us. They're like the chatter I used to hear through the walls of my real dorm: guys having nightmares or talking on their cell phones or muttering to themselves in the hallway on the way to the lav.

Or, like I said, crying. Always someone, many someones, crying, in every form of the word you can look up on Thesaurus.com: wailing, bleating, bawling, blubbering, sniveling, howling, whimpering.

It's like living in a day care center, says Caleb.

This is living? says Steve.

It might be better than living, says Leo.

Because we're souls? asks Caleb.

Is that what we are?

Soul brothers?

Soul food?

Lost souls?

Found souls, Leo offers, Mr. Bright Side Leo, who'd been miserable in the Before and trying in his own way to get here, or a place like here, a place of beyondness, for years, slowly cutting toward it, toward us, one sharp blade at a time. He used to drive to parking lots with his brown leather bag of razors and cotton pads on the seat beside him like a girl he was taking on a date. He'd park in a corner under a broken streetlamp and pull down his shorts and slice a perfect em dash, just enough to feel the jolt from the inside of his thigh to his throat, that gulp of hard air like he'd bolted upright from a bad dream, except *this* was the bad dream—the car, the busted light, his nonstop mind, his junkie mother, everything but the jolt. Then he'd write in a spiral notebook, blasting heat from the vents and his Brujeria CD from the speakers, until the gas meter got to the line just before the *E* or a security van pulled in, whichever came first.

Until, one night, willing but unready, blindly pacing the woods behind the parking lot of the Light of Christ Church, Leo found himself at the bottom of the Rum, swallowing the frigid water and then breathing it back out as expertly as a fish, feeling, unlike every other one of us, not terror, not surprise, but the jolt, that same rush of relief of the blade slicing the skin. The woods fell away and his vision went black and he kicked his feet and flapped his arms until some unfamiliar instinct told him not to swim or fight but to float, to rest, and, when he did, the first words that came to him were not *what the fuck* (that was Caleb), or *who pushed me, I'll kill him* (that was Steve), or *Mom! Mom!* (that was me), but *finally, yes, thank you God thank you thank you.*

Most of us believe this fucked-up situation to be Death. A few of us, Leo and sometimes Caleb and sometimes me, have convinced ourselves it's Real Life, and that the Before, what we *used* to call Real Life, aka Our Lives, was actually Pre-Life, a kind of practice test. Practice for what, and when the final exam was scheduled, though, nobody can say. We are waiting forever and forever waiting for the next part. The big divides are among the guys who think it will be better, the guys who think it will be worse, and the guys who think there is no "next part" at all, that this yapping and floating and gradual blurring and fading of voices isn't some Between Life but our permanent condition, a never-ending frat party without the beer pong or the girls or the community service. And then among that particular group of guys, there's another, deeper, divide between the ones who think it's a punishment and the ones who think it's a reward.

There's even this one dude, Jeremy, in the Connecticut, who believes we're in some sort of superhero cryogenic incubation bath, orchestrated by aliens and/or the United States government, and that the reason we don't hear as much from the blurry guys, the reason why their voices go faint and gibberishy, is because they got pulled out and solved and they're off fighting crime back in their old neighborhoods or on some distant planet. They're fucking *busy*, says Jeremy, with the confidence of the dim and underinformed. I wish I could tell you Jeremy is the youngest, but the sad truth is that he's twenty-three and what my mom used to call "touched." The other sad truth is that sometimes I choose to think Jeremy is a prophet, that we're not dead but *recruited*, that this viscous numbing liquid above and below and all around me every minute isn't the same stupid Huron I used to swim and tube and piss in, but a magic soup of space nutrients brewed by an intergalactic creature monitoring me *right now* with one of the thousand eyes in its mile-wide Death Star–like head, pulling levers and pressing buttons to mold me, transform me, prep me for great acts of heroism and valor the likes of which even my honors-level brain can't yet comprehend.

No matter what you believe, Leo is always reminding us, you can't deny that, in the Before, we were just ourselves, measly people with one measly little life, stuck in a measly body that could see and hear and touch only what was directly in front of it. If you really think about our former selves, he says, we were pathetic, like our parents' old computers, with functionality as basic as two plus two, just heavy clunky calculators. *Now look at us!* He's almost singing. *Measly no more! Look at how much we can see and hear! Look at what we can do!*

Yeah, look at me, says Steve.

It took me a while to warm up to Steve, mainly because he's not the smartest in our quad, at least when it comes to books and school, and he's definitely the scariest—that is, until I figured out how badly he needs everyone to like him, especially the ones who fear him. He talks like a total bully, one of those guys who you think slams the nerdy kid into his locker on a daily basis. But the more you hear from Steve, you realize he'd never do that to a kid. Some guys just get the crawlies, and the only way they can get rid of them is to inflict pain on someone else, or fantasize about the pain they'll inflict when they get the chance. Some of my wrestling buddies were like that. Steve was the type who'd buy that nerdy kid an ice-cream cone after school, who'd slip him money to fix the glasses the bully smashed. Even so, you can't make Steve Donovan cry or hope, and you can't get him to stop calling the rest of us fags whenever we do, and you can't convince him that the world isn't one fat raw deal for him and every other white guy without a Harvard degree or family money to live off of. The guy's funny as hell, though, and sappy like a drunk "I love you, man" bro, whether he means to be or not, with one of those crazy *Good Will Hunting* Boston accents, and he does have this intelligence, like I said, not genius like in that movie, an old-man kind of intelligence. To Steve, all teachers are lazy and college is for chumps and Caleb, had he lived, would have wasted his life trying to save the planet from its slow but totally unpreventable collapse. Needless to say, Caleb's not Steve's number one fan, but Steve shows Caleb no personal disrespect other than the gay jokes, which he applies to all of us anyway, and listening to them talk shit to each other and argue about politics and history and the Real World versus the Ivory Tower helps pass the time.

The last thing Steve remembers, he says, was standing outside the Bell in Hand Tavern smoking a cigarette. He was looking across the cobblestoned street into the window of the Green Dragon, where the woman he'd been fucking in the afternoons—his boss, Monica—was dancing with her husband. Steve had followed Monica to the Green Dragon on a Saturday night not to spy on her or inflict any damage on the husband, whose name was Arthur. The guy was already such a sad sack with his horseshoe balding head and his gut spilling over his designer jeans that Steve wouldn't give him the satisfaction of a fat lip, even though he deserved one just for existing. Steve went to the Green Dragon not for Arthur but to see how Monica acted around her husband, how different it would be from how she acted around him, the man she actually loved, except that when Steve saw them together, it was Arthur he couldn't take his eyes off of: his chunky watch, his shirt unbuttoned to the tits like he wasn't a fat-ass middle-aged limp-dick cuck, his hairy arm around Monica's neck in a grizzly headlock. The sight of Arthur made Steve so sick to his stomach that he was about to puke right there on the cobblestoned streets of Old Boston. But then instead of puking he felt a stab of pain in his neck, and he dropped his cigarette, which somehow landed not on the sidewalk of Union Street but floated away from him in the Charles River a mile off. And now he wasn't only about to freeze to death—*who pushed me, I'll kill him*—he was fucking *littering*, a thing he hated, a thing he'd never do, because he was going to be the mayor or a crypto trader or a celebrity chef, or maybe the first mayor-crypto-trader-celebrity-chef in history, and Boston was an awesome place he wasn't going to let get ruined by soulless zillionaire developers like Arthur Binswanger. Saving anybody or anything was impossible, though, Steve complained, and just for trying he'd ended up in this shithole of a purgatory or Cryogenic Superhero Incubator or Poor Man's Heaven or whatever it was, and all that time picking up people's pizza plates from the street and placing them in trash cans two feet away where they belonged, and all that time on the internet reading up on the disintermediation of currency and filling out online applications for desk jobs nobody called him back for, and all that well-paid time tutoring a rich little boy who couldn't speak and all that minimum-wage time at the Boys & Girls Club playing kickball with kids of deadbeat drugged-out parents—in other words, all that time spent doing the stuff Monica Binswanger, she of the coconut-scented hair and wrists of gold bracelets that made music when she raised them above her head, said made him a "piece of work with a piece that worked really great"—turned out to be one big fucking waste.

We should be screaming, says Steve. We should be on fire. Plotting revenge. Figuring shit out. *Doing something.* Not crying for our moms and pops who never did jack shit for us except make promises they couldn't keep. Don't get him started on priests, nuns, teachers, principals, bosses, coaches, army recruiters, Big Brothers, Big Sisters, social workers, rich aunts, pervy uncles, or any fucking *counselor.* He never trusted anybody but himself, he said, never counted on anything but his own brain and body, until Monica and Arthur Binswanger came along and messed with his head.

He should have killed them both when he had the chance, he says.

But I don't believe him. The guys here who talk rough like that, and there are lots of them, are just blowing smoke. In my experience, the guys with the biggest mouths run away the fastest. It's the quiet ones you have to watch out for, which I know sounds weird coming from me because *quiet* is a word most people used to describe me. *Quiet* or *reserved*, like I was saving myself up. It's not that I haven't thought about it, by which I mean killing or hurting somebody. Or myself. Find me a guy, or even a girl, who hasn't. But there's a big difference between a thought and an act, between showing up at Ravens or the Gaze or the Light of Christ Church or the Green Dragon and actually following through on the crazy thoughts looping around in your head. Sticks and stones, right? A thought not only never broke your bones, it never even hurt you, did it? Because you had no clue it existed.

Listen to me when I say that this very day you brushed past a guy like one of us, a guy with a crazy idea in his head. He turned to look back at you and considered acting on that crazy idea for a flash of a second. There was something about you that hooked him: your sad eyes, or your fear, or the attitude in your walk, like you owned the whole fucking world. Whatever it was, he hated it, or he pitied it, and he needed to address it. That's probably happened to you hundreds, thousands, of times in your life, and will keep happening unless your luck runs out and you brush past one of the few guys who'll actually follow through. My point is that most people are decent and act decent, but if you held them responsible for their thoughts, even their plans, even their plans they *almost* followed through on, you'd have to throw every last one of them—of us—in jail. What matters is what you do. What you *did.*

Like, for a while, I guess you could say I had an obsession with Tessa. She used that word, not me, but the description was a fair one. When you load up your backpack with a bunch of random textbooks and tell your roommate, "off to the library!" but instead you walk up and down the path in front of the dorm of a girl you've never met in case she comes out, and then when she does you can't talk to her, you can't even look her in the eyes or lift your chin in greeting, so you hang back and follow her to the gym even though you don't have your workout clothes with you, so when you get to the gym you wait outside hoping she'll use one of the machines in front of the window, and when she does you can finally relax because it's nighttime and she can't see you sitting on the grass with your heavy bag in your lap watching her on the elliptical, you can watch her as long as you want, some call that romantic. Tessa herself used that word, a few months later, when we were finally, officially, boyfriend and girlfriend, watching *Say Anything* in the dorm lounge for her Film in Culture class with our whole crew of friends, and John Cusack stood outside Ione Skye's bedroom and held that boom box over his head and blared music for her from the street.

"Totally something you would do," said Tessa, snuggling closer to me in her footie pajamas. "My little stalker."

Okay, so maybe she didn't actually use the word *romantic* that night, or any night, but she implied it. It was all clear in context. Even her friends Chloe and Mia cooed when she compared me to that guy in the movie, Lloyd Gobbler or whatever his character's name was, whose whole deal was that he wanted to do nothing in life—not work, not join the army, not even achieve his dream of boxing professionally—except hang with Ione Skye. That was Lloyd's entire ambition, and, at the time, it was mine, too: to hang with Tessa Timmins.

You should have seen how Chloe and Mia looked at her when she said that stalker thing about me out loud. They weren't freaked out or disapproving or even jealous. They were like, you're so lucky to have a guy like Matt who follows you around everywhere and brings you hot homemade waffles from the dining hall so you can sleep in and takes your car to the shop and pays for your fake ID and your Lollapalooza ticket and your almost-real-pearl earrings and new duck boots and our girls' weekend hotel room in Detroit. It was all endorsed, the way I was with Tessa, my role, my place, and I didn't mind it one bit, the running around I did for her. The opposite. I ran around all day feeling *satisfied.*

It wasn't just that Tessa was hands-down the prettiest girl I'd ever seen. I'm not that shallow. Also: pretty is easy, especially at UMich. Throw a rock on that campus and you'll hit a pretty blonde who looks exactly like the pretty blonde standing next to her. Tessa stood out. She had both a purity and a wildness that I associated with Oklahoma, where she grew up. I didn't know anything about

Oklahoma, but in my mind it was a land of vast open spaces and horses and apples and wheat fields and tough women in pigtails driving stagecoaches and shooting at bank robbers. Somehow, these all found their way into Tessa, her cheeks round and pink as apples, her golden hair that fell to the middle of her back in untamed curls, her broad shoulders and wide coltish hips and skin that looked and tasted of dark honey. Even her big feet of which she was ashamed. How she stuffed those big feet into high heels for the Christmas Formal and strapped herself in and then danced heavily on them for hours and then snapped them in two with her bare hands at the end of the night, this was Oklahoma to me, and this was Tessa.

I'd first noticed her through the window from my seat in the back row of Roman Kings and Emperors. I loved that course—it was the one that convinced me to major in Classics—but the prof had a spittle problem that made the front of the room a danger zone you had to show up early to avoid. I never had a problem with punctuality, but focus was another ball of wax, even in a class that interested me. The girl at the picnic table a few feet and a thick pane of glass away, though: her I had no trouble focusing on. She was a head taller than her two friends, who turned out to be Chloe and Mia, two of the many flimsy and forgettable girls who competed with me for Tessa's shadow. The prof was spitting away about Nero, "seventeen, and already an emperor!" trying to inspire us to greatness, but the sun was breaking over the quad and this giantess at the picnic table was pulling off her anorak and flashing me with the soft flesh just below her sports bra, the surprise of her pierced belly button, and then she was rubbing her fingers up and down under the straps of her skintight Wolverines Volleyball tank top, and then she was absently gathering her hair above her head and lifting it and letting it fall, and Rome was burning down all around me.

In my preferred version of the events of that day, I raise my hand and tell Professor Attix, in perfect Latin, that I finally get why Nero didn't give a shit that flames were engulfing his city. *That dude was in love!* I say triumphantly, and then I throw open the window and jump through it onto the quad. I grab Chloe by her armpits and gently deposit her onto the grass. I sit beside the giantess. I play her a song on my fiddle. *Amāmus, amantes, amābimus.* I let her scoop me into her arms and carry me across the quad through the parking lot and the soccer field and up the five flights of stairs to my little room. I shut the doors and seal the windows and we imprison ourselves for centuries. We look out on all the poor unloved suckers of the world and we wave. We're naked all the time. She lies on her stomach to study her chemistry textbook and I write my papers on the small of her back, my forearm at rest on her ass. I finish a page and throw it to the floor for her to pick up and read back to me. When we need food she lets down her hair and I wrap myself in a sheet and climb down to procure it for us. Fried chicken and blocks of orange cheese and McDonald's apple pies. Our fingers and lips and chins are slick and tacky with sugar and grease, and when we sleep we wrap our arms and legs around each other and make a big ball of sticky candy and we sweat and drool and dream identical dreams.

Amārer, amātus sim, amātus essem.

The real version of the day went a bit differently. I didn't hear another word Professor Attix said about Nero other than that he probably lit on purpose the match that started the fire that destroyed his own empire. That was the point of the day's lecture, I learned later from notes I borrowed from the kid next to me. (I have always been responsible, even in a mania.) Don't make decisions like a reckless teenager, Attix warned us; in other words, "don't shit where you eat," another of the "life lessons" he offered us from time to time in poignant attempts to make his underenrolled Classics courses more relevant to the modern world. Anyway, the moment I saw through the window the giantess start packing up her stuff, I slunk out of Attix's class with my hand over my stomach and a floopy expression on my face to indicate intestinal distress. I planned to go up to her and introduce myself and offer to escort her to her next destination, a move I'd learned from my freshman year roommate and had executed successfully with girls in the past, though, more often than not, I lost interest in the girl by the time we reached our destination. As I approached the giantess, though, and heard her throaty booming laugh and saw how she commanded the attention of her friends, conducting those two girls like she was waving a baton, I lost my nerve. I hung back to observe, keeping pace with her at close enough distance long enough to pick up her name on one of the girls' tongues. It was the first time I'd ever heard it, Tessa, and I assumed it was short for something, but it turned out not to be. Tessa. The name sounded vaguely imperial itself, hard and soft at the same time, a head whose smooth curls appear to be flowing though they're carved in stone. Once I had that information—the name and the volleyball shirt would be more than enough to go on to find her again—I turned back toward Roman Kings and Emperors, but instead of reclaiming my seat in the back row, I ducked into the men's room, where I was supposed to be anyway, and jacked off in the last stall to Tessa's big ass in her Wolverines sweats and the fantasy of her turning around and catching me following her and then scooping me up and then the naked candy ball and me climbing on top of her and her pressing her sticky lips to mine. I can't say for sure that was what I imagined that first of a thousand times I jacked off to visions of Tessa—I'm reconstructing it now the best I can based on the limited info I had available to me that day—but I can say that, then and ever after, the act wasn't so much a fun erotic reverie I did out of boredom or procrastination but a form of demon exorcism necessary to function as a student / competitive wrestler / young adult in need of rent money. The only way to accomplish the exorcism was to lock myself in the nearest stall and get myself off as fast as possible and then immediately dive into homework / practice / the Dewey decimal system for a few minutes of relative peace before she came roaring back into my consciousness.

I googled *Tessa + Michigan volleyball + women's + roster* and two seconds later she appeared on my phone: *Tessa Timmins, middle blocker, 6'0". Hometown: Bristow, OK. High school: Eagle Point Christian Academy.* I didn't know the first thing about kills and aces and digs, but, according to her stats, she'd had a lot of them last season, which got me hard again. Before I spoke a word to her, I described her to everyone: my housemates, the guys in the wrestling club, our neighbors, Frankie at Joe's Pizza, even my mom. None of them had heard of her or anyone who'd gone out with her, and none of her nameless faceless friends I described to them rang a bell. It's possible these people weren't really listening. Tessa wasn't the first girl I'd fallen for through a window or made out with blitzed at a party then tried to find for days after with no luck. She wasn't the first girl—young woman, I guess I should say—whose business card I lost after she visited campus sophomore year to recruit interns. When it came to love, I think my buddies considered me the boy who cried wolf, since I was always puppy dog for somebody, and so, with this Tessa Timmins Who Played Volleyball, they figured I'd be on to someone new before finals started. But I wasn't, not for the two whole weeks that went by before I saw her again on campus, stepping off the shuttle, and not for the eight and a half months we dated, off and on, soon after that, and not for the three days after we broke up for the last time when I was doing and saying everything I could to win her back.

It's some kind of shitty cosmic luck that Tessa was just starting to come around to my point of view, and that she'd agreed to meet me at the Ravens Club to talk things over—in public, she'd insisted, and not at a scuzzy bar like Skeeps, and Chloe had to be with her for support, sitting somewhere close but not close enough to eavesdrop—the very same night I got put here. Honestly, that's the main reason I sometimes think this is all some sort of long religious dream. The timing was just too perfect, Tessa and me on the verge of patching things up, her this close to forgiving me, me waiting on her at the bar that last night, watching through the window for her white Mustang with Oklahoma plates to finally turn onto Main Street, my leg shaking, this creepy-drunk-bearded-professor type sitting too close to me asking, "you okay, young fella?" and me saying, "yeah, my *girlfriend*'s just super late like always," and him going, "you sure she's coming, it's last call, one more Mich Ultra for you, this one's on me?" and me wanting to take him by the lapels of his stupid brown corduroy jacket and smash his gay ass against the mirror.

If there's one thing I wish I knew, it's where Tessa really was that night, what made her so late. My money's on the clutch on that shitty Mustang I'd been saving up to replace for her, or on Chloe, who always had some mental crisis, who never liked me to begin with. No matter what Caleb and Leo and Steve say, I don't and won't believe she stood me up. She wasn't the type to lock herself in her room and sit cross-legged on her bed crying with Chloe and avoiding her problems. She was the type to finish her Econ paper by 9:50 p.m., throw on her sweats and her earmuffs and the duck boots I bought her, wrap her pink scarf around her neck a couple times, and drive the ten minutes to the Ravens Club to deal with me once and for all. Where was she? We can see the present, but we can't see the past, though things we don't remember doing or having done to us come back in flashes like they're happening for the first time. This, too, is just as it was in the Before.

I'm training myself not to think about what she's doing right now, this very minute. Not to wonder all the time if she misses me. Not to wonder why, when all those people lined up with my mom to search for me in the woods, I didn't see her among them. Did she just keep on studying and finishing her papers and playing her volleyball matches and making caramel corn for girls' movie night as if nothing had happened? Did she see my name and face on the news and open the door when the cops showed up to ask her questions? Did she wonder why she gave up on the only guy who loved her before she even knew he was gone? I can't know because she hasn't been given to me, not the way Monica has been given to Steve, or Leo's baby sister, Katie, has been given to him. Not the way James Hahn, this super-old guy at his college, has been given to Caleb. We never see the only thing we want to see, which is ourselves alive again reuniting with those people we loved most: Steve taking the stairs two at a time up to Monica's bedroom, pushing open the door to find her sprawled on her bed like a damsel in distress; Leo crouched on the linoleum kitchen floor as Katie comes wobbling toward him with her little jazz hands going and that big unpolluted smile on her face; Caleb hopping into the passenger seat of James Hahn's car for an escape to Montreal. Instead, what Steve sees is Monica Binswanger on her knees debasing herself between Arthur's manspread legs, his hairy balls slapping her chin. Oh, and for you, Leo, here's Katie left screaming in her room with the TV as babysitter, rattling the bars of her crib while his mother shoots up in the kitchen. What poor Caleb sees is James Hahn in a TROPHY HUSBAND apron sautéing shallots for his wife's tenure party, taking a swig from a bottle of wine before he splashes some in the pan, grabbing the champagne flutes from the china cabinet, and rushing into the living room with them bunched in his right hand. These people don't know we're steps behind them, watching them. Or, if they do, they can't or won't let on, they're so preoccupied, so distracted. Taking their mind off things. Busy, so very busy moving on with their lives. Moving on and on.

I used to wish I was in a wheelchair so that people would feel sorry for me instead of envy me. I've had trouble with that—envy—for as long as I can remember, friends talking shit about me because of my looks, because people paid attention to me, because I was good in school and at sports, whereas most guys I knew got one or the other or neither. I was aware that being good at both school and sports on top of having what my track coach once called a "Greek god" body and what Tessa called a "Roman nose" and decent height is pretty obnoxious, especially for a Classics major, so I never held anybody's envy of me against them. The opposite. In my driveway as a kid, playing HORSE with the guys on the block, I'd keep things competitive until at least one other person got to HORS with me, and then I'd miss the *E* on purpose. In Calc senior year, when Mr. Mullins would list all the grades on the chalkboard in descending order, and then write our names beside them starting from the bottom, I used to sit there at my desk praying he'd write *Matt C* before he got to the top. The truth is, I like playing games but not winning them. I like taking tests and getting the answers right, especially in math and languages, but not getting awards. People must have asked me a million times to run for class president, but the idea of getting the most votes and standing at a podium in front of everyone to thank them for picking me over my "opponents"—guys and girls who probably tried way harder and cared way more than I did, and who didn't have my natural advantages—made me sick to my stomach. Except penmanship and baseball and golf and Biology and, weirdly enough, driver's ed, which I sucked at, everything I trained and studied for came easy, which always made me feel, on an average day just walking into class or home from practice, like I had more than my fair share, like I was getting away with something.

That's probably why I fell so hard for girls like Tessa who looked straight through me as if I were nothing, who called me ordinary and basic if they called me anything at all, or, better yet, girls who were even more obnoxious than I was, like this girl Sophia who'd swum for Canada in the Olympics and who'll most definitely be prime minister someday. (Remember this name: Sophia Sanders.) Or that hot recruiter I mentioned, Molly, who eye-fucked me in my suit when I almost walked past the Jackson Financial table. I stopped, obviously even though I had no interest in economics. By the time her recruits showed up in Lansing this fall, she told me, she'd be long gone, lighting up Wall Street. Take my advice, she said, and get out of Michigan as soon as you graduate. Forget Ann Arbor. Forget Detroit. Even Chicago's too Podunk. Move to LA. Or Tokyo! Life was one big pond full of lily pads; the trick was never to stay on one too long or you'd sink. You really want to end up some dusty old professor?

Kinda? I said, staring down at my shiny shoes, because the truth was she scared the shit out of me. I don't want to forget this place, I thought. These people. My friends, my mom and dad. I was only a sophomore, but I already felt old.

Okay, Molly said. Pro tip. She glanced around, leaned over the table, her cheek an inch from mine, and whispered, you're a straight white man in America; the only thing that can stop you is you.

I wish I could ask her now: Is that what happened, Molly? I stopped myself? That's what fucking happened?

I don't like it, but lately my mind's been going dark. I mean that in every way imaginable, including the literal one, as in when I open my eyes I see thin black stripes on the edges of my vision, like a border around my own personal stretch of sky and clouds. The border itself is blurry and vibrating and makes a kind of humming sound, not like normal humming to a song but like a person is trying to talk or sing except their lips are sewn shut. At first I don't understand what they're saying, the song they're singing, but then, suddenly, I do, and when I do, I blink to make it stop, but instead of correcting itself, the edges of the frame get thicker and the painting gets smaller and the humming gets louder and more strangled sounding and horrible, and my field of vision shrinks to just a sharp and distant stamp-sized square of blue sky surrounded on all sides by that black thundering hum. I'm scared to summon Caleb or Leo or Steve or anyone. I sense that this frame is an entity unto itself, a malevolent force encroaching upon my consciousness, trying to break me, to separate me, to take me over, another possession. I hate opening my eyes because when I do, the closing-in starts again, and the humming, in particular, is so awful, not so much for how it sounds, but for what it tells me, what it reveals, before it finally stops.

Okay, so now you know, says Steve. What are you going to do about it?

What I want to do is shut off my mind completely. To go back to the deep sleep of the back seat of our family car summer nights driving home from my grandfather's cabin. I remember my dad at the wheel, my mom next to me with her hand on my back to feel its rise and fall. I'd had aortic stenosis as a baby, two surgeries on my heart valves before the age of one, so even though I grew up to be normal and strong, my parents always treated me like there was a live grenade in my chest. *Don't push Matty too hard, that's too much pressure on that boy, don't yell at him, don't aggravate him, he'll break.*

All that handle-with-care stuff for what?

So I could end up broken anyway? Lost anyway? Dead anyway?

It wasn't my heart. Those glitchy valves did not send me here. I know that now. I am getting solved. My right palm rests on my chest at all times hoping for a rise and fall. *Pulso, pulso, pulso.*

My mother, beside my sleeping little body in the car, picked up the book in her lap, sighed, looked out the window, wondered which of those blistered towns between the city and the lake we were passing through, but if she asked my father he would answer, and then she'd have to bear his unbearable voice, so she turned back to her mystery, but she wasn't reading it, she didn't care who the murderer was, she was planning her escape. My chest rose and fell under her hand, a reassurance, an obligation.

Every single time she passed the portrait of me framed on the wall of the hallway, my mother kissed her two fingers and touched them to my lips. The first time she passes me without a kiss, without even glancing in my direction, I forgive her; she's on the phone with her friend Naomi, the phone trapped between her ear and shoulder, carrying a box of files up from the cellar. The second time, she has no such excuse. Then it keeps happening: a third time, a fourth. On and on. Makes me so angry, the angriest I've been since the humming started. I'm so angry that—I almost don't believe it myself—the picture shakes a little on its hook. It sticks there, just slightly off, my soft serious face looking just over my right shoulder when I stare into it. It's the same photo the *Free Press* ran with the headline STILL MISSING above it, the photo with my zits airbrushed out and my hair all shiny with gel, except now the headline reads MISSING MICHIGAN STUDENT WAS MURDERED, and now it reads SLAIN HONORS STUDENT LAID TO REST.

Occidere? Interficere? Caedere? There's a difference, but it doesn't matter anymore.

My mother doesn't notice the tilted photo, or she doesn't bother to fix it. That doesn't matter either. She's so busy. Telemarketing, now, from the kitchen table, between shifts at the grocery store. Rushing to the front door for packages without stopping to kiss me. A tenth time, a twenty-fifth. I lose track of the times, the time. Days, weeks, months. A year? I'm getting blurrier, the guys tell me, but I can't feel it. All I feel is rage. She passes me a fiftieth time. A hundredth. A thousandth.

When the rage comes, it takes me over as wholly and suddenly as a possession. It's like the demon I had to get out of me by jacking off, except there's no way to get this rage out. I get angry a lot—my coaches and teachers used to warn me about my temper; Tessa used to say it freaked her out—but rage is like anger all roided up.

It's loud and cold and heavy as the river.

It crushes the sadness and horniness and boredom and the anger, too, like a boot crushes a beetle.

It sends my portrait crashing to the floor.

I watch my mother sweep up the glass, fit me into a different frame, put me back up, kiss me for the first time in how long, then pass me again unnoticed a first time. A second time. Another thousand times. I send it down again. This is how rage works, I'm learning; it puts people on notice. Maybe it's the only thing that does. Except it doesn't last. She puts me back up again. She finds a reason for why I keep falling. Soft plaster. A truck going by. God. Any reason that makes her feel better. Meanwhile, I hang there, the same face fading under different glass. There will never be another.

The new silver frame has curlicues in the corners. My mother gets busier. More packages come. More files. A second phone line. She signs her emails:

> Onward!
>
> *Lori Whitford Cardullo*
>
> **Telesales Representative**
> **Elite Insurance Partners**

At the end of her calls, no matter who she's talking to, she says, "Make it a g*lor*i*o*us day." She's so cheerful. She stops biting her nails. She turns the TV off rather than falls asleep to it. She watches pay-per-view boxing matches. She reads prayers out loud from a little gilt-edged book the size of a deck of cards. She brings men home and leads them upstairs by the hand. Onward. I want to punish her, so for a while I stop visiting her, stop putting her on notice with my rage. I keep still. The most powerful thing you can do with power is to not use it.

Steve's the one I talk to most about the rage I've come to feel not just at my mother but at Tessa and every girl and young woman I ever loved, every last one of them. I used to think Caleb understood me best, but now I wonder if Steve and I are the most alike.

They should be afraid, he says.

Of what?

Of you, he says. Of us.

I'd never hurt anyone, I say.

Are you sure?

Of course I'm sure. Who do you think I am?

I have no fucking idea, Steve says.

Likewise.

You can make shit fall off walls, Steve says. I still can't do that.

I'm not even really trying, I say.

Fuck off, says Steve.

I'm sorry.

He's been trying, he says, but he can't reach Monica no matter how close he stands to her as she checks herself in her bathroom mirror, so close he can almost smell her coconut shampoo. It's not rage so much that overcomes Steve when he sees her, but longing. Desire. They look so good together, he tells me, they always have, her brown skin mottled with moles and freckles across her neck and shoulders, his pale and pink and pocked as an unripe strawberry. When he wraps his arms around her from behind, he feels what we all feel, by which I mean nothing but numbness, as if they're both encased in plastic. He craves the electricity of Monica's skin, but it's her smell he misses most, not just the coconut in her hair but every part of her he has burrowed into with his tongue and lips and teeth and nose. Her hungry little pig, she'd called him. No other woman had had this effect on him. No other armpits, kneepits, bottoms of feet, no other warm pools of slick sweat under breasts and at the tip of the crack at the base of the back, between ass cheeks, between holes. No other moles and freckles and patches of hair and scars and chewed-off nails. No other Monica. So unlike me, I think, me who kept falling for different girls in different windows, girls just beyond the glass but unreachable until I stopped whatever I was doing and jumped through it.

Monica's let her hair grow long, he tells me. Then she cut it short.

Now it's long again, with faint streaks of white. Time has gone by. The months and years leap from and back into his hands, but still he can't shatter the mirror she cranes her neck toward, smoothing cream under her eyes with the tip of her finger. He can't shake loose the leaf that falls and catches in her curls as she crosses the Public Garden.

Why can't I do one fucking thing? he wails to me. Why you and not me? What makes you so special?

I tell him I don't know. Because I don't.

Even Leo can do it, says Steve.

You can?

You're not the only special one, Leo says. He tells us a story.

He was on the school bus with his sister, Katie, he says, sitting between her and her friend Audrey. The other kids at CloudView Elementary recoiled from Katie, but Audrey was different because she was new and unaware that Katie was the class punching bag, the girl who stunk from unwashed underwear and unbrushed teeth and whose persistent impetigo reddened and crusted her lips and nostrils. Before long, Audrey would join the coven of girls who taunt and spit at Katie, but that day on the bus she dumped the contents of the front pocket of her purple backpack onto the rubbery seat and directed Katie to do the same with her black knapsack so they could play show-and-tell. They arranged their respective stashes on Leo's lap, their chubby arms passing through him. Audrey held up a heavy silver unicorn with rainbow hair she'd fallen in love with at a museum shop in Chicago and purchased with her entire monthly allowance; Katie a Canadian dollar her mother had brought back for her from a trip to Thunder Bay. Audrey flashed a rabbit's-foot key chain off of which hung three keys of different sizes: the big one to the front door of her house, the medium one to the door of her private tree house, the small one to the trunk at the foot of her bed, where she kept secret treasures she casually promises to show Katie one afternoon after school. Giddy with the prospects of a trunk of secrets and a real friend, Katie produced a creased postcard of a night sky thick with stars and striated with wavy green clouds. Her mother had mailed this card to her at her aunt's house when she was away for so long on that same trip to Thunder Bay. The dollar and the postcard were Katie's sole trinkets, but Audrey's show went on: a lipstick-like tube containing fifty-six dollars in rolled-up bills in different denominations; a fun-sized packet of Red Hots she dared Katie to put in her mouth all at once; and a half-empty bottle of black nail polish she'd stolen from her older sister, Farah, who now went only by the letter *F*.

Leo followed Katie and Audrey from the bus to their classroom to the lunchroom to the playground, wishing he could fill the front pocket of Katie's knapsack with all the riches of the world. The principal's diamond engagement ring. The glittery camouflage shoelaces that belonged to Hannah, the head witch in the band of little tormenting witches. The gold credit card that fell out of Mr. Coleman's pocket onto the cafeteria floor when he paid for his slice of pizza. Leo looked everywhere for colorful, impressive things to slip into Katie's backpack until it was stuffed to bursting and she was rich and grown-up enough to take a train by herself and not get off until the train delivered her far away from this town to a place where she was free and safe and adored. Instead, he could only sit dumbly, uselessly, on the school bus between Katie and Audrey, then, some time after, in the same seat between Katie and no one, and then between her and the visibly pregnant newlywed principal, who was giving Katie news about her mother that made her cry.

And then he did something for that little girl, Steve interrupts.

Yeah, I fucking did.

What did you do?

I showed her she wasn't alone, said Leo. I sent her a sign.

How did she know it was from you? I ask.

She knew, says Leo.

We've each been granted someone. My mother. Monica. Trophy husband James Hahn. Leo has Katie, alone in the world now that their mother's heart has stopped in the back seat of a van in the same church parking lot behind the woods where Leo was last alive. This is the news the pregnant principal has given Katie and why she clutches her backpack and won't get up from her chair. Later, when Katie finds the ring in the front pocket of the backpack, she thinks it's fake, a token of sympathy from Audrey. She slips it on her finger and holds it up to the light and for a few seconds she forgets she's an orphan. It doesn't matter that she loses the ring in the move to her aunt Alice's. She hangs on to the black backpack, in which she continues to find random precious objects, and now she knows for sure who's putting them there.

What does she believe in, my mother? Soft plaster. God. Trucks. Justice. Not forgiveness. Not luck. I send the picture crashing down, dumbly, uselessly. I'm telling her something, over and over, except not even I know what it is.

But why can't *I* do it, Steve keeps whining. He knows what he wants to say to Monica, the question he needs to ask her.

This goes on and on. Days, months, a year? From Caleb we hear less and less, and then, suddenly, we hear nothing at all. What was true in the Before is true here, too: a person can just disappear. One moment he's the random guy next to you in Physics class getting on your last nerve shaking his knee; or he's your loser cousin texting you and calling you just because he's bored and showing up at your house all the time with nothing to say; or, in this case, he's your best friend, the one gay guy you've ever had a real conversation with, talking environmental justice with you from the other side of eternity, and then the next moment that same guy is completely silent, invisible, unreachable.

There is a period in which none of us can summon Caleb at all.

And then, out of nowhere, we hear him.

The volume of his voice has been turned down. It comes unattached to his body, as if through the waves of the river itself. I can barely see his face. Maybe the longer you go unsolved, the more quickly you disappear once they drag you out. I was wrong when I said he'd stay jammed under that rock in Dog River forever, tangled in the vines.

It's late at night in Vermont, Caleb says. He's with James Hahn, who is seated at his desk in front of his computer in his upstairs office. On the screen is the *Burlington Free Press* online report on Caleb Aldrich, the young man gone missing so long ago, and now, finally, confirmed dead, dragged from the floor of the Dog.

James zooms in on Caleb's face, and together they look at him. He is tanned from a long summer in Vinalhaven, where he'd volunteered for the Nature Conservancy before returning to college for his senior year. He was super into my eyes, Caleb reminds us for the thousandth time, but now even he himself is struck by their blueness and bigness and turbulence. We can almost hear him blush.

Conceited much? jokes Steve, who, though he'll never admit it, has been missing Caleb as much as I've been.

In the photo on James's computer, Caleb smiles from ear to ear and holds a live lobster the color of his eyes. His sandy hair is mussed by the ocean wind, which has turned up the left flap of the collar on his yellow polo. He's goofy with pride, as if he'd not trapped the rare iridescent blue lobster accidentally, a stroke of pure luck, but lured it to their boat with his cleverness.

I wish I could see you when you looked like that, I tell Caleb.

He's so blurry I wish I could see him at all.

I'd have turned you, he says to me, in front of everybody.

Oh yeah?

You wouldn't be the first.

So I'm your type, then? I joke.

I mean, not really? he says, laughing. Your dad, maybe? But still. I'd have turned you. Believe me. We'd have had fun.

We can barely hear you, Aldrich, Steve says.

His tinny voice is like music on a distant ship.

Where are you? Leo asks. What do you see?

He sees James Hahn reach down and pull open the file drawer of documents he's printed out. The files in the drawer are labeled with dreary names meant to throw off any snoops, such as his wife. *Lib Admin. Abernathy Collection. Robert Frost.* As James riffles through the documents, scribbling in the margins, Caleb peers closer, trying to gather information on himself. It's dates he craves. Times. He scans the pages James clicks through on the CNN and *Dateline* websites for them, furious that they are still blurred or scrambled or missing altogether. The top right corner of the computer screen is a jumble of the unreadable runelike shapes we've all gotten used to finding in the places where numbers should be.

He sees my face flash past on James's screen. He sees Steve and Leo and Ryan Sumter and Brian Price and Jeremy Dix and, after uncountable nights of this, he sees most, if not all, of the others. He sees the Excel sheet with our names and hometowns and the accounts of our disappearances and discoveries cataloged down and across color-coded columns. He sees the Word documents with our photos cut and pasted and captioned:

> Last seen by cashier Mo Blevins at the Sunoco gas station on State Street on—
>
> Last seen "visibly intoxicated" and "belligerent" at the Ravens Club cocktail lounge on—
>
> A counselor in the after-school program at the Boys & Girls Club of Roxbury, Mr. Donovan, last seen by housemate Archie Echols on—, was known for his "irreverent" sense of humor . . .
>
> "Smiley Face" killer suspected in the case of Leopold "Leo" Ridgeway, last seen by Clint Ousley, security guard at Minneapolis-based ACT Solutions—

The blinking of the cursor at the bottom of the page tortures Caleb. He keeps trying to type *it's caleb, i'm here* by pressing the tip of his finger onto the keys, but even now, finally solved, he can manipulate no material object, he can send no message. There will be time.

So here we are, knowers of the great mystery, but also, somehow, still in the dark, still just boys, still waiting, dumbly, uselessly, to find out who we will become. If you knew we were standing behind you, calling out to you, right now, lungless, lonely, would you stop moving for one fucking second? Would you turn around?

FIRST SEEN

James was not surprised when the blond boy in shorts and a T-shirt crossed the parking lot carrying a McDonald's bag. The surprise came from the lingering look the boy gave James through his windshield as he dropped the bag in the trash can. What sealed it was the trash can in front of the boy's own car, which gave him no good reason to cross the lot except to get a look at the man in the front seat.

It had come to this. It had kept coming to this for several years. James was the man alone in the front seat. He was one of those men who sat alone in the front seat of his car in various parking lots in the middle of the day. He was in athletic gear, too—his jacket and tie and dress slacks on hangers in the back—but, to the trained eye, it was obvious neither man had any intention of running.

Except, this morning, James did have that intention. When he'd told Iris about his dreaded 9 a.m. breakfast with the Abernathys and the calls to the trustees he needed to make before hitting the gym over lunch, the effortless truth of each word had thrilled him. Then his 2 p.m. canceled, and his assistant, Maud, who kept close tabs on him, went home sick, and with the rare luxury of an empty afternoon came the urge. Instead of walking from the campus library to the fitness center after the calls to the trustees, he'd gotten into his car and headed north to Bristol. He'd turned right at River Road and pulled into the cemetery to change clothes. Then the car had made a sharp right into Sycamore Park and crossed the parking lot, the spot in the corner near the trash can and the trailhead looming like a holy place.

The boy was stretching now. Quads. Hamstrings. His palm pressed to his passenger-side window for balance. At the start of each move, he fixed his gaze on James's car, and each time the gaze lasted a moment longer. If James could have assembled a boy for himself from scratch, he'd have treated himself to this very one: sky-blue eyes, broad shoulders, soccer-player legs. My God, he thought, I'm not this lucky. He took a deep breath and tapped his brakes—a signal subtle enough to miss or ignore, but unmistakable if the boy was looking for it.

He was looking for it. Quit his routine. Jogged over. "How's it going?" he asked.

"Good," James said. When it happened, it happened this quickly. "Good day for a run."

"Yeah." He rubbed his hands together. "Kinda chilly, but nice."

"Chilly's good, though."

"Yeah, chilly can be good."

How to make the transition? The boy looked down; James looked down. The boy shuffled his feet; James rubbed his face. A flock of geese landed on the empty field.

"You want some company?" the boy asked. "On—on your run? Makes the time go by."

"Um, sure," James said. It was more than possible he was just a normal college guy who wouldn't mind a running partner, someone to shoot the breeze with and talk sports, and that James was a filthy middle-aged pervert about to get his face bashed in. "I'm no pro or anything, though," James said, stalling. To stand up at this moment would give it all away.

"Don't worry," the boy said. He patted his belly. "I'm not, like, on the track team. More like Model UN." He blushed. "I'm blowing off Debate for this, to be honest."

"I, too, am blowing off work," James said. *I, too?* Soon the kid would notice he was a hundred years old.

"What do you do?"

He hesitated. Everything was traceable. "I'm a chemist. Up in Burlington."

"Cool," the boy said, unconvincingly. He kicked at a pebble like he was bored to death. "I suck at chemistry."

Here was an opportunity. Not an elegant one, certainly not a decent one, but James's foot was on the pedal; he could peel out before the fist hit his face. "Is that all you suck at?"

"Dude," he said, and laughed. Looked down at himself. "Follow me."

James rolled up his window, quick, locked the car, and followed him into the trailhead and then across the field toward the mouth of the woods. He was fast for a Debate kid. Or maybe he was just as big a liar as James was. *A chemist up in Burlington?* Why was his brother's job the first that came to mind? Why did it matter? He kept up with the boy rather well for a hundred-year-old man, gliding over the rocky trails and muddy fields of Sycamore Park graceful as a cheetah. No one was around. Just a lone white farmhouse on the other side of the road. A water tower. The murky river. The silent geese.

The boy spotted a potential site up ahead off the trail, stopped, pointed, shrugged. James shrugged back. There was much crackling as they forged a new path over brambles and fallen branches, all business now. Lewis and Clark. The boy held back some thorny vines so James could pass through.

They reached a small clearing shaded by six or seven scattered pines. "What do you think?" the boy asked.

He thought, God yes. He thought, what a sad creature I am. He thought, you promised yourself no Midd kids. He said, with practiced nonchalance, "Works for me."

They faced each other on a carpet of brown needles. The boy pulled off his T-shirt. His skin was smooth, even his pits. There was that adorable tummy over the lip of his shorts, and the miracle of an inside-out belly button. He tossed the shirt onto a branch, pulled James's up over his head.

"How old are you?" James asked.

"You're not breaking the law," he said. He pressed his chest against his and laid his head on his shoulder. For a while they stayed like that, like a real couple, like slow dancing.

For once, James felt no panic, and, given the assured serenity—rather like a sculptor at his craft—with which the boy lowered and removed his shorts and busied himself with James's body, given his firm and wordless directives that soon had James face-up, then face-down, then face-up again, on the bed of sappy and scratchy needles, neither did he.

"You've got incredible eyes," James said. His thumb drew rings around them.

"You've got incredible . . . everything," said the boy.

"Me?"

He pretended to look around. "You see anybody else here?"

"I just mean, no one's ever called me 'incredible.' Not even when I was your age."

He thought a moment. "That makes me sad," he said.

On the trek back, James learned his name, Caleb, that he'd grown up in Poughkeepsie, that his parents had been diagnosed within months of each other with different cancers due to pollution, that his aunt was a nun, that he could distinguish between different species of pine trees and tall grasses and mushrooms, that he was a talker. He offered James half a Vicodin, which he refused. "I should tell you," said Caleb. "I have a girlfriend. She can't keep up with me. I only came here to clear my head. It's like all this gunk builds up and builds up and makes my brain all heavy, but then I come here and the gunk goes away."

"For me the gunk comes after," said James.

"Because you're married? Most guys are married."

"Oh, well—I'm not."

"And I've got this big Debate tournament at school next week," Caleb said, "which is messing with my head. Against Vanderbilt. Their team's flying here from Nashville, and I'm against flying on principle except under emergency circumstances. My dad was in a plane crash when I was fifteen and it freaked us all out even though he was fine—it was a little plane, they weren't even very high up yet—but then a month later he got leukemia. I'm only doing Debate because I think it'll help me later, in my career, to convince people of things, like how fucked we are on this planet, like how everything we eat is basically poison. Even so-called organic meat and fish. I'm not in it for the trophies. Does a place like Vanderbilt, or Middlebury for that matter, even think about the emissions involved in flying kids all over the country for something as inconsequential as a debate between teenagers? Like, why is it even necessary? We're not smart enough to debate ourselves?"

"One of my clients hosted a teleconference on Skype last month for that very reason," said James, impressed by his own facility with new technology and by how comfortable he'd felt on-screen. "Have you heard of it?"

"Um, yeah," he said. "That's how college kids call their parents nowadays so it doesn't cost anything. But point taken."

They approached the edge of the woods, where Caleb would run ahead and James would wait a few decorous minutes before breaking into a run and emerging onto the open field. They'd followed the same path over the branches they trampled earlier.

"I'm sorry about your mom and dad," James said. "You seem like a nice kid. You don't deserve that. Nobody deserves that."

"Thanks," Caleb said, distracted. "You don't do, like, pharmaceuticals, do you?"

Did he? What did his little brother, Michael Hahn, actually do? James, who considered himself the curious type, didn't pay much attention when he droned on and on about it. Michael's company was called Axis BioSciences (maybe), which sounded like pharmaceuticals, something Caleb surely disapproved of, despite the Vicodin. And the McDonald's bag. Oh, the hypocrisy of youth. "No," he said decisively. "We do . . . toxicology. For bodies. And . . . for water."

"Oh, that's excellent," said Caleb. He seemed relieved, and to be formulating another question, potentially about the levels of toxins in the New Haven River burbling on the other side of the trees, the one they'd washed their hands in afterward. So James interrupted his thoughts, sure he wouldn't have the wits to come up with a convincing answer to any of his questions, and then the jig would really be up.

"When's your tournament against Vanderbilt?" he asked.

"How old are you?" Caleb asked back.

"Don't worry," said James. "You're not breaking the law."

"Haha," he said. "Seriously, I want to know."

"Next time."

This quieted him. He rubbed his face again, slowly, deep in contemplation. He was in no rush. The luxury of youth. Or maybe the Vicodin was kicking in. Maybe he was doing the math in his head, as tough for him as chemistry. *What year was my dad born? What year was this chemist guy born?* "If it's cool," he finally said, turning to meet James's eyes. "Don't, like, show up at my debate or anything. It's open to the public, but don't show up. I'll notice. I get freaked out easy. And don't wait for me here in case I come back one day. I've had, like, a problem with guys doing that. Asking for me by name and stuff. Getting all weird and obvious. I told you my real name, which I don't usually do. I don't know why I did that. I need to be more careful. So should you probably."

James would have to shower at the fitness center. Iris could sense the slightest disturbance in his scent. She wasn't suspicious; she just liked to be included. It was one of the thousand reasons he loved her, which he did. Extravagantly. And for most of his life. He'd never loved anyone but Iris. He certainly felt nothing like love for this chattering arrogant boy; and, at the moment, he never wanted to touch another man as long as he lived.

"Don't worry," James said. "I'm not desperate. I'm just . . . bored."

Caleb smiled and cast his eyes to the sky. "'Who but an idiot could be bored in this perpetually astonishing world?'" he said. "Samuel Johnson."

James stared at him.

"My English prof put that quote on our syllabus. I used it in a speech once against Williams."

"I'll just run ahead," James said.

"He doesn't mean 'idiot' like moron," Caleb continued. "He means the original definition. Like a mute. Somebody deaf and dumb. I'm not insulting you. You can't be an idiot and be a toxicology scientist."

"Good luck in your debate," James said, and took off.

When he and Iris first met, she was in grad school neck-deep in eighteenth-century novels. In all their years together, twenty-six as of this February, she'd never been able to convince him of their charms, not her beloved *Clarissa*, not even *Tristram Shandy.* He'd longed to be convinced. He'd sat through her talks as an adjunct and then associate and then assistant and then full professor, marveling at her passion for what seemed to him the most mundane and bloated and low stakes of narratives. The way she'd argued with her counterparts at Swarthmore and Stanford onstage at MLA as if the very foundations of the world depended on her rightness about Frances Burney's influence on Jane Austen. James had no such passion for anything except, maybe, order, the right things in their right places, which was where he believed he'd found himself, finally, as an archivist in Special Collections at the Middlebury College Library. A pointless job, in the grand scheme of things, but one that gave his days a certain dignity his other career attempts had not. A semester of law school. A year at the New England Culinary Institute. Two as a functionary in state government. Even Michael, his colorless kid brother, lit up when he talked about whatever it was he did with chemicals at Axis BioSciences up in Burlington. When you had only urges, and no true passions of your own, other people's were unbearable.

At the lot, he paced awhile with his hands on his hips, head down, fake-breathing hard. It got busier here in late afternoon. An old graybeard eyed him from a Volvo. Two cars sat side by side on the far end, empty to the untrained eye. If he walked over, what might he find in the back seat? More sad creatures; more runaways; men who, like him, couldn't imagine their lives without their women, and yet couldn't shake the vicious invincible urge. Instead he would slip into his car, swing by the gym, finish out his day in the library, and try to obliterate this afternoon and the many before it, and the ones sure to come.

Don't show up at my debate, the kid had said. Who did he think he was?

For years, when you asked Monica Binswanger, née Alberti, what she wanted to do with her life, she'd give a simple answer: to live free. Her father and brothers had chained themselves to the manufacturing of silks, her mother to her father, and her three sisters to husbands in his image. Being born the youngest and least remarkable Alberti daughter, of whom little was needed and nothing expected, when her parents were too old and too established in Neapolitan society to care, had been Monica's great fortune. Who'd ever heard of a fourth daughter, anyway? In fairy tales, there are only ever three or twelve; if a fourth or a thirteenth comes along, she is evil or disfigured or cursed. Monica was none of these; she was simply unexpected and unnecessary. Hers was a childhood hidden in the heavy folds of draperies, in the narrow passages behind cypress trees in their walled garden, under colossal wooden tables onto which her family slammed their fists. How she memorized her sisters' jeweled ankles. Her brothers' gleaming leather shoes. Her parents' knees angled away from each other's. Their voices hoarse and choked from cigarettes and screeching and gorging themselves on the bounty Textile Alberti had provided. How she longed for them when her mother shipped her off to school, first to Germany, then to Switzerland, and finally to the States, Boston University, where she met, too young, an older man in her father's image, and, too predictably, as in a fairy tale, chained herself to him before she figured out what she'd meant all that time about living free.

Today she was on a tour of the Boys & Girls Club of Roxbury, one of the dozens of worthy nonprofits she and Arthur have supported through the charitable arm of his company—*their* company—simply called Binswanger, which, like Textile Alberti, had thrived as a family business long before Monica met Arthur, and would outlive them and their young son no matter how badly they played their cards. The irony that Monica was a kept woman, chained to her husband by a stingy prenup and to her child by an inconveniently indestructible love, was lost on no one who knew her, least of all herself. How she'd gotten here—to Arthur, to the parking lot / play area of the Boys & Girls Club of Roxbury, to the first year of her forties—was less interesting than what was about to happen to her after someone grabbed her wrist and tried to drag her toward a group of Black girls jumping rope.

"Oh, I don't think so," she said to the someone, a young man, one of the counselors, in something close to a shriek, as she pulled her wrist from his grip. His stick-on name tag read HELLO MY NAME IS STEVEN. One of his fingernails had pierced her skin, pink and faint as a paper cut, in that tender valley at the base of her palm where her wristbone met the end of her life line. That he'd touched her—*helped himself to her* is how she later described it to her yoga friend Kurt—was outrageous enough, but not half as outrageous as the idea of her strutting over to the girls and jumping up and down on the concrete in her heels in front of everyone, including her six-year-old son, Shane, who was holding her other hand; Cora Gutierrez, the horror-struck director of development; and the girls themselves, who regarded her with weariness bordering on contempt.

"Come on, lady, have some fun!" Steven insisted, palms out in playful supplication, a sniffly little boy clinging to each of his legs and looking up at her, Dickensian, flanked by more boys behind them peering over their heads. Hip-hop booming on the loudspeakers. Car horns. Cora muttering apologies in her ear. Shane oblivious. When her eyes went instinctively from Steven's pimply face to his broad chest to his crotch to what looked like tennis balls stuffed into the sleeves of his polo shirt and then back to his eyes again, he caught and held her there, busted, and broke into a brash smile, aware, as they all were, of the effect of a tight shirt and jeans on a body basking in its twenties. He stepped toward her.

Her jump-roping was disastrous. A humiliation. The girls twirled as slowly as physics would allow, but still Monica's heels tripped the ropes. She kicked the heels off, bridesmaid-style, and everyone cheered, even Cora and Shane, but she was no better in her stockings, which would be ruined. So what! She was a good sport, was she not? She was laughing along. She wasn't some snooty socialite who couldn't get down and dirty with the people. The ropes slapped slapped slapped her ankles, and she stumbled, but instead of falling she managed a sarcastic curtsy. They clapped and whooped, she thought she was done, but then Steven appeared with her in the circle, and the clapping got louder. He steadied her, his caveman hands surprisingly delicate, then raised them so that his palms hovered just above her shoulders.

"I got you," he said, and when the girls recommenced their twirling, he tapped her shoulders just as the ropes came down, and together they jumped. It took a minute, it took some more stumbling, some feeble protestations, but look at her now, she'd found the rhythm, she could follow. The girls twirled a little faster. A little faster still. More whooping. Monica couldn't look down or she'd break the streak. She could look only at him, into his encouraging eyes, an arm's length away. That same satisfied grin, impressed at her or himself, she couldn't tell. The coarse ginger hairs, not quite organized enough to be called a mustache, above his upper lip. The clogged zits on his cheeks and neck and forehead, his teeth this way and that, his hair floppy and red, the color of the zits, he was so ugly, he should have been so ugly.

When it was over, he asked, "No harm, no foul? You're okay, right?"

Before she could answer, she felt Cora's hand on her wrist, and again she was whisked away, first to Shane, who leapt into her arms, then through a set of heavy glass doors into the gymnasium, where rows of draped tables had been set up in anticipation of some sort of job fair. WAKE UP TO A BETTER FUTURE! sang the banner strung across the scoreboard. She looked back once through the doors and saw Steven lift one of his Dickensian boys onto his shoulders.

"Please stop apologizing," she said to Cora. "No harm. No foul."

"Stevie's our very own Pied Piper," Cora went on. "The kids adore him. More importantly, they *listen* to him. You can imagine how important that is for us. Clubs like this basically raised him. No parents to speak of. A cousin, I think. Maybe an uncle. All before my time. A sad story. I'll make sure Lexi gives him a talking-to, but I want to assure you: we thoroughly vet every counselor and volunteer—anyone who works directly with a child—and we have a zero-tolerance policy for any infraction. You met Lexi? She makes it her personal mission—"

"I'm not a delicate flower," said Monica.

"Of course not!"

"I don't want him to get in trouble," she said. "He's fine." She turned again and spotted him immediately through the glass, his red hair like a flare, at the opposite end of the lot under the basketball net, leaping up to grab the hoop. "He's got a lot of energy."

"There's no energy crisis here!" said Cora, which helped launch her into the reason she'd invited Monica on this tour in the first place: the renovation of the gym they were sitting in—she pointed out the leak stains on the ceiling, the dangerous divots in the floor—and the imperative to build an aquatic center on the site of the concrete lot across which Steven now led a troop of older boys. The opportunity for naming rights. The importance of exercise, noncompetitive team sports, motor skills training, etc., to the developing body and mind. The unconscionable lack of such facilities in these kids' own public taxpayer-funded schools. Surely Monica was well aware of the crisis facing underprivileged youth in Boston. Surely Binswanger's long-standing commitment to various mission-aligned institutions across the city was loud evidence for their shared values and their belief in a better future. Cora explained that they were in the quiet phase of an ambitious capital campaign, but that, with Monica and Arthur's help, they could finally "make some noise" and drum up enough resources—in nearly fifteen years of suffering through pitches like this, Monica had never once heard anyone use the vulgar word *money*, let alone *cash*—to close the gap and meet their goal.

This was just the first of many conversations, Cora promised, as if that was a selling point. She encouraged Monica to talk things over with her husband and the other trustees of the Binswanger Foundation and to be on the lookout for further communications and documents from her in the coming weeks, including a prospectus, a robust strategic plan, testimonials, and a giving pyramid. "We won't make you trek out here again," she said. "We're well equipped with video conferencing . . ."

"Oh, I don't mind," Monica interrupted. "Do we, Shane? Do we mind?" She picked her son up from off the floor and lifted him onto her lap. Shane had spent the entirety of Cora's impassioned speech face-down on the grime, making snow angels and humming a strange melody. Monica was unable sing along to any of Shane's songs because they were all original compositions and rarely repeated. Nor could she know for sure if he'd mind coming back here to the Boys & Girls Club of Roxbury to discuss their capital campaign because, in his six years as her child, he had never spoken a word to her.

"It's an inspiring place, right?" said Cora. "Some days, working here"—she shook her head, jangling her long gold earrings—"it's like I'm addicted. I'm not just saying this because you're a donor, Monica; I feel that I can speak directly to you as a friend. I'm addicted to the *hope*, you know? The *potential.* Whatever I say will sound like a pitch, I'm aware, I'm very aware, but again, we're friends, we've talked about where we come from, how it shapes us. You know the power of place."

What was this quality in Monica that, without effort or even desire on her part, convinced other people, mostly women, not only that she was their friend but that she would hold their secrets as closely as a friend would hold them, when, in truth, she wanted no part of either friendship or secrecy? Where did it come from? As a girl, she neither spoke nor was spoken to, not in the way that Shane never spoke, but in that way of unwanted children who've internalized their redundancy. To step onstage and announce yourself in your small voice was to confirm for the audience why you'd been silent so long. Did women like Cora attach themselves to Monica and confess to abusive husbands and affairs and various vices because they suspected that, if Monica were to repeat what they'd told her, no one would listen? She was a wealthy and powerful woman, a Mama Bear, not unbeautiful, from a prominent family, socially adept and proper, thanks to a decade in European finishing schools. In other words, she should be feared. She should be *intimidating.* What did people smell on her? The must in the drapes? The dirt in the walled garden, the odor of her sisters' feet? How did this boy, this Steven, this sad orphan, know he could just help himself to her wrist? That all he had to do was tap her shoulders and she'd jump?

She saw him one last time before she left. He was crouched in a corner, elbows on his knees, pulling at the skin on his face to try to get a laugh from a little girl Shane's age who was crying her heart out. She rubbed her eyes with her fists, but you could see her peeking through them at Steven's goofy contortions, barely able to contain herself, and when she did finally break he fell over onto his back and pretended to die. He crossed his arms and shut his eyes and lolled out his tongue like a horse and then she climbed on top of him and thumped his chest with those little fists. Monica could hear her yell, "Wake up! Wake up!" but he wouldn't open his eyes, he wouldn't move a muscle, he was torturing the poor kid, until she started to cry again and his face burst to life. He wrapped his arms around her and together they rolled around on the floor, and Monica could feel Shane watching her watch them, his thumb in his mouth, tugging at her sleeve, asking himself, probably, because how would she know, *why can't I do that*, which, if she's honest, is what Monica herself was wondering as she shook herself loose from the moment and hurried out the door.

"Tell me about your brother, Leo," asked this new doctor, Margaret Mead Ashe. She knew about him already, of course, from Katie's file, which was forever outrunning her from doctor's office to doctor's office, from one intake interview to the next, tattling on her and shaping her before she could shape herself. There must have been a time in human history, she thought, back before AI and digital networks and cameras and hieroglyphics, when a clean slate was possible, but that time is long gone and will only come again when the earth collapses. Though she deleted all her social media accounts and carried only a dumbphone, Katie Starks still felt exposed and projected upon everywhere she went, and nowhere felt worse than in an armchair face-to-face with another doctor, her file aglow from the tablet on the woman's lap.

Katie squinted to read the diploma framed on the wall behind her and to the left, just out of her field of vision if she looked straight at Dr. Ashe, which she tried not to do. "Your parents really named you after Margaret Mead?" she asked.

"You're familiar with her work?" was her reply.

These people never gave you a straight answer.

"Not really," said Katie. "But I've heard of the name. It's historically famous."

"Yes it is," she said. "And yes, they did. My parents were Quakers. Are you familiar with Quakerism?"

"I'm not familiar with much," said Katie. "Most things are strange to me. And most people."

"Tell me about that, then. And please call me Margaret."

"I'd rather talk about Leo," she said. She gestured toward the tablet, now between them on the coffee table. "Maybe you should just read me what's in there and I'll tell you what they got wrong."

Katie had enough self-awareness to recognize that she was performing her hostility. She wasn't angry at Dr. Ashe—Margaret—who meant well enough, or at herself or Leo or anyone in particular. She was just tired of her own story, which bored her and would surely bore Margaret, whose wavy gray curls and deep-rutted crow's-feet had seen it all. If Katie had tried harder in creative writing classes, maybe she could come up with something to shake Margaret out of her self-satisfied slouch, but, even in those workshops, she'd recycled her dead-older-brother material and her dead-druggie-mother material and her kind-but-weird Aunt Alice material, picked through them for shards to shape into poems, and slapped different names on the characters in her "fiction." She'd liked her professors—they meant well enough, too—but she didn't buy their whole hero's journey thing, or their reverence for the imagination, something she'd never had much of. Even as a kid, her stuffed animals or her dolls were just literally themselves—a carrot with green fronds made of yarn, a fat plastic baby—until Leo drew a face on the carrot with Magic Marker and turned the fronds into long flowing hair made of emeralds, and until he twisted the fat plastic baby's head around and around in its neck socket going, "I'm an owl! I'm possessed! I'm the Daughter of Frankenstein! I'm Ivanka Trump!"

That's my first memory of him, she told Margaret: her brother, Leo, bringing her bedroom to life. Katie hadn't had many actual toys, but when Leo was around every object became a plaything: a pencil between his fingers a slithery eel swimming up to her from the deep lake, a toilet roll a telephone through which they confessed their secrets. Leo had made her a tree swing from rope, a big white bucket, and a saw; he'd made her a castle out of cardboard boxes dug out from the neighbor's trash bins, duct-taped together, and painted with their mom's makeup; he'd written her name in glitter above the door of the castle and told her no harm could come to her there, which, as far as she knew, was the only time he'd lied to her.

She'd been too young to remember his face. She knew it only from the online news reports and the three or four photos her mother had printed out from her phone and pressed into one of those old sticky albums with a red cover soft as a couch cushion. Her mother was gone, but Katie had kept the album. It wasn't Leo's face, but his voice—or, more accurately, his voices—that she was able to recall with perfect accuracy. Put her in a voice lineup, if that was a thing, and she could identify his without hesitation. His natural voice had been deep as the lake where the eel came from, but he could turn it into a posh British lady's vibrato, an old man's toothy whistle, a monster's growl, a piggy snarfle like he was talking through his nose, anything she requested. She'd get inside her castle and he'd knock on the door and she'd say, "Who goes there?" and every time it was some new disguise. He never ran out.

She remembered his hair, dyed inky black and longer than a girl's, longer than Katie's was then or now, but no one ever mistook him for a girl when he used his regular voice. His hair was wavier than yours, she told Margaret. Their mother hated it, which was probably why he never cut it or stopped dyeing it. The truth was that Katie didn't know him at all, at least not in the way an adult, or even an older child, could know a person. He'd been less a person to her than a presence.

"And then that presence was suddenly gone," Margaret interrupted, predictably. "And, soon after, so was your mother's."

"Yup," said Katie. "And those twin absences, just a few years apart, have defined my life and my self-narrative by giving me abandonment issues, depression, multiple forms of anxiety, a daddy complex, a mommy complex, gender dysphoria, and hyperattachment disorder, making me more prone to substance abuse, masochism, suicidal ideation, and panic attacks, all of which is detailed in that fat file." She pointed to the tablet. "I'm not here because I think you can cure me or even make me feel better by teaching me coping strategies or reevaluating my medication regimen. I'm here because I don't want to bore people with this stuff any more than I already have. And because I'm lonely. And probably a narcissist."

"Do you mean *reactive* attachment disorder?" asked Margaret. "You should get the details right if you want to be as good and clever company as you think you are."

"Cute," Katie said. So Margaret was going to be the type who tried to win her over by calling her on her bullshit, like Jennifer and Grady before her, like every daytime-TV therapist. She wouldn't be as maternal as Felicity or as cerebral as Dr. Boutelle. Katie quickly adjusted her expectations. She'd hoped that a doctor named after Margaret Mead—about whom she knew absolutely everything since reading about her in Lily King's awesome novel *Euphoria*—might show her something a little different. Why else had Katie chosen her from the drop-down menu of profiles on the Psychology Today website? It wasn't her degree from UChicago, or her acceptance of Katie's shitty insurance, or even that her office was conveniently located across the street from the bookstore. Katie's deep dive into the life and works of Margaret Mead had come during one of her manic phases. Or was that her OCD? Should she ask? Instead she tried a version of her usual opening salvo to see where it got her.

"That presence?" Katie said. "Leo's presence, I mean? It's not gone."

"Where is it?"

"What does the file say?"

"I'd rather hear it in your words. The context in these reports is useful, of course, and important, but, as far as I'm concerned, we're at the very beginning of your process, not the middle and certainly not the end. You've had a number of well-meaning folks trying to help you over the years. But I believe in self-authorship."

She stopped there, as if the concept of self-authorship was obvious.

"By which you mean . . . ?"

"Your story your way. Your metaphors. No therapy speak. No diagnoses. No prepackaged narratives. No additional meds—"

"—You're not authorized to prescribe them anyway."

"Yes, fine, do you *want* more meds? Do you feel that you *need* more meds?"

"No."

"I didn't think so."

"This doesn't sound any different than what I've always done. Spin my sad tales. Watch you nod along. Answer your follow-up questions. Try to keep you awake and interested. Promise to use this or that strategy. Promise to exercise. Promise not to get stoned so much. Pay you a small fortune."

"I did see that your co-pay is quite high."

"Yeah, shock of the century, neither my part-time bookstore job nor my part-time Goodwill job nor my part-time waitressing job come with platinum medical plans."

"You must find the counseling process valuable if you're willing to sacrifice so much income."

"I'm trying to keep myself alive," said Katie.

She'd spoken these words to a doctor before, and just as casually. What scared her now, though, what caused her to shield her face with her hand and turn it away from Margaret Mead Ashe, was that, for the first time in a long while, she wasn't sure they were true.

"You identify strongly with your brother and you're afraid something terrible will happen to you the way it did to him. That this terrible thing will jump out at you like a beast in the jungle."

"Yes, sure," said Katie to the wall of hanging herbs at the window. The basil was overwhelming. She closed her eyes. No, that was rosemary.

"Though an overdose was your mother's official cause of death, you consider this a form of suicide, and therefore you're worried the beast might just be yourself."

"Yes," said Katie. "Beast sounds about right." All the herbs were growing strong except the spearmint, which was odd because it was basically a weed.

"You had a lonely childhood."

"To say the least."

"Your aunt, the one who took you in, has recently passed."

"Yes."

"You have no other family."

"No."

Margaret scooted around the table toward her in her swively chair. "If I were you, I'd probably feel cursed, too," she said. "I'd say you've had more than your fair share, honey."

Once, in high school, Katie's guidance counselor had used that very same phrase: *more than your fair share.* As if any share might be considered fair. Would one family suicide have been fair? Reasonable, even? How about a single overdose? A stretch of just a few friendless, self-hating, panicked years? The high school counselor had given Katie the good news that life was long and had a way of balancing itself out, that it was a kind of luck—yes, luck!—for these awful things to have happened to her so early on. Not only did it build resilience—You're much stronger than you realize! You're developing a thick coat of armor!—it put the odds in her favor that the worst had already happened. Was that any comfort at all?

No, it was not.

"I'm not a very good doctor," said Margaret Mead Ashe, which was the first thing any doctor had ever said that surprised Katie. "At least, not anymore. Not by the book's standards. I don't believe in certain approaches and frameworks the way I once did. I haven't read this closely." She picked up the tablet and tossed it onto the desk behind her, like a flamboyant lawyer dismissing evidence. "Only enough to get the basic facts. I promise to listen to you, to welcome your story into my story. So tell me, Leo, where does your story really start?"

Tues, Mar 12, 2019 at 4:21 PM

That was weird

CHLOE

Dude was definitely following us

MIA

Right?? Totally thought you were being paranoid

CHLOE

I have a Spidey sense

He's after you Tessa

Doubtful

MIA

He's hot though?

Hot Creeper!!!

CHLOE

Creeping is NOT HOT I don't care what he looks like

Jk

Sorta

CHLOE

Where r u rn Tessa? R u alone?

I'm home. Doors locked. Don't stress.

MIA

He turned around when we got to the Cube

CHLOE

OK

Watch your back, Tessa

MIA

I'll take him if you don't want him

CHLOE

Seriously Mia stop

Mon, Mar 18, 2019 at 6:04 PM

Hot Creeper sighting!

MIA

OMG where

Keen!! Sitting on steps when I got off bus

I'm with team so no biggie

My dykes say don't smash lol but everyone else is like get it girl

MIA

I say get it!

CHLOE

I'm telling you I get a vibe

but you do you

I'm gonna say hi

CHLOE

Of course you are

What about Officer Friendly?

I can't say hi to a guy?

6:44 PM

CHLOE

???

8:02 PM

Proof Of Life!

CHLOE

Oh thank god

MIA

So what's his deal

Verdict is in: not creepy!

We sat talking forever

His name is Matt

@mattycardullo

Junior. Lives on Elm

Short but crazy cute smile

Seems sweet

Wrestles?? Kinda random

CHLOE

Ew

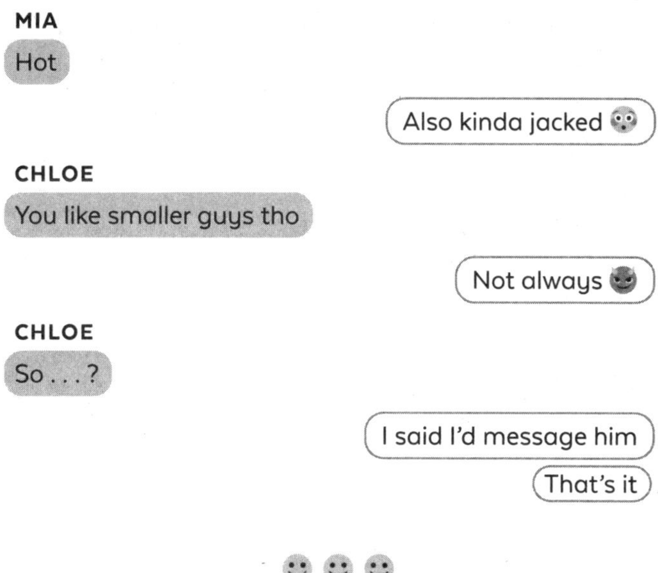

For years, when you asked Lori Whitford what she wanted to do with her life, she'd say it didn't matter if she was rich or poor or skinny or fat, what job she worked, how nice her house was, which foreign countries she got to visit—it didn't matter if she never left the great state of Michigan—as long as she had someone to love. At thirty-eight, her wish still ungranted, she married Gus Cardullo. It wasn't so much that he was in the right place at the right time; it was that he'd been there all along, waiting for Lori to come to her senses. If she held out any longer, Lori reasoned, she might miss her chance to feel for a child what she'd never felt for Gus or any of the men before him. Not even for Jesus Christ, her first crush, who didn't count, for obvious reasons. Jesus started showing up again in those years, too, though, like a friend from childhood who'd moved back to town, and Lori took His return as a sign that she had two choices left: the convent or trusty old Gus Cardullo.

On their wedding day, she was already eight weeks pregnant with Matthew, named for the first book of the New Testament. If born a girl, he'd have been Angela, after Gus's mother, but also after angels, which Lori collected. From Easter to Christmas that year, 1999, in the anxious final months of a cursed millennium, she carried Matthew in her womb like a gift some magical Giver had forbidden her to open. This Giver she imagined as some amalgamation of Gus, God, Destiny, and her own Forbearance. She had a strong attachment to the glorious gift inside her, a supposedly real thing unseen and unheld, but the attachment wasn't yet love; it was closer to faith, to hope.

It wasn't love even when, finally, she first held him. She can admit this now. *So this is you*, went her own voice in her head. *So this is it.* He was perfect in all the ways a baby boy should be: chunky legs and arms, strong loud cry, thumping giant bean of a chest. He'd done his job getting born, and now she was supposed to want to eat him. Gus and Mamma Angela and the Cardullo aunts and uncles couldn't keep his feet and fingers out of their mouths, gnawing on his thighs, sucking his fat cheeks. They passed him back and forth like a ham, and together they feasted.

One of the nurses eyed Lori knowingly. "One day at a time," she whispered to her, pressing her thumb into Lori's palm as she adjusted her pillow, like they were two alcoholics. In her words Lori heard one of her favorite songs, "Day by Day," from *Godspell*, not quite a hymn but close enough, and sang it to herself and to Matthew over and over, replacing the Lord with the name of her son, begging to see him more clearly, to love him more dearly, as the Cardullos swelled around them, fleshy and loud, mouths gaping, swallowing him along with all the air in the increasingly crowded room.

It quickly came time to bring Matthew home. Christmas was a few days away, and, as a surprise, Gus told her, he'd put up a second tree in the nursery and wrapped it in blue lights. He'd tested the lights, but, superstitious, he wouldn't plug them in or leave them on until Matthew lay safely in his crib—like the candle that always burned beside the tabernacle when it contained the consecrated Host. But the idea of the hot flickering tree, smothered by one of her angels at the top, crammed with red and gold balls, dripping tinsel, terrified Lori. What if it caught fire? What if it fell over onto the crib? What if it was too much for her son to live up to, all this joy and hunger? Take it down, she begged Gus. Move it out, at least. She wouldn't leave Matty in his room alone for one second if that tree was there.

She wasn't breathing right. She couldn't get enough air into her lungs without the air needing to push itself back out, like it was rejecting her. Could you be allergic to hospital air? To the odorless, colorless breath of your firstborn child, like carbon monoxide? She sweated through her gown. The room tilted. No one noticed except the alcoholic nurse. She slipped Lori a pill. By the time it worked, it was too late. She'd already infected Matthew, who, suddenly, wasn't breathing right either. She—his mother, the person who knew him best—was the first to sense that his bean chest didn't thump the way it had been thumping. He felt all wrong, looked all wrong. Shrunken. Not sucking with the same gusto. He wasn't the same child. He'd been switched. She stared directly into his face, trying to match it to the face she'd met the day before. She held him up by his armpits for the nurse to inspect, begging her to show him to the doctor one more time before they took him home. Whosever kid this was, hers or another mother's, he was sick, he was suffocating, why couldn't they see?

Standing around the bed, already in their puffy coats, Gus and Angela were laughing at her. Matty's been checked out six ways to Sunday, said Gus. He's perfect, said Angela. They shook their heads. Don't be scared, they said. He's not made of glass.

"He's made of gold," said Angela. "Pure gold."

Later that day, just before the doctor took the baby to surgery, he let Lori hold him. He assured her that this child was her son, Matthew Agosto Cardullo, and made her read the full name and date of birth out loud for him from the band around his wrist. And where are we right now? he asked her, and when she replied, Jackson Hospital, he said very good and promised her, the way a father promises a treat after Mass for a bratty toddler, that the procedure they were about to perform on her two-day-old son was highly routine.

It was simple, really, the doctor explained, turning to Gus, his back to her as if she'd left the room. Matthew's aortic valve had narrowed, or had already been too narrow when he was born, so now they needed to go in through the groin with a catheter and stretch the valve by inflating a tiny balloon. This would allow the blood to flow more easily to and from the heart. A basic plumbing job, the two men joked. In a few hours, Matthew would be good as new, and then tomorrow morning—or maybe even later tonight, in plenty of time for Santa Claus—they could bring him home. In all likelihood, they'd need to come back here to Jackson for a follow-up procedure that would patch him up permanently. But that wouldn't be necessary until he was a little older. You hear *heart surgery* and you think *danger!* said the doctor, but in this case the bark was worse than the bite.

Nothing this man said sounded simple or even logical to Lori. A balloon? The groin that was nowhere near the heart? The patch. The bite. The jokes, brawny and ghoulish. She held Matthew more tightly. Angela scrutinized her from the chair in the corner, legs crossed, still in her fur. Accusing her. Lori didn't entirely trust herself as a mother, but she trusted this doctor less, and Gus not at all. She'd seen the movies where a new mom presses her child to her chest, flees out the door, runs through the echoing halls, chased by her husband and men in green masks and scrubs. The husband turns the corner and the rebel nurse trips him. The mother reaches the elevator and frantically pushes the button, the baby wailing in her arms. There's a ding, and then the doors close, and then she's busting through the emergency exit into an alley, and they're safe, they're on their way. Everyone in the theater thinks the mother is crazy, but by the end of the movie you find out the doctor and the husband and the old *strega* in the fur coat were all in cahoots, they were going to sell the baby and tell the mother he died. They acted like good people on the outside, but in fact they were agents of the devil. The mother in the movie isn't stupid; she gets the boy's heart checked just in case. It's strong as an ox, says a kindly country doctor. She's in Iowa. She goes farther west. Colorado. It's her and her son against the world. She's a hero.

The urge to crush Matthew was no different in degree from the urge to protect him, and either action would result in the same outcome: she'd save him from the laughing men and the evil old lady and the falling blue Christmas tree and the computers exploding and the crazies shooting up schools, and all the various unpredictable terrors of the next millennium. With either action, she, his only mother, who suddenly loved him with a fierceness that armored and emboldened her, would be the instrument of his freedom. She had delivered him once and would do so again, here, in Jackson Hospital, the pillow pressed down mercifully over his sleeping face, or there, on their farm in Colorado, his little legs running through tall grass. Two choices, two equal acts of love she'd commit if necessary, without hesitation, no matter the outcome to her body or her soul.

This was how it felt, after all those years, to finally get her wish.

LAST SEEN (II)

James drove to the Cactus Tree Motel in the gathering snow. Floyd, the owner and manager, was surprised to see him, not only because of the weather but because today was a Sunday and the next day was Christmas Eve. Floyd was used to James and Caleb's frequent no-shows and last-minute cancellations, but as long as the Cactus Tree wasn't sold out, which it never was, he didn't charge a penalty.

"I sympathize with your plight, Jim" was how Floyd once phrased it. Why had James given a fake name that was just the common shortened form of his real name? Why not Jake, at least? Or Jeremy? He'd never been a good liar, despite how much practice he had at it. As for Floyd, ever since Vermonters "showed their asses" on gay marriage back in 2000, he'd gotten more and more shifty and separatist in his ideology. "It's us or them" was Floyd's mantra. This mantra didn't sit quite right with Caleb, who found Floyd creepy, and who believed—ah, the naivete of youth!—that the healing of cultural divides was not only achievable but necessary for the survival of the earth. James didn't mind that Floyd was a little vulgar and extreme in his politics as long as he continued to rent him rooms for cheap, accept cash without checking or recording their IDs, and keep it all between "consenting adults."

Floyd wished Jim a Merry Christmas and handed him the key for 202, the corner room in the back, which overlooked the woods. Even by roadside motel standards, the Cactus Tree was not a decent establishment, but its incongruous Southwest decor (red, orange, and turquoise striped carpets; a lamp made from a bison skull; phallic succulents large and small in dusty terra-cotta pots) showed that Floyd, who'd grown up with money outside Santa Fe, had once at least put some effort into the place. Caleb had found Floyd and the Cactus Tree more than a year ago by searching and chatting online, something James was afraid to do either on his work computer or the desktop he shared with Iris.

It had been six weeks since James and Caleb last touched, but such a cold fact was impossible to believe for two men who were on each other's minds every minute of every day. This, at least, was what they confessed to each other in text messages, which James deleted from his BlackBerry immediately upon reading them, and then made sure Caleb did the same. Even when they were stuck in their respective alternate universes—Caleb in his dorm room, which he'd petitioned the college to let him share with a girl; the nineteenth-century farmhouse in Weybridge James occupied with Iris—they connected in the increasingly intimate and seductive virtual world of 2007, texting and sending grainy photos in the middle of the night, talking on James's drive home or on their lunch breaks as they ate in separate dining halls two buildings apart.

There was nothing alternate or virtual about the Cactus Tree, and now that the cold weather had come and made meeting outdoors impossible, the drab motel was all they had of the real world. James had come to hate the winter for the loss of Sycamore Park (another real world), their semiprivate bed of pine needles, their barefoot walks across the rocks in the stream, his running shoes in one hand, his other hand on Caleb's bare shoulder. The park closed at sundown, which came as early as four fifteen some days, so even if the trees hadn't lost their protective leaves, their presence at the park was itself a crime. Equally impossible were their weekend hikes on the Long Trail, where they could hold hands on the narrow paths that led to Lake Pleiad and then take turns jumping from the rocks. They kept a decorous distance when they were swimming in the lake itself, while, under the surface of the muddy water, legs entwined, their feet found each other's crotches. And on the off chance someone James recognized did show up at the popular swimming hole, a person who wasn't a nudist or a stoner or another of life's dropouts, he'd just say the two had met along the way and struck up a conversation to pass the time. (Tell me your name again, kid?)

In these colder months—oh, how James resented them! He resented them still, for the precious hours they stole from them both—it was mission impossible to find enough time in the middle of the weekday when a class or a club didn't obligate Caleb *and* when James could slip away from the library *and* they could drive the hour and a half round trip to Rutland for a few minutes of frantic fucking in the Cactus Tree. Not to mention that James's body was not built for quickies, or the constant nagging worry that Iris would swing by his office unannounced or invite him to lunch, or that Iris would call and need him home in the five minutes it took to get there from campus because she'd finally found an electrician to fix the lights in the stairwell, or that Iris would hear from a colleague, some gossip like her frenemy Carmen Agarwal, that she'd seen James—it was definitely James!—pulling onto Route 7 down in Rutland the other day . . .

This Christmas gift of a Sunday to themselves had actually come from the dreaded Carmen, who'd arranged a social outing for Iris and a few other women professors on the 23rd. Carmen was to drive the ladies up to Burlington for a late brunch followed by some shopping and a secular holiday performance by the Vermont Symphony Orchestra. When Iris woke that Sunday to the snow coating their bedroom window, she exclaimed, "Oh, thank God," but Carmen wasn't about to let her workaholic best friend get off that easy. We live in the mountains of Vermont, Carmen reminded her; a little snow and wind was no excuse to spend another weekend day grading papers or working on her next book. Besides, the worst of it wasn't expected until the holiday.

"The weather gods are no match for Carmen Agarwal," James said when she pulled into their driveway in a white college-issued van.

"Do something fun," Iris said back. "And pick up some rock salt?"

In the cellar, in a large box marked DUNCAN STREET, full of sentimental items from his childhood home, waited Caleb's Christmas present: a blue scarf with exposed white stitching, matching gloves, and a leather "warrior bracelet," all purchased from the Roots Fair

Trade store in Brandon. The saleswoman had assured James that the materials were sustainable, that the workers who made them were well compensated, and that the jasper stones in the warrior bracelet offered spiritual healing benefits. The stones didn't offer protection, she said, but they did free the wearer from fear and doubt. James was confident in the scarf and gloves—the blue was the exact blue of Caleb's eyes—but he hesitated on the bracelet.

"Do you have anything with protection stones?" he heard himself, a forty-six-year-old man with an advanced degree in library science, ask the saleswoman.

She cast a glance over the rack. "Not for men," she said.

James had forbidden Caleb to buy him a gift. Not only did he not want the broke college boy to spend money on him, he didn't want to be forced to hide the gift in the DUNCAN STREET box or, worse, toss it in some rest stop trash can on the way home from Rutland.

The moment Carmen's van drove off with Iris, he went straight to the basement, stuffed the bracelet and scarf and gloves in a Hannaford's bag (no time to wrap them), and drove to the motel, which took an extra twenty minutes with the snow.

Waiting in the lobby with the key to room 202 in his pocket, James grew more and more worried about Caleb's old Toyota on those slick country roads. He made himself a coffee from the ancient machine in the lobby and stirred two packs of whitener into the Styrofoam cup, trying to avoid Floyd's pitying gaze. He checked his phone every ten seconds. He should have insisted Caleb follow him. Then, finally, thank God, look, there he was, pulling into the parking lot in his perfectly un-crashed car, and now, look, he was grabbing something from the back seat, a paper bag overflowing with white tissue paper.

"You hit the jackpot with that one," said Floyd, as they watched him flip up the wipers.

"He's a good kid," said James defensively. "It's not like that."

"What's it like, then?" asked Floyd. "I'd sure like to know."

If they'd both arrived on time, they'd have had exactly seven hours. Now they had only six. They climbed the outdoor stairs, where they could finally kiss. Caleb didn't like to show any affection in front of Floyd. In the frigid room, they didn't bother at first to take off their coats, they were too busy with all that kissing, rolling around on the bed like children down a hill, unable to let go, greedy already for more hours, more minutes, because once you have six hours like this you simply must have more or you will die.

Eventually, the radiator spitting, their skin slicked with sweat, they relieved each other of their bulky hooded parkas, his Middlebury sweatshirt, James's wool cardigan, their belts, their jeans, his boxers, James's thermal underwear, his white sneaker socks with holes in the heels, James's argyles. Then, from the mysterious red bag, Caleb pulled out an unwrapped condom, held it up for a moment, then put it not on himself, which was their usual practice, but on James, saying, *Surprise, Merry Christmas from Santa*, and, for the first time, he climbed on top of James and let him ease his cock in.

"Why now?"

"Because you want to."

"I've wanted to for a while. From the beginning."

"You've been really patient."

"You're not bored with me?"

"No way!"

"I don't know."

"You told me not to give you anything you'd have to throw away. Is this better than a new wallet?"

"This is better than a new wallet."

"I'm doing okay?"

"You're doing great."

"I came prepared."

"I noticed."

"That's why I was late."

"Oh, Caleb."

"James?"

"I'm here. You're doing so great."

"It's not my first time."

"That's all right. I figured. I can't blame you."

"I wanted it to be you. But you're not available. You're never available."

"It's all right. You've been careful, though?"

"Always."

"Good."

"The first time was this dumb kid from Debate."

"Shhh."

"I get so restless and lonely."

"Me too."

"I didn't even like him. He voted for George Bush. He's a Nazi."

"He's probably not a Nazi."

"No, he's an actual Nazi."

"Okay."

"You're bigger than him."

"That poor kid."

"Don't say that. You're perfect. Every part of you. You're my favorite man I've ever met. You know that, right?"

"You'll meet someone so much better. Someone available. Someone your age."

"I won't. I don't want that. I only want you."

"Shhh."

"I don't want to graduate. I don't want to move away. I don't want to be twenty-one."

"Yes you do, Peter Pan. You'll see."

"I'm talking too much again. I'm being negative."

"It's okay. I like when you talk. I didn't at first, but I do now. It's nice to hear your voice."

"Can we do it like this every time from now on?"

"Yes."

"And the other way, too."

"Sure."

"Which do you like better?"

"I like you each and every way."

"Even though I'm fat."

"You're not fat!"

"Look at this gut."

"I'm looking right at it."

"I've got a fucking beer belly!"

"It's not a beer belly."

"Can we find a different hotel?"

"Sure."

"Will you take me to Montreal?"

"Sure."

"Really?"

"Yes. Someday. We just have to plan it."

"Will you always be around? No matter what?"

"Yes."

"I love you."

"I love you."

They'd set the alarm on the nightstand for 6:50 p.m., just in case they dozed off, which they sometimes did, drunk on each other, James on his back, Caleb along his side, one arm thrown over his chest, his head nuzzling his left shoulder. When the alarm went off, they gathered their clothes from the floor and, precisely at 7 p.m., exited room 202, dropped the plastic key card in the slot of the wooden box in the lobby, and hurried outside to avoid Floyd. They stood between their cars and exchanged a quick, chaste hug, playing uncle and nephew for any passersby. James half noticed the stray candy wrappers and fast-food bags and textbooks that littered the floor of Caleb's car, his knapsack tossed onto the back seat, the stuffed brown teddy bear sitting up watchfully in a blue Middlebury sweater. When Caleb got in, he placed the bear in the red bag with white tissue paper that six hours earlier had contained James's Christmas present.

They pulled out of the Cactus Tree parking lot at the same time. James's last glimpse of him was through the window as he took the exit for 7 South just before he himself went north. He assumed what the boy had told him was true: that he was headed home for the holiday in Poughkeepsie; that he was looking forward to pinching the cheeks of his newborn niece; that, as instructed, he wouldn't text James until after the new year.

Strange now to think of the fugitive joy of that day, of the wonder James had felt at his inexplicable luck. What did the boy see in his ordinary body, in his mind and dick that were only slightly above average, in his J-grade personality, in his decent-at-best face? The closest to comprehension James could come to that night, driving home alone in the increasingly heavy snow, was that his ordinariness itself, his thudding sturdiness, was the real world in which Caleb felt most alive. A common house, like the ones he passed, warm and safe and only dimly aglow. He doubted that Caleb knowingly sought out this quality in him, or in men in general, despite a self-awareness far beyond his twenty-one years. James had made him many promises he couldn't keep, but he'd never lied to him. Not once. Not even that first day in Sycamore Park, when he'd invented a career in pharmaceuticals. In the shadow of those protective trees, as a bored single chemist from Burlington, he'd shown Caleb the truest truth of him; it was upon coming home to Weybridge that he'd dressed himself back up in lies.

The only other explanation for the two of them was love. But nobody was satisfied with love as an answer anymore. James always figured it must have been something else.

On the last day Monica saw Steven alive, he left their room at the agreed-upon time, five o'clock sharp. She insisted on this hour of buffer, even though, in all her years married to Arthur, he'd never once come home from the office in daylight. A reverse vampire, she called him, whatever that would be. A lizard maybe? A workaholic lizard? No, that was unkind, and not even clever, and, these days, Monica was trying to suppress her instinct for viciousness when it came to Arthur. It was more accurate and generous to say that Arthur's reliable absence gave shape and permission to her days. That, upon his arrival, she welcomed his Hollywood kiss followed by the fixing of drinks (bourbon on the rocks for him, Campari and soda for her), followed by the rote accounting of their days as Stefano prepared the dinner they ate alone with their son. This was often followed by a second dinner at some charity event in a hotel ballroom downtown or, better, in their TV room upstairs, Arthur nodding off beside her in front of a melting bowl of butter pecan ice cream. It was accurate, and generous enough, to say that this was her mostly satisfying life, and that the addition of Steven had not depreciated it but enriched it.

Earlier that afternoon, the heavy shadows that appeared on the guest room wall brought on that flutter of panic she associated with Arthur's end-of-the-weekday return. But when she realized it was just the bleak Boston midwinter, just February up to its usual tricks of light, just 3:22 p.m., and she still had more than an hour to go in Steven's "Italian lesson," the flutter evaporated. She switched on the lamp. Her phone had fallen onto the floor. Before she could reach it, Steven stopped her arm, his grip on her as tight and proprietary as it had been that first day at the Boys & Girls Club. The sound and vibrate were both on, he reminded her, as was the 4:55

alarm; if someone needed her, they'd hear it go off; when the time came, he'd make it out no problem, as always. He was on alert, too. Did she think he wanted someone to walk in any more than she did?

A few measly afternoon hours a week, he complained. No time together outside this room, this wing of the house, like prisoners. It was a waste of their precious lives not to spend every second like this, her skin stuck to his, their limbs intertwined, his tongue in her holes. (This was how he talked; this was how he taught her to talk.) It was a waste for her to focus even one percent of her attention on her stupid fucking phone while they were together, he said. It was a waste to complain, he said, though what was he doing if not complaining? Don't even swat that fly away, he said. Let him taste us, too. Get him drunk on our sweat.

They had different ideas about what these afternoons meant, and where they were headed, but on one fact they agreed: they had reached the third point.

The first point, nearly a year ago now, entailed a set of internal calculations that led Monica to call Cora Gutierrez and request a follow-up meeting about the Boys & Girls Club's capital campaign. She'd just found the tour and the Club's ambitious renovation plans so inspiring, she cooed to Cora; Shane, too, had lit up at the place, all that energy. Tuesday afternoon worked for her, yes, same as the other day. No, there was no need to bring Arthur along for this one. She had plenty of decision-making power when it came to their philanthropic expenses.

She drove to Roxbury. She parked, as instructed, in the spot reserved for the director. Then she sat in her car for a minute, the radio still on, Shane punching the child lock, a caged animal. She reminded herself of the promise she'd made that if Steven wasn't there that day, she'd accept the clear sign from Fate and avoid potential humiliation. She understood that she had only approached this first point; she had not yet reached it.

But then, over the net of a makeshift tennis court chalked onto the lot, Steven's eyes and hers found each other. He stopped mid-serve, nodded neutrally as she walked past, like he'd been expecting her, and then completed a graceful gentle lob to the five or six kids on the other side of the net, two of whom crashed into each other to return it.

The meeting with Cora took twenty minutes. Monica pledged a bigger donation to the club than she and Arthur had discussed, and then Cora clapped her on the back and pulled her close like she'd just won their team the title. In the room marked GIRLS, Monica checked her teeth for lipstick and smoothed her skirt. Then, back straight, tits up, one strappy-heeled foot in front of the other, she marched back through the heavy double doors onto the lot and, before she lost her nerve, straight to Steven. She reintroduced herself as the Jump Rope Lady, offered her hand, remarked upon his extraordinary rapport with the kids, and inquired as to whether he ever took on special cases one-on-one outside of the Club.

"Special cases?" he asked. He squatted to meet Shane face-to-face. "You a special case, little dude?"

Shane's thumb went right into his mouth. Instant regression. But—Monica wasn't just imagining it—his face did brighten when Steven's got close to it. Color did rise to his cheeks, and the corners of his lips did eke their way into a natural smile.

He's nonverbal, Monica mouthed.

"I'm not a babysitter."

"That's not what I'm looking for," she said. "Or what my son needs." She picked Shane up, balanced him on her hip, an awkward feat at his age and weight, but one he often demanded so that he could cling to her with his head tucked behind her back and his cheek pressed between her shoulder blades, shielding himself from the world. "I've seen how good you are with the kids here. I have a feeling you can get through to Shane in ways that my husband and I can't. He doesn't have any brothers or sisters yet so our house can be . . . a little lonely."

She explained that Shane attended a private school in Newton in the mornings, but that his afternoons were mostly free and unstructured, and that she and Arthur had been debating what more they could do for him at his age: tutors, skills coaches, music lessons, life lessons, summer camp, even boarding school. Shane had an army of doctors and therapists, she said, trained in the textbook, but what he needed most was a friend. A buddy. Someone who wasn't his mother, someone who was also a boy. All of this was easy to tell Steven because it had the benefit of being true.

"I'm not certified in anything," he said.

"Cora says you're a 'wonder,'" said Monica. "And I think a wonder is what we most need here."

"Miss G is good people."

"I'd still have to talk this over with my husband, of course," Monica went on. "To set it in stone. But, before we even take that step, I was thinking Shane and I could take you to lunch. Get to know each other. Make sure it's a good fit. Would you be open to that?

Not today, of course, but soon. I realize this is out of the blue—I was just so inspired—"

He thought a moment. Rubbed his rough chin. "My pops taught me never say no to a free meal," he said.

"And mine taught me there was no such thing," said Monica.

This caught him off guard, which was surely what she wanted, though she didn't realize that until she spoke. Steven had taken charge from the moment they'd met—his hand on her wrist, drawing the faintest hint of blood, each time she replayed it in her mind it was more outrageous—so it was now her turn to make her own grab. She was the adult, after all. She had the money. She had more to lose, yes, but less time left on earth in which to lose it and to face the consequences. On paper, she was better-looking, with a smoother complexion, and she was tight as a drum in the waist, not from Pilates or a tummy tuck, but from genetics. He had youth, of course. For now. In this economy, who would you say was in the stronger position? Did his youth just automatically trump her experience and money and Sabine genes?

Her offer of employment, followed by the invitation to lunch, constituted the first point. Monica knew it the way you know, just after the death of someone you love, that the life you'd been living until that moment could no longer be lived the same way. It wasn't just that you'd passed through a gate, it was that it locked automatically behind you. There was nowhere to go but forward into the territory on the other side.

At South Street Diner, he ordered something called the Chocolate Fantasy French Toast, onto which he drizzled half a jar of maple syrup and smeared multiple pats of butter. For Shane, Monica ordered a square of warm banana bread and a large fruit bowl, which they split. When it came to breakfast, if not much else, Monica was resolutely Italian: a whole milk cappuccino within a half hour of waking, taken with a biscotto on a ceramic plate, followed by a four-hour fast. She considered this the secret to maintaining her figure, but, just in case, she transformed into an American by lunch so as to avoid the heaviness of *pranzo*, opting for a veggie-packed salad topped with three ounces of a lean protein, washed down and cleansed with lemon water. She ate dinner like a socialite: the white parts of a Statler chicken, blanched unbuttered asparagus, a single bite of the mashed potatoes, and three glasses of white wine plucked from the platter of a circulating waiter. Those pre-dinners with Shane and Arthur, handmade by Stefano—fresh pasta carbonara, fried meatballs with orange and mint, mile-deep Sicilian pizza, all of which she devoured in strained silence punctuated by various tantrums (theirs, hers, depending on the night)—didn't factor into her accounting of the day's calorie intake.

She watched Steven stuff a forkful of the fluffy bread into his mouth, chocolate dripping onto his plate. "You and Shane have something in common already," she said.

"What's that?"

"A sweet tooth."

He wiped his mouth and held up another forkful meant for Shane. "With your permission?" he asked.

"I'd prefer that you didn't," she said. "We don't want him to know what he's missing."

"How do you know he's got a sweet tooth then?"

She turned to Shane. "Where do we find candy wrappers?" she asked him. "Do we find them under your bed?"

Steven laughed. "A little sugar won't kill him."

"That's what Stefano says. And Erma. Stefano's our cook; Erma manages the house. They both spoil him, which makes my husband and me the bad guys. I pretend not to notice, but it bothers Arthur. He believes in a more . . . military approach to child-rearing. It's important for you to know these things before you come work for us."

Steven leaned in and whispered to her, "You can just talk like this in front of him? Say whatever you want about him and your house? How much does he understand?"

"Well, he's six," said Monica. "How much does a six-year-old understand, let alone remember?"

"Depends on the kid," said Steven proudly. "Ask me about any day in my sixth year of life and I can tell you what I did and what it looked like. I've got a photographic memory."

"Oh that's a*ma*zing," said Monica, because it reminded her of that movie about the sexy janitor from Southie who turned out to be a math genius, and because her own memory was fuzzy at best, especially when it came to names and basic information about her friends and acquaintances. How many kids they had, where they grew up, where they summered, none of it stayed in her head. Her mother blamed this not on her limited capacity for the retention of facts but on her narcissism.

"It didn't help me get good grades," said Steven, "but I could always impress my teachers by knowing more than they thought I did. I'd pull some date out of my ass and they'd let me slide. Or I'd tell them their license plate number or what was in their lunch sandwich a week ago, and if it didn't freak them out they'd sit me down and say, *with a gift like that*, and shake their heads like I was pissing my life away right there in front of them." He laughed. "Anyway, last week you had on a black-and-white dress in little diamond patterns and pink fingernail polish that matched your pink toenails, and the third toe on your left foot—the little piggy who ate roast beef—had a Band-Aid around it. You were wearing this same necklace"—he pointed to the gold cross that hung from the chain around her neck—"except nobody told you it got twisted around and landed on your shoulder after you jump-roped. And you, buddy"—he turned to Shane—"you had a couple boo-boos, too, one on your left knee, and one on your right elbow. How'd you manage that? Fightin' the street gangs of Chestnut Hill?"

Shane regarded Steven with the kind of wonder Monica saw only when they took him out on their boat or let him watch an action movie. For such a stoic child, he loved speed, and twists and turns, and bright blurry bursts of color, if not the loud noises that often accompanied them.

"Would you like it if Steven here was your teacher?" Monica asked him.

Shane nodded. Back into his mouth went his thumb.

"Like I said—"

"I know, I know," said Monica, waving him off. "You're not certified in anything. But you have experience. And you have references, right? Teachers, counselors, a current employer? You've already passed Miss G's test with flying colors."

"She's a softy," he said. "The person you need to talk to is Mr. Forsythe. He's known me my whole life. Give me your phone."

Before she could say okay, he grabbed it and held it up to her face to unlock it, and then he got into her contacts and tapped out a new entry: *John Forsythe, Reference for Steven Donovan*. In the memo field he wrote, *Best Guy You'll Ever Meet*. He explained that Mr. Forsythe had been looking out for him since he was Shane's age, and started finding employment for him once he spotted his talents.

Monica would ask this Mr. Forsythe pointed questions about Steven's character. She would learn from Mr. Forsythe whether the young man before her could be trusted with her child, in her house. She would get from Mr. Forsythe a reliable account of Steven's history, education, work performance, and connection to children. In Mr. Forsythe—whoever he was, a solid-named man—she would trust, but she would also ask the Binswanger family lawyer to do a background check. She didn't need to do all this to convince Arthur that Steven was the right person for the job, because Arthur would never question her judgment. Arthur trusted her. If he couldn't trust Shane's devoted mother with his care and development and safety, who else could he trust? She needed to do all this for the other mothers, the better mothers, who'd inevitably ask, how'd you find this great guy? An agency?

No, Monica will say to the mothers. It was the craziest thing! I just had a gut feeling. You should see them! Besties. Like two drops of water. And Shane, he's like a different boy. Shot up a foot in a month! And he's *talking*! You can't shut him up!

All of that happened, a version of it at least. Enough of a version to make the story true.

When the check came at the South Street Diner, Steven pulled a crumpled fist of bills from his jeans. He made no real effort to pay, but the gesture alone signaled to Monica that he didn't have the Entitlement of the Disadvantaged she'd come to expect from her years of charity work. This boy was no charity case. He could take her or leave her. As he uncurled his fist to count the bills, she knew that, when they reached the second point, as they surely would, his body pressed against hers, she would welcome it no differently from Arthur's nightly kiss in the foyer of their grand house. Steven pinning her wrists to the wall of the guest room, his tongue in her mouth for the first time after weeks of brushing past each other on the stairs, her locking the door against Shane and Erma and anyone else who might wander upstairs, had the same inevitability. The next scene in the script she'd already written.

All along she'd known the third point would come, the point at which they'd give each other up. He'd get bored, or she would. One of them would disappoint the other. He'd blackmail her for some outrageous sum of money, or she'd fire him for not taking adequate care of Shane. She'd grow obsessed with him, addicted to him, and he'd recoil from her neediness. She'd get pregnant. Arthur would discover them, either on his own or through Erma or Stefano or (most likely) Shane, and they'd suffer through a round of couples counseling, that thoroughly American solution that, like most American solutions, gave you the satisfaction of self-righteousness in exchange for letting you hold fast to your misery. On that day in the diner, she was prepared, as much as any person could be, for whichever of these predictable eventualities would come to pass.

The Italian lessons had been her idea, an excuse to turn one of the rooms in the guest wing into a classroom and shut themselves behind its doors. Was this not far better than sneaking into the cabana for a few minutes of anxious groping, like teenagers? Three hours a week—one on Mondays, two on Wednesdays—was a luxury. Three hours was more than some people got in an entire month. A lifetime. She'd bought them a textbook—*Prego! An Invitation to Italian*—and painted one of the walls with chalkboard paint. She'd bought chalk. Yellow legal pads. Red pens, green pens. She'd bought a framed map of Italy and hung it next to the chalkboard.

Arthur liked the idea. If it gave her something to do, and if it helped the young man, whom he'd never met, then why not. He wouldn't be surprised if he had a little crush on her, said Arthur; he wouldn't be surprised if he'd made up that whole story about wanting to attend culinary school in Italy next year just to spend time alone with her. You can't blame him, Arthur said, and she read his stroking of her hair, his thumb sliding across her cheek, as permission that would give shape to her late afternoons. This part she did not tell Steven, who preferred a hotel, except her credit cards were in Arthur's name, she explained, and she was unwilling to hand over wads of cash at the front desk like a *puttana*. She dismissed outright his invitations to his double-decker in Dorchester, which he shared with at least two other boys. She encouraged him to be happy with their current arrangement. In addition to his tutoring salary, paid by check out of their joint account, she'd been giving him a little bit of extra cash from the ATM. He said he was saving all of it to start his own business, but that was a long way off. In the meantime, from the stories he told her, she suspected he spent too much of that money on takeout and partying with his best friend Archie and seemingly identical designer sneakers—every week, was it possible, a new bright white pair—and paying back people who'd done him favors.

Somehow, through all this, it never occurred to Monica that not only would Steven fall in love with her, but that, rather than disappoint him, rather than risk the loss of him entirely, she'd choose to pretend she loved him back in equal measure. Most surprisingly, she found that it was her deception, her playing of the part—all her declarations, her absurd romantic promises, the words *I love you* on her lips more taboo than any of his dirty talk—that thrilled her most, that kept her in the game, as much as, if not more than, real love itself ever had. Was this just her instinct for viciousness again, or was it something else?

That last day, a Wednesday, he'd been in a foul mood. Sulkier than usual. Needy. Dissatisfied with the terms of their arrangement, terms that should have pleased him. She blamed it on Valentine's Day, never a good day for complicated lovers. At 3:22 p.m., when she switched on the lamp to look for her phone, he gripped her arm, and then he reached under his pillow and produced of all things, a ring.

"It's not real," he said, by which he meant not only the gems—a chunky cushion-cut diamond flanked by rubies—but, he made clear, the engagement itself. "I know you can't really wear it. But I was thinking, for today at least, maybe you can put it on while we're in here and we can pretend to be, like, normal?" He got onto his knees on the bed. His cock was sticking straight up.

Why not, she thought. She held out her hand and he removed her real rings, first the single oval Badgley Mischka she'd picked out herself, and then the encrusted gold band inscribed *Monica ♥ Arthur* on the inside. He dropped them into her palm and she closed her fist over them and quickly kissed them. She placed them on the nightstand, where they sparkled, confusedly, in the February half-light.

Then he slipped his ring into their place, smiling at the fit. "I didn't know your size," he said. "But I can draw your hands from memory, down to the length and width of the finger, so I did that for the guy in the store, and he was like, 'are you sure,' and I was like, 'yeah,' and see, I was right. And don't worry, it was cheap, but not *cheap* cheap."

She held it out to him and wiggled her fingers. "It's beautiful," she said. "Really. But you shouldn't spend your money on me."

"I know," he said. "But it's Valentine's. I had to do *something*. To be honest, I almost wussed out. But now that the deed is done—" Smiling, he again reached under his pillow. He pulled out another ring, a men's chunky class ring with a dull blue stone, and slipped it on his own finger. "My dad's," he said. "Pissed away every penny he ever made but he held on to this for some reason. My gran wanted to bury him in it, but I said fuck that, the one valuable thing he owned should belong to me."

"You never wear it."

"I forgot I had it!" he said. "That guy didn't mean shit to me. Then when I got this idea for us for today, for Valentine's, I remembered.

Listen. I know where I stand. I know nothing's real. You're using me, I'm using you. Fine. This is America."

"Steven—"

"It's fine. People use each other. We're gonna be so much more than that someday, but you're not ready yet. I get it. I'm young, I can wait. In the meantime—"

Once again he reached under the pillow. What else did he have back there, and when did he hide it? He opened his right palm, like a magician, and in it was a small wrist corsage of white baby roses, mangled and browned at the edges.

"What's this?"

"It's prom night," he said, taking her wrist and tying the white silk ribbon around it. "We just got back to our hotel. The Ritz. That's why it's all crushed."

"Ah," she said. "I hope we had fun. Did we dance?"

"I'm your rich boyfriend," he said, not really listening. "Miles Meriwether III. No, fuck that. Steven Donovan III. See my fancy ring? I've got a bunch of them in every color. You're my high school sweetheart, Monica Alberti. You moved here freshman year from Italy. A poor exchange student. You, like, clean motel rooms after school. You had a crush on me as soon as you saw me."

She laughed. "This is what you call normal?"

"I'm serious," he said.

There was anger in his voice. Frustration, at least. Still, she played along. She stroked the inside of his thigh, where he was ticklish, hoping he'd lighten up.

"Go along with what I say," he said. "Aren't I always good about your games?"

"Okay," she said.

"I proposed to you in the middle of the dance floor and everybody clapped. Your dress was basically a rag. People in school made fun of you. So me proposing was like Cinderella, or like the fifties. I got us this penthouse suite. That's what all the kids in my high school did after the prom: rented hotel rooms and devirginized their girlfriends."

"Am I a virgin?"

"Of course," he said. He climbed on top of her. "You think my mom and dad would let me marry some slut?"

"Steven—"

"Come on," he said. "Just go with it." When he kissed her, she tasted the anger. "Don't I always go with it?"

Later, when he finally let her check her phone, she put their favorite album through the speaker, a band he'd introduced her to, to settle him down, to take them through the third point, but all it did was get him more agitated. "The thing is," he said, lying on his back with his arms behind his head, "it *should* be like that, you know? Normal. Us meeting in high school, going to prom, buying a house together. It wouldn't have to be big like this one. I wouldn't even have to be rich. I could just be me. We could have a mortgage, I wouldn't mind that. I'm not afraid to work."

"You're funny, you know that?" Monica teased. "A mortgage? That's what you're dreaming about when you're in bed with me? Seriously, I bet you every guy from your high school class would kill for this arrangement we have."

"I'd be such a good dad, too," he said, a million miles away. "Don't you think?"

"Shane worships you," she said, which was the truth. Somehow this made his cock stand up again.

"It's fucking mutual," he said. He turned to her. And when he kissed her now, all the anger had melted away.

Steven Donovan had a compass tattooed over his heart. To remind him, he once told her, to "always let love lead the way." She'd found it touching. Against type. She'd kissed it in every direction. But now, suddenly, it scared her, the sharp arrows pointing every which way, his moody eyes and insistent cock, the garish red stones he'd foisted on her, the damage at the core of him.

Which was why, when the 4:55 alarm went off, and he started rooting around for his clothes, she felt—did she know this then?—ready to let him go.

Where did Leo's story really start?

Dr. Ashe wanted to know, and so did Leo himself, and sooner or later his new girlfriend, Bonnie, was going to ask him. Maybe that was the point of therapy after all—to come up with the right answer, or close enough, at least, for when someone asked, *Who are you? Where'd you come from?*

Katie's answer used to sputter out like: my brother died when I was six, and then my mother died when I was ten, and then my aunt Alice took me in like a stray dog, and one doctor gave me pills for sadness, and another doctor gave me pills for restlessness, and another doctor gave me seminars on mindfulness to watch before I went to sleep, and this girl Audrey called me freak, and a boy named

Thomas called me a fat fuck, and once my manager at Spaghetti Warehouse . . . and just the other day my boss at the bookstore . . .

It took Dr. Ashe to point out that in none of these statements did Katie make herself the subject. "Are you an object?" she asked, in a way that was almost mocking. "Are you a person who is authored, or are you an author?"

"I guess Katie's a person who is authored. *Was* authored."

"And who are you now?" asked Dr. Ashe. "Leo? That's your name?"

"Yes."

"Okay, Leo, so tell me, and make yourself the subject this time. Where did your story really start?"

"In the sewing room at Aunt Alice's," Leo said. "The spring he turned fourteen."

There was a tall dresser in the back of the sewing room where Aunt Alice stored his brother's old T-shirts, books, and CDs—the stuff she couldn't sell or donate after she cleaned out their mother's place, and which the lady at the Salvation Army back in Saint Paul had called "too Satanic-looking." This only made Aunt Alice want to hang on to the stuff because, she declared, Leo Ridgeway Jr., her great-nephew, the only son of her only niece, was no Satan worshipper; he was a good, sweet boy, misunderstood, dealt a bad hand in the immediate family department. Her biggest regret in life was not rescuing him from her niece's clutches, but at least now she had a chance to rescue his sister.

Living at Aunt Alice's was scary at first, not only because of that dresser of dead people's stuff and the stories about her brother that Katie overheard, but because of the sewing room itself, packed with bolts of fabric and dolls and medical equipment, the carpet and wallpaper blotched with stains and curling at the seams, the giant oval mirror in a wooden stand scratched up by cats, stacks of newspapers and magazines so old they cracked when you turned the pages. The stacks were taller than ten-year-old Katie and made a kind of tunnel system that led to the dresser, to the sewing machine table often left humming, to the bookshelf of boxes of blue latex gloves and needles and small plastic tubs, to the mirror so cloudy she had to squint to find herself in the reflection.

It wasn't until high school, when Aunt Alice took in a series of foster girls and offered them, one at a time, the other half of Katie's bedroom, that the sewing room became her refuge. After she Windexed the thick wooden table and wiped off the grime, it made for a decent place to do her homework and draw on pads of colored construction paper. Sue Ellen Armitage, the old lady who'd lived with Aunt Alice and died upstairs, had been the sick one and the seamstress and the collector. The dolls, once spookily lifelike, now kept Katie better company than her skittish foster sisters in the opposite bed or even Aunt Alice herself, who went gray and dotty and a little mean after Sue Ellen finally died.

Katie named Sue Ellen's dolls after the wives of the presidents, whom she'd taken a shine to in her American History class. She sat Martha Washington at one end of the wooden sewing table and Abigail Adams at the other and remembered, looking back and forth between the two, that it was Leo who'd taught her to bring the objects around her to life. She wished Leo could come through the door and sit between her and Martha and Abigail and make them fight with each other in their old-timey voices, and when she made her best attempt at those voices herself, a sudden ache overcame her, like an upset stomach but way worse, deeper down in her gut. The ache didn't go away; in fact, it came to live inside her, like a baby she was carrying. Aunt Alice would catch her holding her stomach and give her ginger ale and tell her not to eat so many sweets.

One day Dolley Madison was teaching Eleanor Roosevelt the foxtrot, whatever that was. They needed a bigger dance floor, so Katie cleared the top of the dresser and got them twirling and hooting across it. She was fifteen, too old for this sort of play, but the truth is that she believed the dolls protected her. If not the dolls, then the sewing room itself. It was the only place she felt safe in the world. Which is why when the top drawer of the dresser flew open all by itself, not just a crack but all the way out, so far it hung down about to fall, she felt no fear. The opposite.

It was the drawer that held Leo's old shirts. She'd almost forgotten his stuff was in there, it had been so long since anyone else had come into the room, let alone taken anything out of the dresser, which also held some of Sue Ellen's pattern books and photo albums and even a pair of their mother's jeans. Aunt Alice kept these artifacts out of respect, she said to Katie; the dead deserved our respect no matter how weak they were or what sorts of lives they led or how many people they'd hurt.

She couldn't say why, but all her life Katie had been expecting Leo to come back and find her. Even during those years just after their mother died, when her absence had swallowed his, and Katie had mostly stopped thinking and dreaming of him, then too she'd been waiting for him. What form would he take, she used to wonder, when he visited her? The hiker who'd found him in Rum River thought at first he was alive. He was lying on his back on a flat rock staring straight up at the sky. When he came to her, would he look like this? Would she recognize his voice, or would he try to trick her?

These were the questions young Katie had asked herself under the blankets in her cardboard castle in the weeks after the hiker found him, her mother raging on the other side of their house, and they were the same questions she asked again in the sewing room, as she picked up one of his T-shirts and held it open before her. MANOWAR—HELL ONSTAGE was ironed onto a black background, in big yellow and red letters licked by flames, the edges of the letters curling up from the fabric like the carpet under her feet. The scent—his scent, cigarettes and sweat, pine trees, Leo—buckled her knees under the weight of the ache.

She was wearing the blue-and-yellow plaid jumper and white button-down blouse required by Sacred Trinity, the Christian school Aunt Alice was paying a lot of money to send her to. The blouse had a frilly ruffled collar like Dolley Madison's. She felt Leo's disapproval. No, it wasn't disapproval, nothing so mild; it was rage at her for walking around alive in the world in this getup. Scorn. Disappointment. She locked the door. Quickly she pulled the jumper up over her shoulders and shimmied out of it. She unbuttoned and removed the blouse.

She slipped on Leo's T-shirt and, as she smoothed it over her chest and adjusted the fit on the shoulders, the ache lifted. She was light. She stood taller. Though the shirt was too tight across her breasts and in the rolls of her waist, and so long, even with the sausage-like tightness in the middle, that it nearly reached her thighs, it fit perfectly. Taking off her bra made it even more perfect, her nipples announcing themselves like the newly swollen muscles on the boys at the Y. For years it had been those boys' bodies she always felt she was growing toward, not her mother's body or Aunt Alice's. They were skinny and flat and short and pointy, like origami birds, not at all like Katie. Her brother had been a bird, too, but a strong one, an ostrich, a cassowary. Katie would dwarf them all.

Her routine became: come home from school, go straight to the sewing room, change into one of Leo's shirts, and do her homework or read or listen to Sue Ellen's warbly tapes on her ancient boom box. As hard as she tried, Katie couldn't get into Leo's music, but she sensed that was okay with him; he wanted her to find something of her own. Of Sue Ellen's stash, she liked Donovan and the Doors and especially Janis Joplin; she didn't like Sonny and Cher or Simon and Garfunkel or anyone, it seemed, that sang as a couple. She played the music very low in case hearing Sue Ellen's songs flowing out from the sewing room would make Aunt Alice sad.

Even after the stream of foster girls dried up and she got her bedroom all to herself, Katie retreated to the sewing room. By then the shirts—DANZIG, OBITUARY, TYPE O NEGATIVE—which she kept mostly in her backpack, had lost all trace of Leo and now smelled like her: the clove cigarettes she smoked in Edgewood Park after school, her garlicky sweat, and the Prell shampoo she used to secretly wash the shirts in the bathroom sink. The fabric tore at the seams, and the neck holes stretched out, and she grew, too, as if to keep pace, up to five foot seven and past one hundred sixty pounds.

Unlike the girls in her class, though, she didn't starve herself; she sat with the boys at lunch and ate what they ate, burgers and pepperoni pizza and mac and cheese, and felt pride, not shame, when they teased her for "putting it away." She wasn't Katie anymore, after all; she was Leo, though she hadn't told anyone yet.

Her first job was on weekends in the office of Jenks Lumber Supply, where she was surrounded by men in hard hats and orange vests. No one ever tried to touch this girl they called Katie. The most they wanted from her was her cigarettes and a few bucks now and then and any gory detail she could give them about her dead junkie mother and her dead Satan-worshipping brother, who, they'd heard, got himself murdered by the Smiley Face Killer. Was that true? It sure was, said Katie, and not only that, it was kill*ers*, not killer, and they'd never been caught. Tell your boys to stay away from rivers and lakes; tell them to cover their Solo cups.

On that flat rock where the hiker found Leo: a spray-painted pink smiley face, closed circle for the head, two dots for the eyes, wide *U* for the mouth. The work not of a killer, or of Leo's killer, but of some Cro-Mag playing a prank, someone like one of those Jenks guys' sons or the boys at lunch. Leo wasn't special enough to be murdered, Katie could have told them. He was just a super-sad kid. He'd had more than his fair share. But Katie never told anyone this. Leo's story was a currency she couldn't afford to lose. It specialized her. It protected her, as he once tried to do. People hated her otherwise, the boys and the girls, the men and the women. They hated her smell and her pervy dyke aunt and her superior attitude that made no sense given that she had nothing going for her—not good grades, not a nice body or pretty face, not even God's mercy.

Only the therapists her schools assigned her cared about her brother's silly voices or his kindness to her as a child. Until Margaret Mead Ashe, she told no one that not only had he opened the drawer for her, he'd turned the branches down in the woods behind Light of Christ Church to lead her to the place where he died. Thank you, Leo, she told him as she followed the trail, touching each broken branch as if it were his shoulder as she walked along the bank of the Rum. When she reached the rock, she sat and smoked and read out loud for him her favorite lines from the books that were uniquely her own, books that belonged to no one else in the world but her—Hermann Hesse's *Siddhartha*, Ginsberg's *Howl*, Djuna Barnes's *Nightwood*, the play *Equus* by Peter Shaffer, the story "Rappaccini's Daughter" by Hawthorne, the poem "Patterns" by Amy Lowell—

In Summer and in Winter I shall walk
Up and down
The patterned garden paths
In my stiff, brocaded gown.
The squills and daffodils
Will give place to pillared roses, and to asters, and to snow.
I shall go
Up and down,
In my gown.
Gorgeously arrayed,

Boned and stayed.
And the softness of my body will be guarded from embrace
By each button, hook, and lace.
For the man who should loose me is dead,
Fighting with the Duke in Flanders,
In a pattern called a war.
Christ! What are patterns for?

How could Katie explain to anyone but Leo that she was the rich English lady in this poem, gorgeously arrayed, forced to pace around in whalebone and brocade, and that she was also the man off fighting the war to free her? In the sewing room, she used a razor blade to cut out the map of Belgium from an old atlas and then, at the rock, set the page on the water and watched it float down the river.

In front of the oval mirror, she snipped the curls off her hair, removed the Covergirl makeup Aunt Alice insisted she dab on to hide her zits, and suddenly there was her face; she didn't need to squint into the silver at all.

She found a pair of clippers and buzzed away what was left. She stopped painting her chewed-up nails. She ghosted Grady, the grief counselor who looked too young to order a beer.

She wasn't invited to the graduation ceremony at Sacred Trinity, not because of her long rap sheet of uniform violations or her dismal grades, but because Aunt Alice hadn't made a single tuition payment in seven months. They would be holding Katharine Starks's diploma hostage until the account could be settled. What was more important, though? A meaningless piece of paper with the wrong name on it or enough money for an old lady's groceries and medicines and cable TV, all of which she'd need even more once Katie moved away and left her alone?

The summer and fall after graduation, she picked up evening shifts at Potbelly and used the Jenks computer to search for jobs and cheap apartments far enough from Aunt Alice's to live free of her but close enough to bus back in an afternoon. Madison, Milwaukee, Duluth. The names vibrated on the screen like pornography. She added every cent of the Potbelly money to the stash she'd already set aside for herself and used the Jenks salary for the upkeep of Aunt Alice. On January 2, 2029, she was on the morning bus to La Crosse.

A funny thing, Leo told Dr. Ashe: nobody ever asks for proof you graduated from high school. They just assume because you speak English and spell your words correctly and produce a social security card for them to scan that at some point in the recent past you also knew well enough the order of the presidents and the symbolism in *To Kill a Mockingbird* and how to solve quadratic equations, all of which is supposed to prepare your brain to learn whatever outmoded computer system they use in their bookstore or consignment shop or at Spaghetti Warehouse. Landlords assume you'll pay your rent on time once you wire them in advance the two months' worth you've saved up, and prove you're in good standing in the much-coveted role of server at Spaghetti Warehouse, where, on weekends, you can make hundreds of dollars in cash without once applying your knowledge of the periodic table. And if you work at Wilder's, the used bookstore where the burnout owner pays you under the table and smokes weed with you on slow afternoons and strokes your thigh in your cutoff jeans, you don't even need your social security card or your driver's license. You can be anyone you want, and then you can get a third job or a better second job and be another person in those fine establishments.

Even in a smallish Wisconsin town, Leo went on, people don't pay as much attention to you as you fear they will. It helps when you have nothing going for you—not a nice body or a pretty or a handsome face, not even God's mercy—and the only thing you can do for people is what someone is already paying you to do: hand them their change, take their ticket, point them to the toilet, give them a smile, wish them a blessed day, a lovely weekend, good luck with that.

Sat, Feb 22, 2020 at 11:32 PM

CHLOE
So???

Nothing yet

Just a million texts from M

Phone

MATTHEW
Missed call 1 hr ago

MATTHEW
Missed call 40 min ago

MATTHEW
Missed call 9 min ago

Messages

MATTHEW
Are you running late? 1 hr ago

MATTHEW
I don't see you. Did you drive? 1 hr ago

MATTHEW
Come on Tessa don't stand me up
You said you'd come 1 hr ago

MATTHEW
You said you'd do this one
thing for me but it's not for me
it's for US 42 min ago

MATTHEW
Where are you 25 min ago

MATTHEW
Tessa come on 12 min ago

MATTHEW
I'm still here just come Tessa
please 8 min ago

CHLOE

WTAF

You said you blocked him

Trying not to freak out

CHLOE

Don't freak out

Ken Doll will come through

He's not responding

CHLOE

He's handling it

Or maybe he got called in

He's not on call tonight

CHLOE

Emergencies do happen you know

I checked Twitter

There's nothing

He'd text me if he got called in

CHLOE

To be fair he's not a big texter

The elderly aren't good with technology

Not funny

CHLOE

Sorry

You know what I say

Hottest 50 year old in Michigan

By far

He's 43

CHLOE

Once you cross the 40-yard line . . .

How would you know

You date children

CHLOE

All men are children

Sun, Feb 23, 2020 at 12:22 AM

I went to Ravens

CHLOE

Tell me you didn't

I needed to see

CHLOE

Tessa why

Don't hate me

I just wanted to make sure M was OK

CHLOE

Wait WHEN did you go

Right at 10

CHLOE

When K was supposed to show up???

When you were texting me before??

Yeah

I parked where I could watch through the window

CHLOE

He knows your car!

Like ALL TOO WELL

I borrowed Mia's

CHLOE

Mia???

We couldn't tell you

We knew you'd freak out

CHLOE

Damn right

I'd have come down and taken the keys

Like right out of your hand

Exactly

CHLOE

So then what

I waited forever

K didn't know I was there either

So I didn't text him

Well I did text him after I didn't see him go in

But I was just like, did you leave yet, did you see Matt, tell me what's going on

All I got was "don't stress"

CHLOE

So he didn't call or text back after that?

How long did you stay there?

No

I called him but it went straight to voicemail

CHLOE

I'm sure it's some dumb reason

I have a bad feeling

M looked really wasted

CHLOE

What else is new

I was like WATCHING him message me

And call me

It felt so weird

I stayed until midnight

I should have just gone in and told him myself

CHLOE

No

Also you did tell him

Like a million times

Yes and no

CHLOE

??

I'm the worst breaker-upper

I always make it seem like, maybe things can work out later

If he acted different

Calmed down

Stopped getting so blotto when he drinks

Stopped checking up on me so much

Stopped worshipping me so much lol

CHLOE

Stopped being Matt Cardullo so much

That's mean

CHLOE

He can't be different

Guys don't change

Girls always think they do but they don't

They just lie better

You never liked him

CHLOE

Obvi

True confession?

CHLOE

What

Forget it

CHLOE

WHAT

I meant it about things working out later

I still do love him a little bit

CHLOE

That's your confession?

K is so great but where's that going??

I'm not changing his diaper when he gets really old

Matthew makes more sense

Boyfriend-wise

CHLOE

Your only two choices in life

are not a hot daddy cop

or a drunk jock stalker

This is all totally my fault

I'm the one who cheated

I'm the one who sent mixed signals

I'm the one who used him

All he did was be super into me

CHLOE

Classic abuser narrative

That is NOT all he did

You're conveniently forgetting like a million creepy things

He's not an abuser

Even K says

And he knows

CHLOE

So why'd you send him down there

I thought if K told him himself he'd have no choice but to back off

Scare him a little

Knock some sense into him

Not literally but you know

Maybe I'm just a wimp

CHLOE

And?

And what?

CHLOE

And YOU WERE AFRAID OF HIM

I'm afraid of conflict in general

CHLOE

YOU WERE AFRAID OF *HIM*

I really had no reason to be

CHLOE

My God Tessa you're the one who needs help

He would never hurt me

Honestly

I just didn't want to be the one to break his heart

CHLOE

And yet you went down to watch your boyfriend do it for you

Did you bring popcorn?

I mean REALLY break it

I couldn't take that

I couldn't do that to a person's face

He's the sweetest guy you have to admit that

The most emotional

I think it's so cute what a Mama's boy he is

Always sharing his feelings and asking about mine and telling me about hers, how she can't find a man, her money problems

I think we're not conditioned to accept all that from boys

We pathologize their emotions like they can't have too many

I've been thinking about this a lot LOL

I misjudged him maybe and I let you all misjudge him

Name one thing he did to me that was actually wrong

Not just cringe or annoying but wrong wrong

CHLOE

Girl you're spinning

Am I right though?

CHLOE

About him not doing anything wrong?

Yeah

CHLOE

No

Definitions of wrong:

Following you around #1

Basically not letting you breathe without informing him #2

Talking over you all the time telling his same stories #3

READING YOUR TEXTS

That should be #1

READING YOUR TEXTS

Making you text him goodnight and good morning like he's your dad and your six years old

And if your late he freaks out and worries and comes over because he thinks you're dead

Contacting your parents!! xInfinity!!

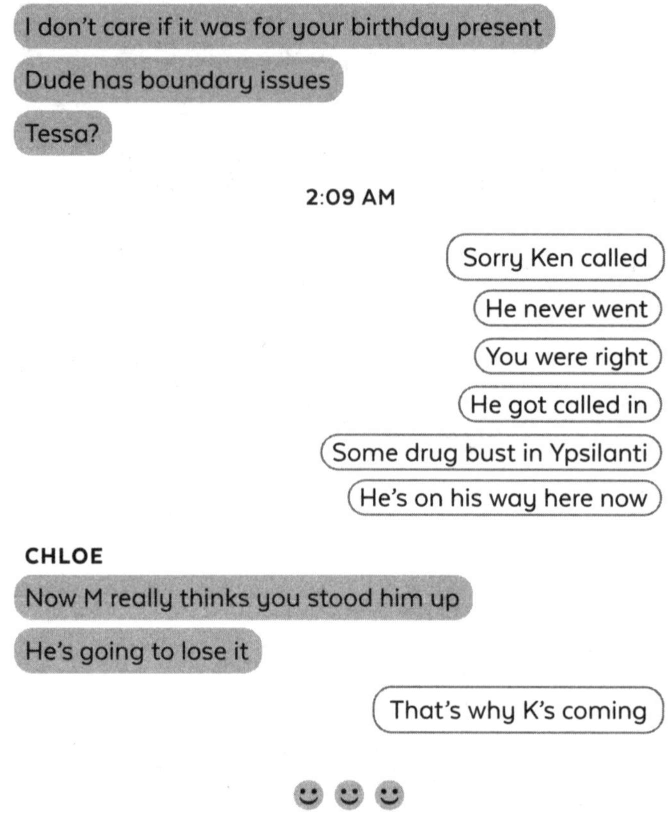

The last time Lori saw her son alive, he had his head and his fist held high. That's what she chose to remember. He'd been victorious. Declared the winner. He'd beaten the unbeatable guy from State with a sick fall. There was the sound of the ref slapping his palm on the mat, like a clap of thunder, and then the crowd exploded. Matty tore off his chin strap and threw his headgear down and found her and Gus in the first row and pointed at them. Then, though he'd been warned about bragging, he did one of his backflips, high and solid, and the crowd exploded again. Even the ref couldn't resist him. Lori saw it on the man's face, the pride or envy or lust or some other officially sinful thing, like the backflip itself. He grabbed Matty by the wrist and lifted his arm over his head, his fist pumping, and paraded him in a circle, showing him off. Who was unbeatable now? Who, with a little more effort, could finally make the D1 team his senior year? That smile a mile wide, that humongous heart, that son of hers, that's who.

She and Gus had almost not driven out from Jackson to watch the match. The forecast had called for windy conditions and more snow, and Gus didn't see well at night, and Lori was tired from a long day at Grayson's. The same excuses they'd given for missing Matty's other matches all season after showing up for the first few. Lori and Gus got along fine these days, but she was in no hurry to play chauffeur for him again, to take his charity dollars to put gas in her truck, and to sit through hours of sweaty guys grabbing each other's butts, just to watch their son get his clock cleaned. She had to admit that's what she expected would happen with the brute from State, but Matthew had texted her—he'd even called Gus, which shocked them both—and begged them to come anyway. He'd improved so much since they were last there in October, he said; he had so many more tools now; he was more focused, more aggressive, more strategic; wait until they saw; they wouldn't even recognize him. He said he could feel something big coming in his life, a turning point. He was the underdog, yeah, no question, but he was not going to lose.

Oh, how Lori had missed that cockiness! You could even call it arrogance and she wouldn't mind; it was one of her favorite qualities in her son. Call it bravado, swagger; whatever it was, it was setting him on the right path in life. Lately, that girl Tessa had been draining so much of his swagger he could barely get out of bed in the morning. A hundred girls had dumped him, and she bet he'd dumped two hundred more, but Tessa—were they even still dating? She couldn't get a straight answer—had shrunk her son down to half his size. Until now, it sounded like. Lori wanted to see for herself, which was the only reason she answered the phone when Gus called to bum a ride.

Lori Cardullo would never win Mother of the Year, according to certain other women, but she did start to worry when Matty called her more than once late at night crying over Tessa. When he told her he'd skipped some classes and couldn't remember a word of Latin and had to ask for extensions on a couple papers because every time he tried to write a sentence all he could think was *where is Tessa, what's Tessa up to, should he call her, why'd she stop calling him*, Lori even offered to come pick him up and let him stay in his old room for the weekend. She promised him waffles with big scoops of Chunky Monkey, his favorite, on top. She volunteered to play that shoot-'em-up video game with him even though all that cartoon blood gave her nightmares. They'd pretend he was ten years old again, she said, when his wrinkled old mama was the only girl who mattered to him. The situation seemed to call for that kind of emergency action, and Lori took it.

When Matty didn't say yes right away and beg her to come get him that minute, she was surprised and more than a little relieved. More importantly, she was also impressed, as much with herself as a mother as with her boy. Sooner or later he'd need to figure out how to deal in a manly way with heartbreak, with girls too air-headed to appreciate his value, and, good for him, he'd chosen sooner. After his aortic stenosis resolved itself at six years old, and the doctors mostly convinced Lori his heart was just as strong as any other normal kid's, her biggest fear became not that Matty would die young but that he'd grow up into too much of a mama's boy, and that it would be her fault for treating him like a porcelain doll when he was a baby. So she'd worked extra hard early on to encourage independence and self-reliance. She considered the necessity of every hug before granting him one. She taught him how to wash and dry and iron his clothes and cook basic meals and sleep with the lights off without TV or radio for soothing. She made him ride his bike home from practice even in the dark and rain and sleet; if a mailman could do it, so could he. She didn't overpraise him for his grades. Yes, of course, she acknowledged with appreciation the B+s and A–s, but with the reminder that these were the minimum. If he had any intention of standing out from the crowd, he'd not only need to exceed that minimum but make a name for himself in football, wrestling, hockey, or any sport he took to. It could be badminton for all she cared, as long as he stuck with it.

Matty had his mother to thank for his obsession with Latin and Classics, which was going to make him into a real college professor someday, the first in either her or Gus's family. She'd told him about an article she'd read in one of her magazines about the hardest languages to learn, and then one day he came home from school and stood on the kitchen table all *veni vindi vitchi* or whatever. What the heck are you talking about, she asked him. He'd found a book on Latin in the school library, he said, and memorized part of a famous speech Julius Caesar made after winning a battle. Memorizing it wasn't hard, he said, but he didn't really understand what it meant or what the battle was about or how the words and letters fit together to make the sentences mean anything, and he found that he wanted to learn all this much more than he wanted to do his Spanish homework. The librarian had told him that what made Latin cool was that it was a dead language and would never change, not to mention that all the Romance languages came from it. Matthew figured if he learned Latin on his own—Jackson High didn't teach it anymore—Spanish and every other language would come easy. He'd be ahead of the game. Stealth. The fact that nobody else had thought of this made him feel, at fourteen, like he'd stumbled upon a powerful secret weapon. But he hadn't just stumbled upon it; Lori had *handed* it to him. She deserved a little credit for that.

When Matty went above and beyond, those were the times she'd kiss him on the lips and muss up his hair and throw her arms around him. She'd even let herself hold him a moment too long, luxuriating in him, his muscles and bones and brain. Then, and only then, in recognition of the above-and-beyondness, did she allow herself such an extravagance. Everything in proportion. Otherwise, this boy would make a worse husband for his future wife than his father had made for her. You don't think she wanted to climb into bed with him every night, keep him safe from the horrors of the world, and follow him around all day, hiding behind trees with a shotgun, ready to take out anyone who tried to hurt him? You don't think she wanted to lock the doors of their house and never let him out? Of course she did. But she loved him too much to ruin him the way Angela Cardullo had ruined Gus.

Nobody understood this approach, least of all Gus, which was one of the many walls that shot up between them once Matthew started school. He accused her of coldness, of riding the boy too hard, of forgetting he was a kid; she accused him of being naive about how hard it was for young white men in twenty-first-century America. Their son wasn't going to work like a chump in a commercial bakery the way he did, she told Gus, letting a union boss decide the number of hours he could work and how much he deserved to get paid and what time of day he could take a shit. He wasn't going to wait around for his mother to tell him when his life could start. Marrying Lori Whitford was the only time Gus ever went against Mamma Angela's wishes, and Lori swore the old lady got cancer that very day and died on their two-year anniversary just to punish him for it.

Her conversation with Gus on the drive out and back to Ann Arbor that night—Friday, February 21, 2020—was memorable only for its ordinariness. The ancient truck's tape deck playing their old songs in that ever-so-slightly-warped warble that brought them back to summer nights on Houghton Lake, before they married, when things made sense. The gossip over the friends who used to meet them there, all divorced or sick or dead or moved away, nobody together anymore except the ones who swapped or went gay. His complaints about his milky vision. Her complaints about her salary. His offers to shovel her driveway, to call Sam Anzio about her furnace, to send her a monthly check, to take her out for a nice meal sometime, didn't have to be dinner, didn't have to be romantic. Her refusals: her snowblower worked just fine, as did her arms; Sam Anzio shouldn't be trusted around a toaster, let alone a furnace; she was getting by with some telemarketing hours she could do from the kitchen table before and after her shifts at Grayson's; they could stop at Metzger's on the way back like they always did, and only because she'll be hungry after hours sitting around on those bleachers.

That the Metzger's dinner ended up being a celebration of Matthew's triumph over the guy from State and also their last meal together as parents of a living child didn't make it any more remarkable, no matter how many times Lori replayed it in her mind, searching for some kind of sign God had sent to mark it. She got the stuffed cabbage; Gus got the smoked salmon pasta. They split a stein of dark beer. It could have been any Friday night. They didn't know the hole that was about to swallow them up. Did anyone ever?

If she'd drunk too much beer that night and swerved too fast and slammed her old pickup into the side of a tractor trailer, she'd be a luckier woman than she was today. And what a jackpot that would have been for Gus, the glass slicing his head off at the neck, a clean break. So much better it would have been for the both of them to die like that—their legs snapped in two, their arms twisted and crushed, the gashes in their chests—than to go on living like it. Every time she met a new man, invited him into her house, she wondered how long it would take for his eyes to adjust and notice all the blood on her. She kept the lights low. He'd use her and be gone by morning. She specialized in men who talked rough, who had wives already. Afterward, she prayed not for forgiveness or mercy or salvation but punishment. But she had no luck, she'd always attracted the most decent of men, even now. They swept the hair from her eyes as they made love to her, caressed her cheek with their thumb like this was *Pretty Woman*. They hung their bath towels neatly on the shower rod after washing all trace of her off their skin. They asked if she had kids. They said oh, that's great, my boy's a senior at Michigan too, maybe they're friends haha, let's not find out, hahaha.

The last time she saw her son, he had his hand and his fist held high. He'd thrown off his headgear and done an illegal backflip and swaggered over to his mother and father. His father gave him the high five and bear hug he'd have given him for doing nothing at all. His mother took his face in her hands and squeezed it like an Italian does, put her forehead against his sweaty forehead, gazed deeply into his eyes, and said, "I'm so proud of you." She would never embarrass him here by kissing him on the lips.

"You saw that, right?" he asked. "You saw every second?"

"Every second," she said.

"Every second," parroted Gus. His hand was on Matty's shoulder. Lori would remember this as the last time God's energy flowed between all three of their bodies at the same time. She thought of His energy like a current of electricity that traveled through their cells, in and out of their organs. The first time they'd felt that energy was up at the lake, she and Gus in the back of the very same pickup truck, Matty a brand-new cell they'd electrified into life under the stars, which weren't stars at all but the eyes of angels.

"I knew I had him from the jump," Matty said, and followed it with technical terms Lori could never keep straight and now would never need to. "He was cocky. He underestimated me."

"He's a wuss," said Gus.

"He's a fucking beast," Matty corrected him. "I slayed the motherfucking *beast*."

"Yes you did, I'm sorry," said Gus.

"So what are we doing? Where we going?" he asked.

"What do you mean?" asked Lori.

"You're taking me out for a beer, are you not?"

Gus looked at her, all *yes* in his eyebrows.

She asked Matty, "Aren't you—celebrating with the team?"

"I'll meet up with them later," he said, shrugging. "I see these guys in my sleep. I never see you."

She remembered that he directed this last comment at her, even though, less than two weeks before, she'd offered again to rescue him from that awful girl and take him into her home for an entire weekend.

"The weather's looking bad, honey," said Lori, rubbing his arms.

"Come on," he said. "One beer."

She looked at her watch. She was starving. She had her heart set on that Metzger's stuffed cabbage with extra marinara sauce. She was bone-tired from talking, first on the 5 a.m. phone shift, then seven hours at the store. All day explaining the benefits of various insurance plans, answering questions for people who hadn't paid attention and now wanted her to fix their mistakes. She had another 5 a.m. shift tomorrow, and this one would go all day, followed by her girlfriend Lu's sixtieth. And she wasn't exaggerating: the wind was fierce. All the way to Ann Arbor, she'd gripped the wheel so tight that her neck hurt.

"Next time," she said. "Go celebrate with the team. They should carry you on their shoulders."

"That shit doesn't matter to me," said Matty. "I don't do it for that."

"What do you do it for?" said Gus.

"*She's* not here, is she?" Lori asked. "Should I even bring her up?"

"No, she's not," said Matty. "And no, you shouldn't." He started shaking a little, but she blamed it on the fact that he was half naked, with sweat cooling on all that exposed skin.

"What girl?" asked Gus, for once remembering to play dumb. Lori had told him all about Tessa on the way out there. Matty never shared his troubles with Gus. Not only would Gus make himself sick with worry, he'd go overboard trying to fix the troubles and end up making them ten times worse.

"Fine," said Matty. "You're not driving, are you, Dad?"

"No sir."

"Okay then," he said. "You can go."

He looked out at the bleachers, up and down from one end to the other, past the snack bar and the coaches and staff gathering up the equipment, but he didn't seem to find what he was looking for. A group of his teammates stood watching from a little ways off, flicking their singlets, adjusting their balls, whispering in each other's ears, waiting for Matthew Cardullo, the star of the night, to be done with his parents. They'd take him out and get him wasted, Lori was sure, and girls would throw themselves at him, and pretty soon he'd forget all about Tessa and his boring old mother and father and remember only the glory of the ref's thunderclap. She wanted him addicted to it. She wanted him to wake up in the middle of the night hungry for it. I'll drive over and take him out for a beer next Friday, she thought to herself, win or lose. If—when—he wins, no one will question whether he's a one-hit wonder.

"Okay then," Matthew said again, leaning in for a hug. "Well, I guess that's it."

CRIME SEEN (II)

The Cardullo case still tugs at James. He's fallen for plenty of solved boys before—Leo Ridgeway comes to mind, as does Steven Donovan, and Ryan Sumter in the Susquehanna, and Dylan Flack with the skull tattoo—but, as time passes, their circumstances and hometowns and even their features blur together. When Derrick forwards him some coda about a solved boy from a Wikipedia entry or a Smiley Face Reddit thread—a copycat murder in the same New Hampshire town, a new ordinance named for a long-deceased boy—James sometimes has to consult his files to match the original case to the details.

Not so for Matthew Cardullo, who, almost a year after he's found, continues to show up in James's dreams, talking to him as if they'd been neighbors or college buddies, asking questions about Caleb and Derrick and even Iris. Suspicious. Angry. Accusatory. Like he knows James has been watching and rewatching his wrestling matches on YouTube. Like he knows James has been reading his girlfriend Tessa Timmins's text messages that are now in the public record, and following the progress of the trial, less interested in the verdict—which seems hardly in doubt—than in the stories of the victim emerging from the evidence. Like he knows how useless James has been in the search for Caleb.

It began like a dream itself, that winter of 2008, an awful dream James could not wake from then or now, Caleb's face suddenly on flyers stapled to trees and telephone poles all over the Middlebury campus, the profiles of him in the newspapers, the college email alerts, the police cars circling the town, closing in. The unshakable fear James bore alone, too afraid to call or text or tell anyone what he knew, which, in his version of the story, was nothing at all. It would have no bearing on the case, he reasoned, that he'd seen the missing boy turn south onto Route 7 around seven fifteen on the night of the 23rd: his Mastercard had already been traced to the Sunoco station a few miles down the road. Everyone was more than aware of the bad weather, the temperature dropping, the snow picking up, the roads that were growing increasingly unmanageable, especially for the crappy car Caleb had saved up for and bought with his own money and registered in the state of Vermont.

James's further, more intimate, knowledge of the boy was also not worth sharing. It was no one's business that Caleb loved an old man who loved him back more fiercely than he'd ever loved anyone in the world. That on the day before Christmas Eve, the man had given him a scarf and gloves that matched the color of his eyes, as well as a warrior bracelet with jasper stones that could not protect him. That Caleb was self-aware and resourceful, but too trusting, too romantic, with little fear. That, at 8:47 a.m. on the 24th, he texted James a Merry Christmas message but never answered James's reply.

That, a few weeks later, in the midst of a multistate hunt for Caleb, the most that this cowardly old man would do for him was drive to a gas station just over the New York border, find a pay phone, and place an anonymous tip to investigate a man named Derrick who ran an underground club called the Gaze, somewhere up near the Northeast Kingdom. That this worthless man traded in his new blue Subaru for a used black Audi and started wearing contacts and dyeing out his grays and making love to his wife again, and that he blamed this strange behavior on a midlife crisis, on fifty looming like a chasm into which he refused to fall. That none of that mattered anyway because, according to the official reports and the online speculation, there turned out to be plenty of old men to choose from on Caleb Aldrich's dorm computer.

In James's panic, sitting across from the detective at his own kitchen table, Iris in the next room, it came naturally to defame Caleb, to turn him into a boy he never was, someone troubled, disturbed, possibly even dangerous. "On dope probably," James said with a shrug. Hadn't he read in the paper that his username on some sex site was OzoneKid? And wasn't ozone some kind of party drug? Yes, he admitted, he'd met him in Sycamore Park once or twice; yes, he was ashamed of those actions and would have to answer to his wife about them; yes, they'd exchanged numbers and a few texts afterward, but James assured the detective that he'd tried to end it; he never expected the kid would get obsessed with him, make up stories about him, stalk his wife, a professor at his own college! Their fling, if you could even call it that, went on for a few months maybe and then it stopped, probably when Caleb became obsessed with the guy who killed him? What did James know, he wasn't a detective! To be honest, said James, he'd forgotten about the kid until he saw his name and face in the paper. He wasn't surprised, though. Boys like that bring danger on themselves. Yes, they could speak to his wife. She could provide an alibi, if he needed one; they'd been together every minute of the Christmas holiday. And now that certain information had come out, he had nothing to hide from her.

The detectives claimed to put no stock in the Smiley Face theory, but after receiving numerous tips pointing them to unsolved nearby cases like Jeremy Dix and Brian Kearns, they grudgingly dragged Otter Creek and Sturgeon Pool and parts of the Hudson. They tracked the newly released felons and registered sex offenders within a hundred miles of both Middlebury and Poughkeepsie. When the case dragged on and the *Burlington Free Press* hounded them for leads, they referenced recent cases of murdered college kids—boys and girls—all over the country, kids abducted and mutilated for reasons best described as "random." It comforted James, in a way, the presence of so much evil in the world. It made his own weakness and cowardice bearable by comparison. He wasn't one of those cold-blooded killers. He was a decent man, respectable, worthy enough of the love Caleb and Iris had shown him.

He'd been such a credible witness that even Iris believed the full story, or claimed to. At his suggestion, they found a counselor, a well-regarded woman named Libby, to help them map out the territory of the rest of their marriage, should they choose to light out for it. Every marriage is a plot of a hundred acres, Libby told them, with the calm assurance of a teacher explaining a simple concept to a child. Ten acres, Libby said, there on the outskirts of their property, belonged exclusively to James; far on the other side, ten belonged exclusively to Iris. The remaining eighty acres in the middle—the bulk of their property, that is—they tended together, which made these rich fertile acres the most important. Sacred ground, in fact. But if sometimes husband or wife wandered out alone to their private acres, that space the other couldn't enter, a space that was holy, too, in its own way, and mysterious, what did it matter, as long as neither husband nor wife was away for too long, and knew the way back?

"How is that not compartmentalization?" Iris had asked.

"I didn't say it wasn't," Libby replied. "Does it make you uncomfortable?"

"A little," said Iris.

"Why?"

"Because the compartments never stay separate. They spill over eventually. Weeds spread. People trespass. Pick your metaphor."

"All of that will happen," said Libby. "My goal here is for you not to require my services when it does."

On April 6, 2021, one year to the day that Matt Cardullo was dragged from the Huron, the remains of Caleb Aldrich are discovered in Dog River, fifty miles northeast of James's home in Weybridge, Vermont. When he reads the news, James leaves the library in the middle of the afternoon without a word to Maud or to Iris. He drives to the nearest branch of the Dog and wades into the murky water still in his dress pants and shoes and coat and tie. He wants the numbness of frozen bones. He wants to be shocked into forgetting the thirteen years he has waited for this moment. No. He wants to find the warmth of Caleb's legs intertwining with his under the surface of the Dog. This strange behavior, too, he will blame on his advanced age, if there is someone watching him, which, as far as he knows, there is not.

LOVE SEEN

Caleb Alexander Aldrich

(December 7, 1986–December 24, 2007)

I am one of those boys they keep finding in the river. If you're around my age, you already know my name—Caleb Aldrich—as in, *Don't end up like Caleb Aldrich.* You're in the woods or at a bar or about to send pix to some guy online, and my name pops into your head like an alarm going off. Caleb Aldrich with the blue-lobster eyes and blond curls and toothpaste-commercial smile. Caleb Aldrich who was too beautiful to live. You're not as beautiful as I was, or as smart, but you're not as dumb, either. Lucky you. So you block the guy's profile, refuse his free drink. You run back to the parking lot as fast as you can, wondering what he must have looked like, the beautiful Caleb Aldrich, as he rotted for thirteen years in Dog River. How much of him was even left?

When I was a kid, a cop came to my school every year to show us the same movie about men who drove around in white vans. *Stranger Danger*, it was called, the movie, the cop's presentation, the Life Lesson itself. In his dark uniform, weighed down by a gun and a club and a heavy hat, the cop warned us never to get into any vehicle driven by a person who was not a parent, a teacher, or a police officer wearing a badge like the one he passed around for us to inspect. For months afterward, walking home alone from the bus stop, I saw white vans everywhere: turning into gas stations, parked at the 7-Eleven, slowing to get a better look at me. I peered into the windows at the faces of the men behind the wheel, their beards and baseball caps and mirrored sunglasses, knowing somehow that one day one of them would stop and open his door and I'd climb willingly in.

Except that's not what happened to me, no matter what the papers say, or what, all these years later, James still believes. No stranger ever put Caleb Aldrich in danger. Not Derrick, not those guys from the Gaze, not even creepy old Floyd. I was never their victim. The danger was encoded in my genes. Predestined. So if you're looking for someone to blame, try God, or try Heidi and Raymond Aldrich of Poughkeepsie, New York. Try all the moms and dads before them who amalgamated their DNA over generations to produce me.

I was driving home to see them the night before Christmas Eve, but even as I pulled out of the Cactus Tree Motel and took the ramp onto Route 7 South, and calculated that if it took the usual three hours to get to Poughkeepsie, I'd arrive well before midnight, I knew I'd never make it. I didn't have some sort of death premonition—I'm not the mystical type or religious in any way; in fact, I blame religion, blind faith at least, for literally every historical disaster and human heartache—I just couldn't bear the sight of my old house, the split-levelness of it, or the Niceness of the people waiting for me inside, by which I mean Mom and Dad; my older brother, Kyle; his wife, Tracey; and their baby, Emma, all of them radioactive with holiday cheer. It filled me with rage, actually, the vision of us sitting around in red sweaters gnawing at slabs of sweet shiny ham while the world burned down around us, and that none of the facts I'd quote for them from actual scientific studies about sea level predictions and avian flu and the northwest-shifting jet stream would penetrate their brains deep enough to make them care. Instead, they'd roll their eyes at each other behind my back and flash me condescending smiles like I was some kook when *they were the kooks* for believing fairy tales like the Bible and American exceptionalism and, worst of all, the lazy middle-class lies that (a) they were powerless against global forces and (b) "everything happens for a reason."

"All I want is for things to be nice for Emma" was my mom's answer when, on our weekly call, I'd asked what I should get my little niece for Christmas.

"She won't remember one single second of it," I replied.

"That's no reason to cause trouble," she said.

"You know who are super nice and never cause trouble?" I asked her. "The lobotomized. Maybe I should invite a few of them over."

"Just get Emma a teddy bear or something," she said. "I'll reimburse you."

Like all people with means and resources and spare time but zero interest in using any of them to improve the world, the Aldriches of

Poughkeepsie were disappointing and despicable. My mother especially. I came to this realization slowly, nudged along by my roommate, Raya. It was Raya who introduced me to the fundamental narcissism of Heidi and Raymond's prioritization of Niceness and Security over Intelligence and Social Justice ("in other words, the preservation of the status quo over a better, bolder future that might not include them"). Even worse, said Raya, dishonest and repressed parents who never raised their voices or fists in front of their kids, or never tried to beat the gayness out of them, fucked them up way worse than the parents who let their demons and revulsion play out in the open. Were my parents even *awake*? What kind of people didn't fight back when their son called them zombies and drones and collaborators?

Raya's mother and father, on the other hand, had been arrested several times. They refused ownership of land or dwelling on principle and now lived in a commune outside Johannesburg. Growing up in the shadow of their angry activism and art had made for a kick-ass admissions essay that won Raya a full ride to Middlebury. Raya's parents never called or wrote or showed up for family weekends. They were perfect; mine were part of the problem.

The older I got, the harder I tried to suppress the severe Nice Guy tendencies Heidi and Raymond instilled in me. I knew where nice guys finished, and that "well-behaved men [*sic*] seldom make history," and that we can blame going along to get along for the rise of every dictator and the progress of every war, but still, not being nice was tough for me. I wanted the calculating and the clueless actors alike to be held accountable for the wreckage their respective evil and indifference had wrought upon the world; I wanted to shake them until they saw the light; but I also wanted them to thank me for shaking them, and to like me afterward. No, to love me. To think me a good person, at least, and noble, and, yes, nice, too. Oh, and to write me recommendation letters, offer me internships. Even when I won a round in Debate, I felt super shitty for the kid I'd just wiped the floor with, especially if it was an elim, and then I found myself going up to them afterward, saying, "You made some great points, you had me sweating in the flow, you'll get 'em next time." This need to please, which is all Nice Guyness is, by the way, not some index of moral character, was as ingrained in me as the compulsion to wake people the fuck up.

"This is why you have no friends," Raya would say.

"I have no friends because I hang out with you," I'd say back.

"I have no friends because I'm a freak."

"We're freaks because we don't care what anybody thinks." (This was untrue.)

"Fuck these people," she'd say, lighting a clove cigarette.

"Yeah, fuck these people," I'd say.

Raya didn't know I drove out to Rutland to see James that Christmas because she didn't know I was seeing James at all. She got all quiet and judgmental whenever I tried to tell her about the guys I chatted with on AOL or cruised at Sycamore Park, even though she spared me no gory details about the Midd girls she hooked up with, an endless parade of preppy tennis players from Connecticut cheating on their boyfriends. She had an issue with the age difference, I guessed, so I kept That Part of My Life separate, and lied to her about where I disappeared to in the late afternoons and what I was typing in the gray glow of my desktop late at night with her passed out on *Guns, Germs, and Steel* in the bed across the room, all of which made That Part of My Life lonelier than it deserved to be. I had no in-person person to tell about the man I couldn't live without except the man I couldn't live without. And I had no one to ask how you tell the man you can't live without that you can't live without him without scaring him off forever. Do you see how that would make a boy do stupid things even though the boy is not stupid?

James and I had been seeing each other since the afternoon we met at Sycamore Park my sophomore spring. *Seeing* is a weird word to describe what we were doing, but it is also the perfect word.

I saw him through the glass walls of his library office as I sat studying at a table.

I saw him walk to the staff parking lot with his arm around his wife.

I saw him step out of Royal Oak Bakery carrying a little white bag that I knew contained the single high-calorie, high-sugar blueberry muffin he treated himself to each weekday, half in the morning with an espresso, half at lunch for dessert.

Through the windshield of his car in the Sycamore Park lot, he saw me appear at the trailhead like a woodland creature and beckon him in.

In grainy pix on his BlackBerry, he saw my naked headless body reflected in my bathroom mirror, from the front and from the back, making a muscle, lifting my leg on the toilet, crossing my arms.

He saw his name for me—Elliott Abernathy—pop up on his phone and he smiled.

I saw my name for him—James Chemist Sycamore—pop up on

my phone and I smiled. I was too sentimental to update it, like it was a ticket stub from our first date. Our texts were like:

JAMES CHEMIST SYCAMORE

Tuesday's supposed to be warm!

Might you have some time for a hike?

Ooh lemme see

Raya away until Wednesday sneak up?

JAMES CHEMIST SYCAMORE

I need to see.

JAMES CHEMIST SYCAMORE

McCardell last stall @ 2:20, after 2:15 Psych Seminar starts. No other classes going on.

I'll see!

I wasn't freaked out when, two days after we met, I spotted James in the back row of the auditorium, slunk down in his seat, arms crossed, that dorky tweed cap low over his forehead, glasses on, the opposite of subtle, when I'd told him in no uncertain terms not to show up at my debate. Instead, a warm calm settled over my body up there on the stage, a kind of confirmation, like a teacher handing me back a paper with a big fat A on it, like the out-of-nowhere granting of a secret wish. Here was love, I thought, not at first sight, but—better—at second, when it's come more clearly into focus. It took the form of the man in the back row looking straight into me, eyes shining.

Like I said, I had no one in real life I could talk to like this about James. I had to rely on the guys in the Vermontm4m AOL chat room, mostly older guys who warned me over and over to be careful, to keep my wits about me, to play it cool, to have some self-respect, to hang out with them instead. It was sad, they had no romance left over from their youth. Early on, I struck a deal with one of them, VTGeorge802, a username so boring and redundant it inspired both confidence and affection. I promised to send him a proof of life message immediately before and after all of my IRL meetups, including any with this shadowy straight/married "J" I'd met in a cruisey park (I never said which one). If I was ever more than twelve hours late with my proof of life message, VTGeorge802 was directed to call a certain number (the pay phone in the third-floor common room in LaForce dormitory, though he didn't know that) and relay the following message to whoever answered: the blond gay guy with the first initial *C* who lived with the pierced tattooed girl was in trouble, and it was time to alert the authorities. I agreed to this hammy cloak-and-dagger scheme more out of kindness to VTGeorge802 than self-protection; he struck me as the type who needed someone to watch over.

Months into seeing James, long after we'd established a rock-solid mutual trust, I still sent VTGeorge802 a proof of life text every time I got home from meeting him in one of our usual places: the always-empty Frost Cabin up on Bread Loaf Mountain, the parking spot by the dumpster in the lot behind the Ames, the backyard of an abandoned farmhouse off Meadow Glen Drive. When I got back to my dorm, I tapped *I'm fine* to VTGeorge802, but let me tell you I was so very much more than fine—I was as happy as a boy could be. My J had been a perfect gentleman and a hot fuck. We'd made love in the back seat of his car in a field near Rivers Bend Campground. My shirt still held the scent of his smoky cologne. I wore it to bed so I could sleep with my sweet old man. Don't you worry, VTGeorge802! We know what we're doing! We're destined for each other! Send me your PO Box and one day you'll get a postcard from Montreal and that postcard will be from us.

Okay so maybe this J guy won't kill you after all, said VTGeorge802, said most of my cyberfriends after months of such reports. But they also said *mark my words!*—because that's how they talked, like characters on a black-and-white TV show—a married man will *smash your heart to smithereens*. A married man will *panic*. A married man will *always choose his wife*. And then this married man will *drop you like a hot potato. Take it from us*, they said: a married man is a *dead end*.

They're just jealous, I thought. Just bitter. They refused to understand what I saw in this "J," and, to be fair, what specifics could I offer to convince them he was worthy of me? The color of his hair, his height, the make of his car, his job? I scrambled all these details into unrecognizability. This was small-college-town Vermont after all, total population one hundred, homosexual population ten, or so it felt. James could be their neighbor, their childhood friend, their sister's husband. I couldn't risk exposing him. Or his wife, who did nothing wrong except get born.

At some point, VTGeorge802 created a private chat room for our little group of regulars. He called the room A-OK—for "Adventures of OzoneKid," which was my username—and together we populated it with the friendlier guys from Vermontm4m. No, I explained over and over to the group, J didn't give me money or presents. No, he didn't have a huge dick. No, he didn't forbid me from seeing other men. In fact, he encouraged me to find a boy my own age, or a slightly older man who was out and single and stable. He urged me to go to campus parties, to "find my people," to not harsh so much on the guys in LaForce and in Debate and Civics in Action. To be less judgmental and dramatic and more patient. And yes, as a matter of fact, after I described in detail the direness of the global warming situation and insisted J watch *An Inconvenient Truth*, he did start to care about the seals and the glaciers and the skyrocketing carbon emissions that would one day cook the world like the famous frog in the stockpot. Thanks to me, J was becoming a climate activist. In other words, I was influencing him as much as he was influencing me. Our relationship was a two-way street. Yeah yeah I know, I told them, everything I say about him sounds like a line from a musical: *When I'm in his arms, I see only him*, and *In his eyes, I see forever. I can't help it!* I wrote in the little text boxes. *I'm only nineteen, remember? Cut me some slack! :)*

It took no time at all to discover that James's wife was Professor Iris Lind, PhD, Department of English. Like I said, population one hundred. Professor Lind wore purple fingerless gloves and had purple streaks in her hair and didn't kiss her husband goodbye after he gallantly escorted her to her car on Tuesday and Thursday afternoons at four when her office hours ended. Fall of junior year I came this close to taking one of her seminars—Intruders on the Rights of Men: Eighteenth-Century Women Novelists—but the subject matter had exactly zero bearing on the real world or its future, and the credit wouldn't have counted toward my major, and I would have had to lie to James about it, and also *why*? So Iris could fall in love with me, like all my professors did, and invite our class to her house for end-of-the-semester cookies and cider? So she could introduce us all to her husband when he walked through the door at six o'clock carrying his brown leather satchel and his decontaminated cell phone and his guilt?

One night I started chatting off and on with this guy Derrick, who went by GodsJoke on AOL. His username, like OzoneKid, stood out for not having cock or ass or fuck or some dirty pun in it, which drew me to him right off the bat. I IM'd him first, which I never did because usually I had my hands full with guys private-messaging me as soon as I logged on. In retrospect, I should have taken "kid" out of my profile—it attracted the wrong element—and people thought "ozone" was some new party drug. Anyway, I could tell Derrick was normal not only because he didn't call me "son" or hit me up to get high, but because of the rock-solid judgment of character that is my unique superpower. Have I mentioned this? That I have a quasi-magical ability to immediately determine if someone is friend or foe? I've had it for as long as I can remember, and I haven't been wrong yet; it's why "stranger danger" never scared me; it's how I'd seen right away deep into the heart of James Hahn; not to mention Matt and Leo and Steve. I trusted that superpower more than the rise and set of the sun. I still do.

Derrick was sixty-six years old, much older than I usually went for, though the way men lie about their ages, I'm sure he wasn't the oldest guy I'd befriended in my time. I asked him the meaning of his username—specifically what "God's joke" was—and he said the joke was homosexuality itself. This strange condition we both shared, he wrote, was one of God's many methods of kicking the cocky and prideful down a peg or two and reminding us we were under His control, the control of His design at least. This unironic talk of God and retribution triggered my superpower in a negative way, but then, like he sensed it, Derrick assured me he'd given up religion and the church a long time ago, and that his username and philosophy were less a declaration of faith than a surrender to an agnostic Fate. As much as we want to believe the opposite, he said, in long paragraphs of messages that just sort of flowed out of him, each of us has an essential nature we'll never be able to change no matter how hard we try. We can be no kinder, and no more evil, and no stronger and no weaker than our essential nature permits. The script is already written, and life is just a daily receiving of the lines, like we're actors in a soap opera. *Would you change being gay if you could?* he asked me, and I told him probably not, but that I hadn't thought much about it, which was the truth, and to that he said that when he was my age, he used to beg God to either make him normal or kill him. *Then I fell in love*, he wrote to me. *Once love happened, I didn't need God anymore.*

Derrick never asked to meet IRL or talk on the phone or do cyber. We IM'd pretty much every night for the entire fall semester, always after 1 or 2 a.m., these long, lopsided conversations with his memory and philosophy faucets turned on full blast, me "listening," barely typing a word, which you think would have been boring as hell but totally wasn't. It was my own memories and ideas and anecdotes, my own history, that bored me. Who cared about a straight-A, straight-faced kid from Poughkeepsie who'd gone nowhere and done nothing when you'd lived a life like Derrick's?

His handsomeness had been legendary, he told me, his real name synonymous with Beauty itself. He wouldn't tell me that real name, only that it wasn't Derrick. But it was said that the young man who went by this name was the best looking in all of New York and Fire Island, that, like some kind of modern Medusa / gay porn flick, just to meet his eyes turned men rock-hard. His prime had been the late 1970s, early '80s, just before all the gay boys started dying from mysterious causes, disappearing one by one. He used to go dancing in secret clubs in dark smoky rooms high above Manhattan every night of the week until the sun came up, and then instead of walking home to his Greenwich Village apartment he'd check himself into the baths just so men hungry for a glimpse of him could follow him up and down the halls. He didn't remember sleep. He didn't remember dreams. He didn't remember a job, though a job had made him rich. He didn't remember paying a bill or packing a lunch or walking through a subway turnstile, and yet he must have done these things as regularly as an ordinary man. They must have happened in the daylight, he said, a light he hadn't had much use for anyway, unless it was the holy sunlight that warmed the sand on the beaches of Fire Island Pines.

I am a creature of the night, he wrote to me.

He was at the height of his beauty on that late-summer morning he dove into the sea at Fire Island and never reappeared. He'd danced through the night at a party at which every living friend he'd ever made had shown up, a party of glowing red rooms engorged with men spilling out into hallways onto pulsing wooden decks and moonlit beaches, a party with the sense if not the promise of an era ending. At least one of these friends watched him from the terrace as he floated for a while and then swam farther and farther out. Eventually, the friend must have given up and gone back in the house, only vaguely concerned; the sea was calm and Derrick was a strong swimmer and he'd yet to say goodbye to this friend or any of his friends; he'd left his shoes and his green polo shirt on the sand.

Derrick had planned to return to the house eventually, to take the afternoon ferry and then the train to the city, and then to dance again later that night, and to stay young and gorgeous forever. But when he emerged from the water, he was not in New York. He was in Idaho. He gazed up at the snowy mountains that hugged him from all sides. He recognized these mountains, these woods, though he'd never been to Idaho or west of the Mississippi. He carried an axe in his right hand. He searched for his face in the stream. He'd grown a beard. His cheeks were flushed, his skin mottled. There was meat stuck in his teeth. Was he alone? Where had everyone gone? With the axe he built himself a cabin. He hunted and grew cabbage and tomatoes and for money extracted molars from the elderly villagers. He took walks and studied the birds. He had a decent life spent mostly alone. Every few years he drifted east for a change of light, pulled by the ocean he remembered like a dream. The mountains grew greener as he floated in and out of houses, some he built himself, some built by others. He'd found the house in Vermont exactly as it now stood: sagging, overgrown, drafty, haunted. The very night he arrived there, the men pulled up in their trucks, as if they'd been expecting him. A few remembered him from back in the day in the city, the parks, the baths, the beach, though of them Derrick had no recollection. The others were strangers who became friends. Everyone else he'd known was dead. *I made it to Idaho in the nick of time*, said Derrick. *Why me and not them? What was the argument? My beauty didn't save me. It never saved anyone. It won't save you*, he said.

I asked him repeatedly for a pic of himself from now or from back then, but he claimed to be too shy. And he was too gentlemanly to ask for my pic if he wasn't willing to reciprocate. He was too old and craggy for the camera now anyway, he said; besides, he wasn't even sure he owned a camera anymore or would know how to transfer a photo from it to his personal computer. Many months passed, over which I guess he came to trust me, because finally he agreed to send me a Polaroid he'd dug up and then scanned.

It was late at night, as it always was when we spoke, when the pic downloaded onto my screen. I stood up so fast my desk chair crashed to the floor, waking Raya. This image he'd sent wasn't of the wrinkled old man I'd been chatting with, or his younger self, it was a photograph of me, Caleb Alexander Aldrich: my same blond hair and square jaw and high cheekbones, my wide eyes, the soft curves of my lips.

How did you get this? I fired back at him. *How do you know who I am? Is this some kind of joke? What the fuck?*

"Are you okay?" I heard Raya ask. "What's going on?"

That's not you, son, hahaha, wrote Derrick. *That's yours truly if you can believe it. Summer of 1978. Maybe '79.*

I looked closer. This was, in fact, a photo of myself. It couldn't *not* be me. I enlarged it on my screen. "Come tell me who this is," I asked Raya.

She staggered over in her pajamas and glanced at it sleepily, squinting. "I have no clue," she said. "Why?"

"You wouldn't say this is me? You don't think this guy looks *exactly* like me?"

She grabbed her glasses. "I mean, yeah, in that generic pretty-boy way, sure. Could be your brother maybe? Why? Are you into this guy? You crack me up, Caleb. First you're out chasing old men, now you're hitting up your doppelgänger? Talk about narcissism!"

I looked again.

Cal? Derrick was asking on the screen. *Cal? Are you still there? What's going on? Did I do something wrong?*

When I go to James, he's sleeping in his big wooden bed on the blue summer sheets. His ankles are entwined with Iris's, but their bodies stretch in opposite directions to seek the cool air, making a big *V* that spans the entire bed. The windows are open on both sides of the room, surrounded by trees as still as paintings of trees. The only sound is the squeak of the fan that spins on full blast above us. Iris wears a black mask over her eyes. James's chest hair is polar bear white and rhythmic in its rise and fall. His belly is round and spongy. They live somewhere in North Carolina now, where she teaches at a different college, one with gray stone buildings not unlike Middlebury's. I never see him in an office. I see him sleep late and join her for lunch in a dining hall, where students stop and ask her questions. He eats an entire muffin the size of a fist all at once, and then a Reuben sandwich, the cheese dripping down his chin, and then he wipes himself down and brushes her lips with a greasy kiss goodbye and walks along the shallow creek that meanders through the campus.

Sometimes he drives to a hilly park and sits in his car in the far corner of the lot with the radio on. Looking. Still looking. Forever looking. I've watched him score with boys my age, with men his own age, with older, with everybody in between. The routine's the same: the taps of the brakes, the nervous fumblings with zippers, the running off after. There are also the total strikeouts, the boys who walk right past him on the trail without meeting his eye, who shoo him away, who sneer and snicker. My James is beautiful and pudgy and pathetic in his rolled-up jeans and brand-new hiking boots and Coke-bottle glasses and trim white beard and barn jacket, out in the cold among the bare transparent trees. Now he's wiping the mud from those boots. Now he's in his too-long gym shorts that just barely cover his knobby knees one shade whiter than the rest of his skin. He wraps his ankle before stepping out of his car. He sprays his limbs with tick repellent. He asks another guy on the trail if he's tracked any bears. He walks so much slower than he used to. He's had hip surgery. He woke from it saying my name. Iris was not there. Maybe she had died by then. I lay my hand on James's chest as it rises and falls, hoping it will keep rising and falling and also hoping it will stop, thinking if it stops I will see him again. Is that what will happen? When the beating of his heart does cease, someday soon—we're getting so close, I can sense it—will he come to me here? Or is that when we'll both disappear for good? I have many questions, but this is the one that consumes me.

When James packed up his house in Weybridge, he put his files about me and the other boys in a box marked DUNCAN STREET. The next time I saw that box, he'd retrieved it from the back of a storage unit somewhere in North Carolina, set the files on the passenger seat of his car, and driven it to a Waffle House off the highway, where he sat the box next to him in a corner booth. He looked at every page once, some for just a moment, some for a long while, without making any notes. The pages with my name and pictures he put in a single manila folder. The rest he tossed in the dumpster behind the Waffle House.

Was this before his hip surgery, or after? He still had some hair that day. He had on the blue windbreaker I once told him made him look like a weatherman. Was he living in the house with the mulberry tree or had he already moved into the apartment with the cracked mirror? I can't get the story straight. Memory here works like a game of 52 pickup. Those countless times I've looked in on him, each and every one of those hours we've spent together since the boom, are playing cards floating all around me in the water. I don't know where in the order of James's life he will be when I reach for him.

Memory didn't used to work like this, of course. I used to be able to say how and when one event in my life led to the next. Like, in April of my senior year of high school, I got all four wisdom teeth pulled, which led directly to my dentist putting three refills on my Vicodin. Because my parents trusted me and didn't keep track of stuff like that, I stocked up on the pills and carried them around with me in my backpack in an Altoids tin, taking them only on special occasions like my birthday and prom and when I needed to slow my heart down before a big debate or interview. I'd hide in a bathroom stall and place a pill on my tongue like a Communion wafer, knowing it would make me all floaty, and that I deserved to float on that day and that day only, not every day, because I had too much to accomplish in life to waste it riding the clouds. This made those floaty days so extra special to me that I marked them down in my datebook with a big smiley face that I alone understood meant a Vicodin Day. On each Vicodin Day, I took stock of how far I'd come since the last one. What had I learned in those months? How was I different, if at all? Was I progressing toward my goals and ambitions or was I sliding backward, wasting my precious time? How much closer was I to academic success, to community/global impact, to finding true love?

The thing about 52 pickup is that it isn't even a real game. More like a prank played by some asswipe bully at middle school birthday parties. I fell for it every time, and then there I was on my hands and knees on the basement carpet, fifty-one cards in my hand, sweaty, degraded, searching under the couches for that last card that the bully always hid in his fucking pocket. I hated his stupid grinning face, and now I hate that I'm still playing this game-that's-not-a-game, with the final card still floating out there somewhere.

I started with twenty-four pills. When I left the Cactus Tree, I had five left in the Altoids tin. I'd probably have polished them off over break just to get through the two weeks in Poughkeepsie, especially after the texts I sent to James. I'm not saying I'd have swallowed all five at once; I'm not Leo; I wasn't depressed; I wasn't afraid. I'm saying I'd have craved the who-gives-a-fuck-ness the drug gave me, that glorious high I treated myself to so rarely. Because (you know this by now, right? Or do I have to keep showing my work?) my biggest problem—much bigger than my Nice Guy tendencies—was my giving-a-fuck-ness. I gave so many fucks about every living creature that their endless needs and starvations and oppressions grew heavier and heavier on me until they squeezed out all my breath. Like, on Tuesday I'd be at my normal one hundred fifty-five pounds, but by Friday I'd get up to four hundred, grouchy and wheezing and gasping for air under the weight of the fucks. And here's the truth only I will tell you: once you start to suffocate a Nice Guy, he won't just shrug you off. He'll *jettison* you so far and with such force your head will split open when it hits the ground. He does this so you won't come back.

We Nice Guys are the angriest people in the world.

I jettisoned a lot of people over the course of my twenty-one years: my brother, my best friends Meghan and Paul from high school, Mr. Corbett and the kids in Poughkeepsie Peacemakers of the World (what a joke that club was! They barely bothered to attend the meetings!), every one of them a letdown and a faker. I threw them off for a reason. I was the only one who did any real work, the only one having nightmares about the African girls who got their private parts cut out of them; that tsunami that killed over 200,000 people—as many as Hiroshima and Nagasaki combined!—on a sunny day at the beach in Thailand; those little kids with their legs blown off from land mines; AIDS, SARS, Ebola. What if Meghan's mom's breast cancer came back? What if Paul snapped his neck skiing? Worry built up in my head like gunk in the shower drain.

There were only a few places my head never got gunky:

1. Sycamore Park, on the chase.
2. With Raya in our room in LaForce, bitching about the snobs and Neanderthals down the hall.
3. In the gray glow of my computer, reading Derrick's stories.
4. The corner table in the library next to the heater, making notes for an argument.
5. The beach at Vinalhaven, spearing trash, tracking turtles, frolicking with the seals.
6. With James, didn't matter where.

The gunk just kind of melted out of me when we were together, making me so thin, so light, carefree but also powerful, like my bones were hollow and my muscles made of wire. Like I was Spider-Man. James and I had so much to worry about—Iris's growing suspicions, me giving him some infection he'd pass along to her, a cop busting us on whatever private property we trespassed onto—and yet, in the preciousness of our hours, I never wasted one second worrying. That's love, right? After hearing these other guys' dumb definitions over all these years, I think this one comes closest? Because honestly? I'm *still* not worried. Even here. I'm good right where I am next to sleeping James on the blue sheets, reaching for memories, asking myself what will happen when his heart does finally stop.

We are getting so close to that moment. I have actual hope.

Mr. Corbett, who wasn't just the moderator of Poughkeepsie

Peacemakers but also my AP English teacher, used to say, when we discussed books, "every character is an argument." Jay Gatsby, Jane Eyre, Clarissa Dalloway, their authors were making arguments when they unleashed them on the world. If they didn't have a strong case, they would never have endured, Mr. Corbett preached; we wouldn't still be scrutinizing them a hundred years later, writing papers about them for college credit. So lately, as I wait and watch and ruminate, I've been wondering if the same is true for every real person, if each of *us* is an argument, and if it's the weak arguments that don't endure. Like how I always thought I had such important stuff to say and world-altering work to do, but what if my words were pointless, and my actions, whatever they'd have turned out to be, only made life worse for people and the planet? And what if the only way to learn this tragic destiny was to die at twenty-one? What if my best argument wasn't my mind at all, but my body?

To be honest, that's not even my own question. Derrick asked it once over AOL. *What if our bodies are our best arguments?* The question stuck with me, and just now I tried to claim it as my own. The question came up when I told Derrick how I jettisoned Mr. Corbett, the closest person I had to a mentor, after I got to college; how I ignored his emails and birthday cards and stopped showing up to the potlucks and George W. Bush Resistance Fundraisers he threw over holiday breaks for his favorite alumni. I didn't care that Mr. Corbett secretly pocketed a not-insignificant percentage of those resistance funds—I considered it a form of protest against our high school, which paid him half as much as they paid the football coach—I cared that he spent more time shaking us down for weed and regaling us with stories of his hippie youth than firing us up for meaningful action against an increasingly fascist and homophobic regime. It enraged me, actually, his comfort level with incremental change, with the long arc of justice, because when this man was my teacher he filled me with *passion*. Nobody but Mr. Corbett could get me emotional about a *poet*. It was like he picked the poets our class studied just for me: Wilfred Owen and Allen Ginsberg and Langston Hughes, men who turned the injustices and indignities they faced and the horrors of their era into literature that woke up generations. For me, that was the main purpose of poems and of characters in novels: to get people to *do* something, not just go *aww, poor Jane Eyre*, and close the book.

I used to type out my favorite lines of poetry for Derrick. *I've heard of this one*, he said, but I could tell he was too embarrassed to admit he wasn't a big reader. He didn't watch films either ("only movies") or go to museums or follow politics or history. When he did, he said, he felt accused of wasting his life. I tried to sell him on reading history or sociology books, at least, mainly to convince myself he wasn't a Neanderthal, but he said no thanks, he didn't need to check out *Guns, Germs, and Steel*, he already knew enough about human history and behavior from his daily observations of the turkey vulture.

Listen to me, he'd write, whenever he riled himself up with a story.

All day the turkey vulture flies the skies sniffing and scoping out rotting flesh to feast on. He fills his belly to bursting, and then, ugly bastard though he is, retching up gastric juices ten times more acidic than humans', he never fails to find another bird to smash himself up against and shoot his wad into, and then a committee of buddies to roost in some trees with for a while, and then, for good measure, another carcass to stuff himself with before conking out for the night, just to wake up the next day and repeat his mindless cycle of urges again and again until he dies. Here we all are, Derrick went on, flexing our biceps and puckering our lips in the mirror, drunk on our own exquisiteness, and there's God looking down on us seeing not beautiful men but flocks of identical hideous turkey vultures crafted in His own image. *He must have laughed his ass off at me!* he wrote. *He's probably still laughing.*

I grab a card from the deck and it's James in that tweed beret and a long suede coat standing on Derrick's front porch. He carries his brown leather satchel with his files, like a *Law & Order* citizen detective. He's not super old yet. He's got a beard and mustache and has dyed out all the specks of gray. We wait for the door to open. I put my arms around his waist, my chin on his shoulder. He knocks a bunch more times and peers into the windows, and when Derrick finally appears, I watch James's face for a reaction, a thrill, a shock, when he sees me in him, but there isn't one.

He spreads the files on Derrick's kitchen table, and there's Ryan Sumter and Brian Price and Jeremy Dix and the two other Brians and the other Matthew and there's me, of course, holding my fucking lobster, all of us smiling back at James and Derrick from the front pages of newspapers. It must not be Matthew's time yet, or Leo's or Steve's. They must be off somewhere still alive, a few more years ahead of them, as James unfolds his map with dozens of *X*s and crisscrossed lines from Boston to Milwaukee. He plays him part of a documentary he found—*Our Nation Under Cover*—which features two real detectives hot on the trail of the monsters who supposedly killed us. There's Brian Price's mug shot from his DUI. Now me and my lobster again. Now Ryan Sumter in overalls, hands on the straps like a parachute pack. His bawling mother. Mine. The smiley faces on boulders and bridges and the sides of silos. I'm watching the screen, still on the alert for something new, anything new, but it's the same footage, the same last-known whereabouts, the same blurry dates and grouchy cops and faded MISSING posters flapping on telephone poles.

"These 'detectives' are wackos," says Derrick. He and James are sitting together on the couch. I'm on the arm next to James, knees up to my chin, arms around my legs. "You know that, right?"

James doesn't seem to know that. We watch one of the detectives squat at a stream and dip a test tube into the murky water. He points to the trestle bridge in the distance. The camera zooms in on the graffiti. Now there's a computer-generated composite of all our faces, dozens of us blended into one boy, and it's weird how in this boy you can see all of us and none of us.

"There must be some connection," says James. "It's too many coincidences."

"You're taking the bait. Those boys don't even look that much alike."

Derrick's wrong about that, though. The first thing I noticed after I'd met everyone, and new ones kept coming, was that we could be cousins, if not brothers. Even me, one of only three (Ryan, this kid Alfie) with blond hair.

"I get why he came here," James says. He's looking at the woodstove and the stacks of records and the tapestries on the walls. The sunset on the mountain through the sliding glass doors. The stained-glass lampshades. The vases of wildflowers. "It's homey."

"He didn't know what he was walking into," says Derrick. "But he took to it right away. The guys really liked him."

"I'll bet."

"It wasn't like that."

"One of those guys knows something."

Derrick shrugs. "If he does, he won't tell. Listen, Greg, none of those guys would hurt a fly. They *are* the flies. If they're guilty of any crime, it's not wanting their names in some gay story in the newspaper. Can you blame them? You think you're the only one with a wife? A few of them are schoolteachers. Their involvement would only gum up the works and throw off the search."

"*One* of them, at least, knows something."

"You know what I think? I think our Caleb's in Key West living on a boat with some rich old Daddy Warbucks he adores and who adores him right back. He's a lifeguard by day, and when the sun goes down he sneaks around to all the piers freeing fish from their traps. He's got a shaved head and pink toenails and his skin's brown as an Arab's. The locals call him Ganymede and bring him offerings of wine and wildflowers. The last thing he wants is to be found."

James shakes his head. "I've been so—" But he can't finish the sentence.

"I know," says Derrick. "But listen to me, Greg. All my boys are dead. Every one. I can't—no, I *won't*—allow myself to accept the fact that their beautiful bodies are disintegrating in the dirt. Let me tell you what I do when something reminds me of one of them—a song, a voice behind me in line at the grocery store—and I ache for him so bad I have to hold my belly to keep myself upright. I tell myself a simple story about him and I pretend that story's true: he's off doing the thing he most loves to do. He doesn't need me calling him or dropping by and getting in his way. Why would Cal miss you when he's down in Key West freeing the fish? Why would any of my dead miss me? I want to show up at my friend's apartment on Twelfth Street, but he's in a bathtub filled with candles and anatomy books and he can't answer the door. I want to call my other friend, but he's building a fire in his cabin in the Pine Barrens. I want to check up on another friend, but he's nineteen under the flashing disco lights, the DJ's playing his song, and I'm not so selfish as to drag him off the dance floor."

"My mind doesn't work like that," says James, like he's mad about it. "I need facts. I need reality. This Smiley Face stuff—it feels like an answer."

"A roving gang of serial killers with cans of spray paint feels like an answer? Aren't you supposed to be a professor?"

"Aren't you supposed to be a *human being*?" asks James. He grabs the remote control and hits Eject, gets up, and puts the DVD back in his satchel. "My wife's the professor," he says. "Chemistry. Up at UVM. I'm—in fundraising."

"Well, even a fundraiser can see that Smiley Face stuff's a load of crap. Mark my words, it's those detectives who'll turn out to be the perverts. Not us. It's not ever the ones you suspect."

"You being so sure about every little thing is what makes me nervous."

"About me?"

"I was afraid to drive up here. I really was. I didn't even know you existed. Caleb never mentioned you. Not once. Does that surprise you? Seems like you knew each other extremely well. He kept his life in lots of little boxes. That's what I've come to realize. Otherwise he'd have been found by now, right? Then I was chatting with this guy on AOL—"

"George. I heard."

"He assumed I'd already been here, and why wouldn't he? I must be the last guy on the internet to know about this place."

"Maybe you are," Derrick says, and now he's the one who sounds mad. "And he was Cal to me, by the way. He said he went to UVM. He told me your name started with a *J*, and that you worked in a library. That's the only biographical data about you I could get out of him. Told me he loved J so much it ate up his insides. Told me he ran track and had a girlfriend—'R'—and that he was 'confused' about whether he liked boys more than her. Almost none of that was true, was it? Lots of little boxes."

"Did you say all that to the cops?"

"Of course I did. I told them every fact I knew. Over and over. Just like I'm telling you now. 'The kid who called himself Cal showed up on my doorstep the evening of December twenty-third around eight o'clock. We talked and played records and watched TV. He liked my stories. He put off going home as long as he could. In my opinion, he was troubled and sad but not desperate or suicidal or on any sort of drugs. He drank a couple beers and crashed on the couch and when I woke up the next morning, he was gone. No note.' I let them go through my recycling and read every single one of our AOL messages. I gave them my fucking password, for Godssakes. I have nothing to hide. *Greg*."

"He texted me at 8:47 the next morning."

"I don't know anything about that. They never found his phone, as you know. I guess that's lucky for you. He was probably past Hartford by the time he texted you, en route to Key West. He drove through the night. Delirious. Imagine how happy he must be on those white beaches."

"It was an extremely ugly message," says James. "He didn't sound like himself. He sounded like someone had put some thoughts in his head."

Derrick stares at him. "Might be time for you to get going," he says. "These roads ice up really quick."

James grabs his coat. It's heavy and I want to help it on him. "Dumb question," he says, like he's just thought of it. "Can I ask—did you notice if he was wearing a bracelet?"

"He was, yeah," says Derrick, right away. "And yes, I mentioned that to the cops, too. They asked me for every detail of his clothes. I remembered the bracelet because one of the guys teased him about it. He asked if he was part Indian, which Caleb didn't find too funny. He got kind of weepy and said the bracelet belonged to his favorite uncle who'd hung himself because he was gay. I've got a good memory, but that really made an impression."

When his heart stops, will James come to me here? If the other boys know the answer, they won't tell. I keep asking. I keep trying to tell them about James and what he's doing and where he's going, but all they do is shout the names of people and places I don't recognize. Either they can't hear me, or they're not listening. I ask them why, after so long (years, decades, a lifetime?), after getting pulled out and solved, after the awful humming, we don't know it all. I ask them when this endless asking, this spinning of the wheel, will be over. I miss how I used to just log on to a computer and get answers and instructions from friends who'd made a private room just for my adventures. I miss James telling me one day I'd alter the course of the world. I miss Raya calling bullshit on my bullshit. I miss VTGeorge802 waiting up for me to prove I was still alive. I miss Derrick, even though he wasn't real.

I did make him up, didn't I? GodsJoke? I must have read about him in a book. I must have been inventing a different future for myself—a better one, a longer script. It was fuzzy then and keeps getting fuzzier. It's been so long since I talked to him, to anyone but Matt, Leo, Steve. I was only nineteen. And then, I was only twenty. And then, before I knew it, I was writing to the guys in A-OK: *Next month I'll finally be twenty-one! December 7! Don't forget! Should we finally all meet in person? Safety in numbers?!?*

How can I determine, in all this noise, what's a memory and what's a dream and what's a wish? I don't believe myself. I don't believe that, on the morning of the day before Christmas Eve, I tore out the page of directions I'd scribbled in my Econ notebook and stuffed it in my backpack, and then, instead of driving straight home to see my nice family of Aldriches who loved me, I met James at the Cactus Tree Motel. I don't believe I said goodbye to him in the parking lot in the falling snow, promising through tears not to text him at all, not even with the most innocuous message, over the holidays, when Iris sometimes borrowed his phone to snap pictures. I didn't put the directions on the passenger's seat and follow them north over icy country hills around steep curves to a falling-down house deep in the woods. When the man who'd renamed himself Derrick opened the door, and I looked into my own future face lined and weathered, and he outstretched his arms, I didn't fall sobbingly into them. Derrick didn't say, patting my back, pulling me closer, "There there, young man, now what's the trouble?"

He didn't try to cheer me up by feeding me peanut butter cookies and mixing up a pitcher of eggnog and making some calls to his friends, while over and over promising me everything would be okay, that all I had to do was grow up, that in a few years, probably sooner, I'd forget this "J" I couldn't stop crying about—and come on, why not tell us J's real name, now that we're friends? Not only would I forget J, according to Derrick, I'd forget Derrick, too, and all the stories of his youth and the blizzard gathering outside and my lovesick heart; that's how life worked; that's the wisdom of the old, we who know that time will dull and dissolve every single moment no matter its radiance.

Derrick didn't talk like that to me that night. Nobody talks like that ever. Men in trucks did not start arriving one after the other carrying six-packs of beer and bags of weed and Saran-Wrapped slices of pineapple cake for a party thrown in my honor. I didn't get a little tipsy on the eggnog and beer and dance in the kitchen to "Feliz Navidad" with a leathery dude in a tuxedo and candy cane tie. Or play spin the bottle in a circle of bearded flanneled men, their beards soft on my cheeks when they pressed their lips to mine for the smooches. I didn't argue with the tuxedoed man—a total douche, it turned out—about the private plane Al Gore flew in to his speeches. I didn't let the men hug me goodbye so tight or laugh when they made quick, sheepish grabs of my ass. I didn't wonder what James was doing at that very moment. I didn't forget to call my brother long-distance to say the roads were too icy, I'll see you tomorrow, I'm sorry, tell Mom not to worry, kiss Emma's fat cheeks for me. I didn't spend the night lying on a lumpy sofa under an afghan beside a roaring fire, the room drunk-spinning, Christmas music low on the stereo, Derrick snoring in his bed at the other end of the room.

The next morning, when I woke just before sunrise to passable roads but still couldn't bring myself to drive them, I didn't kill time by hiking down to the river I could hear but not see from Derrick's back deck. I didn't go over and over in my head the injustice of my separation from James, and my hatred for the societal and cultural and familial forces that enforced that separation, and then break my promise to him by sending him this text:

Merry Christmas to my hot daddy, my one true love

I absolutely did not follow this text moments later with:

Iris if you're reading this then now you know our secret so FUCK YOU!!

And then: I didn't panic. I didn't frantically type:

I'm so sorry, I didn't mean that. It was a joke.

I'm so fucked up

Please don't hate me

When the rain started, out of nowhere, first lightly, then in warm steady sheets, making puddles and mud pits of the snow, I didn't double back on the hiking path and scramble up a slippery hill and then down another slippery hill and then double back again until I couldn't tell which way was back and which was ahead. I didn't find my way to a high flat rock in the middle of the creek to try to see my way up and down (east and west? north and south? I'm no Boy Scout) through the blinding rain, soaked to the skin through my jeans and sweater and the same boxers I'd had on since James tossed them back to me over our bed at the Cactus Tree.

I blamed my pounding head and wobbly legs on my hunger and my hangover and the aftershocks of my texts to James. I'd had the spins and wobblies like that before, usually after a night of bong hits and Southern Comfort shots with Raya, sometimes so bad I couldn't get out of bed. I'd called up friends and said things I shouldn't have said, shot flames out in all directions, burned them at the stake. Teen-boy tantrums. Friendly fire. Whatever this attack on my body was in the woods behind the Gaze on Christmas Eve 2007, it felt different from the wobblies. The attack was cataclysmic. A separation. In my head, all at once, came an electric fizziness; a lurchy jolt, like stepping onto a stopped escalator; and an excruciating boom. *Well, there goes my brain*, I said out loud, but there was no one around but myself and the wind kicking up and up, bending the trees toward me from the riverbanks, whipping my face, drowning my words in the roar. It was as if I'd expected them all along—the fizziness, the jolt, the boom. Like the men in their trucks, like the love that would obliterate God. When they went off—fireworks!—I clutched my skull with one hand, and my foot slipped off the rock. As I fell, I reached up with my other hand for one of those twisting branches, like it was a jungle vine and I was fucking Tarzan, like I could just pull myself onto it and swing over the raging river onto the land where I'd be safe. Like I wasn't just some ordinary kid whose luck had finally run out.

Leopold "Leo" Ridgeway Jr.

(September 29, 1995–January 11, 2016)

I am one of those boys they keep finding in the river. For four days, I lay on my back in the Rum on a flat rock that jutted out from the eastern bank. The lower half of my body was submerged in the water, like I was both sunning and cooling myself, except I still had all my clothes on—black jeans, black shirt, silver belt, silver chain, black socks, black puffer vest—and my arms were in an *X* over my chest. My boots and hat were long gone. My hair was in my eyes, obscuring my view of the sky over Saint Paul that was not the actual Saint Paul sky but my idea of the sky.

I didn't see the fuckwads who fixed me up like this and stole my wallet and keys and Fluevogs and spray-painted the pink smiley face on the rock. I didn't see the hiker or hear him call 911 and shout the words *dead kid dead kid* that echoed into the woods. I only know about all that from the stories that came way later, told by Katie to the men at Jenks Lumber Supply and her boss at the bookstore and her high priestess of a therapist Margaret Mead Ashe and, well, anybody who even hinted at it. Katie talks about me more than I ever talked about myself, more than anyone talked about me before I disappeared, and, no doubt, more than people will talk about me in all the years to come.

I'm with Katie most of the time. Summoning Matt and Caleb and Steve takes so much concentration and effort, and even when one of us, usually Matt, manages to wrangle us together, we shout as loud as we can and talk so fast to catch each other up that we can't or won't follow the conversations the way we used to when Matt first got here. I don't recognize all the names and places they shout about, and they've lost track of me and Katie, they haven't even met Leo, and yet they don't ask me questions, and they don't slow down. I'm just as guilty, to be honest. It's like we've stopped caring about communication with each other at all. We just shout our own shit, even though, like I said, we can barely hear ourselves or each other over the shouting.

But I miss those guys, which makes me angry and lonely all over again, so I follow Katie and Leo around. Who I find depends on the moment of the day and place I look in on them, a moment that never lasts long. Just when I'm sure Leo can sense my presence, my elbow on his shoulder—just when he catches that shiver—he's gone, and suddenly I'm in some other moment of some other day in some other place with him. Matt describes time here like a frog jumping in and out of your hands, but to me it feels more like dreams dissolving into other dreams. You know how you don't remember any of your dreams coming to an end—like, there's no credits rolling at the end of them? You're just already in the next one, and everything's out of order? That's how it is for me, because in one dream Leo's still calling himself Katie and she's half his size and her hair's a mess of curls. Then the dream switches and her hair's buzzed on the sides and bleached blond and she's sucking down a Frappuccino labeled *Leo.* Then she's asleep on a bus back to Saint Paul, wearing red lipstick and black nail polish and a flowy dress, *Mrs. Dalloway* open in her lap. Cut from the bus to the stage of a karaoke bar, Leo standing tall and straight and super stiff except for his left foot stomping to the beat, screeching Janis Joplin's "Piece of My Heart" into a microphone. Then he's looking for seats at a movie theater holding hands with a pretty blond older lady, laughing about the flask and candy bars they've smuggled in their coat pockets.

Standing behind Leo when he squeezes that lady's hand, leans forward to kiss her, grins that shit-eating grin as we step over the knees of the people in our row, basically erases my loneliness. It melts most of the anger away, too. I stay a long time, as long as I can, admiring his moves, the film flickering and booming, the audience laughing, but then I get distracted again—I'm still so easily distracted; I'm still myself—and my brain brings up some shit I pulled when I was Leo's age, a guy or girl I stole from or screwed over, someone more fucked-up than I was, whose name I never even knew. I'm sorry, I say to them, but it's too late for that, too. It makes me feel so low.

The next time I find Leo, he's in a backyard I don't recognize, and on his arm is a different blond lady than the one he took to the movies. He's a few years older than me, early twenties at least, wearing black jeans, black sneakers, a yellow button-down dress shirt untucked, sleeves rolled up to the elbow, a yellow tractor hat, and a fat silver watch. His head is high, periscoping to check out who else is at the barbecue. My first thought is that they're leaving me behind, Leo and Katie, that one day I'll look in on them and they'll be so old they'll be strangers. My next thought is that, right now, in his prime, in that getup, Leo looks like a bumblebee, round and bouncy, introducing his date to one circle after another under rows of chili pepper lights strung from heavy trees. He takes a big bite from a double-stacked burger and talks while chewing, wiping ketchup from the corner of his lips. His old lady tucks a paper napkin under his chin just before he drips more ketchup onto it, and they laugh, him saying *Bonnie Bonnie, oh Bonnie, Bonnie's the best, Bonnie always saves me in the nick of time, what would I do without Bonnie.*

They met at Wilder's, Leo tells a pair of college-aged girls. She came in looking for something to help her sleep. She'd been having trouble in that department lately, Bonnie says, and she'd always heard of people falling asleep with books open on their chest, so she thought why not try that little trick before filling an expensive prescription that supported the pharmaceutical industry. Bonnie hadn't owned a book since high school, she told Leo that day, and Wilder's was en route to her job. She wanted a book to last the rest of her life, Leo continues. She wanted it to be so long she could read a page or two each night before it put her to sleep and then pick up where she left off the night after. Something not too boring, but not too interesting either. The last thing she needed, she'd told him, was another thing to occupy her mind.

What could Leo say? The woman was practical and stern and blond and a weirdo and yeah, he shrugged, a total MILF, sure, he had a type and she was it and somehow they both knew it. He led her in circles to keep her talking and then to the literature section and the store's single copy of *Clarissa* by Samuel Richardson, a book so wide and heavy it slipped from between his thumb and forefinger when he pulled it out from under its shroud of dust. Leo had had his eye on *Clarissa* for a while, more for the challenge of it than its subject matter, the "History of a Young Lady" in eighteenth-century England.

"Here it comes," Bonnie said to the college party girls, squeezing Leo's arm, "his big pickup line."

"So I handed it to her," said Leo, "and I go, 'Live long and slumber.'"

The party girls looked at each other. "We don't get it," one of them said.

"It's from *Star Trek*," said Bonnie, and they said, "Ohhhh okay," and she said, "Don't worry, my daughters didn't laugh, either. But I totally LOL'd."

"I even did the Spock voice," said Leo.

"And you know what?" Bonnie went on. "That night I read the first page of the book, and then another page the night after, and both times I conked right out lickety-split. Problem solved."

"Next day here she comes with a pineapple cake baked just for me."

"Aww," says one of the girls, "that's so sweet," but when Leo and Bonnie walk off I catch them snickering behind their Solo cups. No matter, though, because now Leo's in the bathroom of the house not giving a fuck about what some random college girls think of him and his taste in women. He removes his Minneapolis-Moline hat to check his fade in the mirror. He rubs his hand over the fuzzy part and flicks off some lint and scratches his gut and straightens his big bumblebee-yellow shirt over the chest he's (mostly) flattened with a kind of tight tank-top bra thing. He runs the faucet over a paper towel and dabs at the shirt where some ketchup seeped through. When he washes his hands, he hums. On the other side of the door waits Bonnie.

If I'd lived, some Bonnie would have probably come for me, too, carrying her pineapple cake. She'd have fed me, washed and waxed me, stood guard on our front porch with a broom in one hand and the other on her hip, daring the zombies to just try to come inside and mess with her man. The world is lousy with kind people, women especially. Could she have saved me, though? I thought I knew the answer to this question. Nobody ever wanted to hear it. They still don't. I'll say it anyway.

I was named after my father, Leopold Ridgeway. He played drums for Wild Horses, a Rolling Stones cover band that got regular gigs all over the U.S. and Europe and even South Africa—everywhere, it seemed, but Saint Paul. My first few years of life, he quit the band to move in with Patricia and me and provide for us by teaching drums out of our basement and painting cars at Maaco, but by the start of my earliest memories he'd rejoined Wild Horses and spent most weeks on the road. He called me from pay phones and hotel rooms to ask about school and friends and how long my hair was getting (*the longer the better*, he'd say, *it's not long enough until people mistake you for a girl*) and to tell me he loved me and missed me and couldn't wait to come home, and that he was only in the band for the money, which he was doing his damnedest to save for my college fund. One minute he'd be talking, and the next the phone would go dead and I wouldn't hear from him again until he got to the next city. We never said goodbye.

Wild Horses had huge followings in Florida and Germany. Every few months he mailed us a cardboard tube with rolled-up posters that advertised their shows. Patricia would take the envelope of cash he'd hidden between the posters (he didn't trust banks) and then crack the tube over her knee and stuff the posters in the trash. When I was still young enough to believe everything he said, I fished out the posters and memorized the names of the cool-sounding bars he played in—Howl at the Moon, the Green Parrot, HausHaus—and imagined him on a stage bashing miserably at his drums, beaten down by the months of holidays and birthdays he spent apart from his beloved wife and son. Some nights, after Patricia went to bed, I'd slip downstairs and spin the hands of the grandfather clock around and around, thinking that would speed up time and bring me closer to eighteen, that mythic faraway age Patricia said I'd need to be if I really wanted my wish to come true, which was to move to Orlando, where my father and his bandmates shared a rented house with a pool.

But by the time I reached eighteen, he'd divorced Patricia, and the house in Orlando he rented with Wild Horses became the flat in London he owned with his new wife, a German bartender named Ingrid. According to Patricia, he owed us "millions" in alimony and child support, but "good luck tracking that deadbeat down." The return address on his envelopes didn't show up on MapQuest. Wild Horses's internet presence had dwindled to a handful of listings for small venues and festivals throughout Northern Europe. The few times a year my father called, he dodged any and all questions about upcoming gigs, Ingrid, my college fund, or flying me to London for a visit. He told hurried unglamorous stories about British drivers and greedy pub owners and the effect of the damp weather on the arthritis in his hands. All he wanted to hear from me was how well Patricia and me were doing, if she had a serious boyfriend, how much better off we both were without him, as if he'd been just an old roommate and not the source of my existence.

And so, in some senseless hope he'd get jealous and come fight to win us back, I spun tall tales of our awesome life: Sunday afternoons at the skate park showing off disco flips for my proud mother watching from a bench; summer trips to Lake Minnetonka with her new friend Bruce, who had a boat the size of a building; the brand-new Jeep she stuck a giant red bow on and surprised me with at Christmas. No mention that Patricia lost her job at the diocese, that she got headaches so bad she slept most of the day in her room with the lights off and the door locked. No mention that her hands were often shaking when she zipped up my coat. That her wrists had burn marks from when she tried to cook. No mention that, most nights after dinner, if we had dinner at all, she walked to the park at the end of our street to meet up with friends whose names she wouldn't tell me, and that she rarely made it home before I fell asleep. That one of the times I followed her to the park, I saw a girl from my high school pick her up on the side of the road and drive off with the music blaring. That another time I watched her get into the passenger seat of a different car, except the car didn't go anywhere. No mention that, one by one, various items in our house were disappearing—Grandma's old-timey gold lamp, the framed photographs of Thunder Bay over the rec room TV, the DVD player, the TV itself. The grandfather clock. No mention that I started to hide my stuff from her. That her headaches went away. That she got so thin her veins glowed blue. That police officers parked outside our house a lot, knew my name, told me my mother was "troubled," called our house a "sinkhole." No mention to my absent father that, early on, I regularly found her stash on her nightstand, innocent as a book, and buried it in the woods in his old metal lunch box. I know now I should have flushed the pills down the toilet, but I sensed, even then, that someday I'd want them for myself.

When I tried to hurt Patricia, as I so often did, nearly as often as I tried to protect her, I'd sneer at her in my father's voice, call her by all the sweet names I'd heard him use on her in phone calls years back: *Pattycakes*, *Dolly*, *Babylove*. His face I'd long forgotten, but his voice I could mimic flawlessly. The slow, throaty drawl with a faint whistle on the *s*'s, the quick sniff at the end of each of his sentences, like he couldn't get enough air. Depending on how far gone she was, Patricia would either run at me fists flying, or she'd crumple to the floor like one of those stick puppets dropped by its master, her wooden arms and legs piled on top of themselves, wrecked by bruises and divots.

Patricia's voice was easier to imitate, so much cleaner and crisper than my dad's, all back-of-the-throat yaps and rounded *o*'s, my tongue curled to the roof of my mouth. I used it to call the pharmacies, the banks, CloudView Middle, then CloudView High. I used it to call the Piercing Pagoda to tell her boss, "Oh, Meryl, I can't shake this damn flu." After Piercing Pagoda fired her the second time and she managed to get a job in the checkout line at Kowalski's, I called Sam Kowalski to tell him my son, Leo, was sick, he had strep, I might be contagious, too, I'm so sorry this keeps happening to me. Before I left for school each morning, I wrote notes to remind her of the excuses I'd made for her missing work the days before. I stepped over her on the floor of the rec room in time to make the bus. In the afternoons, I stepped back over her in the same spot, her limbs slightly rearranged, her mouth hanging open, my note on the coffee table next to her cell phone displaying a full screen of missed calls. I locked myself in my room upstairs and listened for hours to the iPod I'd stolen from a guy in homeroom even though his music sucked, and then, at seven thirty, I rode my bike across the highway to Penza's Pizza, where I swept up and took out the trash for Mr. Penza himself, who paid me in free subs and slices and sodas and the occasional wad of cash because at that time I was only thirteen.

Sam Kowalski had a high tolerance for Patricia's bullshit. On the phone with her (me), he credited the virtue of Charity, which granted him infinite patience with the "ill-fated and indigent," as well as the fact that, on the days Patricia did make it in, her pretty smile and sad stories and heartfelt vows to do better—not to mention her rock-solid belief in the awesome power of the Lord our God—won him and everybody else over, especially the widowers buying frozen dinners and the high school boys who bagged them up. *We all just want what's best for you*, he said on the phone to Patricia (me). *My wife and I pray for you every single night.*

"Thank you, Sam," I'd yap back, my throat raspy from fake strep. "See you tomorrow, God willing."

"God willing!"

I give her credit for getting herself clean once Dom, another addict, knocked her up with Katie and then skipped town when she told him she was keeping her. That fuckwad sent no cash, never once called Katie, and, as far as I know, never tried to contact any of us. At least my dad pretended to care about me for a while. Patricia never married Dom, of course; she took back Starks, the last name she grew up with, and made it Katie's, too, and tried to convince me to take it, but, at the time, Leopold Ridgeway Sr. was the one person in our house who'd made something of his name, and I aimed to bank some of that potential for myself.

Those months Patricia was pregnant with Katie, and the year or so after she was born, around the time I turned fifteen, were the best of our lives together. We came as close as we ever would to being those happy people I pretended to be for my father, the ones who cannonballed into Lake Minnetonka from a boat the size of a building. Little by little, our house filled with objects again. Weekends, Aunt Alice drove out from Eden Prairie and slept on the fold-out and brought us stuff we'd soon need: baby clothes she'd saved from her many foster girls, an extra TV to replace the one Patricia pawned, and a garbage bag filled with mildewy stuffed animals we aired out in the front yard. Driving by, you'd have thought our place was on Sesame Street, all those googly-eyed creatures propped up on chairs, peeking out at the road from between the bars of the railing. We painted my bedroom pink and put my dusty old crib back together and moved my mattress and dresser and nightstand to the basement, where I hung my Mastodon and Iron Maiden posters on the cinder-block walls and plugged in a mini-fridge and a stereo.

I remember how every morning at six, Patricia brought baby Katie down and set her next to me on my bed, then got into Sam Kowalski's waiting car for the first meeting of the day at Church of the Redeemer. I was too afraid I'd roll over and smother Katie if I kept sleeping, so the two of us just chilled out in my cinder-block palace watching the room fill with light. Somehow, lying there on our backs with her little hand wrapped around my finger, listening for the garbage truck, the sun and branches making patterns on the walls and ceiling—a different pattern every single day, like a new episode of a TV show—made me wish that time, which I used to want so badly to speed up, would actually stop instead, right then and there. If only we could live for a long while like this, I thought: us two stink bugs wiggling our toes to the tune of a Minnesota morning, waiting for Patricia's white sweat suit and white sneakers to appear in the window on their way up the driveway, the turn of her key in the lock—*whoozat? 'Zat Mommy?*—the thwack of the front door, the sight of her on the stairs, arms folded, fake-mad, *what are you bums still doing in bed?* Her cheeks fleshy and pink from the cold, her eyes alive. If only mother and son could always just be getting our schedules synced before she shooed me off to school—her day shift at Kowalski's, my night shift at Penza's, weekends the opposite; sometimes we needed a neighbor or Aunt Alice to watch Katie; worst case Patricia took her with her to the store. If only my grades could stay not terrible. If only we could have a few dollars in the bank, splurges on dinners at Spaghetti Warehouse. Snow days, my favorite, all three of us home. Game shows on the new TV. Katie a purple puffball I could pull around on a trash can lid. Talk of a new used car, with decent heat. Talk of getting a dog.

But then came July 19, 2013. I remember the exact date because, throughout the short but happy period that preceded it, I kept handwritten journals, mostly song lyrics, but also pencil sketches and calligraphy and "Dear Leo" letters addressed not to my absent father but to my all-too-present self. On that day, I was sitting on the edge of my bed in the middle of the afternoon in just my boxer shorts and bare feet, elbows on my knees, head in my hands, doing absolutely nothing. Like sitting-there-smelling-my-pits-but-not-wanting-to-shower-absolutely-nothing. I got like that a lot, lost in thought about my life or some girl, tired but fidgety, lazy but jammed with ideas. *Where are you going?* Journal Leo asked again and again in his letters to me, more of an accusation than a question. I should mention that Journal Leo was often disgusted with Real Leo, and felt strongly that he spent too much time on the edge of his bed in the middle of the afternoon half stoned, half hard, half awake, half thinking about college, half planning to start a band of his own. Journal Leo felt that, when Real Leo did finally leave the house, he should be going somewhere other than Penza's to scrape the grill and sign for deliveries, or to Electric Fetus to sift through rows of shrink-wrapped imported albums he couldn't afford. But neither boy could conjure any images of Leo Ridgeway at twenty, let alone Leo Ridgeway at twenty-five, that looked any different from what he was then: the junior manager at Penza's Pizza, the skinny stringy-haired dude on the sidewalk outside Electric Fetus bumming a cigarette. My future was like my window high up near the ceiling on that summer afternoon: unreachable, unopenable, full of glare. Staring at it hurt my eyes.

Then, on July 19, 2013, I got seized.

I wrote that word—*seized*—in my journal like it was a kidnapping, because that's exactly how it felt when that basement window shattered and into my room dropped the hooded man who held me down and pressed the barrel of his gun against the notch at the base of my throat, choking all the air out. When I tried to breathe, he pressed the gun harder, and cupped my mouth and nose with his fat sweaty hand, making my heart go berserk. I threw him off me, gulped in all the air I could, and for a few seconds breathed normal, but he kept coming back at me and back at me, and I kept pushing him off. He'd give me a few minutes, a few sips of air, until, again, there he was, his gun at my throat, his fist in my mouth. We went on and on like that until I got so tired my limbs ached, even though I hadn't moved from that spot on the edge of my bed, where I sat with my hand over my heart, drenched in sweat.

I looked around the room. Everything was right where it was—the rain-streaked glass in the unbroken windows, the plastic crates of records and CDs at the bottom of the stairs, the piles of dirty clothes on the floor, the white cube alarm clock on my bedside table next to the lamp next to my watch—but I didn't recognize any of it anymore. It was all strange and faraway and possessed of a threatening energy. The blue numbers on the face of the clock scared me. The branches just beyond the window, covered in thick green leaves, swaying in the breeze, scared me. My balled-up socks scared me. I couldn't turn on the lamp because the little black switch scared me. The click it would make scared me. The shade scared me. The sheets. The sash. That sound—*sh*—scared me. The carpet scared me. The smooth grooves between the stone blocks of the wall scared me. The green in the leaves. The words in my head. The words in my head. The words in my head that wouldn't stop jumping around up there, body-slamming each other, trying to get out, but they couldn't, they were trapped there, and then again the glass shattered, and again the hooded man swooped down, and again I choked on the unavailable air. What was happening to me?

I pulled on a pair of shorts. I ran up the stairs, out the front door. I expected to find a hole in the sky. The trees on fire. Chariots. But nothing had changed out there, either, not the parked cars, not the crack in the asphalt down the middle of the driveway, not the rabbit masticating the weeds that grew up through the crack, except all of this, too, emitted malevolent vibrations. All of this came at me, suffocated me. The crack. The rabbit's black eyes, locked on mine as it chomped and twitched. This is a dream, I thought. A night terror. I'd had them as a kid, around the time my dad left. But it was the middle of a summer day, a Friday in July, and I was seventeen years old, and I'd stopped caring that my father ditched us. I hardly thought of him anymore. My life was just starting to get good. I had tomorrow off. I'd saved the good weed to smoke with this girl Marisa. I was just about to jerk off thinking about her. I'd read somewhere that I was on the precipice of my sexual peak. Now the thought of Marisa scared me. The necklace she wore against her throat scared me. And the weed. And touching my dick. And shooting. And tomorrow scared me, that time off, all those hours. What would I do with them? How would I survive them? I walked over the cool crunchy grass back into the house and closed the door, scared of the crunch and the click, remembering the hooded man, the first time his hand closed over my mouth. When I remembered him, he came again. He kept coming.

Right away, I knew two things: some sort of chemical change had occurred, and I had to hide it from the people around me. The problem was I needed people around me. Being alone scared me. I rode my bike to Penza's and sat in a booth and ate my free employee slices and tried to act normal. The regulars smiled at me, said *hello*, said *how's your summer*, like they couldn't see my soaked pits or the ripple of my pounding heart against my shirt. My shift started. The straight line of the hands on the clock scared me. I tied my hair back and put on my apron. The red paisley swirls in the bandanna scared me, and the loops of the apron. We got Friday-night busy right from the jump, and I got lost in the rush of customers, forgetting myself for a few precious minutes. There I was, warming up slices, changing the CO_2 tank in the soda machine, running credit cards, all the while drinking in the delicious greasy air as easily as water from a garden hose. Then we got a lull, and I remembered I couldn't breathe, I remembered the fucked-up cells inside my skull, dividing and multiplying, I remembered the self-ness of me, the Leo Ridgeway of me, and that I couldn't escape him, I was stuck with him in this heavy head, and the room tilted, and the people slid away, and I gripped the counter to stay upright, and kept swallowing so hard I could hear the glugs in my throat over the lip-smacking, chewing, and spitting at the tables all around me, the spiky mandolin music, the sizzle of the grill. Still, nobody saw the terror on me. It was as invisible to them as the hooded man. We got busy again. Relief. We got another lull. Terror. The same pattern, over and over, relief terror relief terror, for the rest of the night, for the rest of my life.

Later, in the early hours of the morning, the 20th of July, I couldn't sleep, so I went up to Katie's room. I needed her protection, though she was barely two years old, barely a person at all. I lay on the carpet beside her crib, clutching my pillow. The hooded man slipped in anyway, like a molester. He'd find me everywhere, wouldn't he? Afterward, I stood at her crib, white-knuckling the bars, choking on the air, watching the peacefulness of her slumber, hoping I wouldn't disturb her, also willing her to wake. When she finally did, I picked her up and held her close, her legs long enough now that they wrapped around my waist, her chubby arms around my neck. I held her tightly to my chest and carried her from one end of the room to the other, back and forth, back and forth, crying into her hair.

I'm going crazy, I said to her. I'm so sorry. I can't make it stop.

Maybe speaking the words would make them untrue.

I'm so scared, I said. I'm so fucking scared.

When I laid her back down, she opened her eyes and said my name.

You just had a little nightmare, I told her.

She blinked back at me and smiled.

Every night for weeks, I climbed the stairs as softly as I could, me and my pillow, like a child hiding from a thunderstorm, and curled up on the floor beside her. I slept so close to the surface of consciousness that her slightest stir or faintest whimper woke me, and when I sat up on my knees and peeked in on her through the bars of the crib, she was always okay, always just dreaming a normal kid dream or turning onto her other side to make herself more comfortable, oblivious to the storms in my brain, to the dangers and evils of the world.

On the really bad nights, I carried her half-awake body around the room, telling myself it was good for her, telling her what I'd learned from the internet, which is that I was the exact right age for schizophrenia and had every warning sign: *Extreme hostility. Depression / unrelenting sadness. Deterioration of personal hygiene.* I hadn't heard voices yet, but my ear was always cocked for anything strange, anyone I didn't recognize; once they spoke to me, I assured her, I'd check myself into a hospital, or I'd run away, or I'd blow my brains out. I promised her that much.

I had to tell someone. Why not Katie? She was too young to understand or to remember. She was goodness itself. Untouched. She was helping me.

You don't have to worry, I whispered to her, just in case. I'd never hurt you or mommy or anybody. Please never worry about anything.

I'm so sorry, I said to her. I wanted to watch you grow up. I wanted to be the best big brother ever.

Check yourself into the hospital right now today this minute, Journal Leo wrote to me, the words underlined in thick marker. If you wait too long, it'll be too late. The cells are dividing faster and faster, amassing themselves like armies at the gate of a castle, and soon the doctors will have to dope you up on horse-grade pills and shock you so bad it burns the light out of you and leaves you some vegetable version of yourself babbling, *yes please sir thank you sir yes please thank you sir.* Do you want to be no good to no one? Journal Leo's letters were furious like that, calling me a crazy fuck, a total goddamn psycho. Stop smoking so much weed, he said, it makes you even crazier, more paranoid. Find a real person to tell, not some innocent sleeping child who can't help you. Are you listening? You are torturing that poor kid and you don't even realize it.

But who could I tell? Not my teachers (they were already afraid of me), not the school nurse (she was like ninety), not Mr. Penza (he'd just tell me to eat more), not Sam Kowalski (he'd just tell me to pray more, plus he was probably having an affair with Patricia), not Patricia (obviously). I trusted none of those people. This was a warning sign, too, wasn't it? The fear—the *certainty*—that the people in my own house who loved me, and the well-meaning men and women around me, everyone but Katie, not only couldn't help me but would themselves be the ones gleefully flipping the switch that sent the shocks to burn the Leo Light out of me.

Guys on Reddit had smart things to say about it. I trusted them. At first, I—or "Metallick651"—just did a lot of lurking. Then, one really rough afternoon, one of those afternoons when I felt the dust motes floating around in the sunlight choking me, and I stuffed a rag in my mouth to keep from breathing them, I broke down and went on the subreddit TooAfraidToAsk, and confessed everything: the hooded man, the rag in my mouth, how scared I got of colors and letters and numbers and voices, of just turning a doorknob. Patricia. Katie. My dad. I was like, *here's my guts, good people of Reddit.* I cried all the time, I wrote, my fingers shaking over the keys. I titled the post, "Am I Schizophrenic?"

I sat there and waited for a response. Minutes. Hours. Nothing. Then, finally, this dude KillerDolphin upvoted and made a comment. I recognized him from a Brujeria subreddit. We liked a lot of the same bands, and his life looked exactly like mine—deadbeat father, strung-out mother, shitty house, a kid sister an angel on the earth—only he was older, twenty-six, and lived in Phoenix, or so he said. Until we IM'd in real time about music, I thought I'd blacked out and posted as him and was upvoting my own posts. Turns out KillerDolphin was a bona fide schizo and I didn't even know it. He took aripiprazole and a bunch of other pills every single day, he said, pills that gave him man-tits and screwed up his blood sugar.

His comment: *When you're crazy, you don't realize you're crazy.* Something I'd always heard but figured was way too simple to be true.

KillerDolphin had a lot of karma, so comments popped up fast after that.

Smoke Buddy: *They're called panic attacks, bro. BIG FUCKING DEAL. I've had them since I was in diapers.* (Forty upvotes.)

Xcommunicatd: *Call me when you stab your best friend in the forehead with a pencil because you think he's the Demogorgon. Then we'll talk.* (One upvote.)

Brother of Mercy: *A fork, an ice cube, and some klonopin. That's all you need.* 💊💊💊💊 *DM me.* (Comment later deleted.)

Xcommunicatd again: *Man the fuck up.* (Forty-six upvotes.)

Just reading those words, even the mean ones, let the air in. I read them over and over, filling my lungs, and, for a long time, months, into the fall, over Christmas, the Reddit words alone, and my long IM convos with KillerDolphin and Smoke Buddy and even Xcommunicatd, who wasn't as big a dick as I first thought, all of whom told me, someone they'd never met in person, that I was "fine," did more to help me than all the "scientific" articles Journal Leo copied out from WebMD, more, I'm convinced to this day, than my mother or any therapist or any well-meaning Bonnie could have done.

Then came winter, and the numbers in the new year—2014—scared me, all those hours, all those weeks and months that make up a new year scared me. The guys' words wore off, and the hooded man kept finding me, except I no longer thought of him as the hooded man, as some person or entity separate from myself; the hooded man was me, my defective brain, the sickness in my blood, the Leo Ridgeway I was stuck with and would be stuck with forever.

I DM'd Brother of Mercy.

Along the way, Brother of Mercy had taught me a trick with ice and a fork. When I felt an attack coming on, I'd jam the fork into my palm and focus on the points where the tines met the skin. The idea was to divert every ounce of brain energy to those four sources of pain on my palm, to make them four giant whirlpools of pain in my mind, which would leave no energy left to go to my lungs, my heart, my throat that was closing closing closing, my legs where the heat was surging upward, my forehead breaking out in a cold sweat. Without brain energy, the attack had no fuel, he explained.

I could do it with an ice cube, too, he said: hold it to the back of my neck and press on it until it burned, send my energy to the melted water that dripped down my back, make the drips into raging rivers, the burn into the brand of an iron, myself into a steer, until I forgot I was human at all, and once I forgot my humanness I could breathe again.

This worked, too, until it didn't.

Lucky for me, Brother of Mercy had an associate in Minneapolis, Abe, who could hook me up with some Klonopin. I drove to his apartment in Farview Park and handed him one hundred dollars in tens and fives, the first-timer's discount, in exchange for a three-month supply. I couldn't help thinking I was another Leopold Ridgeway Sr., making himself feel better by hiding cash in a plain white envelope. Fuck you, I said to my father, as I popped the first pill into my mouth in Abe's stairwell. *You'll feel it in an hour*, he'd said, but the whole day went by and nothing. Then we got a lull at Penza's and I slipped into the bathroom and took another, and as the night wore on I felt like somebody had covered my entire body in one of those lead vests the dentist throws on you. Next morning in homeroom, I took another. "I'm on Adderall now," I said, popping one at lunch with my Coke, like anybody cared. Three weeks later, I raided Patricia's purse for cash and went back to Abe for another ninety-day supply at double the price.

It's amazing how decent you can make your life when you're on the right drugs. It requires not much effort. A pill when you wake up in the morning, a second when you get home from school, a third and final mid-shift. In the meantime, you sleep pretty good in your own bed, do just enough homework to stay above the F line, show up on time for your job, even get promoted to manager, skim some cash from the register once you figure out how to get away with it, date a girl (Missy), don't freak out when she breaks up with you for no reason, date a different girl (Becca), take her to senior prom, don't freak out when she calls you a burnout druggie and breaks up with you, graduate, help Abe out with some of his deliveries, babysit your sister days and weekends, give her giggle fits by bringing stuffed carrots and hippos to life, build her a castle out of cardboard, make her a swing from a plastic tub and push her and catch her and clap for her when she jumps off and sticks the landing. If I could handle my shit this well, why couldn't Patricia, when she was using? Was she not a grown woman? It made me hate her all the more, how weak she was, how badly she fucked up my childhood by ditching me once she got ditched. My dad must have sensed the low quality of her humanness. I blamed her more than him for the sinkhole she turned our house into, which is how the hooded man snuck in. I couldn't forgive her. I didn't care that she'd gotten herself clean. I knew it wouldn't last. We didn't need her anyway, Katie and me; we'd be better off without her.

Amazing what a good game the drugs talk. They convince you they'll always be enough, like the words and the fork and the ice cube. But the drugs wear off, too, and you need a new trick if you want to keep handling your shit at the same level. I learned the new trick by accident. A single tine of the fork pierced the skin in the middle of my palm and drew a drop of blood. The sting, followed by the instinctive vampiric sucking, and then, sweeter, throughout the day, the shiver of the cut in the tender skin tearing and healing and tearing again, blood on the steering wheel, the cash register, the sharp edge of the album as it spun on the turntable. Accidents, like I said, at first, until I started to crave the shiver and how easily I could achieve it. Why wait for the unintentional brush of the palm against the album edge. Why not just take the fork and dig it deeper into the cut and twist. Why not make a second cut. A third. Three would be enough, right? Three holes in my left palm, three pills a day? It wasn't.

I should have known the pattern by then, that I'd keep needing another new trick, and another, and that I'd be good at it, and that days, weeks, months, a year would evaporate like my breath on the mirror. I looked into it, straight at myself, and slapped hard. Harder. So hard I lost my footing, so hard I had to grab the sink to break my fall. Where did I learn to treat myself like that, by which I mean to reward myself like that, with the tickle that spread from my ears to my throat, with the knock to the teeth? Smacked awake. I miss it even now, the soreness in my cheekbone and jawbone, the tears, the vibration of my skin, like it was rising, soft and hot as bread. One side of my face flushed and bruised and wetly alive. But it never lasted long enough. The ache in the bones dulled so fast. The sizzle across my cheeks faded to a tingle. The tears stopped coming. The body is so desperate to heal, to prove over and over its capacity to heal.

I rooted for my body to disappoint itself. To rupture completely. To give up. Waging such a war on your own body takes every second of your time, day and night. In the mirror of my bedroom, I stood before Leo Ridgeway's pale white face, smooth as a girl's, almost pretty, with that little metal barbell pierced under the dead center of my bottom lip, those slippery eyes, and I punched him hard. Harder. I was aiming to knock him out. Give him some rest. Stop being him. It was worth a try. I punched my temple, hard. Harder. Hard (finally!) enough. Patricia heard the thud and ran downstairs, Katie behind her. I came to and there they were standing over me screaming. My head an inch from the nightstand. Did Katie learn from me, then and there, to fight her body? For a year, now two, I'd been trying so hard to hide my tricks from her. I did them alone in my room, door locked, or in the bathroom, door locked, or in my car, doors locked, late at night, after my shifts, early mornings, in parking lots, in parks. But she was getting so big, so sharp. A real person. Kindergarten already. Her memory would kick in soon. In the meantime, the tricks kept working and kept working, until they didn't. Trapped in the pattern. I needed the next thing. So I went to the woods. I dug up my dad's lunch box.

They were still in there, Patricia's old stash of pills. A rainbow of colors and flavors. I didn't take one right away. I had more sense than that! And then I didn't. And then I disappeared.

I don't believe the guys who say they don't remember the very *very* end, just before they woke up in the water. If you ask me, those guys are ashamed or embarrassed or acting all macho, even here, even now, like it matters. Like we're still in fucking high school. For example, I remember every single second of my last night, January 11, 2016, but when I'm around them, I pretend I don't. I go along that it's some big mystery. That's how you know I'm trustworthy: I'm literally telling you I lie to those guys, even to Matt and Caleb and Steve. I get it, we want to believe we were chosen for some higher purpose, that we're connected, that we're special. But I certainly wasn't, and, from what I've seen and heard so far, I doubt any of them were, either, no matter what they say. They think they're entitled to these long complicated life stories, with the how and the why spelled out for them, but, in the end, even the very *very* end, the story is always way simpler and way shorter than we care to admit. So we don't.

My story: terror relief terror relief. The rest is just details.

Some details you already know, like how New Year's always freaked me out, the numbers strange and scary, and how the time that attached itself to the numbers stretched into a black hole that sucked me deeper and deeper into it. What I haven't told you yet is that Mr. Penza fired me just before Thanksgiving, not for cooking the books—which he never noticed—but for finding me passed out one morning on a stack of flour bags in the storeroom, lights still on from the night before, ovens ablaze. That's when I started spending more time at Abe's, where the money was better anyway, and where I could do my tricks in peace. At home, all people did was hound me. Drown me in Concern. Even Katie, her little scrunched-up confused face. I avoided it. Not that I was allowed to be alone with her. Mother-of-the-Year Patricia Starks herself removed the lock from my bedroom door and ransacked my closets and crates and in behind her came Sam Kowalski to sit me down like the Divine Redeemer himself, promising peace, threatening hellfire if I didn't take a little trip with him to a place of redemption.

No surprise, then, why that night, the 11th, I pried the car keys out of Patricia's bony fist and pushed her out of my way and drove to my usual spot at Light of Christ. I parked under the busted lamppost and sat there for a hundred years bawling my eyes out, the heat blasting, the terror closing me in like the snow on the windshield. I wished the snow would bury me. I was on day three of nothing harder than benzos, just to see if I could go back, not for me, but for Katie, and now I was seeing I could not. Patricia and Sam had cleaned me out when they raided my room, but I still had a few tricks literally up my sleeve, dropped into the small hole I'd cut in the lining of my jacket. I shook one perfect blueberry into the cup holder.

It was then that an amber glow filled the car and someone started banging on my window, yelling "Open up!" I'd never seen a security van in that lot before, which was the main reason, along with the irony of Light of Christ's busted lamp, that I parked there.

I popped the pill into my mouth and rolled the window down to see an elfish man, barely as tall as the car, wearing thick glasses and a red parka emblazoned with the logo of ACT Solutions.

"You okay in there?" he said, and shone a flashlight directly into my eyes and then at the passenger seat and then down at my crotch.

I'm fine, I told him, I just wanted to be alone.

"This is private property, son," he said, like the very idea of it bored him to death. "You're gonna have to be alone somewhere else. I'll follow you out."

"Can you give me just five more minutes?"

"For what?"

I shrugged. I can't explain why, but that moment is when I understood what I'd come there to do, what I was always going to do one of these nights. Why not this one? "I just need five more minutes," I said.

He looked down at my crotch again. "Oh okay, I get it," he said with a grandfatherly smile. "Make it quick. I'm not gonna watch you."

He got back in his little van and, after a moment, true to his word, he drove out of the lot, slowly, and turned onto Elkins Avenue. I shook the rest of the pills out of my jacket, shut off the car, and stepped out into the snow. It was movie snow, fat flakes that hung in the air, no wind, and I felt like I'd pressed Pause on the movie of my life and stepped into it, walking under the buzzing lampposts toward the church. My toes and the tips of my fingers went immediately numb, but my dick was so hard it pushed against the zipper of my jeans. I walked in the tracks of the van. I climbed the steps to the entrance of the church and peered through the glass door into the blackness. A sign taped to the inside read NEW YEAR, SAME GOD! I fingered each blue in my right pocket, counting.

No, not here.

It was so quiet I could hear the river. I walked toward it, under a pavilion of picnic tables and grills, onto a path that led past a jungle gym into the woods. By the time I reached the ridge, the first blue had kicked in, and my eyes had fully adjusted to the shapes of the branches and the gradations of gray in the endless clouds. The sky had entered me, taking up the space left by the hooded man, which was the prime benefit of the trick. I couldn't stop staring at it, the last real sky I ever saw, which is probably why I slipped and landed on my ass and slid down the ridge and planted my feet in the icy water. I lay there shivering, my back on the ground, my boots in the ankle-deep muck, the water up to my shins, the snow burning my cheeks, the sky so close now that when I reached up I parted the clouds and found the moon hiding.

Here. This place that smelled of rotten pine. This place unholy as any.

I sat up, dazed by the blue and by the sudden memory of the time I took Katie tubing down the bunny slope at Hyland Hills, holding her tight around her waist on an inflatable red doughnut. When we veered off course and crashed into a drift and watched the doughnut roll all the way down on its side, she asked, now how will we get home? We'll be all right, I said to her then, and I said it again now, as I took off my watch and buried it in the dirt. I held the nine blues from my pocket in the cup I made of my muddy hands. Then, like I was splashing water on my face or praying or playing peekaboo, I brought my cupped hands to my lips and licked them clean. I held the pills in my mouth for a moment, tasting the metallic sweetness of the earth, and then swallowed them.

I remember standing. I remember unsticking my boots from the muck. The sucking sound it made. I remember stepping up onto a rock, then another, then another, until I reached the middle of the river. The rocks, I remember, were slippery, the water black in all directions except for interruptions of snow. The clouds lighter shades of gray. I reached up and parted them and there was the sun, blushing, unready. No snow, no wind. My heart slow but fearless. The air thin but enough. The trees buried but singing. The river still as a lake. All of it spinning. Which world did this belong to? The old or the new? I couldn't say and still can't. Then I slipped beneath the surface and swam, and my lungs filled and refilled with water, and I could hear the sounds of boys crying, and that's when I knew I'd entered the next part. I wasn't afraid. I was at rest, at play, making eyes with strange fish, testing my arms, calling out, which is when the others noticed me, and the dreams began.

This wasn't the first dream, but it was the first that convinced me.

Katie at the Bowl-a-Rama for Audrey's tenth birthday party. She's been invited not because she and Audrey have become friends since that day on the bus to CloudView Elementary, when they sat beside each other comparing amulets, but because Katie's mother has recently been found dead, and Audrey, neither angel nor monster, has taken pity on her.

Audrey's parents have provided her with a giant heart-shaped cake that the girls are feasting on. Everything in the four reserved lanes is purple: streamers, napkins, plates, cups. Even the heart cake is as purple as Audrey's slinky sequined dress that has no business on a little girl, in my opinion. And there's Katie in lane three sitting on the edge of one of those plastic bucket seats in front of where the balls pop out, head down, back erect, like she could bolt at any moment. She cuts her cake into squares but doesn't eat. The girl next to her (not Audrey, but with Audrey's same giraffe limbs and metal teeth) squeaks at her about her pet ferret that her dumb brother stepped on, asking Katie whether she herself has any pets? Not even a goldfish? A bird? A brother or sister? She's making an *effort*, this giraffe, but Katie won't even lift her head to smile or give her the simple true answer—"my mom bought me a cat once, we called him Smoochie, but he ran away"—and honestly I want to shake Katie for this, for acting exactly like I used to act at every classmate's birthday party Patricia forced on me back when I was her age, which is just sit there like a zombie sheepdog with my hair in front of my eyes, pissed at the world, hoping the kid next to me would just get it over with and do what he was eventually going to do anyway, like call me a weirdo loser freak, like drop a ten-pound ball on my foot, like bash the bars of my rib cage and rip out my heart, like pick up his bazooka and blow me to smithereens.

I'm crouched next to Katie in this dream that's not a dream, willing her to do better than I did. She has this opportunity here, today, at the Bowl-a-Rama, with Audrey's kindness and the giraffe's inquiring mind, with Patricia dead, to chart a different course in her life. But instead she just sits there, smacking the heels of her shoes on the underside of her seat, staring down at the mashed-up heart cake like it's a hymnal she's being forced to follow. I hear myself call her a weirdo, a loser, a freak. She can't hear me, of course, though now I'm sitting beside her in the empty seat the giraffe abandoned. She doesn't need to hear me. She already knows what she is.

Then all of a sudden she stands up and pushes through the circle of girls without a word to any of them and walks toward the bathroom, her hand over her heart. She locks herself in a stall and sits on the toilet seat with all her clothes on. Her cheeks are flushed and her chest is heaving like she's been chased over the rooftops of buildings. She makes suffocating sounds. Then she unbolts the door and flies out of the stall and stares at herself in the mirror, brings her face close to the glass, turns her head one way and then the other as if searching for something, her eyes bugged out in terror, her mouth slung open. She paces back and forth in front of the row of sinks, swallowing hard and pressing two fingers to that gully at the base of her throat, the exact spot where the hooded man likes to press the barrel of his gun, until Audrey bursts in to say *it's your turn, you're holding everybody up, jeez, what's wrong with you.* She can't see the man. Only Katie and I know he's there.

How then could fear not take root in me, trapped and useless, watching the man put his sweaty hand over my sister's mouth, stifling her scream? How, in the endless rush of dreams-that-weren't-dreams that came after, could my fear not grow and consume me as I watched Katie, more silent and alone than even I ever was, still talking to dolls at fourteen? As I watched crazy Aunt Alice push her aside once her younger, even-more-fucked-up girls showed up? As I watched Katie stuff herself into her Sacred Trinity uniform like a virgin nun-in-training, ready to believe all the shit those priests poisoned her brain with day after day?

Worst of all, as I watched her stare at herself in the oval mirror in that moldy sewing room and slap herself across the face?

How does fear for the life of someone you love not, eventually, turn to rage?

Look! It sends the dresser drawer flying open.

Look! I'm not so useless after all.

It's strange. Until Katie put on the MANOWAR shirt, I hadn't seen our resemblance. Her curly brown hair fooled me, her breasts, her chubbiness, the fact that she was just my half sister and technically a girl. But it's like we both met Leo for the first time that day, the other Leo, the Leo who was and wasn't me, who was and wasn't there all along. So we can thank the rage for that, too, and for the days, weeks, months (a year?) afterward, when she ran home from Sacred Trinity straight to the sewing room and shut and locked the door and tore off her frilly blouse and skirt and became him. Became me. Became us.

Steven Francis Donovan
(June 4, 1996–February 17, 2018)

I am one of those boys they keep finding in the river. In my case, it's the mighty Charles, all that dirty water. *Oh, Boston, you're my home* damn right, but the problem is I'm not home. I'm in California on a shelf in my uncle Owen's house, scooped into an urn he haggled down to five bucks at a yard sale but could probably sell for five hundred, stuck next to his wigs and Madonna CDs. Believe me when I say I don't care that I got cremated, or that the cremator FedExed my ashes in a Glad freezer bag, or that Uncle Owen's the faggiest of fags. What bothers me is California. Palm Springs, to be specific, because I never went there and so can't bring the place into my mind. Worse, the way the guys here describe it—a big hot desert with golf courses and brown mountains and pink Cadillacs and rich retired people mingling with old leathery movie stars—doesn't sound like Steven Donovan's kind of town. Scatter me in the Charles with the syringes and oil slicks and clams and duck boats and chunks of gray ice. My home.

I'm hunching the fine print here. The headlines—Palm Springs, Uncle Owen—I got direct from Monica one night at dinner. Arthur was sitting at the head of the table, as usual, Monica on his left, Shane across from his mother. I sat far away at the other head watching them eat. The Binswangers have these crazy high-backed chairs with gold studs and purple padding so thick it pitches you forward into your soup. "Oh, so they found his next of kin," Monica said, super casual, like it was gossip from her yoga class. "His mother's brother. In Palm Springs." She spooned her minestrone away from her in the bowl from the closer end to the far end, like high-class people do, and brought it to her mouth.

"Is that right," said Arthur.

"I called that 'mentor' of his," Monica explained. "John Forsythe. I'd been feeling so . . . unsettled, since no family came forward to claim him. It was just—"

"But you feel better now?"

"I do," she said. "Like a loop's been closed."

"Good."

"I'd been having those nightmares," she added.

What I don't understand is why I wasn't boxed up the normal way and put in Mount Benedict's next to Gran and Pops and the other Donovans. Mr. Forsythe would have paid for it. I could draw you a map of every little road winding through that cemetery, every elm tree and white stone cross and zinker and statue of Mary, but give me a million dollars and I couldn't name a single street in Palm Springs, or tell you what the air smells like, or the food it's famous for, or what I'd see if I could look out Uncle Owen's window.

This is unsettled, Monica. You're just lost.

I may not have known where I was going in life, but I always knew where I was.

Like right now I'm waiting for her to say my name. It's been so long since that Binswanger family dinner when her loop got closed—five years? Ten? More? How can I tell? More white streaks in her hair, that adorable little belly, and she hasn't said it—*Steven, Steve, Stevie*—not even in her sleep. But she will. She knows, somehow she must know, how hungry I am, hungry as ever, to be on her lips.

"Steven's missing persons report," she'd said once, to a woman across from her in a swanky bar. "Arthur and I were the ones to file it."

"And then they found Steven's body by the Salt and Pepper Bridge," she'd said another time, to a different woman, in the same bar. "He washed up a day later. What's the real name of that bridge anyway? That's right, the Longfellow. Stop, that's not funny."

Two cops showed up at her door, she went on. They took off their hats to break the news to her, thinking she was closer to Steve Donovan—Steven—than she was. It was so awkward, so sad, they had no one else to call, Steven had no real family, just his coworkers, his boss, that mentor, roommates too stoned to notice if he came or went. No, I can't believe it myself, she'd said, how I got myself mixed up in a situation like that.

Another time, at a different swanky bar, darker, wood-paneled walls, red wallpaper, she happened to mention her donation to the Steven F. Donovan College Fund. The least she and Arthur could do, she said, considering, was write a check. What a shame it all was, and such a shock for Shane, but she thought—she hoped!—he would eventually forget Steven, or that, if he did remember him, it would be like the memory of a happy dream, not one of those gut losses that followed him for the rest of his life, that haunted him, that did damage.

"Before what age can you get away with that, do you think?" she'd asked a different woman, a blonde in yoga pants, in a coffee shop. "Like, when does your actual memory start? Do we know? I don't mean what your parents tell you that you said or did, those scenes you cast yourself in at parties when you're narrating the story of your life. I mean the things you're a hundred percent sure actually happened to you, that you play on a loop in your mind. Is six already too old?"

The blond woman—where did these friends come from, by the way? She never seemed to have any when I knew her; in the story of her life she played for me, she'd cast herself as "Poor Little Rich Girl"—scrunched her eyes and nodded in a way that wasn't a yes or a no. She tore her croissant in half and handed a piece to Monica and licked the chocolate from her fingers. Monica left it on her plate uneaten. Then Shane was seven. Shane was nine. Shane was twelve (I counted the candles), and along the way Monica had stopped asking such questions, stopped asking about Steven at all.

Of course I'd already answered the question that day she threw herself at me at the South Street Diner. Either she didn't believe me when I said I remembered every day of my childhood, or she needed an educated rich lady like herself to tell her that was impossible, that I was a bullshitter, and, oh, sweetie, don't you worry for one second, your precious Shane will have no scars and no damage and no ghosts will visit him over his long happy life.

To none of those ladies—to nobody ever—not to Shane as he slept—not to the couples counselor she dragged Arthur to—not to her mother on the phone from Italy—not to herself in the mirror—did I ever hear Monica ever say the words *I miss Steven.* I can't forgive her for that.

To be honest, I can't forgive her for any of the shit she pulled, but still I'm stuck with her like I'm stuck in Palm Springs. My punishment for being a first-class asshole most of my life, I guess. For loving the wrong people. Trusting them. Believing them when they made promises. Her. Gran and Pops. Mr. Forsythe. For not knowing how good I had it the whole time, even when, by anybody's standard, I had it pretty shitty. For how fucking nuts I got over another man's wife, another kid's mom. Punishment is the only possible explanation for my current unsettled situation. What gets me, though, is that every guy here, maybe every guy ever, dead or alive, is just varying degrees of asshole. For example, if I had to rank my four best friends, I'd say Caleb's the next biggest asshole after me, then Leo, then, way far down the list, Matt. My point is: they all *still make the list.* Not one of them's a shining example of humanity no matter what story they sell you. What really gets me, though, what makes me rage, is that the people those guys loved, the people they get to see grow up and grow old and bring flowers to their graves and kiss their pictures and write poems and letters to the editor about them, every single one of their people, at some point when they were alive, loved them back. Monica never did. She even sucked at pretending to. Why.

I'd never have met Monica if it weren't for Mr. Forsythe, so I guess I should blame him as much as her. Mr. Forsythe ran the youth center in Dorchester where Gran and Pops sent me for swim lessons when I was really little, then kept sending me because they couldn't afford anyone else to watch me after school. Mr. Forsythe founded the youth center, actually, with his own money from his business as a big-time lawyer. He was a tall, bald, clean-shaven Black guy who always wore a suit and tie with squeaky-clean new sneakers, like a retired basketball player doing commentary on ESPN. Everybody at Open Dor, which was the (kinda dumb, tbh) name he gave his youth center, bowed down to Mr. Forsythe, and not only because of his height and millionaire status and the fact that he still lived in the same house on the same rough street in Dorchester he grew up on. The man just gave off a quality of Extreme Goodness, the kind of Goodness that people immediately assume a man in a priest outfit will have until he gets you alone. With Mr. Forsythe, the Goodness was authentic and didn't wear off. And when you were in his presence, and he sent his words and attention in your direction, you could physically feel that Goodness land on you and stick to you.

The first time I remember it was the day Mr. Forsythe came to watch me dive. I'd gotten a reputation at Open Dor for progressing from Tadpole to Guppy to Dolphin to Shark in record time, and Lula, the swim teacher, had even let me skip a fish step or two so I could get up to the diving board faster. I'd never been in an airplane, so diving was the closest I got to flying. I'd stand on the bouncy board with my heels on the edge and look down at the kids who started with me in Tadpole still clinging to their paddleboards to stay afloat, kicking away with their little legs, and I'd make my body into an arrow, aim it right for them, and then burst out of the water at the other end of the pool before they could blink.

One day, I was up there on the board taking a second to gather myself when, out of nowhere, I felt a sudden lightness in my chest and legs, like I weighed no more than a feather. I looked over at the bleachers and there was Mr. Forsythe, arms folded over his suit, big smile on his face, beaming his Goodness at me. It charged me. I pushed off and did a perfect tuck, but then I over-rotated and landed with a huge splat. When I climbed out of the pool all embarrassed, he raised two fists and shouted, "You'll get 'em next time, Steven Donovan!" so loud it ricocheted off the walls. I was shocked he knew my name. I was nine, maybe ten? He came back to watch me the next day, and the day after that, and each time I felt that lightness again, that charge, and it made me better. I had major skills compared to the other Sharks and Dolphins, but not even Mr. Forsythe, who believed in kids nobody else believed in, saw Olympic gold in my future. For some reason, though, I stuck in his mind, and from that day forward his Goodness followed me, sticking to the back of my neck as I walked the halls. He looked out for me and called me Stevie Spitz (after some famous swimmer) and hugged me when Gran died and then when Pops died and got me a job helping Lula teach the Tadpoles and the Guppies. Those little shits drove me nuts with their whining and their goofassery, but somehow, with me holding their chubby bodies up, they found their strides, they *progressed*, and I had all this patience with them that I had with nobody else on earth over the age of six.

It bugs me that when you're good with kids like I am, people tell you it's because you're a big kid yourself. Gran and Pops described me like that to people; Lula did, too; and the parents who came to pick up their kids from the Club and Open Dor; and, of course, Monica said it to me all the time, including in the midst of fucking, even after I told her it wasn't just creepy to call me a big kid, it was false. Well, half-false. I wasn't a big kid; I was a grumpy old man who displayed childish behavior. You know how old guys get so tired and fed up they quit caring what anybody thinks? That was me from the day I was born, solidly aware that life's a joke, that most people are chumps and doormats, and that fuck-you money is required if you don't want to end up one of those hundred-year-olds on their deathbeds telling the *Today Show*, "Life goes by in the blink of an eye! Stop working so hard! See the Pyramids! Don't postpone joy!" Little kids have this attitude twenty-four seven, all take take take, now now now, gimme gimme gimme, except kids don't smell bad and won't stab you in the back, and also they're hilarious. Kids make fun of your pimples to your face; they clue you in when they love you and when they hate you; they hug your legs real hard when they're happy and also when they're sad; and then they go away or grow up and don't bother you.

When I'd make up dumb games to play with the kids at the Dor or the Club, or teach them to swim or play tennis or do math, I forgot for a second that on the inside I was an old man who didn't care if they sank or stunk or flunked out of school. I forgot I was a bad person who'd one day make that fuck-you money in the crypto economy or from Mr. Forsythe's will or by opening the first all-ages casino; however it happened, once it did I'd ditch everybody so I could spend my millions on my own pleasure.

Then Monica came along and just kind of helped herself to me, picked me out and popped me in her mouth like candy from a trick-or-treat bag. At first—I admit it—I thought, here's my ticket, this chick with fuck-you money for the taking. Right away I clocked her as one of those starving sad weak women who'd melt under a little male heat. When she showed up a second time at the Club with that trumped-up babysitting job, I figured it was her lame way of getting a closer look at me over lunch and then, if we vibed, she'd slip me a key to a fancy hotel room. Instead, she acted all proper and business-like, taking notes and asking me legit interview questions—where do you see yourself in five years? What are your dreams?—and then made me sweat it out while her husband's secretary checked my references (Mr. Forsythe, of course, and Miss Abrams, the one guidance counselor with a functioning heart). When Monica called my cell phone a week later with the official offer, she put on this crisp voice like the receptionist at a fancy restaurant confirming a reservation. Her patience surprised me, and how formal and in charge of the long game she believed herself to be.

Normally I can't keep my mouth shut about anything, but the day I met Monica, my Spidey-sense told me I couldn't brag about her wanting me to Archie, my best friend, or the guys who lived with me. Couldn't even whisper it into some little kid's ear just to confess to someone who wouldn't understand it. Definitely couldn't tell a priest, not that I ever went to church after Gran and Pops died. The whole deal with Monica was dangerous, for her and for me, but the main reason I couldn't talk about it was because I didn't want to wreck it. The money was too good. And there was a kid involved, one I fell for just as hard as I fell for Monica, except in a different way, obviously.

I'd run into Mr. Forsythe at Open Dor reeking of her, my lips chewed-up and neck skin all blotchy, and he'd look at me like *all right, spill it, Spitz*, but I never spilled it. I just shrugged and grinned and chalked it up to my studly ways. He'd slap me on the back and say something basic like, "be careful," which meant don't get anyone pregnant or catch gonorrhea or let the multiple girls I must be juggling find out about each other. He had a Spidey-sense, too—it kicked in whenever I had sins to get off my chest—but somehow he didn't connect the bruises on my arm to my new gold chain and the smirk-I-couldn't-wipe-away-as-hard-as-I-tried to my new job at the Binswanger mansion. For whatever reason, he'd made it his personal project to make sure I not just survive my teens but come out of them a decent full-grown man, and he had pride in that accomplishment, and that pride totally screwed up his Spidey-sense and blinded him to my true nature.

It was Mr. Forsythe who'd insisted I apply for the counselor job at the Boys & Girls Club, where nobody knew me and nobody would be tempted to coddle me. When Gran died, Mr. Forsythe was the first person to show up at our door. Then when Pops got sick, Mr. Forsythe explained dialysis to me, and living wills, and probate. He cosigned insurance documents. He ran interference with DHS and hooked me up with a free lawyer and tax lady. He came up with the idea for me to rent out the bedrooms in Gran and Pops's house that became my house. I was the only twenty-year-old I knew with a deed and a safety deposit box and a book of long business checks I used to pay roofers and pest control. Mr. Forsythe "staunchly disapproved" of some of the guys I rented my rooms to, and that I charged other guys to sleep on the couch and in the basement and even the garage sometimes, and that I let these guys pay me—or promise to, at least—in cash or other trade-offs, but he didn't interfere with any of that. He picked his battles. Some lessons he wanted me to learn on my own.

What he did very much approve of was my job with the Binswangers. To have secured it without even applying for it meant I'd distinguished myself among "quality people" who might one day connect me to a bigger, more adult job or, if I opened my mind a little, pave my way to college. He put a ton of faith in the Binswangers without ever having met them. In fact, he was jealous that Miss Gutierrez and the Boys & Girls Club got their "greedy little hands" on Monica before he'd had a chance to sniff her and Arthur out for a big donation to Open Dor. He asked me to introduce him to her sometime, maybe bring her around the center, maybe mention how much Open Dor meant to me personally and to the entire Dorchester community. He was hoping to score a dinner invitation to her house so he could convince her that the "level of support" she and her husband could offer would be "transformational." He'd get all jazzed up about this and use all these business terms and I'd nod, feeling tall and adult and important, like now it was me in the bleachers watching him on the diving board.

The longer my thing with Monica went on, though, the stronger my own Spidey-sense got about keeping her and Mr. Forsythe apart. I was afraid she'd poison his Goodness, I think, or that, in the bright light of it, I'd see her for the person she really was. A bad person. A bad person like me. Another user. I wanted to ask Mr. Forsythe if a man could hate a woman and still love her, or love a woman and still hate her, and I wanted him to reply *yes, Steven, that's how you know the love is real*, because that's the answer I'd already settled on. I wanted to tell him that even fuck-you money like Arthur Binswanger's couldn't buy this real love Monica and I had. I wanted to show him the rings in the little velvet box I kept with me at all times in my backpack, to get his blessing the way they do in real families and on TV, but I must have known he'd refuse to give it. This is why I avoided him when things got super complicated those last few months, didn't return his calls and texts, stayed tight-lipped with Archie and the guys at home, and put all my energies into her and Shane and the future we were building together.

My first day at the Binswangers', I wore brand-new Chuck Taylors, a white dress shirt, and my one pair of jeans without fashion holes, but I still felt like a handyman, which I guess I was? Erma answered the door in a man's white shirt of her own and led me through a courtyard as big as a parking lot with an actual fountain in the middle. The house—Erma called it "the Hacienda"—had a bunch of add-ons and different levels and "breezeways" filled with sculptures and human-sized potted plants and rocking chairs that faced out onto patios crowded with more rocking chairs. It had those wavy clay tiles on the roofs and rough outside walls that scraped off a layer of skin if you sideswiped them. At the bottom of a big hill that dropped down from the back deck was a pool with a slide and a diving board and a mini-house in the same style surrounded by trees and flowers, which looked like a hotel you could sleep over at if you were too tired to trek back up the hill. All of it made me kinda sick, to be honest. Not disgusted sick—Mr. Forsythe bought the house next door to him just to knock it down and put in a tennis court with a ten-foot fence around it—I mean sick like I'd just looked up after stealing a soda and noticed a security camera.

It was chilly, the middle of September, back-to-school weather, but there was Monica—I still called her Mrs. Binswanger then—horsing around with Shane in the shallow end of the pool like it was eighty degrees out. When Erma opened the gate, Monica pulled him close to her and put her arms around his neck as if I'd come to take him away.

"Did I get the date wrong?" I asked her.

"No, no," she said, and kissed the top of his head about ten times. "Mother's instinct."

She had on a black bathing suit and sunglasses and one of those tight turbans women wore in old movies. I think now that she opted for the turban just so she could slowly pull it off as she climbed the steps up and out of the pool, shaking her dark hair loose and letting it fall onto her shoulders. I'd seen this porno before and: five stars. Erma passed her a towel and she dried herself off and then held my hand and told me how lucky she and Arthur were to have me and how excited Shane was for these afternoons with his new best friend.

I crouched at the edge of the pool to make eye contact with the boy. He showed no sign that he recognized me or expected me or cared that I'd shown up. We'd had plenty of autistic kids come through the Club and Open Dor—people even used to tell me I probably had a touch of it myself, like it was the flu or Indian blood, and also like it was something I could get fixed if I wanted—but in all the years I'd spent around kids, I'd never met one with such a Grand Canyon of Nothingness behind his expression. It didn't freak me out, though. The opposite. It made me even more determined than I already was to break through. To fill that Grand Canyon with something. Whether I'd be doing that for Shane, or to prove a point to Monica, or to Mr. Forsythe, or to myself, I didn't know. (Update: all of the above.)

"You won't need a suit," Monica said, as she settled herself on a lounge chair next to a small table stacked with magazines.

I must have blushed, which I hate, because she quickly explained that what she meant was that they had a bunch of extra bathing suits in the "cabana" because their guests kept leaving them behind, and that these suits were washed and came in all shapes and sizes. She apologized for forgetting to mention that Shane was "part fish," and that I'd be spending the bulk of my hours with him in the water, where he was happiest. They kept the pool heated into the middle of winter, she said, when only a crazy person would still be out here, but that's what you do for your *angelo* of a child. If Shane kept it up, they'd put a roof over this pool or just build another one indoors. "It's not like we don't have the room," she said, sweeping her arm out toward the lawn. I told her they were in luck because I was part fish, too: part Dolphin, part Shark. I'd fit right in.

Shane was drawing pictures on the surface of the water with his index finger. He stared at the pictures for a few seconds, no expression on his face, then erased them with the palm of his hand and started over. I thought, this is your kid at his happiest?

I changed into a pair of board shorts and folded my jeans and shirt and laid them out nice and neat on the giant bed that took up most of the cabana. I balled up my socks and underwear and tucked them into my shoes and set them on the floor facing out from the right side of the bed. I smell-checked my pits and feet and did a few push-ups and admired my naked chest in the mirror. Already I felt like the cabana and the pool and everything that came with it, Monica and Shane included, belonged to me, and that I'd earned them from all those years working with Lula and the kids at the Club. I remembered Mr. Forsythe saying that sometimes life hands you a trophy for a race you didn't even realize you were running. The important thing, he said, was to accept the trophy like you'd been training for it and expecting it all along, to never ever admit that it wasn't already part of your plan. People said Mr. Forsythe made his fortune with one lucky break after another, that he was charmed, but it wasn't just charm; he'd been smart enough to recognize his first big break as the trophy it was and then figure out ways to make more trophies for himself.

For a kid who loved the water so much, Shane seemed uninterested in swimming. Mainly he liked to stand or sit in the shallow end and draw his invisible pictures while I asked him questions about them that he wouldn't or couldn't answer. Occasionally Monica peered over the top of her magazine to praise one of the pictures and then beg Shane to teach me a different game, like maybe something athletic that involved the equipment in the giant mesh bin at the side of the cabana? So for a while we tossed around a neon-green foam football in a way that felt like a punishment. The only times Shane smiled were when I fake-missed catching the ball and fell onto my back, making bigger and bigger splashes. The closer the splash got to Monica's legs the better—her pink toenails, the thin gold chain around her ankle—until finally I managed to soak her all the way up to her thigh, and Shane's eyes went happy and wide. Still, that game got old fast, and wasn't exactly the best use of my advanced youth counselor skills, but before I could come up with some better way to spend our time, it was five o'clock, and Erma was calling them up the mountain to dinner.

Just like Shane wasn't like other boys, Monica and Arthur weren't like other mothers and fathers, or so she explained to me from her lounge chair over those first few weeks. Their own parents—hers in Italy, his in Germany—had completely ignored them, and look what well-adjusted and successful adults they'd grown up to be! Meanwhile, the American parents in their friend group were as pale, underfed, overmedicated, depressed, and anxious as their kids. Pyromaniacs. Cutters. Hair-pullers. The Binswangers, she said proudly, were none of these. Arthur had his work and his golf, Monica had her charities and a budding interior design business, and Shane had his entire universe all to himself. Who were they to say he wasn't the happiest of them all? Just because he didn't talk didn't mean he was miserable. Look how sweet and calm he was with everyone he met! They were confident he'd break out of this quiet phase eventually, and the less they interfered with his process, the better. Yes, they'd brought him in for all his shots and let the doctors scan his brain to make sure he didn't have a tumor or whatever, and, after a big fight with their pediatrician, they'd agreed to take him once a month to the "specialist" for his "autism," words she couldn't say without making quotation marks with her fingers, but they trusted Shane much more than they trusted these people. More specifically, they trusted the strong Alberti and Binswanger genes. Both sets of Shane's grandparents weren't just "thriving" over in Europe, they were so busy with their own well-adjusted, successful lives—companies, cruises, political campaigns—that they hadn't seen Shane in person since the year he was born.

She asked me a million questions about my own family, which, in case it's not obvious, was nothing like hers.

As far as I was concerned, I told her, Gran and Pops were my parents, since my "real" ones—I made the quotation marks to show her I knew how—were out of the picture. She wanted details, sad ones, and the sadder and more violent I made them, the more satisfied and turned on I could see her getting. Her respect for me grew, too, this orphan she'd rescued with his low-class accent and the scar on his jaw and his savage red chest hair and his hard, hard luck. I wanted to tell her that she and Arthur were the ones who sounded like orphans to me, because even though Gran and Pops were broke from the shit my dad put them through and worked a bunch of jobs and were never home and could barely breathe or walk by the end, they made it their *business* to "interfere with my process," which meant riding my ass night and day, and even though I went to bed hungry sometimes and did stupid shit with my buddies, I never for a single second felt alone or scared until both Gran and Pops were actually gone. It broke my heart that this little kid, Shane, who had the full six-pack of parents and grandparents still alive, needed some random dude like me to keep him company.

"We could use some guy time," I'd say to Monica, my signal that we adults had been jabbering on for too long, that Shane was bored, that guy time was what she hired me for. She'd slip on her sandals and cover herself and journey back up to the house and then, ten minutes later, carrying something we didn't ask for—a plate of sandwiches, a bocce set—she'd come back.

"Is guy time over yet?" she'd say.

Some days yes, some days no. It depended on my mood. I liked telling her no and sending her away, putting her in time-out, making her jealous, pissing her off. Just as much, I liked telling her yes and having her there on her back on the lounger, knees up, legs spread, my eyes on those little shaving bumps along her thighs, her eyes on that itch just above my crack when I scratched it.

The cool thing was that the longer I spent with Shane, the better I could see the pictures he drew in the water. I just had to focus and put myself in his head as he moved his fingers, then ask, that was a dragon, wasn't it?

Yes, he'd blink.

For no, he'd lower his head.

Me: "A castle? A sailboat?"

Him: Blink, blink.

Mashing his thumbs together meant he was frustrated. The grunt from his gut meant "absolutely not." The grunt from his throat meant "maybe." Balling and unballing his fists really fast, blinking like crazy, meant "yes let's fuckin' GO!" For an original language, it wasn't all that hard to learn. A smile was a smile. Uncomplicated. When I got an actual laugh out of the kid, even a weak one from between his teeth, I felt like I'd won a prize.

Splashing his mother to get that laugh—anywhere but her face—became the ritual we began our afternoons with, like saying grace. For the hours I let her stick around the pool with us, I put her to work playing different parts: Silly Mom, Blind Mom, Mom Caught in Bear Trap, and, our favorite, Momzilla, the Hideous Monster who creeped around on centipede legs and spit worms when she talked. We knelt in front of Momzilla and begged Her for mercy, holding out in our cupped hands the peace offerings we'd scavenged from around the Binswanger Kingdom: a smooth rock from the courtyard fountain, one of Stefano's metal spatulas, a self-help CD called *Ego Is the Enemy.* She's a good sport, I thought, until I realized, with a kind of thrill, that we couldn't humiliate her enough, that she got off on being the butt of the joke. Like this one day, when she was safely up the hill and out of sight, I raided the cabana drawers, tucked my junk between my legs *Silence of the*

Lambs–style, changed into one of her one-piece black bathing suits, fitted her turban on my head, and came busting out of the door of the cabana shimmying and shaking my ass and tits for Shane the way she was always doing around me. You could have heard his snorts and belly laughs a hundred miles away. In a movie, he'd have spoken his first words to me right then and there: *Oh my God* maybe, or *Stop, that's mean!* I'd have settled for any words at all, some proof I was having an effect on his life.

Monica called later that night to say we needed to talk, and could I show up a few minutes early next Thursday?

"Sure," I said. "Everything cool?"

"It will be," she said.

That Thursday, Erma showed me to Monica's study, which was a mess of boxes and paint chips and different-colored fabrics rolled up and picture frames still wrapped in brown paper. There was nowhere to sit except behind her desk, so I just stood there with my hands behind my back as she closed the door behind her.

She turned to me and folded her arms and put on this super-serious face. "I happened to catch your little performance the other day," she said, in the superior tone of every teacher who ever taught me. "I'm sure you found it funny, but to me it was extremely inappropriate. And embarrassing. If Arthur knew this was what we were—"

"Wait, how'd you even see? Do you have cameras on us?"

"That's not the point."

Of course, I thought, even from time-out she'd been watching us, either from the windows or some closed-circuit command center run by Erma.

"I'm so sorry," I said. "I really am. I didn't mean anything against you. I just wanted us to bond. The more I act like a doof, the more Shane trusts me. The more he trusts me, the more he learns and grows, and that's what this is all about, right? Please don't fire me now, Mrs. Binswanger. I really feel like I'm making progress."

"I'm not going to fire you, Steven. And please call me Monica. Well—except when Shane's around. And Erma. And Arthur, if you ever get to meet him."

"Okay," I said. "So only when we're alone. I get it. I'll do that, Monica. And thank you for not firing me. Thank you so so much. This job means a lot to me. I cut down my hours at the Club so I could come here. And Shane's such a special kid. And your house is really nice. It's like a museum."

"Well, then, consider this a warning. You get"—she did a quick calculation in her head—"two more, I guess. Two more strikes?"

"Fair," I said. "Can I ask, though? Other than this, I'm doing okay? You're getting your money's worth?"

"Oh," she said, looking around, like she'd left my report card on her desk. "Yes, absolutely. You're great with him. Just like I hoped. We hoped. I see a change. A small one, but a change. Other than this incident, yes, I'd say everybody's happy."

"Cool," I said.

"I'm burning that bathing suit, though," she said. She had her back to me, shuffling some papers, but I could hear the smile in her voice.

"I thought I looked kinda pretty in it," I said.

"Stick to trunks," she said. And then, without turning around, "You fill them out better."

On rainy days, or when it got too cold for the pool even for Shane, I'd meet them in what they called the great room. They'd be sitting next to each other on the couch in front of a talk show or the home improvement channel when I got there, and then she'd check her watch, breathe a stressed-out sigh of relief, take out her laptop, and begin the backbreaking work of "sourcing" pillows and vases and wallpaper for other women's houses. She fell into these jobs by accident, she said. After guests found out she decorated the Hacienda on her own, they begged her to rescue their country house, their beach house, their "place in the city." She talked to me about these guests and their houses the same way she talked about Miss Gutierrez and the Boys & Girls Club and the Greater Boston Food Bank—like charities that couldn't exist without her. Meanwhile, I taught Shane to juggle, first with balloons, then with plastic balls and soup cans we raided from the kitchen. The autographed soccer ball he got for Christmas, I taught him to bounce on his knees and ankles. I showed him how to make paper planes, which we graffitied with markers and sent flying at his mother's head when she was trying to concentrate.

Eventually, she'd stop pretending to work and get down with us on the floor. She wore that dress on purpose, I'd think, the tight and stretchy one that stopped just above her knee. The longer one with the slit up the side. The blue one with the loose strap that kept slipping off her shoulder. She let the strap hang there a few seconds to catch me looking and then pulled it up. She crossed right in front of me on all fours to retrieve, like a dog, whatever I dropped from juggling. She stopped mid-crawl, fetched the balloon or ball or can of soup, half turned toward me, and, propping herself up with her left arm, pitched it back at me, missing by a mile.

Later, I instructed her to wait for me in that same position on the bed when I walked through the door. I wanted her looking back over her shoulder at me just like that, sticking her ass out and lifting up her tits and licking her lips, making what I called a buffet line. *Get the buffet ready*, I'd text her. No quotation marks. Then a few minutes later I'd find the buffet all laid out for me, start at the end of the line, and eat my way up.

Back then I didn't give a shit about Arthur, mainly because I never saw him. But also because Monica talked about him the way a high school girl talks about her dad, like, yeah, he might catch us sooner or later, but so what? He'd yell a lot, she'd get grounded, but no big deal, the world won't end, worst-case scenario I lose my job. Risks we were both willing to take. The one other married lady I'd messed around with before her wasn't so chill. I'd meet her for a quickie in a hotel or in her office after it closed, she'd block my number, and then a month later she'd pop up on my phone out of nowhere begging for "another go" or "one last roll in the hay." (Her old-timey expressions gave me a chuckle.) I never expected that when Mrs. Binswanger finally got me alone we'd fuck upstairs in her own house in the middle of the day while her kid played in the yard and her chef cooked my dinner.

Monica had dated a couple guys in boarding school, but mostly she'd fooled around with other girls in her dorm, which of course got me hard just hearing her admit to. By the time she was my age, she was already engaged to Arthur; since they'd been married, though, she said, all shy: nobody. Not even a cater-waiter or a personal trainer or an idiot kid from an app she could block before he put his boxers back on. In other words, for a forty-year-old from a foreign country who was also seriously hot, she didn't have much experience. She let me try all sorts of stuff on her, and I sat back and let her use my body for whatever she could get from it, so in a way we did do some tutoring, just not in Italian. What I taught her I can sum up in three words: do it faster. What she taught me I can sum up in two words: slow down. Everything we did with our naked and sweaty body parts she turned into games with complicated rules and penalties, maybe because she was stuck at girl-age on the inside? Under the Mrs. Binswanger mask and the Shane's Mom mask and the Lady of the Hacienda mask was the nineteen-year-old Monica Alberti who sharpied lightning bolts around my nipples and turned me over on her lap for spankings and cracked up when I farted. My silly goose. Her little rascal.

I was a different person, too, under my Youth Counselor mask. Not such a Big Kid. Not such an old man. A grown-up. I wouldn't admit this to Archie or to any of the guys here, but my favorite times with Monica were those few minutes between the end of her games and five o'clock, when we lay down next to each other naked on those crazy-soft sheets, pillows behind our heads, talking about grown-up things: Selwyn Academy versus Mercer for Shane; if I should rent one of my rooms to this pregnant girl, Melissa Montague; how she'd never had the fried clams at Castle Island; how I always brushed my teeth with hot water; if the DeMarcos' country house bedroom looked better with drapes or plantation shutters ("those are plantation shutters," Monica said, pointing to the window); whether I needed glasses, a new car, a raise, a haircut, a college degree. Discussing this stuff in her cloud bed, all wet and stained and sour-smelling, door locked and shutters cracked open, her always-cold foot on my always-warm foot, turned it from boring to fun. Stuff like the traffic to Watch Hill on the summer Fridays she skipped town and left me so lonely, even though I never had Shane on the weekends. The screaming match she had with Mr. Simms, her neighbor, about his tree that hung over the giant wooden wall that separated their properties, a tree that dropped apples onto her lawn, apples that attracted wild turkeys, which totally freaked her out. Blue Sunshine, this Boston band I introduced her to, whose bassist was the guy who got Melissa Montague pregnant. I'd put my phone on my chest and close my eyes and serenade her with Blue Sunshine songs and she'd run her fingers up and down my ribs like she was strumming a guitar, and by the time I bought her the ring we not only had a favorite song, "Right as Rain," she could sing all the words along with me.

I had the ring in my backpack the day everything changed. Not because I was ready to give it to her, but because I carried it with me everywhere. A trophy. A reminder to keep my cool. A warning not to fuck up. A magic trick for when the perfect moment came to seal the deal. It was around Halloween, that afternoon. I remember because there were fake cobwebs on the stairs. We'd just finished a game where I closed my eyes and guessed what object she stroked my dick with. Give you one guess what the final object was. Anyway, she was lying on her stomach bare-assed, half on half off me in our cloud, complaining about the construction on Route 9, how it made her late for every appointment, and I was just about to blow her mind with a shortcut I'd lucked into off Dudley Road, really exciting stuff, when out of nowhere she said something like wasn't it nice we didn't have to worry about Arthur anymore.

"Wait, what?"

She raised her eyebrows in this fake-evil way, like, *let's not pretend we didn't bury him in the basement.*

"We're free," she said. "Isn't that wonderful?"

I sat straight up. It's weird, but my first feeling was fear. Like all of a sudden I was in charge, not just of her, but of Shane, of this whole entire house. I say weird because this was exactly the future I'd been dreaming about.

The fear didn't last long. It never did with me. As soon as I tasted fear of any kind, I spit it out. "I don't understand," I said. "What happened to him?" Already I was settling into the future of her and me forever, not in this house probably, definitely not in mine, but maybe in one like Mr. Forsythe's, big but in a real neighborhood, with neighbors you could see over the fences and kids in the street for Shane to play with.

"Nothing *happened*," she explained. "We just—had a talk. A big talk. A talk that's been a long time coming. You gave me the courage to initiate that talk, Steven. I bless you for it." She had her elbows on the bed, her chin propped on her palm, hair spilling onto her shoulders, like a mermaid, blinking at me. Then she looked away. "I never lied to you about my marriage, Steven, not really, but I did leave out some information."

She'd practiced that line, and the look away, too. I could tell. Usually it turned me on when she did that. It meant I'd been on her mind ahead of our scheduled meetup. But it didn't turn me on this time. "What kind of 'information'?"

"Don't be mad," she said. "I was ashamed. And no man wants to know the whole story of a woman. We pick and choose what we say to keep us interesting. Otherwise . . ."

"I *do* want to know! I always did!"

"You're not normal," she said in a teasing way. She patted my thigh. "I'm still not used to how not-normal you are." She meant it as a compliment.

"Will you just tell me what's going on?" I said. She sat up on her knees and grabbed my T-shirt from off the floor. As she pulled it on, stretching her arms through the sleeves, fluffing her hair in the back, and started to tell me about the talk, and the years before the talk, her and Arthur's whole story, I remember thinking, *you're right, I don't want to know this*, but by then it was too late.

I'd heard the word for guys like Arthur before, but I thought it meant like "wimp" or "pussy" or "loser." I thought it was the word you'd use for a man whose wife was a high-powered CEO but he flipped burgers. I didn't understand it meant a guy who went along with his wife fucking another guy. When Monica told me that, my first thought was that Arthur wanted to join in, or watch us, both of which made me want to barf, actually. So do you have cameras in here, too? I asked, all frantic, checking the four corners of the ceiling. I looked at the bookshelves directly across from the bed in a new way. The Italian textbooks and DVDs we never watched. The TV. I started to get up to look behind them, but she stopped me, her arms around my waist, laughing. No, *caro*, no, she said. There were people like that, she was sure, but the Binswangers weren't them. It was just the part she'd said about Arthur going along with what they did, looking the other way, that applied to them. To us. Didn't I notice how much older Arthur was than her? Did I think she'd married him for his body? And yes, of course she loved him, now more than ever, in fact. Their talk had reminded her why. And he loved her, too. If you love something, you set it free, yes? You don't squeeze it so hard it explodes. Not to mention the man was Shane's father, the owner of this house, her friend and protector. But why were we talking about love at all? she asked. Love did not factor. Remove love from the conversation. Focus on what I'm telling you, Steven, she said: we're free! It's good news! Why aren't you happy?

Like I said, until that moment I hadn't thought much about Arthur. I'd never met him, never heard his voice. If I passed him on a Boston sidewalk, I wouldn't have recognized him. I guess I'd made a mental note of what he looked like from the photographs in picture frames arranged on little tables and fireplace mantels all over the Hacienda: a guy in a tux next to her at some wedding, a guy in a captain's hat behind the wheel of a boat, shirtless and squinting. I hadn't missed the giant portrait of himself he hung on the wall of the dining room, side by side with the portraits of Monica and Shane in their own gold frames. Three faces taking up the whole wall: baby Shane in the middle, Monica on his right, Arthur on his left. Separate but together. From all that, what stuck in my mind: his droopy tired eyes, saggy cheeks, round glasses, normal nose, maybe a thick neck? But not super-old-looking, not even ugly. How sick did he have to be, this man, to let another guy use his wife like that, like one of those skid-marked Speedos left behind in his cabana?

And yet, there was Monica, hyper and giggly about it like we'd won World Series tickets, going over the "only ifs" at 4:51 p.m. If and only if we obeyed them, she said, Arthur would leave us alone. The first few "only ifs" were the ones we were already obeying because they were common sense, not because we'd ever discussed them much:

1. Only if Arthur was at work or out of town.
2. Only if Shane never ever in a million years found out.
3. Only if we still pretended they were Italian lessons (for Erma's sake, though Erma was no idiot).
4. Only if, according to everybody and anybody who asked or even hinted, I was just Shane's tutor—"mentor" was better, or "life skills coach"—who was doing a great job. Look at Shane! Like night and day! A miracle! No, you can't poach him!
5. Only if I never tried to contact Arthur for any reason.

These were the new ones:

1. Only if we never used their bed (I didn't even know where their bedroom was).
2. Only if I never slept over.
3. Only if nobody saw us in public without Shane.
4. Only if we put nothing in writing: no texts, no incriminating notes, nothing Shane or Erma could find in the

trash. This also meant: no pictures, no videos. (In front of her, I'd have to permanently delete the ones I already had. Right now, in fact. So I did.)

5. Only if she gave me no gifts or money other than my regular paycheck.

6. Only if she told Arthur what we did together. Not *everything* we did, though. Just a little sample. She'd pick and choose. Tone it down. So he didn't get wild ideas about us, or too jealous. It was his right to know at least something, was it not? We owed him that, for this gift?

7. Only if—and this was the most important rule, according to Arthur—we didn't fall in love.

Easy, yes? she said. And such a relief! To have all the details spelled out, like a contract. To agree on the terms. Maybe I'm a businesswoman after all, she said. Sign on the dotted line. Haha! She took off my T-shirt, sniffed the pits, and handed it to me.

I was standing by the bed, listening, already in my shorts and shoes. It was 5:23. I was late for the first time ever. Did it matter anymore? Would I ever come back? The room was a million degrees.

"This is crazy" was all I could say.

"Tell me about it," she said, like I meant good crazy. "We're having our cake and eating it, too!" She flopped back down on the bed and pulled the covers up to her neck. "I never understood that expression," she said. "It's so American to have cake and not eat it. What else would you do with it? Throw it in someone's face?"

I don't remember walking down the stairs after that or fist-bumping Shane goodbye or getting into my car. What I remember is how desperate I was to get to the Dor for the pool and the showers with the superstrong water pressure.

The Dor was the only place I could breathe right. I still spent most nights there with my people: the pizza ladies, the security guards, the janitors, the college kids getting credits, and the juvenile delinquents serving hours. I even slept over once in a while, on a bed of vinyl mats I spread out on the floor of Lula's office, just for the peace and quiet of an empty building more like a home than Gran and Pops's place once Gran and Pops died and this guy I barely knew, Rob Wexler, offered me three hundred dollars a month to rent their old bedroom. Mrs. Forsythe was a minister used to taking in her husband's strays, and they had a bunch of extra bedrooms and no kids of their own, but I had too much pride to move in with them. Making myself a stray was way worse than crashing on smelly mats that kids had been sweating and sneezing on all day.

Lost in thought, I blew past my secret shortcut and got stuck in the construction on Route 9, and I was leaning out of my window cursing at the cars in front of me and the men standing around in their orange vests with their stupid shovels when the lady in the car behind me slammed into me and my head snapped back against my seat then forward smack into the steering wheel, and at that moment I went instantly completely apeshit and jumped out and stood in front of her white tank of an SUV to block it with my body yelling *what the fuck is wrong with you* and *you're gonna pay for this, lady*, banging my fists as hard as I could on her shiny perfect hood making a lot of little dents and dripping my nose blood all over it. We screamed at each other through the window she cracked open an inch for her protection—her husband would kill her; I didn't have insurance—and then when people stuck behind us started blowing their horns and getting out of their cars and walking toward us we figured the cops weren't far behind so we quickly called it even—her dents, my nose—and after that we both drove nice and slow and far apart between the cones like it never happened, and we even waved goodbye to each other when she turned off at the Riverway.

Pride. I had "more than my fair share" of it, according to Monica. Pride came up a lot in our cloud talks, those last few months especially, because, once I got my breathing right at the Dor, once I weighed the pros and cons, I went back to her. We'd taken it too far to throw it away. I was just like her brothers in Italy, she told me, me and my ideas that would wow the world once it wised up and put me in charge. Pride would take me far in life, she said, like it did for Marco and Lucio; men like us strutted onto every field believing we'd already won the game. "I'm jealous," she said, taking me into her, "can you give me some of that pride? Can you give me all you've got?"

We tried to be good. We followed every "only if" except one, the most important one. "I love you," I said, my arms wrapped around her, holding her so tight my muscles throbbed, 4:56, 4:57, on our Mondays and Wednesdays that became also Thursdays, and every once in a while, before the five o'clock alarm went off, she managed to say it back.

"I love you," I said, the nights Arthur was in Denver or London on business, 7:56, 7:57, just before Shane's 8 p.m. bedtime, when she left me, walked the three minutes to the other wing, and read him a story. I said the words in my head as I waited for her to come back, but I never wrote them in a card or a text message, only on her back with my finger, across her closed eyes with my thumb.

My neck hurt all the time. She flipped me over and massaged it and told me I really needed to get it x-rayed.

I wasn't allowed to shower before coming to work at her house or change out of my boxers from the ones I'd slept in. She liked the taste of my BO. I kept a stash of body spray and mouthwash in a Walgreens bag under the bed in case the funk was too much, but it never was.

When we pissed, we left the door open so we could watch each other. It drove her wild.

She showed me her favorite film, *I Vitelloni*, by Fellini, but I was "just resting my eyes" through it, I told her. Pops used to give Gran that line when they watched TV next to each other on the couch. Until the words came out of my own mouth, I didn't realize he was lying. I always took his side when they argued about it.

Three a.m. was the latest I ever stayed at Monica's, but neither of us rested our eyes long enough to break rule number seven. The roads were so empty on the way home I slalomed around the orange cones, veering into the opposite lane, the radio on max.

One time I let the truth slip out that I wished Arthur was dead, and it was like I flipped a switch that made Monica's face go dark and her eyes fill with tears. "Grow up, okay?" she said. "Just be normal for once." I might be wrong, but I think this was the same day she told me that, just before we met, she and Arthur had been expecting their second child, a girl, but the girl died inside her a month before she was due.

I googled Arthur's name and zoomed in on his pathetic face. I held my fingers up to his nose so he could smell his wife. It was funny but not good funny. The guy had all the money in the world but zero fucking pride. I couldn't let Monica know my secret dreams of killing him with my bare hands, of finding him dead on the side of Route 9 in a car wreck, of reading his obituary in the *Herald*. How much I hated him. How it disgusted me, what he let happen in his own house.

Nobody bothered us on our Mondays, Wednesdays, and Thursdays, which also included a few Fridays and Tuesdays here and there when our schedules allowed. We laughed our asses off and didn't care who heard. I walked in and out of the guest rooms and up and down the hallways digging my toes in the plush carpets. I smoked joints out of the bathroom window. My paycheck got bigger with all the added days. My future plans got bigger, too. If Erma or Stefano had a question for me or Monica, they'd text and not expect an answer for a while. Shane had himself and his books and DVDs, his own little kingdom. His needs were simple: a bunch of hours in the pool with us both, some guy time, a story from Mama when the sun went down, a fist bump from me on my way out. If I forgot the fist bump, he'd cry until she got me on FaceTime telling him *I'm sorry buddy, don't worry, double-bump tomorrow!*

Not once did Stefano ask me to practice my Italian. No idiot either, that guy, and probably a fag, too, now that I think about it. He listened to opera when he cooked and on nice days with the windows open the music floated up to us with the aroma of garlic and onions.

Arthur Louis Binswanger, founder and CEO of Binswanger, Inc., born March 4, 1952, in Freiburg, Germany, MBA from MIT. In ten years he'd be seventy-six, the average life expectancy of a man in the United Status in 2018. Not once did he come home early, or pass me on Dudley Road (she gave him my shortcut), or show up at the Dor or the Club or my house in Fields Corner. But I saw him everywhere. In a blue suit waving down a taxi, checking his watch in front of Legal Sea Foods. I woke up in whatever room I was sleeping in and Arthur Binswanger was standing over me, licking his lips, stroking his puny dick.

My neck hurt all the time. Even when she flipped me over and massaged it and told me I had the body of a Roman soldier, and that her hands worked wonders on my war wounds, and that anytime I needed her hands I could come to her and she'd take my pain away.

Since the day I met Shane, I was filling his head with Goodness like Mr. Forsythe did for me, hoping it would stick better. If I'd known that Wednesday, February 14, 2018, would be our last day together, I'd have given him a big hug after the fist bump. I'd have said, I'm gonna miss you kid but you'll be okay. I'd have told him to keep his head up because he had magic in him.

Monica is always saying Shane's name. She visits him at the hotel-like place in the mountains where he lives with other kids who have magic like his, except he's not such a kid anymore. Mother and son walk through the woods and he points at birds and they take their shoes off and cool their feet in the creek. He's still painting castles and dragons but now they're on giant sheets of paper that he tapes to the walls of his room. She takes one every time she leaves and rolls it up and lays it in the back seat.

That Valentine's Day, she didn't get me a gift. The opposite. She let slip, all casual, like it was no biggie, that she'd been playing the Blue Sunshine album for Arthur, and guess what? He really liked it! And guess who was taking her husband out to see them this Saturday at the Green Dragon?

She and Arthur were both too old for the Green Dragon, she went on. They'd have to drink espressos to stay awake. But how could she resist? She had me to thank.

This time, it was her words that flipped the switch.

"I'm sorry it can't be you and me," she said, slow and sweet, the voice she used on Shane when he refused to get out of the pool. "If they play 'Right as Rain,' you know who I'll be thinking of."

I was looking straight ahead, explosions going off in my head. She played with my earlobe and kissed me on the temple. "You're okay, right? You don't mind too much? Things are so good these days: you and me, me and Arthur, us and Shane. I'm not trying to fuck it up."

"I'm okay," I said. I let her kiss me a little longer. Before I left, I took back the gifts I'd given her—a ring, a corsage of white roses—and stuffed them in the pocket of my jeans.

That Saturday night, I don't remember leaving the Dor or paying the fare at Fields Corner or walking through the turnstile at Haymarket, but I do remember how fucking freezing it was walking in my too-thin jacket, and my feet in two layers of socks going instantly numb stepping in slush on the way to the Bell in Hand, where the asshole bartender denied me another beer after just three maybe four, and of course I remember standing in the window that had a perfect view of the Green Dragon waiting and waiting for Monica and Arthur to show up in the line for Blue Sunshine. I remember them holding hands as they walked, huddling in the cold and the wind and the sleet just starting to come down, and by the time I figured out what the fuck I'd come there to do to them, they'd made it into the Green Dragon and bought drinks and appeared in the opposite window laughing and dancing and sloshing their drinks on each other. When I stepped outside, I heard the terrible music coming from the place, not Blue Sunshine at all, some opening act doing '70s covers old people like them went crazy for. I watched Monica raise her arms over her shoulders, close her eyes and make fish lips as she shook her head from side to side. I watched her undo his shirt buttons and paw his chest hair. His belly stuck out over his belt and hung there like a tumor. They bumped hips. He held her chin in his hand and brought her face in for one of those show-off kisses. It broke my heart, her happiness. He didn't deserve it. What he deserved was to get his lights punched out in front of her and Blue Sunshine. I was ready to do it, to fuck everything up. It's what I came there to do, the only thing I was ever going to do. We were already over anyway. From the day she told me the whole story. I had too much pride. She was right about that.

My feet were coming back to life, tingling the way they did on the diving board just before I jumped. People on the sidewalk were watching me watch the window. "You okay, kid?" one of them said. They had no Goodness in them. Did I? I never knew for sure. I needed a cigarette but nobody was smoking. I walked to Washington Street and found a frat guy sparking up under an overhang and stood there with him shivering, trying to get my head right. When I walked off, I said, "Fuck!" and he said, "No worries, bro." Garbage was everywhere, coffee cups and poop bags spilling out of the trash cans on the corners, dirty black mud in the numbing slush. I'm not trying to fuck this up, I said to myself. I'd miss her too much. I missed her already. My neck hurt. One day she'd love me for real. Or pretend better. I was not the cuck. Arthur was the cuck. In ten years he'd be seventy-six and dead and "Right as Rain" would be Monica's and my wedding song. I kept walking. The goal was now to put steps between me and them, to get as far away as possible. I crossed a busy street and ended up in a park with a baseball field all lit up, the bases little frozen ponds. I bummed another cigarette from a guy walking his dog. Now I needed to piss, too. I wanted her to watch me. It drove us wild, exposing ourselves. In real life I'm a shy person and ashamed all the time no matter how I come off. At the Dor I cover myself with two cupped hands. This park had no good place to hide. The jungle gym, the public pool, the bocce courts were all flooded with light, the bathrooms locked, people all around on their way somewhere else. So I walked to the water and jumped the fence and climbed down.

There was a whole world under there, like a cave, a place you could do anything you wanted and not be seen. I expected to find junkies or homeless guys or hookers giving blow jobs or whatever, but my eyes adjusted and I saw I was alone. I pissed for like an hour, staring at the tall ships docked across the river, wondering what voyages they'd been on before they got turned into floating museums. I should have gone back up right away, but it was warmer down there, protected from the wind and sleet, lit by the lights on the ships. Above me was the sidewalk I'd just been walking on. Around me was the sound of water sloshing on the rocks and the roar of cars crossing the bridge. My own little kingdom. I didn't do anything too stupid at the Green Dragon, I thought. I didn't fuck it up. On Monday I'll go back to work and she'll be none the wiser. I took another drag of my cigarette. Somehow I still had half of it left. I jumped from rock to rock in the general direction of home.

Matthew Agosto Cardullo
(December 18, 1999–February 23, 2020)

Memory gets more and more slippery the longer I'm here, as slippery as time itself. Even that little sliver of life I was given—twenty years and sixty-eight days, to be exact—feels like a giant armful of Jell-O the harder I try to hold on to it. But if I don't try, if we don't try, we lose what's left of ourselves completely. No wonder it's so noisy. No wonder we can't hear anything but our own voices.

Until I got here, I didn't pay much attention to the details, and now all I do is go over them like they'll be on the test. I have to say them out loud to memorize them and cement them in my mind like my declensions. *Recordābor. Recordāberis. Recordābimur.* The things I did in my little sliver of life come back to me in flashes, like they're happening for the first time. I can choose to relive them, over and over, as many times as I want, to cement them, too, to see my life for what it was, or I can push them out, try to forget them, lie to the other guys about them, make myself into someone better or worse than I really was, same as I could in the Before.

Like: I had a pet frog named Fritzie. I fell asleep in the back seat of my father's blue Taurus on the way home from Houghton Lake, my mother's hand on my heart. I was on page 4 of a ten-page analysis of Catullus 51 for my junior seminar. I could rep two-fifty on my max bench set. My left ear was going cauliflower. My locker combination was 0724, which was my mom's birthday. When I rubbed Tessa's feet, she threw her head back and moaned and said, clear as a bell, "I love you, Matthew Cardullo." Every time I looked ahead to my life, squinted at the horizon of what I could be, I saw

Tessa coming toward me, like the moon over Houghton Lake. On February 22, 2020, she didn't show up at the Ravens Club at 10 p.m. like we'd agreed she'd do. I sat at the end of the bar and pushed little wedges of lime through the necks of I-lost-track-of-how-many Coronas. When Ravens closed I stumbled out and made my way down Main Street to Packard, my mind consumed by her health and well-being.

One thing I keep forgetting to say is that nobody's entitled to my true story. If they really care so much, let them cross-check my facts, piece them together. What I'm telling you, the best I can remember it, is no lie, though; why would I lie about a story that makes me look like such a chump?

I had my phone up to my ear and Chloe's number was ringing and I was going, "pick up pick up," when I walked straight into a tree on Washtenaw. I heard these drunk idiot frat guys start laughing at me, and their laughter made me so angry I got up and took a swing in their direction, but when I swung I lost my balance and fell back on my ass in the snow. Then I just lay there for what could have been a second or could have been an hour until the frat guys stopped laughing and the old man who'd kept trying to buy me a drink at Ravens showed up out of nowhere and got me up on my feet and asked if I needed help.

The guy had a brown mustache and glasses and a scratchy voice I could barely hear. A red pickup truck like my mom's F-150 was idling behind him, spewing exhaust, and for a second I thought it was her come to rescue me. I was wearing two pairs of socks and the Moosejaw puffer jacket my dad bought me and my blue Michigan hat with the yellow pom-pom. I told the Ravens guy to fuck off

I was fine, but I guess I walked the wrong way into oncoming traffic because there was a loud screech of car brakes and some lady started yelling at me, and then a cop showed up.

The Ravens guy told the cop I was with him, he'd take care of me, but the cop wasn't buying it. He was in uniform but he wasn't a campus cop. He'd jumped out of a black SUV, not a cruiser, so it confused me and for a second I got the two men mixed-up—the Ravens guy and the cop—though they didn't look anything alike. The Ravens guy was scrawny and the cop was your generic white douchebag standing tall and sucking his teeth and resting his hand all tough on his holster in case I wasn't aware cops carried guns. He reminded me of one of those big-dicked guys in the gym shower who play with themselves as they talk to you, like it's not obvious they've got something you don't.

Speaking of which, for some reason my dick was so hard that it hurt, and I didn't want the cop to see me throbbing in my jeans and think it was for him or for the Ravens guy, so when he offered to drive me home I said fine just so he'd have to turn his back to me and walk to the driver's side while I adjusted myself. I should have known right then my neurons had been compromised. I put my seat belt on and told the cop I lived at Elm and Geddes and rested my head against the window, and as we crossed campus and drove down Washtenaw toward Observatory, the streetlights were too bright and swirly and made me nauseous and the last thing I needed was to throw up in a cop's car, so I closed my eyes. When I opened them, I wasn't being dropped off at my apartment, I was being pulled out of the car and dragged on the ground somewhere in complete darkness. Then I was set down on my back in the snow and the douchebag cop was crouched next to me and his face was right up against mine saying Tessa's name.

Tessa? I thought. How's this guy know Tessa?

Stay the fuck away from Tessa were his exact words. *No more calling and texting and showing up at her place, never again, you hear me?*

His spit landed on my lips and I tasted his gum in it. Then he spit the gum at me.

DO YOU HEAR ME?

Who the fuck are you, is what I replied.

He grabbed the front of my coat with his fist, pulled me up toward him, and dragged my body a little farther along the ground. This time when he dropped me back down I felt the shock of frigid water cover my ears and the back of my head through my hat. It took my breath away. I couldn't catch it. He jammed his knee on my chest.

This is your warning, asshole, he said. *Tessa doesn't want you. She wants me. As far as that girl's concerned, you don't exist. Now tell me you hear me or you're going in. Tell me you understand the words I'm saying to you.*

I nodded, my eyes adjusting. I studied his face. The face of some strange guy twice my age who thought Tessa belonged to him. The reason she hadn't shown up for our date that night, and all the other nights. The reason she'd never show up for me again. Not because of anything I'd done or the man I was. Not because of her phone battery, or Chloe, or the clutch in her Mustang. Because of this scumbag who'd messed with her head somehow. Oh, Tessa, what were you thinking, mixing yourself up with him?

He pulled me back onto the riverbank, unballed his fist from the front of my coat, and again let my head smack against the rocky ground. My entire back and legs were covered in ice-cold mud seeping through my clothes. Then he squatted next to me, forearms on his knees, like he was about to take a dump. Shaking his head. Pitying me. Smiling. Eat a dick, I thought. But I didn't say a word. I was gathering my breath. Building energy. *You were made for this moment*, I said to myself. I'd been expecting it all my life. What else did I train so hard for, condition my body into its optimal form for, learn ancient fighting moves for, and practice them four nights a week on sweaty hairy dudes in a room that smelled like dirty socks and dried cum? Not to hold up some dinky trophy. Not for my picture in the paper. Not even to make D1. I did it so I could walk around feeling satisfied, primed for any man who came my way if the need arose, confident that I could defend myself, my girl, my kids (one day) against him. I used to carry this secret knowledge with me everywhere, and whenever I passed a guy bigger and stronger than me on the street, a guy like that beast from State I'd pinned the night before, or some other guy who had no idea what a match I was for him, I'd smirk to myself, maybe give the guy a look that said *I dare you*. And now, here, daring me, was this guy Rafferty, who'd spit on me and messed with Tessa's head and thought he could take her away from me just because he had a uniform and a gun and the element of surprise.

I looked him straight in the eyes, trying to figure out if I knew him, but also faking surrender in my own eyes, faking a plea for mercy; in reality, though, my blood was surging, flooding every muscle in my body with energy spoiling for a fight. In the second it took for Rafferty to scratch his forehead, I'd rolled away from him onto my stomach, then jumped to my feet and got in my stance, hips low, knees bent, elbows in, and charged him while wrapping his knees for the blast double. Tough Guy didn't know what hit him when I speared his chest with my head and took him down hard into the mud. I must have looked to him like one of those horror movie psychos, the ones you think are dead because they've been shot twenty times but still they rise up howling.

I'd knocked the wind out of him, and now I had him on his back. I mounted his torso and punched at his head one fist after another, the hardest ground-and-pound I could muster given my weakened state. I didn't feel weak, though; my adrenaline was pumping, and watching him try to fight me off and protect his face fed my fury. He knew how to defend himself and that pretty face, but he wasn't so skilled at inflicting damage on his opponent. If this were a match, I'd have won every point so far. Still, he was stronger than I thought, and maybe twenty pounds heavier, one ninety at least, probably two hundred. That lopsidedness pissed me off. It also riled me up. I was entirely focused on beating this guy's ass, but I was also simultaneously back at Bahna telling Justin and Travis the chain of moves I hit on him.

We scrambled in the mud, both of us finding ways to get clean punches off on each other. Fucking mutt, those only fueled me. Eventually, he switched his efforts to trying to get away, but by then I had him on his back again, and I was in total control. I don't think Rafferty even realized or could fully believe what was happening to him, what had transpired in the past thirty seconds of his sorry-ass life. I remember wishing he could see the smile on my face when, finally, I got him in a rear naked choke, which had been my goal from the jump, my legs trapping his, my right forearm cinched his throat, my left hand pulling it tighter, him squirming in my grasp. I was truly howling then, blessing every muscle I'd built in my twenty-year-old body, spitting on his pretty right cheek, screaming Tessa's name into his ear, asking him who her daddy was now, who the bitch was now, who was the sick old pig and who was the college boy choking the sick old pig to death, all kinds of crazy shit, which in my mind went on for like an hour but probably took ten seconds tops.

We'd rolled into some branches that were poking us both in the face, but I still had him in my grasp. Just on the other side of the branches was the river. He elbowed me and tried to kick me as he gasped for air, sounding like a cat coughing up a hairball. The water was so close. I remember its eggy smell and the chill it gave off. I remember the smudges of moonlight on the surface, the perfect stillness all around us. I'd slayed another beast. The guy had no way out of his situation. He was fucked. But so was I, right? What was I supposed to do, asphyxiate a cop and then dump his body in the Huron? Then what? Call Tessa and beg her not only to take me back but to wait out my life sentence? It didn't occur to me then that I could kill this guy and then cover it up, not because I had no clue how I'd accomplish a thing, or because it was impossible, but because I believed that if you deliberately commit a crime, you deserve the appropriate punishment. And that right there is the difference between him—them—and me. Yes, I did think about choking Kenneth Rafferty to death, I may have even liked the idea of him going limp in my arms, but not for one second did I consider going through with it.

Instead, I loosened my grip. I gave him some air.

I trusted he'd honor the rules of the fight.

I figured he'd pass out, and then I'd run off.

I figured he had some pride.

But either he was a true psycho, or the substances in my system finally caught up with me once the adrenaline wore off, or I had a secret death wish all along. Because with that little bit of air I gave him, he found the strength to push off me, and the balls to grab his gun. He held the gun at my temple, snarling at me as his chest heaved and he gulped more air, recovering himself, but even at that moment, with the cold steel burning my skin and the wheels turning in his head, I wasn't afraid he'd blow my brains out. We were two men in a duel for the love of a good woman, not an episode of *CSI*. We were supposed to back off, call this part a draw, and then regroup for the next part, whatever and whenever that was.

With the gun still pointed at me, splayed on the ground, he stood up. He kicked the backs of my knees. Then, with the heel of his boot pressing against my ribs, he tried to push me toward the water. Fine, dude. Dunk me in and we'll be done. I'll get hypothermia and then take whatever pills you take to recover from hypothermia and then I'll come for you. He didn't say a word, didn't even meet my eyes, as he kept kicking at me, and so I kind of helped him, wanting this to be over with, using my elbows to scoot away from him. My body was already bruised from the night before, and now I'd have even more bruises all over, war wounds, battle trophies, the only kind of trophy that mattered.

The shock of my elbows hitting the water, shallow and rocky, froze me in place, but he kept kicking, and now my ass was in, now my legs, and now we were both in the river, my whole body, but him only up to his boots. I tried to keep my head above the surface, to scramble to my feet, but my limbs were both jelly and numb somehow, like they weren't even attached to me anymore, like they were floating away into the night, and this time I was the one gasping, watching his face as he calmly slid his gun back into its holster and then stepped onto my bare neck with his heavy boot as casually as you'd squash a spider. With his two hundred pounds on this boot he held my dumb unblinking head under the water until he didn't have to anymore.

CRIME SEEN (III)

James taps *10 Riverview Drive, Northfield Falls, Vermont*, into his GPS and heads up Route 7. He knows the address and the route by heart, but this will be his first trip to the place on Dog River where Caleb's body was found. Determining the precise location wasn't difficult thanks to Google Maps, Zillow, and the multiple news reports, now a year old, that chronicled the construction woes of Riverview Gardens, the high-end fifty-five-plus community delayed first by COVID, then by the discovery of mysterious remains.

Caleb would hate this place, James thinks, as he pulls into the development of identical stone-front townhomes and lawns cut close as fairways, faux Victorian gazebos, heated garages, and paved walking trails that infiltrate the otherwise virgin woods. In one of his letters to the editor of the *Burlington Free Press*, Derrick M., a "concerned neighbor" upriver, called Riverview Gardens a "twenty-first-century Pleasantville" that would "drain rapidly vanishing resources, threaten the natural ecosystem, and emblematize Vermont's stark income inequality." He didn't mention that its location, within eye- and earshot of the Gaze, would also spoil the club's seclusion and relative anonymity forever.

According to the State of Vermont Municipal Directory, a man named Charles Ringgold prepurchased 10 Riverview Drive, a two-bedroom condo with a small yard that bordered the Dog, in February 2020, more than a year before the developers broke ground. Ringgold told the *Free Press* it "didn't faze him" when he later learned that a young man had been buried, perhaps after being murdered, in what was about to be his semiprivate pool of river. He'll probably croak somewhere on the property himself one day, Ringgold said, and besides, where was he supposed to go? Every other unit was taken now that nobody, especially not the fifty-five-plus, wanted to live in a city anymore.

James could knock on Ringgold's door, invent a family connection to Caleb Aldrich, and ask to be permitted onto his property, but he's too cautious even now. Caleb's case remains unsolved, his cause of death still unknown. His car has vanished from the earth. The bones recovered from the Dog showed no signs of major trauma: no blunt force to the head, no broken limbs. In fact, according to the medical examiner, the bones were remarkably intact, "pristine," even, due almost certainly to the body's tomb-like encasement under the giant boulder relocated by the excavator to build Riverview Gardens. The boulder didn't kill Caleb, that much seems obvious; it sealed him, dead or alive, and hid him from view for more than thirteen years. But how did it get there, and how did he, and why? James still has his suspicions, but little hope he'll ever know for sure. From that interview alone, though, Charles Ringgold seems like the type to phone in a tip, and James can't bear another series of interrogations from the police or from Iris. He's survived those interrogations already, as has his marriage, a miracle he still can't quite believe he deserves.

So he parks at the Doghouse, the restaurant / activity center / interfaith gathering space at the heart of the complex, and heads straight for the walking trails. From studying the website, he knows which path meanders closest to unit 10, the corner town house on what they call the Left Bank. By now James is an expert at blending in, dressed for the occasion in tick-safe athletic pants, waterproof hiking boots, and the blue weatherman windbreaker Iris has begged him to retire. He nods hello to a woman his age, sixty-five or so, who remarks upon the beauty of the summer day and coquettishly demands his name and seems just about to invite him inside for a cup of coffee and propose marriage before he quickens his pace and bids her a great afternoon. As he approaches number 10, he peels off the trail and trespasses into Ringgold's backyard.

There are no fences at Riverview Gardens. The developers wanted an open community of neighbors who look out for each other, a landscape and view unbroken by walls of any kind. Only white-painted picnic tables and grills and jungle gyms, presumably for visiting grandchildren. Rope swings hanging from the stronger trees along the Dog. Sitting rocks for contemplation jutting up from the banks. Lampposts. Benches. Little beachlets of coarse sand.

James stands on one of the severed tree trunks at the far edge of the property, watching the water gently foam and eddy on the scattered smooth stones. Were you here? he asks Caleb. Or over there?

Was this the boulder, or was it that one? Boulders are everywhere. Now that James has come this close, he requires the exact spot. He steps onto one of the giant rocks, then another, making his way carefully toward the middle of the river, bowing to peer into its depths—which aren't deep at all—hoping, against his own practical instincts, to sense the answer, that love will act as a divining rod, that he'll feel in his guts the unmistakability of the boy's presence. But there is only the wind in the trees, the shushing of the river, and the minnows nibbling his fingertips when he crouches down to examine them, and he's not mystical enough to believe any of these hold Caleb's spirit.

You were right here the whole time, he says aloud. How did I know, but not know? The question he's never been able to shake.

James could tell you the name of the pizza shop where Leo Ridgeway worked. The Michigan State wrestler Matt Cardullo defeated the night before he went missing. The bar near Faneuil Hall where Steve Donovan was last seen pounding beers. For years he's been tending his acres of these dead boys, decorating their graves, clicking through images of them, cutting and pasting and arranging them, recording if they had a girlfriend, a boyfriend, a drug problem, a personality disorder, if they played an instrument, if they went to the prom. He's clicked and clicked. But not for Caleb. Caleb is the only boy whose history James has wanted to only half know. It's the circumstances of his death he's been after, not his life as others understood it, those men he befriended, the stories he told them, the hearts he won and led on and broke. If, over all these years, James had been after the full picture of Caleb's life, he could have smoked many a joint on Derrick's porch and traded tales of the boy, read over the messages they sent each other, compared notes. They could have invited VTGeorge802 over. James could have written under an alias to Amaraya Sonder, the roommate, now living in South Africa, or that mentor from his high school, Gil Corbett, both of whom were quoted in the papers saying they finally felt "settled" and had "some closure" when they learned that Caleb Aldrich had been found and laid to rest. James could have wrung these people dry and drenched himself in all the Calebs they offered him. But none of those boys would be *his* Caleb, and his Caleb is the only one who matters, not the one his roommate or teacher or lovers constructed of him, and that he constructed for them. This is why we can never fully see another person, he once told Libby in one of his and Iris's counseling sessions, this is why we always appear just a little out of focus to each other; not because we've got something to hide, or we're willfully blind or resistant to the people we love, but because we are always multiple versions of ourselves at once, like the blurry composite photo of all the Smiley Face boys he showed Derrick years ago.

Out of fear, James destroyed any and all evidence of the Caleb he knew until the only trace of him existed in his memories of their few hours together; and these, too, are blurry, reduced to still images faded from overviewing, like paintings exposed to too much light. This must be what he hopes to find in the river behind 10 Riverview Drive: some new piece of him to carry away, a piece that James alone will recognize not only as Caleb's but as theirs.

He's also come to say goodbye, to finally put the boy behind him before he and Iris relocate eight hundred miles south to a different small town, a different college, where she's landed a prestigious deanship. Now retired, James readies himself for a fresh start. Caleb is gone and never coming back. He won't find the boy again here in the mountains of Vermont. He's not down in Key West freeing the lobsters. He's not in Poughkeepsie, either, though surely his parents have claimed his remains and interred them in a family plot complete with a stone and a cross. He'd hate that, too.

What would he have wanted instead? James wonders, making his way back across the rocks. An organic burial, probably. To be returned to Nature, to the Earth. Which, ironically, is exactly what he got. No. That's not right at all. What Caleb would have wanted was to live forever.

James pulls out of Riverview Gardens and drives in the general direction of the Gaze, though he's unsure if he'll actually show up there. When he messaged Derrick a month ago to say he wanted to see him in person for the first time in a decade, maybe the weekend of the 30th if he wasn't too busy, he half hoped he'd rebuff him. But then Derrick didn't write back within minutes, as was his custom, and James noticed that his original message and follow-ups went unread for more than a week, and he found himself strangely disappointed and, eventually, concerned. Derrick was in his eighties at least, highly susceptible to the still-raging virus, and there was also such a thing as natural causes. In the years of their odd association, they'd had too much to say each other, and so they'd said almost nothing substantive at all. James rarely reached out unprovoked, and Derrick contacted James only when another boy went missing; they'd then speculate wildly about him over AIM for a while. Otherwise, their exchanges were brief and concerned local politics, or the price of gas, or the opening of a new restaurant, like two guys thrown together at a party because their wives were friends. Only obliquely did Derrick ever reference Caleb, and when he did James either ignored it or logged off.

Eventually, Derrick did reply, offering no reason for his silence. Yes, he'd be home all weekend, he said, mowing the lawn and setting up tables and chairs for the Fourth of July festivities he was hosting at the Gaze. Yes, he'd be alone. No, he wouldn't mind at all if James stopped by for a chat. What's taken you so long, he said. You don't know what you've been missing.

He'll never admit this to Derrick, but since their first meeting, James has driven past the Gaze once in a while, usually on the Sunday afternoons when the club hosts barbecues. He's stayed on the mailing list under one of his aliases—ColinFirth2010@gmail.com—so he can read the quarterly newsletter, *The Gaze Gossip*, and keep up with Derrick and VTGeorge802 and other men he's yet to find the courage to meet in person. If James doesn't knock on the door of the place, he figures, or pay the daily or monthly membership fee, then he can't be counted as one of those men; he's just a voyeur, a dabbler, a concerned citizen, a vigilante keeping the peace. Which of these James is depends on the day, the month, the year. Sometimes, jealous, he's parked at the gravel turnout a half mile away and walked back along the shoulderless road in his orange safety vest, headphones muted, listening to the laughter and the music that pulsed from behind the hedges of the ramshackle house. Through the leaves he could see the men standing around holding red cups and paper plates, pumping the keg, tending the multiple grills, dancing on the grass. Sometimes, suspicious, he's taken photos of their license plates with his camera phone, though he's done nothing with this data but transfer it to a desktop file. When the discreet ones walk out, he's noticed, they keep their heads down, baseball caps pulled low over their foreheads, avoiding eye contact as they unlock and get into their cars. The indiscreet ones burst through the front door in pairs or groups, still singing along to whatever song was playing, and if they notice James at all they brazenly look him up and down and tell him don't bother with the party, come on home with us.

And sometimes, lustful, James has gone home with them, enough times that he needs two hands to count the number of men whose otherwise forgettable faces he could still recognize anywhere—a street corner, a WANTED poster—but has never seen again. Geography, far more than desire, would dictate whether or not James followed the man or men to their next destination. He couldn't stray so far that it would take too long to get back to Iris, who waited on the front porch of their farmhouse, eyes shaded, scanning their mutual territory for any sign of him. Or, at least, that's how James pictured her as he rooted around for his clothes in the bedroom of the country house in Bristol, the trailer in Jerusalem, the B&B in Hancock.

James behaves like a guilty man even though Iris no longer asks what he's been up to or why he smells like cigars or whether he ran into Carmen Agarwal at the gym. If he picks up groceries from the list they compiled together and puts gas in the car and seems happy to see her, which he always genuinely is, that's enough. Then they read side by side on the sofa in front of the fireplace. They host a dinner party for their colleagues, an end-of-semester celebration for her seminar students. They make love with a new and punishing brutality contingent on the tenderness that comes after, when they luxuriate in licking each other's wounds. For Iris he saves himself for weeks at a time, deletes the apps he downloaded onto his phone, steers clear of the Gaze or Sycamore Park. For Iris he arms himself with blue pills. For Iris he gets tested every six months at the anonymous free clinic in Burlington.

Some of this he reports to Libby in their joint counseling sessions, but most of it he keeps to himself. James doesn't believe in radical honesty, only in self-protection, which, he rationalizes, includes the protection of Iris, now that they are one unified body ruling over the vast hundred-acre estate that Libby deeded to them.

"Does your husband know everything about you?" Libby once asked Iris.

"Of course not."

"Would you want him to?"

Iris thought a moment. "I think, I wouldn't mind? I'd probably find it liberating, wouldn't you? If it were possible?" She addressed this question not to Libby, but to him. "It's why people believe in God," she went on. "To feel fully seen by someone who loves them, guts and all. But no one can ever fully see another person. So it's not a fair question."

"You haven't had anything to hide," said James. "That's the difference between us."

"I guess that's true," she said—triumphantly, or wistfully, James couldn't tell—and took his hand. "What bothers me, though," she told Libby, "is that every problem I've struggled with in my life got better after working it through with James. He's a good listener.

Pragmatic, clinical. Big-picture-y. I'm always in the weeds. And the good stuff—anything that's brought me pleasure, joy, mystery—he's always the first person I want to share it with. Why should I have to stick it in some distant field by itself like a monument only I can visit?"

"You're a lucky woman," said Libby.

"Am I? Because I don't hear him saying the same thing. What I keep hearing, time after time, is how happy he is on his ten-acre playground."

James protested, of course, reassuring Iris that she was his best friend in the world, that he'd give up every square inch of this so-called playground for her, that his urges, however potent, were no match for their love. Also, they had history on their side: Virginia and Leonard Woolf, Paul and Jane Bowles, Lou Reed and Laurie Anderson. Did they not consider themselves as evolved, as cosmopolitan, as those intellectuals, despite living in Vermont? He'd have made any argument, any promise, to hang on to Iris. He still would.

Driving the two miles from Riverview Gardens to the Gaze, James feels a kind of stubborn pride in the resilience of their long marriage. As it turned out, the fight was never between their love and his urges; the intervening years have proven those two seemingly oppositional forces to be compatible, separable. He's been able to contain any potential spillover or contamination. And Caleb's fate, as awful as it was, had the effect of sparing Iris the only fight she might conceivably have lost.

After driving in circles for a while, James finally arrives at the Gaze to find Derrick waiting for him on the front porch. He sits in a rocking chair, sucking on a vape, eyeing him as he backs his car in. James has seen glimpses of Derrick through the hedges on his spy missions, but this will be their first face-to-face conversation in fifteen years. Time has turned James's own hair white and shrunk him an inch and a half and woven cobwebs of wrinkles on his neck, but it seems to have left Derrick mostly alone. When James steps onto the porch, the old man springs out of the rocking chair without losing his balance. He offers James a strong handshake that makes his triceps bulge. His tank top, which he wears under a pair of grass-stained overalls, clings to his tight chest and flat middle. The lines across his forehead and around his eyes have stayed shallow; his jaw doesn't sag. So much for natural causes. Where's his ear hair, his liver spots, his missing-molar smile?

"Good timing," Derrick says. "I'm on a smoke break." He sits back down and takes another hit from the vape. "You want some? It's just a little CBD. Helps with the joints and the nerves."

"No thank you," says James.

"Sit a spell, then, as we say up here in the country. I'm a bona fide redneck now, in case it's not obvious." He flicks the straps of his overalls.

"Inside's probably better," says James. Even now, he worries who might drive by. Why else did he instinctively back the car in, if not to hide the license plate. "Or how about the yard? I'd love to check out the grounds."

"Can't see much through those hedges, can you?"

"That's fair," James says. He holds up his hands in surrender. "At least let me help you set up for the party."

"I've got more help than I can use," Derrick says gruffly. Then he softens a little. He launches himself up out of the chair again and puts his hand on James's shoulder. "But sure, I'll give you a tour of the *grounds*. You make our little pigpen sound so grand. I've made some improvements since the last time you were here, but don't expect the gardens of Tivoli."

"We never made it outside," says James. "It was the middle of winter."

"Is that right? My memory's not so hot anymore. But I do recall you were all twitchy."

"I was losing my mind," James says. "The boy had been missing for thirteen months. In my head you were the one responsible, you knew more than you were telling me, you were some kind of ringleader mastermind psychopath getting away with murder. I don't remember half the things I said to you, Derrick, but I'm sure they were as nuts as that. I was this close to buying a gun."

"To do what?"

"To protect myself. From you, from the other guys. The whole network."

"You'd seen too many movies."

"My heart was broken and it made me crazy," James says.

"And now?"

James closes his eyes. "My heart's still broken, but I'm—less crazy?" He manages a smile.

"Well, that's progress," says Derrick.

James follows him into the house, which also hasn't changed much. Maybe a few more blown-glass vases and mood lamps and oil paintings of male nudes in gilt frames. His first time here, he found the entire setup of the place, especially the decor, garish and creepy and incriminating; he felt as though he'd walked into the lion's den.

Now its baroqueness, its shameless excess, offers a kind of comfort. A kinship. Proudly, Derrick points out the sound system wired into the exposed beams in the ceiling, the added security around the windows and doors, and the finished basement/"playroom"—tricked out with leather-covered benches and a mounted sling—requested by the monthly members. Out in the backyard, hidden completely from the road, a working fountain of two life-sized Greco-Roman wrestlers spits and splashes, lulling him into a kind of dreamy numbness. Next to the fountain: a bocce court, a badminton net, a garden of cabbages and kale in straight rows. Far off, at the edge of the woods, a cheap replica of Michelangelo's *David* stands sentinel-like on a three-foot pedestal. James wasn't aware of the vastness of Derrick's property, that it encompasses this backyard, the side yard that faces the road, a freestanding garage nearly hidden by an elm tree, and two windowless sheds big as cottages. "You've got quite the setup out here," he says.

"Our own little old folks' home," says Derrick.

"I just came from that place."

"I figured. You go up there a lot, I guess."

"Actually no," says James. "First time. It took me a full year to work up the nerve."

Derrick looks at him more closely. "You really are a twitchy one."

Ignoring this, James says, "I'm moving out of state right after the fourth. That's why I'm here. To say goodbye to you. To close the loop. And to apologize. I didn't want to do it over email. It's never a good idea, legally or otherwise, to put an apology in writing. I didn't know I had anything to apologize for, but now that I'm here—I feel like I owe it to you."

"You don't owe me anything," Derrick says.

"I never understood what you were trying to do with this place. But he did, I guess."

"You were scared shitless," says Derrick. "I was, too. And worried for him. He had some kind of magic in him, didn't he? I don't blame you for losing your head. He was my friend, too. We were close in that way you can only be with someone you poured your soul out to online and never met in person. Like us, in a way, trading mystery stories back and forth over the years, thinking those missing Smiley Face boys belonged to us or something, that they'd add up. I hadn't even heard of them until you walked in here with your maps and files and paranoia. It's your fault I ended up falling in love with each of them worse than you did. But I'm not mad at you for it."

"That's not why—"

Derrick waves him away. "I swear, I felt more intimacy with Cal—excuse me, *Caleb*—than I did with ninety-nine-point-nine percent of the guys I slept with. When he showed up at my front door and jumped into my arms, he was like my long-lost puppy come home."

"He made you feel like you were the most important person in the world."

"That was the magic," says Derrick.

They're walking across the back lawn now, toward the sheds and the woods and the river. You can't hear the water from here, but you can smell its muskiness. The grass is spongy and slick from a soaking overnight rain, but Derrick has no trouble bounding across it on agile feet that barely disturb the earth. His lightness, his surefootedness, makes James jealous. He craves his usual six o'clock Jameson and ginger, or maybe a hit of the CBD—anything to diffuse the ache that weighs and slows him down.

"Seriously," James says, "how the fuck did he get under that rock? Who put him there? By this point there's always some sort of resolution. A strong theory, at least, right? A reality the parents and loved ones don't want to accept, but one that's plausible, that most people agree to believe so that they can move on? Why not for him?"

Derrick stops and looks him up and down. "You don't expect any answers from me, do you?"

"Not anymore," he says. He reassures Derrick that he hasn't come here on another spy mission, that he no longer suspects that he or any of the guys from the Gaze played a part in Caleb's disappearance. They're too sloppy, he says; they'd have been caught by now. Once again he asks him to forgive him.

"I told you it's not necessary."

And yet, James could say: Caleb was so close to these grounds all these years. And men, they snap so easily. Every man—even you, even me—has it in him to go off. How will James ever be completely settled, without even a likely scenario resolution? How will Derrick?

The old man's been fiddling with the rusty numbers on the padlock on the door of the shed. "Something terrible happened to him," he says, trying various combinations. "That's one thing I might know for sure. I hate saying it, but I feel in my gut that he didn't die easy. He didn't skip town trying to disappear, like some people do, as is their right. He wasn't wasting away in Margaritaville, as much as I convinced myself he was. He was just wasting away. I didn't want to use those words with you the last time you came here in your twitchiness. I spun a pretty tale. But you knew already, didn't you? Didn't we all know, deep down, the moment we met him, that he'd come to no good end? Back in the day, so many boys around me had that same magic in them. Not a single one survived."

"You did."

Finally, the lock clicks open. "Don't remind me."

The shed contains the mowers and truck tires and decommissioned toilets and rakes and shovels and cinder blocks you'd expect to find in the front yard of an actual redneck. Tucked in the back corner sits a small, derelict car filled to its nonexistent roof with cracked flowerpots and bags of soil and rolls of chicken wire. The car is also missing its taillights and passenger-side doors and three of its tires. In the open trunk are VCRs and stereos and speakers and TVs with BB-gun holes in the screens. Taken together, the entire place looks more like an avant-garde art installation, Slab City East, than a "shop," which is how Derrick referred to it when they approached.

"I left you a few things in my will," he says.

"You did?"

James glances around nervously as Derrick clears a path to the back of the shed behind the car, where he'd set up a bench and sawhorses and a worktable in front of one of those large square backstage mirrors with fat bulbs around the perimeter. The shelves above it are crowded with paint cans and pallets of bottled water and discarded dinner plates encrusted with food.

"Yes I did," he says. "But since you've finally decided to grace my home with your presence, and you're taking off to parts unknown,

I might as well give these things to you now. For a while I thought we were the same breed, but now I'm not so sure."

"I don't understand," he says. "I'm just moving to North Carolina."

"If you can't take them today, at least you'll know where to find them after I'm gone."

He flips a switch and the mirror bulbs come on, flooding the room with light. Then he gets on his hands and knees and starts pulling cardboard and plastic boxes out from under the bench one by one. He opens each box, checks its contents, then sets it aside. "I should have labeled these better," he says. "It's here somewhere, I promise."

"What do you mean the same breed?"

He stops and looks up at James and smiles, the shadows from the stage lights softening his face. "You're lucky," he says, peering closer. "You've got no magic at all." And it's then, in just a flash, that James sees the boy in him: Derrick with all the years smoothed away, yes, but also, unmistakably, Caleb. Has this resemblance been there all along, or is it a trick of the eye? Who would have thought to look for it? He blinks and it's gone.

"Wait, are you two related?" James asks.

"Who?"

"You and Caleb."

"Of course not!" says Derrick, like it's the craziest thing he's ever heard. "What would ever give you that idea?"

He stands up and the light changes and there again is an eighty-ish-year-old man with dull blue eyes and lines across his forehead and a salt-and-pepper beard. A man youthful but not young. He sets a plastic file box on the table, and then from that box he pulls out not files but two T-shirts, and a spiral notebook, and a brown teddy bear in a blue Middlebury sweater.

So this is terror, James thinks. Until he feels it, which he hasn't until this moment, he doesn't know its distinction from fear. He backs away from Derrick, into the sawhorses, and nearly falls back onto the car—Caleb's car—the floor sliding out from under him, but Derrick catches him and puts his hands on his shoulders and steadies him and tells him not to be afraid, this isn't what he thinks, this is a gift he could and should have claimed years ago. Listen to me, says Derrick. This is what you came for.

Derrick wasn't surprised, he tells James, when he woke up on Christmas Eve and found Caleb gone. He knew the kid had a long drive ahead of him, that his family expected him, that the roads were bad. Many a time had he himself slipped out of a house before dawn as a man he regretted going to bed with slept off a night of partying. So Derrick went about his day: made coffee and tidied up the kitchen and stood in the window watching the storm cycle through snow and sleet and rain and then back to snow again. The wind twisted and bent the trees nearly in half. Between the rumbly thunder and the cracks of winter lightning, he could hear animal howls from deep in the woods. It wasn't until the wind died down hours later that he went out front to check for any damage and noticed the kid's Toyota still parked at the end of the driveway, the keys in the ignition, the battery dead, the door not quite closed, like he'd gotten in and started the engine and then decided to walk to Poughkeepsie instead.

He put on an extra layer and walked the grounds calling his name, but there was no sign of Caleb anywhere, no surviving footprints, no disturbance to either of the sheds or to the garage. Meanwhile, the snow was falling hard, weighing down the trees already heavy with ice. The lights in the main house flickered. By the time Derrick got back inside, the generator had switched on. He'll be back sooner or later, Derrick thought. Either he went for a walk and got caught in the storm, or one of the guys had come by and taken him to the Skinny Pancake for a greasy hangover breakfast. Caleb seemed like the type to discreetly arrange a date the night before to make sure he'd be fed, kept company. To be helpful, Derrick shoveled out the Toyota, jumped it, and parked it in the covered garage.

When Caleb didn't come back that night or the night after, Derrick searched the car and his backpack and duffel bag for his phone or a note or any indication of where he might have snuck off to. He'd brought few clothes—four pairs of underwear and socks, four T-shirts, a button-down shirt, two sweaters—a bunch of textbooks and spiral notebooks, the teddy bear in a red paper bag, a six-pack of Trojans with two missing, and a leather travel case of CDs. There were five discs in the changer, but the last thing he'd been listening to was 620 AM, presumably for the forecast and the road closures.

On the 26th Derrick's phone rang and kept ringing. Earl and Tim and the others came over and together, without much debate, they decided no good could possibly come from the police knowing that the missing boy had stopped at this house, stayed a few hours dancing and drinking enough to compromise his ability to drive, passed out, and then woke up in the middle of the night and drove off. The poor kid probably skidded into a ditch somewhere off the

Taconic Parkway, they said, but they hoped he was holed up with some secret boyfriend in Burlington or New York City. Derrick had not told them about the car in his garage. He wanted to sniff them out first. He had his own suspicions about these men, none of which were confirmed then or later. He suggested that, as good citizens, as involved individuals whether they liked it or not, they had an obligation to at least search for Caleb, which they did, in earnest, for three days. They found nothing. Snow fell day after day, followed by a weekend of rain and then more snow. Roads had crumbled at their shoulders, rocks had shifted and tumbled. Downed trees were everywhere, crews out repairing power lines, plows scraping and spewing salt on the streets just to scrape and salt them again.

Then suddenly they were weeks into 2008. By the time the police showed up, early February, Derrick had thoroughly dismantled the car. He'd already kept it too long for his reasons to seem innocent to them or to Earl or Tim or to any of the other guys. The reasons no longer sounded innocent or rational even to himself. He disposed of the small and large pieces of the car in various ways in three different states until what was left of it was unrecognizable to itself and, most importantly, untraceable. Most of what you see here is aftermarket, he says to James, rapping his knuckles on the hood like a salesman. Over the years he's been replacing it piece by piece with new and used parts, building it back up from its guts, like Frankenstein. At this point, he hardly remembers what he kept of the original and what he sourced from eBay and local junkyards. He has no plans to drive it—currently it doesn't even have a transmission—but working on it helps him pass the time, like a 3D jigsaw puzzle. Some days, it feels like a tribute. Other days, penance.

For weeks, then months, the authorities paid Derrick regular visits. They went over his messages to Caleb, asked the same questions, got the same answers. They spoke to Earl and Tim and the others, and all their stories checked out. The cops were hostile at first, but, as the visits went on, they got friendlier, almost collaborative. Derrick half expected to see one or two of them back for a barbecue. Briefly, the Gaze was the subject of scrutiny in the *Burlington Free Press*, until Derrick and other "concerned citizens" called out the newspaper on its homophobia and hysteria—though apparently this was a word they shouldn't have used—in letters to the editor and op-eds. The attention only increased the Gaze's popularity and made Derrick a little extra money, which he spent on the security system, the fountain, the playroom equipment, the new roof he needed after Hurricane Irene blew off the original. Based on their conversations with Caleb's roommate, and some of Caleb's internet searches (he didn't keep a journal; his browser history was surprisingly school-focused), the police speculated he drove to Montreal, though they couldn't find any record of his Toyota crossing the border. After a while, they stopped coming around altogether.

It was somewhere in that period that you darkened my doorstep, Derrick says to James. I could have told you all this back then, nice and calm like I'm doing now, but you were too keyed up, you and your videos and maps and spreadsheets and suspicions. I couldn't trust you because you didn't trust me. Maybe even had it out for me, wanted me to be guilty of something. Only after Caleb turned up, alive or dead, his mystery solved, did I expect to have this conversation with you. A few more weeks or months, I figured back then, maybe a year. I never expected thirteen years. Or that you'd skulk around my home and place of business playing Miss Marple. Who'd this guy think he was? the guys and me would wonder. We've been laughing at you, James, calling you the saddest of closet cases, snooping through the hedges in your orange vest thinking it would protect you.

"I'm not a closet case," James says. "My wife—"

"Closets have closets within closets," says Derrick. "Like a Russian doll. I don't judge you. Look at half the guys who show up here, caps pulled down over their eyes, hands in their pockets. The difference is they're in my backyard and you're in the street on the other side of the hedge. But I'm a romantic. I always have been, though that wasn't my reputation. I saw—still see—the love you had for that boy, your version of him, at least, which was as real as any of his other versions. He shook something loose in you. It happens to the luckiest of us."

"You're not the first one to tell me how lucky I should consider myself."

Derrick closes up the box. "Needless to say," he says "the cops started sniffing around again last year after the bones were found, but they found no scent here. Most of his stuff I burned. I'm not just a romantic, I guess; I'm a sentimental fool, given the risk. I thought of you, believe it or not. I thought, he'll want to put that boy's shirts on. He'll want to run his fingers over the letters he formed on the pages with his own hand, the sentences of the notes he took for his research paper on the Peloponnesian War, his doodles of giraffes and sailboats and sharks. The directions he scribbled and tore out and left on the passenger seat of his car. He'll want to curl up at night with the little teddy bear."

He's right.

"I think we take what we can get and then we convince ourselves it's enough," Derrick says, "until something shakes us loose." He flicks off the mirror.

Early evening, the sun shifted so that no light at all comes through the cracks and slats in the walls of the windowless shed. Iris expects him soon. Maybe she's already made her way onto the porch of the farmhouse to look for James's car. He checks his phone: no messages, no missed calls. He picks up the box and wraps his arms around it, holding it tightly to his chest. His instinct is to hide it, bury it on his plot of land somewhere, in a safe spot he'll always know how to find. Then he remembers that nobody is looking for these items anymore; he and Derrick are the only ones for whom they are legible. Can he wear the EARTH DAY 2005 shirt to bed and claim to have found it while packing for the move? Make up a story about that April weekend seventeen years ago, when he'd planted trees for charity, weren't you there, Iris? Of course he can. If it will help him sleep in peace, James can lie his way into and out of anything.

He's standing beside Derrick in the darkness of the shed, the box in his arms, ready to go, when it happens. Derrick is twisting open the cap of a water bottle he's pulled down from the shelf. Both men are silent in their thoughts. Then the car horn in the Toyota sounds—one long sustained honk, like the jerk behind you in traffic the second after the light goes green. The sound makes them jump.

"What the fuck?" says James, but the noise—loud, sustained, insistent—a howl, a whine, a wail—swallows his words.

"It doesn't do this," Derrick says. He rushes toward the front of the car, but when he reaches the driver's side, the horn stops. He places his palm on the steering wheel and applies pressure and the horn sounds again until he takes his hand away.

Leo first heard of Awkworld when one of his crushtomers at Wilder's, a woman named Lily, showed him short videos she'd posted of herself painting her toenails. Lily's feet were jacked-up with corns and bunions, her skin cracked over bulging blue veins, but in the videos—she called them "Awks"—she lovingly painted her hammertoes a bright, sparkly pink as she exorcised her shame with stories from the roads of her life on which those weary feet had traveled. The Awks lasted only a few minutes, but by the end of the first one, Leo was as moved as he was turned on, and into his mind came immediately the shames and triumphs of the rough roads he himself had traversed from his mother's house to the foster home at Aunt Alice's to the split-level he now shared with Bonnie. From Katie to Leo. From schoolgirl freak to boy-toy cub. Twenty-five years old, and Leo's history already felt vast. He signed up on the spot for an Awkworld membership, which gave Lily a referral star; paid the not-small monthly fee meant to keep out assholes and abusers (an impressive percentage of which went to progressive causes); and became Lily's 607th follower. That was three years ago. At last count, she had over 500,000 and counted Birkenstock among her sponsors.

Awkworld started as a nonprofit online Environment created by and for people "like him" who either didn't fit any identity or affiliation category, or who checked so many boxes that no single comprehensive category existed for them, or who just felt singularly awkward in the world. Unlike in every other Environment, the goal wasn't to seamlessly integrate your awkward self with products and businesses and experiences aligned with that awkwardness, or even to hook you up with other awkward selves for love or companionship or sex, but simply to give you a voice. Every other Environment urged you to perform and perfect your best self in your best words, videos, and images; Awkworld claimed to celebrate the messiness of you. Your embarrassments and kinks. Your mistakes and sadnesses. Your terrors and traumas.

For most of Leo's adult life until then, he tried to stay offline as much as possible. The last Environment-type account he had on a handheld device was TikTok on his Android, back when people still called it social media. He didn't miss it. The IRL small-town pool of queers and weirdos he and Bonnie swam in, with their karaoke nights and bowling leagues and potluck dinners, was a satisfactory amount of human connection; anything beyond those weeknight gatherings exhausted him. For a while he'd been flirting with the idea of an ayahuasca retreat, a purging of lifelong griefs and ugliness, as a way of cleaning the slate, but otherwise Leo was happy enough—safe enough, satisfied enough—until Lily and her craggy toes came along.

For those first few months of his subscription, Awkworld truly felt like another small-town friend group of misfits, except these friends talked only of their minor and major betrayals, secret sexual attractions, party fouls, and OCD-type obsessions. Leo was mesmerized by their nakedness and openness. The rawness of their souls. All over the world, people were suffering in a zillion small and unnecessary ways; they lugged their suffering around with them like a box of stones; now they had a shelf to put that box on and display it for all to admire. It didn't make Leo feel less alone, which was what the Environment claimed was a big part of its mission; it made him worry he wasn't maximizing his life. That he was, in fact, wasting it. He used to think working in a vintage bookstore with a robust used section and discounts for students and seniors was making a noble contribution to a country hollowed out by greed and self-interest. His biggest dream was that Mrs. Wilder would sell the place to him someday, and then Leo and Bonnie could expand it into the Laundromat next door, or—better yet—combine both businesses into one called Books & Bubbles or Wash & Read (finding a better name was the first step). That biggest dream came to seem so paltry, though, his hope so low, as Plath put it, it was comfortable.

He quickly came up with a username—🙂LeoTheThird🙃—but it took him a while to muster the courage to make his first Awk. The rules were strict. If an Awk seemed scripted or acted, like a rehearsal for fame or Hugs or a pandering to sponsors, the Awker accrued Scrub Points. An unknowable proprietary algorithm determined how many Scrub Points was too many; at any moment you could be Scrubbed Out, your fee unrefunded, banned from reentering the Environment for six weeks. On the flip side, the more authentically messy and brave you seemed, the more Hugs you earned. Hugs made you more visible, unlocked other benefits, and, inevitably, gained you more followers. Leo told himself he wasn't in it for the Hugs, but once they started coming, along with the messages at all hours in all forms, he understood their addictive power. If he chose to use an HMD, as most Awkers did, he'd get a warm jolt at his temples with every new Hug. For now, though, the earbud and old-fashioned screen on his phone, the muscular arms emoji embracing a pulsing orange heart, were enough.

His first Awk, "Iron Man" (8/1/2034, 1:00), got way more Scrub Points than Hugs. It started with a still shot of the iron-shaped scar between his shoulder blades from the night his mother tried to "warm him up." He'd been eight or nine at the time, lying on his stomach on the shaggy living room rug, coloring. Too old for a so-called girl to be shirtless. Probably too old to be coloring. His big brother was dead, unable to protect the kid he'd known as Katie. Their mother was just playing a game, it was an accident, but she was so fucked-up she didn't realize the iron was still hot when she pressed it onto Katie's flesh. As a story, it was just right for this Environment, but the Awk itself was too staged and too shy: the stationary camera zooming in and out on the scar for exactly one minute, the disembodied voice-over. People needed a face to connect. Pain lived in the eyes, not the skin. A minute was nowhere near enough time to capture them all: Patricia, Katie, Leo.

He tried another, "Cougar & Cub" (9/14/2034, 1:43), about his thing for older ladies, and the looks he and Bonnie got, the annoying questions. He didn't blame Bonnie for refusing to be filmed, but the Awk would have done much better if his thirty-six followers could have met her. Bonnie! Who could meet that woman and not give her a Hug? The thing was, Bonnie was the least awkward person who ever walked the earth. She belonged everywhere *except* this strange Awkworld. All of Bonnie's pieces added up: her cute blond bowl cut under her baseball cap, her fanny pack of mints and energy bars and towelettes, her Venus dimples, her mezzo-soprano singing voice, her twin daughters who were both nurses.

"Unfit" (9/28/2034, 2:02), a Huggier version of "Iron Man," was Leo's turning point. In this Awk, he spent two minutes wordlessly squeezing into the frilly white blouse and tartan skirt of his old Sacred Trinity uniform. He hadn't planned this; he'd just been going through some old boxes. But there he was in the garage, bearded and unbound, his tears overtaking him as he tried to push his thick arms through the sleeves, as the fabric ripped at the seams, as the zipper busted going up the side of his leg, as the snow blew through the open door. He balled the fabric, brought it to his face and breathed it in, sobbing and shivering in his boxers with the little skulls on them, forgetting the camera was even on. Because you think you're a big strong man. You think you're living free. You think Bonnie's the antidote to millennia of human anguish. You think the two of you will have a good life together—years of companionship and copulations, trips to the Florida coast, the launch and then franchising of Clean Sheets Book-o-Mat, walkies with their dachshund, Constance—and that along the way you will complete the return to your pre-birth uncorrupted Self in his fullest form. But what if you'll also always be just a fat girl running from the school bus? What if someone will always be chasing you, shaking you down for your money or your life? These were not the words Leo spoke in the Awk, but this was what the Awk said.

Meanwhile, capitalism was busy licking the asses of Awkworld's otherwise benevolent founders, and it was starting to resemble too many other money-grubbing Environments raking in corporate dollars via lucrative sponsorships. The bar for authenticity got lower and lower. It took worse and worse behavior to get Scrubbed Out. People gave out Hugs like they were free (though they no longer were). Now when Lily, the woman of the goblin feet, came into Wilder's, she had a haughty air about her as she fingered the new hardcovers. Of Awkworld's corruption she sneered, tale as old as time. She herself was the founder of a respected nonprofit chamber choir now considering a program of Beyoncé covers to reach younger audiences, i.e., losing its way in service to the almighty donor dollar. No one seemed to know the way. So, for a time, Leo gave up making Awks. The relative success of "Unfit" was a blessing and a curse. He worried that the border between offline and online was getting blurry. He paused his membership to Awkworld, resumed his flirtation with ayahuasca. One of his chattiest followers, 爿Virago 😊, zapped him a code for a retreat in Peru called Arkana.

Then one day Leo saw a WXOW story about a hometown boy who'd gone missing from his college. For a week nobody could find the kid, whose name was Arvin Ackerman. A blond meathead type, like the corn-fed boys who'd teased Leo back at Sacred Trinity. Arvin's parents flew out to Carnegie Mellon, but by the time the plane landed the boy had turned up dead in the Ohio River. Arvin looked nothing like Leo's older brother, but they used the same words for him—*angry, sullen, troubled, detached, falling behind, forgotten*—as if the words themselves answered the question.

At Wilder's, Leo switched on his camera. He grabbed his brother's copy of *Michelle Remembers*, which he kept under the desk at all times, but, other than that, he didn't think the Awk through too hard. Sticking to the Environment's original ethos, he rambled through a barely coherent three-minute version of what he'd told

Margaret Mead Ashe in their first few sessions five years ago, when he was a kid just out of high school finding his way in the real world. The MANOWAR T-shirt. The journals of his brother's self-hate Aunt Alice finally allowed him to read when he turned eighteen. The same hooded man who came for him after he'd strangled Leo to death. The turned-down branches in the woods behind Light of Christ. The sick joke played by fuckwads in the trussing-up of the body. He called it "The Drawer" (4/9/2035, 3:07).

Leo's 808 followers were already familiar with MMA, as he referred to his therapist. They knew she'd been the first to recognize him as himself, to call him by his proper name, and then to help speed along his return to his pre-birth Self. They knew his panic attacks started getting better once he embarked on that return, and that they'd kept getting better on the journey. But they didn't know about his brother, Leo, because, until now, he'd kept him to himself.

"The Drawer" earned Leo a lot of Hugs, but also an explosion of questions: did 🙂LeoTheThird🙃 really believe his brother Leo (the Second? Junior?) was communicating with him from the beyond? That there's no rational explanation for the disturbances? Did he think he himself could be his own brother reincarnated? If naming the trans self is a political act, a kind of argument, what did 🙂LeoTheThird🙃's naming himself after his brother signify? What was the argument? And how did all of this connect to the Smiley Face Killer(s), who, they reminded him, had never been caught?

You're missing the point, Leo explained in the follow-up Awk, "Sad Face" (5/1/2035, 2:34). His brother, Leo, had not been the victim of a nonexistent mafia of serial killers, but of untreated anxiety and depression. Of pranksters probably high on meth. Of a shitty mother. An absent father. Big Pharma. Crimes as old as time.

And no, Leo added, in "The Watch" (5/4/2035, 2:48), the follow-up to the follow-up, drawers don't fly open on their own. The tips of branches don't turn themselves down as you approach them on a trail; they don't send you scrambling down a ridge, nearly falling on your ass, to a spot where you find a watch poking up from the dirt, a watch you wear every day. See? It still ticks. In "Light of Christ" (6/18/2035, 5:22), he brought them, his now 18,000 followers, patient and adoring, to the very place. He sat on a rock on the bank of the Rum and read "Patterns." He read "Mystic" by Sylvia Plath. He read a few underlined parts from *Michelle Remembers*, a book no one remembered.

In "Debts" (7/4/2035, 4:09), he riffled through the accordion file of documents he'd saved from Aunt Alice's funeral and the sale of her house at 447 Ashby Lane, all of which added up, give or take a few pennies, to zero dollars. The reverse mortgage, the unforgiven Sacred Trinity bill, the visiting nurses he'd hired so Aunt Alice could live until the end surrounded by all her remnants in the house she loved and in the bed she'd shared with Sue Ellen, while Leo himself, pre-Bonnie, lived 150 miles away in La Crosse in a studio across from the Spaghetti Warehouse.

In "Dolley Madison" (8/15/2035, 5:00), he took the bus back to Saint Paul and sat on the stoop of a newly resided 447 Ashby, the shutters cranberry red, a kid's dirt bike lying flat on the front lawn. Just before she died, said Leo, Aunt Alice made Katie promise to discard all of her remnants, and Patricia's and Leo's and Sue Ellen Armitage's, too, not because those people no longer deserved respect, but because the girl would have enough burdens in her life and didn't need to carry her dead aunt's around as well. You'll inherit this house, she'd told Katie, and if she truly desired to thank her properly for taking her in and raising her as right as she knew how, her first order of business should be to sell it, move far away, and keep only a single item that gave her a happy memory of her aunt Alice. Would you do that for me, Katie? she'd asked, and, in the Awk, Leo clutched the doll.

In "Kiss My Name" (10/22/2035, 3:20), he said yes, I do have an argument. His brother was the only good thing about his childhood, the only true happiness he remembered, sorry, Aunt Alice. The only source of joy. That presence. We have so few ways to hold on to it. Remnants, like this watch, Aunt Alice's way. Tributes, like these Awks, little tombstones. Fine. They're fine. But his name! His name Leo could never lose. It can't fade. The Salvation Army lady can't take it or leave it, can't say, *no, that's not you.* The name will lead Leo all the way back to the pre-birth Self. And once he gets there, who knows? Maybe he won't need it anymore. But, for now, he does.

Leo replies to every single message he gets on Awkworld and on his personal Environment, Starksville, population 230,000 and growing. Bonnie worries that his followers and cohabitants find this desperate, even pathetic. These days especially, when everyone is so easily findable, and when people rarely interact with anyone they're not already connected to on at least one platform, you get more cred for aloofness and unreachability. For mystery. You also attract better sponsors. But mystery has never been Leo's brand, and aloofness isn't his click, and he didn't start out telling stories to make money or to hide from people. The opposite. Reachability was and still is the point, and, until he posted his Smiley Face stories and his reputation exploded, he didn't have so many followers that replying to them felt like a burden. To every video message, he dutifully sends back a video message in return, usually from behind the checkout at Wilder's when it's slow. (It's always slow.) To text comments and questions he dictates quick first-thought-best-thought responses into his earbud, either on his drive home or after Bonnie falls asleep or on morning walks with Constance. To the images his followers generate just for him, he generates images back, though lately he just recycles the prompts.

Meanwhile, the border gets blurrier and blurrier. Leo knows it's unhealthy, that he's in danger of disappearing himself into his Environments. It's only temporary, though, he tells himself, and besides, he's making a shit-ton of money, not just from all the Hugs but from the Shatterpoof and Electric Fetus sponsorships. He's doing all this not just for himself but for Bonnie and Constance and for the big dream of Clean Sheets Book-o-Mat, which might just need a bar and restaurant while they're at it. Leo even has a name for the place: Current Location. Because now, more than ever, we need to be reminded that we exist in a Space, and in the Now, and in that current location we are most happy when we've got a book and a whiskey and a basket of fries and clean underwear.

He answers messages late into the night. He buys an expensive

HMD, then tosses it as soon as a faster, lighter model comes on the market. He sees less and less of Bonnie, less of their friends. But it's worth it, this packaging and purging of the past, this building of the future. This buzzing blur. Bonnie understands. She's always encouraged him to find his people. It is, itself, a kind of return. He has all the energy of youth and all the time in the world, and he's becoming a known commodity. And he's helping people, or so people tell him in their messages. Making them feel less alone. Giving them hope.

Like there's this older man, 🌵JimmyH🌲, seventy-four, down in Raleigh, North Carolina, who, ever since "The Drawer" went up more than six months ago, has been Hugging Leo at the Premium rate. Over all that time, though, he's sent Leo only a single video message, one he then deleted before Leo could view it. The guy's home Environment is bleak: no images and no Awks of his own and a few dozen followers. Every time one of his Hugs gave Leo the jolt, he wondered what his story was.

Which is why as soon as Leo notices a new video message from 🌵JimmyH🌲, flashing red for New and Premium Follower in a constellation of static blue messages, he opens it. And then, with just a blink of an eye, the old man appears:

> Hello to you, Leo. My name is Jimmy, and I'm one of those people obsessed with the Smiley Face murders. I understand why you don't believe in them, but I do, because a young man I knew very well might have been one of the victims. Some monster or monsters drugged him or something and left him for dead. That's what I think, at least. We still don't know any-

thing for sure. It was almost thirty years ago, and we still don't know who did it.

I remember your brother, Leo, from 2016. Such a long time ago, but I can still see his face in my mind. The long hair, the piercing on his lip. They tried to make him sound so scary, with all the drugs and the black clothes, but I could see the goodness of his soul. I saved all the clippings of him. I can zap them to you here if you want, but they're nothing new, you probably have them all. I'm not a detective, I'm an archivist. I was an archivist, for my job. I'm retired now and my wife died and I don't do much of anything, but I found this "Environment" after a friend—another "weirdo" obsessed with this stuff—told me you were famous on here saying you're Leo Ridgeway's one surviving relative. I'd been looking for you for a long time to ask you a question and then I go on here and I find out not only did you answer the question, you answered it better than anybody.

The way you always make fun of us "Smiley Face Weirdos," you probably won't believe me or even respond. I've started and stopped so many of these videos to you. I'll probably delete this one, too, before I have the courage to send it. But I think you'll want to know that he visited me, too—not Leo—I mean my friend, the one who was killed. Listen: it's not just you and your brother with this special bond. It's all of them. I've talked to their loved ones, the ones I could find, the ones who would talk to me. They pretty much all say the same thing: they've heard from their boys. Gotten some sign, like the drawer and the branches. But yours is the clearest. You can say they're kooks, fine, but that would make you a kook, too. It's too much of a coincidence, right? Because I don't think if you asked any random person if their dead loved one visited them, they'd immediately say yes the way these Smiley Face people do.

I know you're going to say nobody killed your brother. I must have watched your "Sad Face" Awk a dozen times. It answered a question I always had about Leo. His story didn't sit right with me from the beginning; something was off. Turned out I was right. But I don't think it matters that he wasn't one of the "real" victims. There's a connection anyway, among these boys. I'm sure of it. They were targeted, or targets; they share some other common bond besides turning up in the water. It adds up but it also doesn't.

You might not realize how lucky you are. Leo sent you a message, and you understood it. The rest of us didn't get that. The signs aren't as clear, or we can't read them. My signs don't come anymore. What makes you so special, is what I'm wondering. Why you and not us? Why Leo and not my friend? It feels unfair. Do you have any thoughts on this? If you did, you probably would have said so by now. You say a lot. These days there's no such thing as an unexpressed thought. I keep waiting. I check every day to see if you've got a new Awk. So far, nothing. But I bet you're making a lot of money. I hope I don't sound rude. I do feel terrible about your brother. It breaks my heart to think of a boy so young giving up on himself.

My friend's name was Caleb. Caleb Aldrich. What does it matter anymore if you know his name? That you know mine is James Hahn, that we were lovers? He only visited me once, in a shed in Vermont, but even that was enough. If I told you about it, would you help me understand? I wish we lived closer, or that I could get around better. I have money, but I don't travel well since hip surgery and then knee surgery and then my wife died—I'm sorry, nobody wants to hear all that. To be honest, I never really went anywhere even when I could. Don't make that mistake. You're young. Let Bonnie take you somewhere nice. You talked about the Florida coast the way Caleb and I used to talk about Montreal, except we never got there. Don't make the same mistake. Get yourselves to Florida before it's too late. Life changes so fast. You think you have all this time but you might not.

I knew I'd go on too long. Believe it or not, I practiced this message. I made notes on actual paper! I'm still not used to modern modes of communication. I miss the days of letters and emails. I like that you work in a bookstore. You seem like a fine young man, an old soul, like your brother. You deserve a long life. Please don't give up, and please be careful, okay? You don't have to believe in something for it to get you. If you have time, please send me a message back, but you don't have to. You probably hear from weirdos like me every day.

Leo switches on his HMD and blinks a Reply to 🌵JimmyH🌲. The old guy's story touches him—especially the part about his dead wife—even though, in this line of work, a dead wife story is as common as a story of a son or a brother found floating in the water. In the long queue of messages that wait for Leo, he'll likely find another lonely man asking him to reassure him of what he already knows to be true: that the shadow passing across the ceiling above his bed isn't from a bird or the branches in the wind but from the woman who shared his bed for thirty years.

Of course it's your Julia, Leo will confirm; sleep easy now; she's watching over you.

Lately, it seems, everybody is seeing ghosts. Leo didn't start it; he just helped people find their glasses. He reads and watches and listens to their sad stories, then tells them what they most want to hear. He's in the business not only of self-authorship but of radical comfort. It does no harm.

When it comes to Jimmy, Leo is much too busy to stop and consider whether his brother had any connection to Caleb Aldrich or to that other first wave of Smiley Face guys. He believes in elaborate connections—in patterns at least, even in conspiracies—but he's less interested in the pattern itself than what it reveals about the patternmaker. Each man deserves his own reality. He won't say this to Jimmy, though. In fact, it would be cruel to deprive the man of his myth-making. Instead, he says, *maybe you're onto something.* And: *if you find out anything else from the Smiley Face families, will you let me know?* He's sorry about his friend Caleb, he says, and he means it. (He briefly looked up the kid, who seemed, at first glance, harmless and naive.) He thanks Jimmy for his financial support and his kind words about Leo Jr. and encourages him to keep in touch. He promises he'll take Bonnie to Cocoa Beach someday—*sooner rather than later!*—and then on to Cape Canaveral. She has a thing for rockets, he tells him. He'll make an Awk down there, he promises Jimmy, and dedicate it to him and Caleb, without using their names, of course. *Thanks again*, Leo says, *and good luck!*

They still have one full week left in Sperlonga, but Monica is already on edge. She hears the way she's been barking at Shane the past few days, and at Stefano and Amy—the gentlest of Shane's helpers—and though she always apologized right after, and has tried to be more mindful and patient, here she is again, on their heavenly stretch of Italian beach, barking. This time, again, at Shane, swimming out past where her brother anchored the *Carissima*. "Grab my sandals! No, not those! The pearly ones! No jumping! *Stai attento!*" Her voice a screech. Is she always this harsh, this hard? In Boston—that city of thin lips, stiff backs, vinegar eyes—her hardness is understandable, expected, but not in the gauzy beauty of Here, not on the happy occasion of Now.

The sea at Sperlonga is translucent. There is almost no border between water and air. Whether Shane is pulling himself up onto the stern of the boat or submerged in the ocean frolicking with the other fish, Monica can still make out the checkerboard pattern of his suit, the pink burn of his Binswanger skin, the glint of the gold cross around his neck. She can't take her eyes off him, her child cavorting in the body of a man. No. She's supposed to be working at that, too. Her son is not a child; he is eighteen as of two weeks ago—a man—and a man is a man no matter the childlike structure of his brain. Monica is still a woman and still a mother, of course, but the mother of a man and the mother of a child are not the same animal. The mother of a man has been moved to a different wing of the zoo.

These pearly sandals, a gift from Arthur. August in this six-room villa, a gift from her brother Marco. Shane's gold cross, a gift from their mother, for protection. Grown men still need protection, apparently. More protection than Monica's mother ever offered her.

She agreed to the month in Sperlonga, and to Shane's birthday party on Lucio's *Carissima*, on the one condition that their mother, Giulia, not make an appearance. Monica has forgiven her brothers, and even her dead father, for their neglect of her childhood and their indifference to her American family, but she will never forgive Giulia. Women—mothers—are the levees in the boiling ocean of life; you have to hold them to a higher standard or you'll be cooked alive. This is, perhaps, the reason Monica has had so few of them in her life.

She's self-aware enough to know that she falls far short of her own standards. If she met Monica Binswanger at a party, she might admire her teeth, her skin, her bearing, her savvy, her easy throaty laugh, her hand on your shoulder as she talked to you that made you feel like the only person in the room, but once she got to know Monica? What was behind those smoky eyes? A struggle to care. Indifference to the suffering of millions, to the flooding coastlines, to the disintegration of civility. She single-handedly saved the Boys & Girls Club of Boston, but she has only a passing idea of their actual impact on the lives of children; same with the Sunflower House (dementia) and the Rinsler Foundation (cancer) and the ACRJ. What do those letters even stand for? What does she?

Shane, of course. She stands and will always stand for Shane. You can accuse Monica of shameful acts, of indulging her wildness and even her wickedness, but you can't accuse her of the kind of neglect and abandonment she herself endured in the Alberti house, under Giulia's watch. Even so, her so-called friends, those Other Mothers, have looked askew at her since the day Shane was born, and now, like in a fairy tale, their faces have permanently frozen that way, contorted in distressed judgment. *That* doctor, are you sure, Monica?

Not Ingram, who worked such wonders with my Wylie? That many hours in the pool? You let him eat what? Stay up until when? Did you say Selwyn Academy? Not Mercer? This kid from Dorchester, where'd you find him again? And, finally, the biggest question, the greatest crime, how could you ship that sweet boy off to Pine Mountain like damaged goods? How could you give up on him? *And then she complains about her own mother*, said their sideways faces. *What a hypocrite. How spoiled.* Meanwhile, Monica framed Shane's art and stuck it on the walls of their country houses and charged them a fortune for the privilege.

This is what the last laugh looks like, she thinks, at dinnertime, when her son appears on the terrace of Marco's villa in a blue linen suit. Alberti linen, of course, another of her banished mother's gifts. Guilt works wonders, too. Shane makes for a handsome man. Tall beyond genetic reason. He smiles and bounces on his bare feet. Balls and unballs his fists. Throws his arms around Arthur's neck and nuzzles the side of his head. A happy man who now has some words for his happiness and for the meanings behind his pictures, however abstruse. He can also tell you what he wants to do with his life: marry Amy, swim the English Channel, get more followers on Awkworld, and teach young children to paint and sculpt (though sculpture is his toughest medium). Shane doesn't always use his words, but when he does he means every one of them and demands you take them seriously. Monica can't say the same about herself or anyone else, certainly not the Other Mothers. Back in Boston, on their leafy prep school campuses, their sons' and daughters' boring brains are molding them into little stockbrokers and tax attorneys and AI engineers. They'll move away at the earliest opportunity, rent corporate apartments in New York and Hong Kong, send fruit baskets at Christmas. But in one week, Monica's son will be moving back home to live with his best friends—his parents—where he belongs.

Still, despite this good fortune, she's on edge. In anticipation of Shane's imminent return, she's spent more time in the guest wing in the weeks before Sperlonga—sketching plans, painting and stenciling, supervising the arrangement of new furniture and carpets, the installation of an art studio, a bigger shower—than she has in the past ten years. She replaced every pillow, every quilt, every lamp, every book on the shelf so that there would be no trace of the kid from Dorchester. Not a stray sock or a pair of boxers stuck between the mattresses, not a little swirl of ginger pubic hair. The only concrete evidence he ever existed was his half-empty can of drugstore body spray, which Erma found in a Walgreens bag under the bed and left discreetly in the top drawer of Monica's office desk. The spray that smelled like cheap *balsamico*—peppery and syrupy sweet—was all that remained of him until the day she got rid of that, too.

His actual smell: grass, milk, the faint trace of ammonia. You must be part dog, he used to say. You must be a bloodhound. She misses him telling her who she was. She misses playing Fetch. Guess What. Italian Buffet. She misses his dick. He was her gateway drug. Her game changer. Her prime mover. She is and will forever be grateful to him for bringing Shane to life, and for leading her back to Arthur. She wishes he hadn't slipped and hit his head on the rocks and died; but didn't that itself open up a space, and make the next part easier? If, ten years on, he rarely enters her mind, and, when he does, she feels mostly gratitude and relief, does that make her cruel, or does it mean she's finally settled?

After him, Shane had Samantha and Stephanie and then the staff and a gaggle of friends at Pine Mountain, and now he has Amy.

After him, Monica had Jason and Zach and Mike G and a few forgettable others. She never invited these men to the Hacienda, and they never met Shane. They gave her no rings; they never professed love—only affection, desire, eagerness, interest. They accepted payment via the Environment where she met and selected them. They lived on the other side of a border nobody crossed. She learned her lesson. Guilt worked wonders.

Here, in Sperlonga, the familiarity of Arthur's body, her knock-kneed and blotchy husband soaked in Amouage, his soft belly, his coffee breath, is its own thrill, made more thrilling by the strangeness of him fucking her in her brother's bed to the distant soundtrack of *Kung Fu Panda 6* playing for local families on the public beach. Something old with something new. A comfortable transgression, a transgressive comfort. When Arthur flies back to Boston, he leaves her with the usual licenses and "only ifs," but she can barely recall the last time she indulged herself. Mike G? She doesn't once think of entering the Environment. You know you're free when freedom no longer turns you on.

One night she and Arthur were seated across from John Forsythe at a fundraising dinner for some charity she can't remember. It was during a time not long after the body washed up, when Monica was less settled, more skittish. She avoided making eye contact with the man—she couldn't not think of him as "Mr. Forsythe," couldn't not hear Steven's voice reverently saying his name—through the obscene centerpiece arrangement of magnolias and pussy willows between them. Then, just as the program began, he came over and crouched beside her, his hand on the back of her chair.

"You were his boss, weren't you?" he asked, by way of introduction.

"Yes."

"How are you holding up? And your little boy?"

Monica shrugged. She took a sip of wine to steady herself, unsure what he knew. "It's been incredibly tough, to be honest. Not so much for me and my husband but for Shane." When she was finally able to look directly at Forsythe's face, it was resplendent with Goodness. She felt accused. "How are *you* doing with it all?" she said quickly. "It's been such a shock. He really looked up to you. You did so much for him."

"Likewise," he said. He rubbed his eyes. "In my line of work, you see kids come and go all the time. Good kids, 'bad' kids, it doesn't matter, they're chunks of your heart. You think you've seen every tragedy, but you haven't. I try not to let it make me hard. But sometimes I wish it did. And Stevie was special, wasn't he? Don't you think he had something?"

Monica nodded.

Now he smiled. "If you ask me, I think he had a little crush on you. The way he lit up every Monday—"

"Oh no," she said, startled, blushing. She waved him away.

"Don't worry," he said. "By Tuesday he was lit up on someone else."

She took another sip. "Boys," she said. She leaned back to let Arthur in.

"I don't think he ever wanted the three of us to meet," Forsythe said to both of them. "He was afraid I'd hit you up for money. And he was right! But I won't do that now, even though Open Dor could really use your support. What would it take to get you to come by?"

"We donated generously to the boy's scholarship fund," Arthur said. He turned his attention to the program. "It's good to meet you."

"Of course," said Forsythe. He looked at Monica. Raised his eyebrows. Flashed a conspiratorial smile. *Go through the wife*, he must have been thinking. *She's always the easier target.* In this case, he was wrong.

A few years after that, she got a strange call from the uncle in Palm Springs. Owen Something. Not Donovan. The mother's brother. A man had contacted him asking questions: have you received any messages from your deceased nephew? Have you noticed any disturbances in your house, any odd sensations on your body? Have you felt sometimes that he's in the room with you, that you're not alone?

Owen had not, he'd said to the man, and now relayed to Monica. Owen was hypersensitive to disturbances of any kind; he had some undiagnosed OCD issues and required order and objects in their rightful places; he knew his increasingly decrepit body like he knew the exact location of his records and vintage films, some of which were on reels. Besides, he said, his nephew *was* in the room with him. The best roommate, exceptionally quiet.

The man on the phone hadn't laughed.

Owen loved a good mystery, he told Monica, and he loved when the phone rang in the middle of the afternoon, which it rarely did anymore unless it was a heat advisory or a notification to pick up his prescriptions or a cop asking for donations. Plus, he was a chatterbox; sometimes he made a donation just so he could spend a few minutes in the company of the cop's deep voice. So he kept this inquisitive man on the line—Jimmy, he'd said his name was, from North Carolina—and let him fill his head with all kinds of crackpot theories and weird "coincidences" and ghost stories. Jimmy promised to send Owen news reports and documentaries and transcripts from conversations he'd had with loved ones across the country who'd lost boys to the water. That's how he phrased it, said Owen, *lost boys to the water*, like it was *The Blob*.

Owen told him that he did vaguely recall how, when the police first notified him that they'd found his nephew in the Charles, they mentioned the possibility he'd been the target of a serial killer. The idea had made him shudder. But then, not much later, they relayed the findings from the coroner's report: Steven Donovan was just another drunk chucklehead who'd lost his life from pissing in the river. Was Owen relieved or disappointed? Embarrassed? Probably all three, if he was being honest. Anyway, he figured this Jimmy from North Carolina was either barking up the wrong tree or just a kook, one of those lonely conspiracists with too much time on his hands and nobody to talk to. Jimmy asked who his nephew had been close to, if he had any enemies, if he knew of anyone else in the Donovan family who'd been "contacted." But Owen had virtually no information to impart to him. He was sorry to disappoint the man, but the truth was that his nephew was a stranger to him. Owen was merely the steward of his ashes, by way of a blood connection. The rest of the boy's family was dead. His Donovan side was a bunch of rotten eggs, no bother trying to contact them. And I'll be dead soon, too, he said. Bladder cancer.

The conversation got Owen remembering his teen years in Dorchester "in the Mesozoic era": the fried clams at Castle Island, matinees at the Franklin Park Theatre, cruising the Esplanade at dusk. It got him wondering what his nephew's life had been like. He assumed it was hardscrabble, but what had he done for fun? Did he have a girlfriend? A boyfriend? Hmm. It was strange how seldom Owen thought of the boy, whose urn he took down and dusted once a week along with his other memorabilia. They'd only met in person a handful of times, and never under happy circumstances. He remembered him as a chubby little redhead, sullen, smart-alecky. One of those kids who made you grateful you don't have kids. It felt wrong, all of a sudden, a moral failing on his part, that he'd never taken an interest in him. And if he was being honest, it did spook him a little now, after the man's call, this stranger in his house, this boy lost to the water.

So Owen made inquiries, which was so easy—"too easy"—in this modern era. Everyone, alive or dead, was in plain sight. A few clicks and *bam*, there they were. All roads led to that guy John Forsythe. Of course! How could Owen have forgotten that name? Blake Carrington himself. The Angels' Charlie. He blamed his chemo brain. Or maybe a touch of dementia? It all came rushing back to him: the lawyer who'd handled his brother-in-law's estate back in the day, who'd tried to cut Owen a check from the sale of their old single-family home on Stratton Street. But Owen refused the check; the last thing he needed was money, and he was too superstitious to accept profits from tragedy. Better to set up a fund for orphaned boys or something, put his nephew's assets in deserving hands. What a terrific idea, said John Forsythe, and reminded Owen what he surely already knew, which was how great Steven was with kids, what a big kid he was himself. We'll call it the Donovan Fund, he said; I'll take care of all the details.

And that was the last Owen had heard from John Forsythe until just recently, when it took four days to get him on the phone. His report on the progress of the Donovan Fund brought Owen to tears: as of January 1, 2024, it had helped more than twenty-five young men afford college. These were men Forsythe knew well, who'd grown up at his community center, who were disadvantaged and troubled but had promise that might have gone unrealized. All the good his nephew had done for the world, Owen thought, and he didn't even know it! Shouldn't Forsythe have put him on a mailing list or something? Sent him annual reports? But Owen didn't ask. Forsythe struck him as a very busy man and very serious. His appointments were booked in fifteen-minute increments. No way could Owen bring up disturbances and messages from the beyond. Instead, he thanked John Forsythe for his time and made a Farrah Fawcett joke he regretted and asked offhand if he had any names and numbers of people who'd known his nephew.

One of them, of course, was Monica. Owen apologized for going on and on like this to her. What, if anything, could she tell him?

As far as she knew, Monica told him, his nephew didn't have a girlfriend. She clarified that she was only the young man's employer; they weren't in the habit of discussing their romantic lives. What she did feel qualified to say was that he'd had a transformative effect on her son, Shane, who'd adored him. That he worked hard, put in the hours. That he was responsible, devoted. Yes, *devoted* was the right word, for sure. For his devotion she'd be forever grateful. And no—she laughed—he'd never tried to contact her. Or her son. It would be nice, though, wouldn't it, if that sort of thing were possible? If he could give Shane a fist bump now and then, let him know he was okay up there?

Yes, it would, said Owen.

The good news, Monica said, was that Shane had stopped asking about his former tutor after just a few months, and now, as he entered his teen years, he seemed to have forgotten him completely. He'd had a few tutors since—the current girl, Stephanie, was in med school at BU—and Monica considered it unhealthy to remind Shane he'd ever had anyone else. She was Italian, she explained, raised never to say the name of the person you'd loved and lost. Better to pretend he never existed. She was sure Shane grieved, in his own way, to himself, but that was as it should be. Good practice, unfortunately, for life.

You got me thinking about him again, though, she admitted to Owen. I have fond memories. When he was here, my house had an energy it hasn't had since. Stephanie is good, but the house isn't the same. One thing that's ironic, which I can tell you about, if you want, is that your nephew was a very good swimmer. He and Shane spent all their time in the pool, and I personally watched him do all sorts of acrobatic moves. He could hold his breath so long underwater it made Shane cry with worry. I'm not saying that means anything. Only that it's ironic. And sadder, somehow. But I can't explain why.

His best friend was named Archie, Monica remembered that.

Have you talked to him? And his favorite band was called Blue Sunshine. What else? He said he wanted to learn Italian, she said. Maybe move to Italy one day and apprentice to a chef or a sommelier. But honestly, he only mentioned that once. I never knew how serious he was.

Walking alone now past the sign for Sorella Beatrice in the town of Sperlonga, Monica feels the urge to confess everything. Not to Owen—the man's long dead by now, the whereabouts of his nephew's ashes not a thing she can ever know—but to someone, anyone. It's a familiar urge that has come less frequently with each passing year, but still it comes, unbidden as a craving. To satisfy it, she's told pieces of the story to people who don't care enough about her to care: Mike G; gay Kurt from yoga; the avatars in online chat rooms for the nonmonogamous, sex-addicted, or polyamorous, though she doesn't belong in two out of the three.

I have one amor, she wrote to the poly room; *the rest are just toys.*

What are you doing here then? some user would always ask her. *What do you want from us?*

Monica could never quite say.

On the "Am I a Sex Addict?" quiz, she scored a 3 out of 10. Only the 4s and above were advised to seek help.

Once, she wrote out a list of everything a woman her age could hope for, and next to every item she put a check mark. She already had them all. It terrified her.

The right room for her is out there. Sooner or later she'll find it.

Sorella Beatrice has been on Monica's radar since she arrived in Sperlonga. From what she can gather from the local gossip and the

Yelp reviews, she appears to be the closest approximation to Madame Oana, the mystic who guided Monica through her teen years in Zurich more responsibly than her teachers or any Alberti had done. The only other option in the little town, Divina Ombretta, set up under a tent near the lighthouse, was an obvious scammer.

Sorella Beatrice kept odd hours and didn't take appointments, so there was often a line in front of her door just off the Piazza della Repubblica. Today there is no line. A sign.

"Do you come in joy or sorrow?" is the old *strega*'s greeting.

Right away Monica takes comfort in Sorella Beatrice's accoutrements: the jeweled rings clotting her fingers, her deep wrinkles, heavy makeup, gold eyeglasses wide as a welder's, hair wrapped in a blue turban pinned with a sunburst above the center of her forehead; her room of tapestry-covered walls, curio cabinets, wide shelves crowded with candles and glass eyes and framed sepia photographs; the two carved wooden chairs facing each other in the center, just inside the entrance from the street, where she can hear children playing and a man hawking olives and cantaloupe spears from his wagon.

"Those are my only two options?" Monica asks, with a smile she hopes comes across as friendly. It's as important to get psychics to like you as it is anyone you need a favor from. "*Gioia o dolore? Felicità o tristezza?* There's a whole ocean in between, no? That's where I am. The middle of the ocean." She forks over the hundred euros required for a one-hour session. "I can't imagine what kind of person comes here in joy."

"A woman on her honeymoon!" says Sorella Beatrice. "A woman with a new baby! To share these happy occasions with a loved one who's crossed over!" She kisses the two fifties, smooths them with her hands on the marble table, and leaves them there between them. "But you're not either of those women."

"No," Monica says. "I just want someone to talk to. I have a guilty conscience. But I don't know what my crime was. I'm hoping you—or someone, through you—can tell me."

"Your parents?"

"My mother is still alive."

"Is she?" She looks more closely at Monica. "Give me your hands."

She lets the *strega* hold them. She gives her full name, her date of birth. The woman wants no more information than that, and scolds Monica for saying too much already. She wants to prove her authenticity to her, to establish trust. So Monica waits, regretting this act of self-indulgence, blaming it on the renovations of the guest wing, which dredged up pointless memories, as Sorella Beatrice, eyelids fluttering, chest heaving, summons the available spirits.

Already she misses Madame Oana, who took in seventeen-year-old Monica, homesick and lonely and wandering the streets of Zurich, and let her talk as much as she wanted about the family she left behind in Rome, the mother she called out for in her sleep. Madame Oana used to stroke the tender skin on the inside of Monica's arm with her long fingernails, which sent pleasant shivers all through her body, and let her cry on her satiny shoulder. She let Monica curl up on her daybed in the back bedroom on the afternoons she skipped classes. I see deep love in your future, Madame Oana would say at the end of their sessions, and this love will set you free. You'll meet him very soon, she said, and, I promise, when it happens, you won't come looking for me—or your family—again.

Sorella Beatrice's breathing has slowed to a steady deep rhythm, then a snore. Her hands go limp. "Signora?" Monica asks. "Are you awake?"

Her head jolts backward and her eyes flash open. "No!" she says. "Do not disturb!"

"I'm paying you to sleep?"

The woman looks crossly at her. Sometimes, Sorella Beatrice explains, with haughty impatience, she needs to enter a dream state in order to reach the spirits. This is bad news for the seeker, unfortunately; it means the spirits are either very distant, crossed so far over that they can't find their way back, or that they are too preoccupied to give her the gift of their time. It can also mean they have forgotten the person who summoned them, or never knew them at all. "I don't like to do this," she says, "but I must ask you for the name of the person you want to contact."

"Steven," says Monica. "Steven Francis Donovan." The words feel strange on her lips, like a language she studied in high school but hasn't spoken since. "There's no way he forgot me. He loved me very much, but I—"

"Shh!" says Sorella Beatrice, squeezing Monica's hands so hard she cracks a knuckle. "Too much noise!" Then, so quickly it looks fake, she shuts her eyes and slips back into her snoring dream state.

The night Monica got drinks after yoga with gay Kurt, she confessed to him the games she once played in the upstairs room of her house, years ago, with a twenty-one-year-old redhead who worked for her a couple days a week. If you tell only one part of a story, you can always get the response you need from a person. It's not dishonest to leave out the rest of the story if the part you tell is completely true. Then the part itself becomes the whole story, and feels brand-new, and who doesn't like a brand-new story? In this case, she got all the details right: the oiliness of his face and back slicking her own skin, which even her expensive creams couldn't keep moisturized; the pummeling he gave her, the first few times, until she taught him ways to work her into a full-body shudder; what a quick study he was of those ways, so eager, such a good memory; the thrill of catching his smell on her when she lifted her arm to put it around her husband's shoulders later that night as they watched TV.

"You little slut!" said Kurt, which was the response she knew she'd get with the right part of the story, the response she needed at the time.

With Kurt, she even used his real first name. That way, in the bar on Boylston across from the yoga studio, Steven was still alive. One Monday he just didn't show up for work, she said, and, no, she never found out exactly what happened to him. Yes, she wished she could track him down, but it was probably for the best that she didn't.

"You're my hero," said Kurt.

With Mike G, she played "Right as Rain" through the Bluetooth speakers on the alarm clock on the bedside table at the Verb Hotel. A young man who loved me used to play this song for me, she told him. For a little while she believed she loved him, too; she entertained fantasies of exploding her life for him. But then she realized, with something like a jolt, that it wasn't the boy himself she loved, but the woman she was when she was with him: reckless, puckish, filthy, ravenous. "Like you are with me," Mike G said, and turned her over, which was—it occurs to her now—the response she'd been after.

There's no point in telling Sorella Beatrice the whole story from the beginning. They don't have time, and, besides, what's the beginning? The day she watched Steven from her bedroom window, shimmying out of the cabana in her swimsuit? The moment he grabbed her wrist, his fingernail slicing a pink comma into her skin? Or does she need to go much further back, past Arthur's visit to the first and last business class she took at BU, past her lonely hours in the arms of Madame Oana, to the years of her girlhood when she moved invisibly through the musty rooms of Villa Alberti, knocking over candlesticks, begging to be seen?

"Steven is speaking to me," says Sorella Beatrice now. "He tells me he's been trying to reach you for a long time. He tells me he misses you."

"Okay," Monica says.

"He still loves you," she goes on. "He will never stop. Forever you will be in his heart, but—" She shakes her head.

"But?"

"But—you must forget him," she says. "Let him go."

Monica narrows her eyes. "Are you sure?" she asks. She's no fool. These are the standard messages. The last words are the only ones she knows Steven couldn't possibly have spoken.

"It's very noisy," says Sorella Beatrice. "A lot of static." She covers her ears. "He's alone most of the time, he says. You were the only one who understood him. But he's not angry."

"He was always angry."

"Then he's not angry anymore," she says quickly. She goes quiet again, scrunching her face, biting her painted red lip, like she's constipated. "He is maybe . . . the type who says few words?"

"No," Monica says. "Not at all."

"Hmm," says Sorella Beatrice. "As I said, it's very noisy. He's so far away. I may be misunderstanding him, or he might not want to say more. He was—very young when he crossed over?"

"Yes," Monica says, relieved.

"But—Steven was your son, Signora?"

"No."

"Strange," says the old *strega*. "His voice is like a little boy's. Like he doesn't know all his words yet."

"He was an adult," says Monica. "Twenty-one, but like a big kid."

"Ah yes," she says. "A big kid. It's a tragedy when a young person crosses over. But the tragedy is ours. Not theirs. Your heart is upside down but his soul is at peace. He watches over you and your son. You haven't felt his presence at all?"

"No," she says. "I don't think I'd know how."

"But you've been trying? You call out to him, you dream of him, you talk to him in your head?"

Monica looks at her. "No."

She listens another little while, and then she nods her head. "That's your crime," she finally says to Monica. "But you knew that before you walked in, yes? The reason for your guilty conscience. Obvious. It's not so terrible a crime. Most people are guilty of it." She squeezes Monica's hands, gently this time, like a good mother would. "He tells me he forgives you for that."

"He never forgave anybody," Monica says, rolling her eyes. "He had too much pride. You've got the wrong guy on the line, Sorella. My Steven knew how to hold a grudge. If he's really been watching me, if he were really in this room—which I don't even believe is possible, if you want to know the truth—he'd be fucking furious. He'd want to punish me. Strike me down with a bolt of lightning."

"Is that what you've been waiting for?"

"Yes!" Monica says. She stands and grabs one of the fifties. "What's taking him so long?"

Saturdays are for washing the truck. Sundays are for God. Fridays are for dinner and a movie, with a date if Lori gets lucky. If she doesn't, she goes solo or asks Gus to tag along and that's fine. The weekdays are for work. Thirty-five years at Grayson's, the last eight as full-time store manager, the last three with her holidays and weekends guaranteed off. It's in her contract.

Laundry on Tuesday nights. A standing 6:30 p.m. mani-pedi appointment at Marie's on Whip-'Em-Out Wednesday, the first of the month, when they're twenty percent off. Hair on Thursdays every two months at Gina's next door to Marie's, across from the Shell station owned and operated by Vincent, who insists on running out to squeegee her windows when she fills her tank, Vincent who she'll say yes to if he ever mans up and asks her out for another Friday-night movie.

Saturdays are also for the library. Lori drives over in her gleaming F-150, catches up with Naomi at the circulations desk, then peruses the new-arrivals table and what she still calls "books on tape," though even CDs are long obsolete. At Grayson's she listens to books all day long on her company-issued HMD and none of the customers care or can even tell; most of them are on their own HMDs talking or taking meetings or watching their shows as they drop soda cans and bags of string beans into their carts. Naomi knows to suggest only happy and healing stories for Lori—romance novels, Christian fiction, self-improvement—and often has a few titles at the ready to get her through the week ahead. Once in a while, Naomi persuades her to give another celebrity tell-all a try, but, in Lori's opinion, these writers—most biographers, actually—do too much padding, like, who cares what Taylor Swift served at her wedding brunch? That's not the "all" Lori wants her to tell.

True crime was once their go-to. Hers and Naomi's, not to mention the ladies in the Moms of Mystery Environment, formerly the Moms of Mystery Book Club, which hosts a meetup Lori used to faithfully attend on the first Thursday of the month back before Matthew disappeared. All these years later, it still makes her physically ill to remember the bloodthirsty hours she spent drooling with those women over the missing and murdered bodies of innocent boys and girls. The jokes about taking notes on how to mutilate their ex-husbands and daughters-in-law and get away with it. Their pride, their arrogance. Lori the proudest and most arrogant of the bunch. No one will ever be able to convince her that her own son's murder wasn't punishment for those deadly sins. She brought tragedy upon herself and her son by making him into a little god, a false idol, all while luxuriating in the misfortunes of unlucky lesser humans. By believing he was untouchable. Not even Fr. Wright disagrees with her. These words are mostly his.

Sundays are also for Matthew, which means driving the forty-five minutes to Ann Arbor. First to his old apartment on Elm Street, then down Geddes to the butterfly-and-hummingbird garden in Gallup Park, where the university put up a stone with a bronze plaque in his name. She then walks over the wooden planks and mud to the exact spot he was found, near the marker that says, in both English and Chinese, MAY PEACE PREVAIL ON EARTH.

The marker was not there in February 2020. It showed up a year later, a gift from the Rotary Club to the city and to Gallup Park. Lori used to imagine the killer coming back here and laughing at the words and at the placement of the marker, twelve steps from where he stood with his boot on Matthew's neck, watching him drown.

There are monsters in the world, she knows that much. There's been almost no progress since biblical times. Sundays are for praying that God will punish the monsters adequately. Life in prison won't be enough for Kenneth Rafferty, because life is just the beginning. The eternity that follows, that's what Lori prays for. That's where his true hell will begin.

Mostly she prays for God to nourish the soul of her son. This, though, feels less like praying and more like thanking Him for fulfilling His promise to her as a woman of faith. By allowing Matthew to contact her, God has given her no doubt that her son is enjoying his divine reward, that he is saved. Finally untouchable. Finally, in His mysterious way, home. No matter where you find Lori Cardullo on the days and nights of her week, she'll be striving to summon that gratitude in the storm of all her rage.

Which is one of the many reasons why, at first, she refused to let WDIV interview her for the ten-year anniversary. Give it to God, Fr. Wright advised her, and you will be free. Don't shed any more of your precious blood for the thirsty vampires on earth to drink up.

Don't gratify those who court suffering. But then the same counterarguments were made to her, as they'd been made every other time a reporter or producer had approached her: the more attention Matthew Cardullo received for his innocence, his promise and intelligence and beauty, the longer the flame of his memory would be kept alive not only in the state of Michigan but all over the country. The world! And then, decades from now, when Lori was dead and Kenneth Rafferty was still in prison lifting weights and earning his master's degree—privileges he'd denied her son by his own hand—the parole judge would see these films and show the monster no mercy. Didn't Lori want that most of all? Wouldn't she do everything in her power to ensure that the full course of justice would be served? Yes, she would, it turned out. She always would.

The first interview was scheduled for Saturday, April 6, at 2 p.m., ten years to the day they found Matthew in the Huron, five years since Rafferty's sentencing. On Friday night she puts on a classic movie she's seen a hundred times—*La La Land*—then another—*Bridesmaids*—to force a laugh, to calm herself, while she assembles the usual photographs: Matthew as a baby, Matthew in high school holding a wrestling trophy over his head, Matthew's senior portrait still in its silver frame. She looks through the documents she keeps in labeled folders on her tablet like she's reviewing material for an exam. She rereads the messages she sent back and forth with Jimmy in North Carolina. The next morning, she wakes up an hour early, scrubs and waxes the truck, pays Naomi her usual visit, and gets back in plenty of time before the news van arrives.

She used to make a pot of coffee and set out doughnuts for the reporters and cameramen, thinking that if she made a good impression, if they thought she was a nice lady, they'd work harder on the story; and that the harder they worked, the better it would turn out, and the sooner Matthew would be found; and that the sooner Matthew was found, the greater the chance he'd be found alive. You need a really good story, with the right images and camerawork and voice-overs, to make people care about anybody but themselves. To get them out of their houses combing the woods for a stranger. To make them remember. Now she is giving this part to God, in whose hands it has always been anyway. She washes and puts away the breakfast dishes; she tears open a package of Little Debbie's; that will be enough.

SYDNEY SHARP, WDIV: We're here in the home of Lori Cardullo, mother of slain University of Michigan junior Matthew Cardullo, whose body was discovered at Ann Arbor's Gallup Park on this very day ten years ago. For nearly two years beginning back in 2020, the mystery of Matthew's disappearance, the strange circumstances of his death, and the trial of his killer, disgraced officer Kenneth Rafferty, captivated the greater metro Detroit area. Thanks to the excellent work of local detectives, Officer Rafferty is currently serving a life sentence for second-degree murder at the Ionia Correctional Facility, also known as I-Max, albeit with the eventual possibility of parole. Mrs. Cardullo, first of all, how are you doing?

LORI CARDULLO:

SYDNEY SHARP: I understand this is difficult. We know it's been a while since you've had to sit for one of these interviews. Maybe we can start with an easy question. How old would your son, Matthew, be if he were alive today?

LORI CARDULLO: Matty would have turned thirty years old this past December eighteenth.

SYDNEY SHARP: That must be hard to believe. I know it is for me. As I mentioned to you before we started, Matthew and I were at UMich around the same time. I remember being in my dorm and seeing police cars all over campus. I didn't have the pleasure of knowing your son, Mrs. Cardullo, but I see you've brought out some photos of him for us. Could you show them to our viewers, maybe tell us a little bit about what Matthew was like?

LORI CARDULLO: All right, well you can see here what a good-looking boy he was. What you can't see is how smart, the smartest in our family. Both sides of our families. He did honors his senior year. His father used to call him *genio*, Italian for *genius*. Gus and I weren't school people, but right away we saw that Matty was. Everybody saw it, his teachers, his coaches, the kids in his class. He could have skipped a grade but we wanted to keep him normal. He liked the regular things for whatever age he was at: trucks, sports, girls. It wasn't until high school that he started really getting into old heavy serious things that set him apart, that made him special, like Latin and the Roman Empire and Napoleon. History. Ancient shipwrecks. And wrestling, that's an old thing, too, he used to remind us. He knew the history behind everything. He was perfect, if you want to know the truth. A perfect young man blessed by God.

I'm not just saying that because I'm his mother. When you ask his teachers and coaches and friends they'll use the same word. And his father will say *genio*, like I already said. Matty had plenty of guy friends and the girls were all after him and he had not one single enemy until he met—I won't say her name. Or his, the killer's.

SYDNEY SHARP: Kenneth Rafferty. Tessa Timmins.

LORI CARDULLO: Neither one of them's a human being as far as I'm concerned. But what I've realized the last few years—and I want you to make sure to put this on the air—is that no matter what they say, the reason for what happened was they were jealous of how perfect he was. They couldn't stand it, having somebody that perfect alive. They claimed they were just trying to scare him off, that it was an accident, that things got out of hand, and a bunch of other lies, but deep down they knew what they were doing. Both of them. He wanted to be as perfect as Matthew was, but he knew he wasn't. The thing is, Matty will *always* be perfect. And that man will never be. Not even close. He will always be garbage.

SYDNEY SHARP: Those are strong words, Mrs. Cardullo. Please take all the time you need to—

LORI CARDULLO: I'm fine.

SYDNEY SHARP: All right. You're doing great, by the way. Now I'm wondering if you're ready to take us back to ten years ago around this time. How much of that period do you remember?

LORI CARDULLO: People say it's a blur but I remember every minute. Even the first few days, after the weekend, when I didn't believe he was missing. I said he must have met a new girl and let her drive him up to the lake house; it wouldn't be the first time; they lost power up there; they were snowed in; they'd be so embarrassed when they got back. Denial, I guess, or "magical thinking," whatever you want to call it. Matty had always been so independent, so intelligent; I never worried for one second about him. He was the man of the house since he was a boy. And, you know, he'd just won a big match with his wrestling club against Michigan State the night before; I assumed he was off somewhere celebrating. Then he didn't show up for class on Monday and practice on Tuesday and all of a sudden the nightmare began and Gus and me were on the phone with the cops and the detectives ten times a day. We had people here in this house at all hours. I slept at the station more than once. We were doing those search parties all over campus where you walk in a line with long sticks in the freezing cold in a foot of snow. So many volunteers showed up, so many sweet young people who knew Matty and plenty who'd never met him.

Little by little, though, the volunteers petered out. People were getting scared. It was COVID times, if you remember. Then, overnight, everything stopped because of the lockdown. They called off the search, even though the search was outside, where there was no virus! That was our bad luck. More bad luck. The police will lie and tell you they still worked day and night, even sick with COVID, they didn't stop, but I was *there*. They stopped. They were scared just as shitless—excuse me—as the rest of us. Of course it didn't matter anyway. Matty was already dead. It took until April 6, today, to find him, but they were able to figure out pretty quick that he'd died in February, that same weekend he went missing. When they told me he had boot prints on his forehead and on his throat, I thought that would lead us straight to the killer, that you could identify the type of shoe, but it was a common shape and pattern. And then we lost so much time with that Smiley Face stuff—

SYNDEY SHARP: Tell the viewers what you mean by Smiley Face.

LORI CARDULLO: Does that matter? It wasn't real.

SYDNEY SHARP: It had some bearing on the case, though, as you mentioned. It caused even more of a delay—

LORI CARDULLO: Because of *him*. But fine. The police had three pieces of "evidence" that made it look like a serial killer had done this to Matthew. There was—still is, probably—a theory about "Smiley Face Killers," these men who'd been roaming around for twenty years targeting college-aged boys. None of them has ever been caught. The first piece of "evidence" the cops had was a yellow spray-painted smiley face on a rock upriver from where Matty washed ashore. This was supposedly the serial killers' calling card. The second piece was that Matty had the drug GHB in his system. The third was that his body was found face-up with his arms across his chest, which isn't a normal way to float if you drown from falling down drunk and hitting your head on a rock or if you kill yourself, which is what other people wanted us to believe at first.

So for the first part of the investigation, the detectives had three theories going: drunk accident, suicide, or Smiley Face serial killer. Any idiot could see that none of these made the least bit of sense. The graffiti could have been on that rock for months or years already. Two of the guys in the wrestling club admitted to doing GHB at the victory party the night before, though neither of them saw Matty take it. There were a bunch of reasons why a body might be found face-up and arms crossed. But people *wanted* the serial killer stuff to be true—I understand that from the average person, I used to be one of those people, but shouldn't cops' eyes be clearer? They had all these crackpots online claiming they saw something, bored at home during lockdown calling in tips to the police, saying Matty's case was like the case of the drug addict in Saint Paul or the blond boy in Vermont, and the cops ate it up. Meanwhile, those two monsters were trying to get their stories straight, deleting their text messages, pressuring their friends to lie with them, planning to escape to Canada. People remember the text messages because they were all over the internet, but they forget those came from her friend who ratted them out. After that it all came crashing down on the two of them like a house of cards: the girl's lies, the cop's excessive-force conviction years before. It's pathetic, when you look back, how bad they were at it. Like I said: garbage people.

SYDNEY SHARP: Am I right that it was later revealed that it was Officer Rafferty himself who first floated the Smiley Face theory?

LORI CARDULLO: At the trial, that's right. He—they; the girl never gets enough blame—I don't care that she wasn't there, that he supposedly kept her in the dark at first. *They* did everything they could to push the Smiley Face stuff; that's the only way it was like the Saint Paul boy. *They* dumped Matty in the water just to make sure he was really dead. *They* stomped on his neck and held his head down for so long there was no way he could survive. *They* crossed his arms over his chest. *They* weighed him down even though that never works, even in the cold water. The body always comes up. And then they ate Kung Pao Chicken in a Chinese restaurant and left him in the Huron, where he rotted for more than a month while the cops were all cozy on their couches watching *Tiger King*. That's why he should have gotten first-degree, and they should have tried her as an aider and abettor, not an accessory after the fact. Just because she got scared and guilty and took a plea deal only when the jig was up shouldn't spare her full punishment. But I don't write the law, I just follow it. That's what quality people do. That's what Matthew did.

SYDNEY SHARP: Kenneth Rafferty will likely spend the rest of his life in jail. Tessa Timmins was released on good behavior after three years—

LORI CARDULLO: She's still young enough to have her own children. That's what burns my ass—excuse me. I don't care that she was only twenty years old, that Rafferty was some kind of predator—that's an adult woman who should have known better. I don't care that she flipped, that she cried over Matty, that she begged for forgiveness. Just because I'm a Christian doesn't mean I'm obligated to forgive or have even one ounce of sympathy.

SYDNEY SHARP: She—Tessa—claimed your son had been abusive to her. That Officer Rafferty acted out of self-defense. Matthew was very strong—

LORI CARDULLO:

SYDNEY SHARP: Mrs. Cardullo, I'm just trying—

LORI CARDULLO: You should be ashamed of yourself. Nobody believed a word that girl said. She broke his heart, and he was trying to win her back. He came on strong. He was passionate. The Italian side of him. A man should be allowed to be a man. It was bad back then, and it's even worse now, how the boys get treated. You can't put a rock on a flower and expect it to grow straight. And you say he was strong? That cop had a gun. How strong can you be against a gun? What wrestling move could he make against a gun? Shame on you for bringing this up. The judge didn't believe her and neither should anybody else. If you put this part on the air, I'll sue you for slander.

SYDNEY SHARP: I'm sorry, Mrs. Cardullo. You have my word.

LORI CARDULLO: I don't trust you. You look too young for this. They used to send Gail Benjamin for these interviews.

SYDNEY SHARP: Gail retired in 2027.

LORI CARDULLO: She was a professional.

SYDNEY SHARP: I assure you I'm acting in good faith, Mrs. Cardullo. I'm just trying to do my job. I'm twenty-eight years old; like I said, I went to school with Matthew. I have a master's in media studies from Penn State. The goal here isn't to dredge up bad memories or to put a stain on anybody's good name, only to provide context when necessary. You know the types of pieces I do, right? You said you'd seen me on WDIV before?

LORI CARDULLO: Maybe I did, I don't know. I don't remember. I don't watch a lot of news. I don't have the stomach for it anymore.

SYDNEY SHARP: That's fair. I can't say I blame you. I urge you to watch my stories, though, if you can. The one that aired last week, on the Estonian refugees? I'm very proud of that one. I try to focus on the positive. Serious but positive is my motto.

LORI CARDULLO: Okay.

SYDNEY SHARP: And we're almost through, I swear. I was hoping we could talk about the past five years since the trial, since everything's been settled. If you're willing. Only what you're comfortable with. I have a date with Gus later today, and I've already got some nice footage from a couple of Matthew's old teammates, and—I don't want this to come as a surprise—I might include a clip from Tessa's mother, too, who I know has tried to reach out. You and Matthew are the focus, though. *Matthew* is the focus. My stories are just a few minutes long, but we need a lot to get those minutes. I'd love for you to tell me whatever's on your mind, but—you know how this works—I can't make any guarantees about what will and won't end up in the piece. Only that I'll give you the last word.

LORI CARDULLO: This is how I know you're young, because you use those words *settled* and *comfortable*. It's okay, though. I hope you never understand why those words don't apply to me anymore. Or Gus. Probably to her mother, too, I don't know. I can't think about that woman. I'm sorry, there's just not enough room in my heart.

You want to know how the last five years have been. There are things I could tell you, but I won't. You'll put it on the air even if I ask you not to, and people will laugh at me and say I'm the pathetic one, that I'm a nut. So I'll just tell you Saturdays I wash my truck and go to the library. Sundays I go to church and visit Matthew. The rest of the week I'm at the same grocery store—the Grayson's on Cortland Street—where I've worked my entire adult life. For a while I did two, sometimes three, jobs to pay all the bills that piled up after everything went to shit. Excuse me. Now I'm debt-free. But I'm not settled.

A few months ago, a young man came into Grayson's and bought a bouquet of white roses from the floral section. I couldn't resist, I asked him who they were for, and he said nobody; his grandmother had told him once that a surefire way to get women to smile at him was to carry around a bouquet of flowers, and it worked! So that was how this young man spent his days when he felt lonely or a girl broke his heart, just walking around with a bouquet of flowers in his hand, letting the smiles of women heal his wounds. He'd even gotten a few dates that way, he said.

Of course that made me think of Matty. I started to call him right then and there to give him that grandmother's piece of advice.

I wanted to tell him there were women everywhere ready to smile at him, to ask him who those flowers were for, and if they did he should say, *oh, these are for my mom, just because*, and then she would say, *oh my gosh, how sweet*, and then they'd be off and running. I wanted to tell him life could be so easy for him. He was on a track. He thought what he had with that girl was love, but it wasn't. Love was the trophy at the end of the match, but the match wasn't over yet. *Get up!* I wanted to tell him. *Get UP!* In the few seconds it took to swipe that young man's credit card, I said these things to Matty in my head, and then I sent the boy and his roses on their way. I stood at the window and watched him walk proudly down Cortland, and sure enough, his grandmother was on the money: every woman and girl smiled at him. Even the men kind of nodded at him in a friendly way. I imagined he was Matty, of course, not some boy I'd probably never see again, because for me it's always and forever Friday, February 21, 2020, and he's still walking around somewhere alive, still holding his head high. Not a single day has gone by since then.

✷ZAP CALL✷ from Mia Richter

Mon, Apr 8, 2030 at 9:01 PM

Hey

MIA
Jesus Christ

I know

MIA

You okay?

Yeah I guess

MIA

You don't look okay

Where are you?

It's so dark

My mom's

Walking upstairs

Keeping my voice low

MIA

Did she watch?

On the edge of her seat

I told her they'd cut her out

Anything that makes me look human

MIA

I'm sorry, Tessa

It's Saint Matthew all over again

I mean I get it

How can I *not* get it by now

Still—I hoped maybe this time

With Syd in charge—

MIA

You'd get fair treatment—

I'd settle for *equal* treatment

But it's never gonna happen

MIA

You don't know that

Should I have talked to her?

She left like a hundred messages

MIA

No

You've been down that road

My mom couldn't call her back fast enough

Got her hair done and everything

MIA

She just wants people to know the real you

Not this version of her daughter that's been in the news for ten years

---

And she's a drama queen

MIA

And that

It's all I want, too, but it's impossible

Every time I try, it blows up in my face

MIA

I mean I feel that way at my school?

By the time I get my eighth graders they've heard all these stories about me from the years before, like they've *literally* got my number

---

No offense but that's so not the same thing

You'll never know what it's like

MIA

I know, I'm just—

Even the women in Ypsilanti

Most of them, they get out, move a few towns over, nobody's heard of them or what they were in for

They tell their story the way they want to, no preconceived notions, or they just don't tell it

Me, though, I meet people, and if I decide they're worth confessing to, most of what I end up doing is correcting and explaining, super defensive, and when you're explaining you're losing, right?

Cause they're all, "ohhh" and "really??" and "hmm" and "that's not what I heard," totally unconvinced, and then guess what, all of a sudden they're super busy, they don't text me back, they go cold.

Not all of them, but enough of them

Like there's this new guy, Ethan, I met in St. Augustine. We danced and made out at some Irish pub and exchanged numbers.

Told him I don't do social media or Environments because they're full of liars and they kill the soul

To him I'm Tess Griffin from Gainesville. Now we chat and Zap and send pix and make plans, etc. etc. But when do I tell him my real name, my whole story?

First official date? Fifth? Before or after we fuck?

Meanwhile my paranoid self is sure he already knows, that I'm this joke he has with his buddies, that maybe he even recognized me at O'Briens or whatever it was called and is getting off on it.

You try living in a glass box and see what it does to your psyche

---

MIA

You never talk about this

Because there's no point

MIA

I'm so glad you got out of Michigan, though

No matter what, that stuff has to be easier in Florida

Yeah everybody here's got a conviction or two haha

And the team's great, I don't think the girls give a fuck if the coach did time as long as we win

In fact I think it scares them in a good way

And we're fucking *winning*

MIA

That's so great

You think Matt's mom will really sue Syd?

Doubtful

Plus that wasn't slander what Syd said

It was documented fact

The judge just "deemed it irrelevant"

I get that too

But it's the part of the story no one talks enough about

Except to say, "if Matt Cardullo was so scary, why didn't she report him to campus police? Why didn't she tell her adviser?" Such bullshit

---

MIA

Ugh

Yeah that's not relevant to the law but it was relevant to, like, *your life*. To *truth.*

Exactly

MIA

Syd should have had those other girls on

Yeah right

It still wouldn't have mattered—

That was always the thing with Matt

Nothing he did ever went *beyond* beyond, you know?

He was just *too much*—he gave you a feeling, you knew he was over the top, but you ignored the feeling because technically nothing he was doing was "bad"—

All I had—and all those other girls had—was the *feeling*, and that's not enough

---

MIA

Chloe's "Spidey-sense"

I need to get one myself

I totally didn't feel it with Matt

You always liked him way more than I did

MIA

Chloe used to say, "Tessa loves him but she doesn't actually like him"

Is there some reason you've dropped her name twice in ten seconds?

MIA

Sorry—old habit

Sometimes I forget we're not still in college

The *only* good thing about being a criminal is that you find out who your real friends are

---

MIA

I just think—

Mia don't

It's fine you're still friends with her, but like my therapist says, "no one's entitled to your forgiveness"

They have to earn it, and Chloe has not

MIA

Okay

I wasn't trying to get you worked up

Wait, are those *dolls* behind you?

My mom collects them—don't ask—creepy as fuck, right? When I sleep here I cover them with a sheet

---

MIA

I swear one just winked at me

The one with the teacup

Oh yeah Elsa—she's a flirt

MIA

She can tell I have no Spidey-sense

None whatsoever. But guess what, you also never blamed me for anything that went down

You put the blame on Ken where it belonged and will *always* belong

You're like the *only* one who did that from the beginning even when you had to lie and I'll never forget it

Not even my mom did that

MIA

You know I love you girl

Nothing was your idea

You were like under his spell

And we were scared as shit

You didn't deserve any of it

Neither did Matt to be honest but that's not the point

That's what I mean, you can say that about Matt and it doesn't bother me because I know where it's coming from

When other people say it, talk about how sad and tragic it was—and it fucking was, he didn't deserve to get killed, he wasn't supposed to get killed—what I hear is, ***it's your fault***—no, not just that, what I hear is, ***it should have been you***

MIA

No way, Tessa, why?

Oh come on

A dead girl's on the news every day

Between the weather and sports it's oh by the way, this girl got the shit beat out of her

They splash her senior portrait on CNN for ten seconds and maybe there's a podcast about her life except the episode is super boring because the story's always the same: jealous boyfriend, wacko stranger, was she just stupid or something, did she ask for it, she shouldn't have traveled alone, etc. etc., totally predictable. Maybe she gets her own Environment dedicated to her memory but it's *nothing* like what the boy version of her gets

---

MIA

Maybe

You don't think there's something special about a dead beautiful boy? Something that hits different? All that potential, all that strength gone to waste? He doesn't even have to be captain of the football team or all that good-looking—

Check out the Smiley Face Environments if you've got a spare million hours. They're like altars. The girl equivalents are like pornos. And then in the same breath the people are like, "now she'll never be a mom, which is all she ever wanted."
In 2030!

MIA

If she was white yeah

And if *he* was white, then *of course*

Okay yeah fine that's obviously what I meant

I'm white, you're not, I just know what I see

MIA

If you're saying we care about white guys more than white girls, and every other boy more than every other girl, then yeah, no shit, that's been true forever and will never change. You're not just realizing this, are you?

It just gets back to: I think I'm entitled to some sympathy, too. I earned it. I fucked up, yeah, but I came clean. Eventually. And I got punished for it anyway, and I took my punishment like an adult.

MIA

You did

I was naive. And both guys—*both* guys—did me dirty. One was a stalker, one was a predator. Because that's how I pick 'em. So I was a victim, too. Not a monster. The more I say that, though, the more I explain about the plea deal, etc. etc., the more people hate me. Like I said, explaining equals losing.

MIA

Nobody hates you. Well, Lori Cardullo hates you. But nobody else, nobody who matters.

That's not true, but thank you

MIA

I hate that this show was on tonight. What was the point of it? There was no new info. Who's it supposed to help?

Not me.

Sydney Sharp, I guess

She was always kind of stuck-up

MIA

What do you think Lori meant, *there are things I can't tell you*

Who knows

I try not to think about her

But I do, like I *still* do. It's weird. I dream about her more than Matt

Even with all the shit she's said about me, I feel terrible for her

And so guilty

MIA

Because you're a good person

Yeah, I guess

After a while, you start to believe all the worst things about yourself, question your entire identity, your *soul*, because of what some troll you've never even met says or posts about you. It really does make me want to call Syd.

MIA

Don't. Really. You should just forget about her. And Lori. And the trolls. Focus on you. On Tess Griffin. Your new life. You're not even thirty yet. *We're* not even thirty.

I'm thinking Tess Griffin is forever twenty-nine haha

For four more years at least

MIA

Haha yeah why not? You should get those years back.

Make up for lost time. Look forward only. Speaking of which, when can I fly down there? School's done for me June 14

You know girls were sending Ken love letters? Nobody sent Tessa Timmins any love letters.

MIA

Yeah, it's sick. Did you even hear what I just said?

Anytime before 4th of July. It gets brutal down here after that.

MIA

We need to talk at least once a week, okay? I worry about you.

I'm fine. Honestly. Am I not always fine?

LAST SEEN (III)

We are those boys they keep finding in the river. I floated alone on the surface of the Huron, trapped between ice and sky, my arms hugging my chest because I was terrified, until I heard their voices. Caleb. Leo. Steve. Fellow soldiers telling stories, crying, calling out in the dark to their mothers and fathers, to James and Katie and Leo and Monica, who couldn't hear them. Us. Then we were pulled onto shore, delivered into the arms of Miranda Nelson, chief medical examiner of the Washtenaw County Health Department, and Ernie Evans of Washington County, and Kelly Munson of Ramsey County, and Jim Macone of Suffolk County. When we get solved, it's the men and women of the counties who do the work, who box us up and feed our stats to spokespeople, who spit them out for the reporters, who splash our names and faces across the front pages of the *Detroit Free Press* and the *Burlington Free Press* and the *Star Tribune* and the *Globe*.

Until we know the end of our story, we can't trust the beginning or the middle. What we see coming toward us is just a trick of the eye. Our lives. One trick after another. We fall for it every time. Fuck it up. It takes forever to see a life for what it was, and, lucky us, we've got forever, me and Caleb and Steve and Leo and the other boys lost to the water. Lost and found, two simultaneous states of being, like Liam Auslander, dragged just today from the Des Moines River in Emmetsburg, Iowa. Like this skinny kid Ben who still won't tell us his last name or where he's summoning us from, only that he can hear sirens coming closer. Like the keys and phones and baseball caps in the gray plastic bin behind the circulations desk of Shapiro Library at 919 South University Avenue in Ann Arbor, Michigan 48109, where I didn't show up for my 10 a.m.–1 p.m. shift on Sunday, February 23, 2020, because, in the early hours of that morning, Officer Kenneth Rafferty drowned me in the river.

I am still going over every detail, still trying to hold my life together. I don't look in on my mother anymore. I've trained myself on myself. Like I said once—when? Who was I talking to? Who am I talking to now?—*don't think too hard about the people you miss.* Treat them like they're Roman kings and emperors. The guys who never stop crying are the ones who can't learn that simple lesson, who don't have the self-control and discipline I learned long before I got here, not just from wrestling but from studying Latin and the Classics. What I like about Greek and Roman history is that it's finite. I can't change it and I can't be blamed for it, not only because it happened centuries ago, but because I had nothing to do with it. It didn't touch me. My job as a student, as best I understood it, was to memorize it and analyze it, like a doctor looking at an X-ray. If I worked hard enough and read long, dense books and research articles and went to lectures and took notes and kept my brain filled and fired up, my interpretation would be just as valid as anybody else's.

I'm not Caleb. I didn't dream of "making" history. I didn't hope to play some big part in the future. If I dreamed of anything, it was of making the *present*, of dominating the *moment*, like knights did in the Renaissance. My studies taught me I wasn't special, that my particular historical present had already occurred an infinite number of times before me to men just like me, and that it would keep recurring. *Leave me alone then*, was my message to the world, which really meant leave me alone with Tessa or with my opponent on the mat, not just alone with my books and my Jeep, though honestly most of the time that kind of alone was okay, too. I rarely got lonely, but when I did, I just went by Tessa's, or I invited myself to my mom's, or I headed out to Bahna, where Justin or Travis was always around to spar and shoot the shit with. That's it, that was my sliver of life, which happened to be the exact life I wanted.

I had a plan to teach college kids to love the Classics and analyze them right back to me and make their marks. I wanted to start a Classics Club, like the Wrestling Club, to attract higher enrollment so the major didn't die out at UMich. Virgil and Ovid and Aeschylus have the worst PR! Like I said, I didn't dream big. My hopes were low. My ambitions and expectations were reasonable. I'd already been given my pot of luck, and I was hyperaware of hubris and Fate from studying the Greeks. I believed in my innate goodness, though. I wasn't religious in the way my mom was, juiced up on saints and sacraments, but—I can admit this much now, why the fuck not—deep down I did secretly trust in some version of her Almighty God, whatever form He took. I believed He was like her, like that He admired what He'd made, and that He'd appreciate my humility and lack of pride. I believed that if I ever stumbled off the path, He'd watch out for me. He'd keep me safe.

Listening to Matt, I'm like, must be nice, dude, growing up thinking you had some divine right to safety. It's not just Matt, though; it's most of these guys. I swear some are *still* waiting, even now, for a ship to appear and rescue them from their little deserted island. Keep watching the horizon, morons, I want to say, she's on her way! But I don't bother with the guys much anymore, especially not the new arrivals, because what's the point? Everybody's in his own head, his own world, staring down the empty waves. Not once in my sliver of life, as Matt calls it, did I expect a person other than myself to save me, not Gran or Pops, not even Mr. Forsythe, definitely not Monica. If they helped me out once or twice, lifted me up, cut me a break, they did it in their own way on terms that benefited them somehow, not because of their relative Goodness, or because I asked. Did you ever hear me ask? If I wanted anything from life, it was someone to look out *for*, which is what I got, for a while, with Shane, and the kids at the Club, and with Monica, too, in a way—who was babysitting who in that Hacienda?—and mostly all of that felt pretty great. It felt like enough, at least, more than I'd expected. I wanted it to go on and on, even if we had to pretend it was realer than it was. I was a big kid, remember, all gimme gimme gimme. I'm much wiser now, even though I haven't changed a bit.

I'm not Matt. I don't have his discipline. Which is to say, these days I'm back to my old ways, following Monica around like a dog, lapping my name up off the floor every time it drops from her lips. A Gypsy lady in Italy started it, I think, because since Monica sat down with her she's been calling out to me, and in a way that makes her happy. Like right now, this very moment, a guy whose real name is Mike is placing a red leather collar around her neck. He's attaching the Velcro straps, testing the tug with his finger between the collar and her throat. I'm standing behind her when he turns her around by grabbing both her shoulders. Immediately, she puts her hands behind her back and holds them just over the crack of her beautiful bare ass. She opens her legs a little wider. It's not the first time she's come to this room with Mike, sat for a minute to catch up on their lives like she used to do with her girlfriends, handed him some cash, taken off her clothes and jewelry, and submitted to him; it's not the first time she's stood in the window light facing me as the man velcroes two more red collars, smaller ones, around her wrists.

She breathes deep, relaxes, throws back her head. I wish I could smell her breath, the sweat in her armpits. I wish I could stick my thumb in her mouth, feel her bite down. Now the man takes a belt with what look like key rings at both ends and attaches one end of the belt to the back of the neck collar and the other end through the leather loops of the wrist collars. When he tightens the belt along her spine, making sure she's fully bound, he can't see the big smile that breaks across her face, but I can. It's the smile I'm wearing, too. I put my hands on her waist, ask her if she's okay—she's okay—as he covers her eyes with a mask.

Thank you, Steven, she says at the first crack of the whip. It's not one of those long black whips that cowboys use but a kind of mini-mop he holds in his fist and waves around like a wand. I'd never seen one of those before. Every time he smacks her with it, this guy who's now me, she breaks out in that same ecstatic smile, like she's not just surprised by what he's doing to her again and again, she's *astonished*, she's *grateful*, and she lets out a little yelp to prove it's working, to show her appreciation, to ask for more. The little mop makes pink blotches on her cheeks and back. Every time he smacks her with it, he rubs the new blotch with his bare hand, soothing her, and she says, *thank you, Steven.* He tickles the soles of her feet with it, making her squirm and laugh and shimmy across the bed. He chases her, catches her, holds her by the neck collar, and when he asks if she's had enough, she says, with giggle tears running down from under her mask, *no, Steven! Don't stop, Steven! More, Steven!*

When their time is up, and he pulls off the mask, she seems a little sad. The sadness lingers when he frees her wrists, and he becomes Mike again, and when she puts her rings back on, and when she doesn't move after the gate goes up in the hotel parking garage, and when she steps out of the shower at home and examines the faded blotches in the mirror, and when she falls asleep in her bed beside Arthur watching a soccer match, and when she wakes up alone. To be honest, she seems sad most of the time, which is why I'm trying to help her. Like, if she forgets, I set her phone on its charger so she'll start off the day with a full battery. Like, I switch the shoes on her shoe rack to left-right instead of right-left because it bothers me otherwise and should bother her, too. Like, I flip open one of her Italian magazines and leave it on a page of two people kissing. I'm trying to send a certain message, but she never notices. I shouldn't be surprised; she was never much of a noticer, and I was no expert at communication. Is any guy? But I'll keep trying. I'll get better.

The way I see it, time here is not a jumping frog or a dream or a game of 52 pickup. It's not as complicated as all that, or much different from how it was in the Before, which is why I've never come up with my own theory of how it works. Time is still just one big moment after another big moment, and in between the big moments other stuff happens that you mostly forget. Then you string along the big moments in your memory and turn them into your story. I thought my memory was photographic, but the truth is that only the important stuff stuck. For example, I have no recollection of twisting my ankle on a rock in the Charles River around midnight on Saturday, February 17, 2018; I don't, and probably won't ever, remember how it felt to fall six feet two inches down onto the slab of concrete that cracked my head open. It must not have mattered much, otherwise I'd string it to some other moment and keep going over it the way some of these guys do. Instead, I go over Monica's pink nail polish that first day at the Club. The Band-Aid on Shane's left elbow. The dragons he drew on the surface of the pool. I string the dragons to his fist bump at the bottom of the stairs to Mr. Forsythe in the bleachers expecting big things from the boy on the diving board. I open the door of the bedroom and find a beautiful woman making herself a buffet just for me. We burrow deep inside each other, roll around on her bed like pigs in mud, slick and pink and grunting, as the smell of garlic and olive oil fills the room and opera music floats up from downstairs.

I could have kept all that going for a few more years at least, played her game, but I fucked it up by wanting more than my fair share.

Who did I think I was? She'd made it so easy for me, for us. She'd stuck her neck out. I had it better than anyone I knew, maybe even better than Arthur Binswanger himself. My housemates did drugs and got knocked up and worked shitty jobs; meanwhile, my biggest problem was my sore neck. I'm sorry, I say, when I pry her phone from her sleeping hand and place it on its charger, neaten up her shoes, draw a line in the dust on the spine of the Blue Sunshine CD. I'm sorry, she says to me, when she calls out, *thank you, Steven*, and *don't stop, Steven*, and *more, Steven*. We're still playing our games, and there are more big moments ahead of us, I can feel it.

Like right now, this very day, I'm following her through the crowd in the backyard of the Hacienda. It's hot out, I guess, the middle of summer, because everybody's in white pants and short-sleeved shirts and dresses with their tanned arms showing, but it's not a pool party, it's fancier. Monica drifts from the low tables covered in trays of food to the high tables where people stand around sipping from champagne glasses to the row of paintings on easels that make a giant semicircle on the patio. Shane stands just outside the circle, half behind one of his paintings, his fingers dancing to the piano music that twinkles onto the lawn through the open doors of the living room. He's wearing a crazy-looking suit, paisley I think it's called, all these pink sperm-like swirls, and a fat purple tie, and square black glasses, and he's so tall and skinny, I almost don't recognize him, a young man my age at least, with a big shit-eating grin on his face. Did I teach him that? When he sees Monica, he loops his arm through hers and together they walk up and down the patio, weaving between the easels. Shane walks tall. Monica squeezes her friends' elbows when she passes, saying thank you and what a good choice they made.

I wish she'd slow down a little and let me look more closely at the paintings. They're different from the ones I've seen before: no dragons or castles, no whales or shipwrecks or mermen or monsters. There are real people in these, the same repeating characters: an old man with a mouth so wide open it takes over his entire face, a woman with eyes swirling into rainbows, a naked baby with octopus arms. In at least one of the paintings—slow down!—I see a smiling red-haired man rising up out of blue water; in another, the same man is floating on the edge of the sky. He's got black arrows on his chest going different directions and blotches on his face that match the color of his hair. Not even Monica could miss him.

I finally get it, the older-woman thing. You can't watch Bonnie with Leo all this time, and hear Steve go on and on about Monica, and listen to Matt cursing Tessa and crying out for his mom, and *not* get it. Even Caleb gets it, I bet; no offense, but James Hahn is just his gay version of the old lady who came along. Anyway, my parents were more like bratty kids than responsible adults, and they definitely shortchanged me in the parental love department, but I can't say it's their fault that no Bonnie or Lori or Monica or James ever came along for me, that I had no idea the world was full of Bonnies and Loris and Monicas and Jameses looking for young and messed-up guys to save. I blame myself. My own unworthiness. Good for nothing, Patricia used to say. One of the few times she spoke the truth. Some of us are just born that way.

I get this, too: if you love a person enough, you can live an entire life through them and not miss your own. I'm not Matt; I'm not gripping tight to my cherished childhood memories, my afternoons in Patricia's basement, my nights behind the register at Penza's, roaming the aisles of Electric Fetus, shooting up on Abe's skunky couch, popping pills in the park the lot the yard the woods, all the everywheres I tried to hide from the hooded man, who found me every time. But he can't find me here. He can't find Katie because she's gone, too. It's just me and Leo. I grip tight to him in all the everywheres he and Bonnie don't have to hide. They show up to their potlucks and movie nights and karaoke bars, places they'll want to remember, and the only man following them is me. I walk so close to Leo I almost trip him, I'm almost on top of him, clinging to him like Katie clung to me down the bunny slope at Hyland Hills. Every step I take with Leo I forget more of myself, I shed pieces of my old skin like a snake, until one day—we're getting so close, I can sense it—nothing of the old Leo will be left, and I'll become him. Good for something. That's when I'll really be saved.

Right now we're driving through Orlando on our way to Cape Canaveral. Leo's behind the wheel of a camper that's more like a floating house with big windows I can't stop looking out of. I couldn't wait to turn eighteen so I could move here and live with my dad and work as a roadie for Wild Horses, but now look at me, almost an old man myself, flush with Awkworld money and all the time in the world, hypnotized by the palm trees. Bonnie's hungry and wants to stop and walk Constance and check out the downtown, but we're less than an hour from Cocoa Beach, Leo says, and if we don't hit traffic we'll make it in time to catch the sunset. Constance will be fine, says Leo, and tosses Bonnie a granola bar. She's pissed, but he wins the argument, promising to stop in the city on the way back, and maybe even add an extra day at Disney. He's never seen the ocean, he reminds her. Neither have I.

But then we do hit traffic, and it's like we're literally crawling along the interstate. Bonnie folds her arms in a told-you-so-asshole kind of way, and they don't talk, and Constance barks at seagulls, and the three of us just sit and squirm in our seats, willing the cars in front of us to get out of our way. Then Leo gets the best idea ever and switches the music to Manowar's *Kings of Metal*, which would pump up just about anybody to storm the beaches of Florida.

High and mighty alone we are kings
Whirlwinds of fire we ride

"Must we really?" says Bonnie, when Leo turns up the volume so high the speakers flutter, but there's a smile in her voice. This is what I mean about these older ladies. They're hungry and tired and mad at you, but they still reach over and rub your shoulders and scratch the back of your neck because you've been driving for three days and they know how you're longing to get your toes in the sand. She looks pretty in a flowy yellow dress that hangs off her shoulders and barely covers her knees. She puts her bare feet up on the dashboard and rolls down the window so the people next to us can see her pale fuzzy legs and hear us sing along to "The Crown and the Ring." She knows the words as good as Leo and I do and raises both fists when she belts out, *whirlwinds of fire we ride!* Most people smile at us and honk their horns in a friendly way but then of course there's this one redneck guy who sticks his ugly tongue out at Bonnie and grabs his crotch. She flips him the bird and calls him a dirtbag, which makes me nervous because we're basically trapped next to him on the highway, looking down on him from the heights of our camper. Bonnie's fearless, though. She leans over and plants a kiss on Leo's mouth and then blows it down to the redneck guy. He makes gagging noises and shakes his head and turns up his own crappy music and faces straight ahead ignoring us cracking up at him.

What I'm saying is that we have fun, Leo and Bonnie and me, and the longer I stick with them, the longer the dream stays the same dream and doesn't dissolve the way it used to, which can only mean I'm getting closer. It takes concentration to stay in the dream, to sit patiently in the jolty traffic, to tune out Matt and Steven and Caleb calling to me and the new boys crying for help, but the loud music, and knowing the words to the songs, and reading the billboards, and watching the palm trees bend and sway, helps me focus. I can't let my old life bubble up, force itself on me, so I nuzzle closer to Leo and wrap my arms tighter around him, making myself see what he's seeing, which is usually just Bonnie's face looking back at him, but today it's also the cars on the 528 finally speeding up and the exit for Cocoa Beach and the bright blue water coming into view.

We park and jump down from the camper, and Leo kicks off his shoes and takes off his shirt and runs straight in up to his knees, carrying me on his back. Bonnie and Constance stand at the edge of the surf, Constance afraid of the crashing waves, Bonnie staring up at the clouds that have burst into red-and-orange flames. I climb up onto Leo's shoulders, his head between my legs, my feet kicking his chest, ready to chicken-fight the college guys next to us. "This is amazing!" he says, stretching out his arms, the water up to his big round belly, but of course he's talking to Bonnie, and he means the warm ocean and the breeze on his naked skin and the colors of the sky. "I love you!" he says, and of course it's still Bonnie he's shouting out to, not the brother he can't see or feel but somehow knows is there. It doesn't matter, though; it still makes me happy to hear him say it. The happiest I've ever been.

I'm not on some rich guy's yacht in Key West. I'm with James in Raleigh, I think it's Raleigh, in the bedroom of his first-floor apartment with the cracked mirror and the duck pond. The drapes are pulled shut across sliding doors that lead to the patio. Light forces itself around the edges of the drapes on all sides. The TV is on. James is propped up on pillows on his side of the bed, the right, next to the nightstand crowded with three pairs of eyeglasses, half-finished crossword puzzles printed out, pencils, a pencil sharpener, pill bottles, tubes of lip balm, a cell phone plugged into its charger, and empty plates and mugs. He's wearing my old EARTH DAY T-shirt, frayed around the neck, yellowed in the pits. A hardcover of one of Iris's books—*Austen's Many Mothers: Imagination as Liberation in Eighteenth-Century Women's Writing*—lies face-down on his chest.

I should have taken Iris's class. I might have fallen in love with her, too. James was always praising her intellect. An unsung genius, he called her. "Imagination as liberation" sounds like a fairly obvious concept to me, though. Who doesn't know that if you work hard enough, you can delude yourself into anything? The problem is I was never all that curious about the past. I went through the motions in Debate, of course, arguing one side or the other, full of passion and respect for history, for precedent, for the generations that shaped it, but it was the future I couldn't take my eyes off of.

You might think guys like Matt, Steven, Leo, and me have nothing better to do these days than follow our people around. But that's not true for all of us. We get busy. We have a lot to go over with each other, with ourselves. The choices we made. The choices our families made for us. Our countries. Our so-called friends. Remembering it all, putting it in order, shouting it over the noise. It's work. I'm not Leo. Sometimes I can't stay in the dream. Sometimes James slips my mind. Sometimes I try to force him *out* of my mind. But I'm like the drapes in this room. I can't block all of him.

What I'm trying to say is that the street goes both ways. They come to us, too. James, Lori, Monica, Leo. Our people. When they ache for us so badly it nearly knocks them down, we feel that ache, too, like it's pulling at us from our guts, and that's when we go to them. Walk behind them, sit beside them, try to right them in their chairs. I wish we could tell them this. But some things are impossible to say.

James must have been dreaming about me again because when I got here he was fast asleep, his right arm hanging over the bed's metal bar. Now I'm sitting beside him on the edge of the mattress watching his chest rise and fall. I put my hand over his heart even though I can't feel it. I can only observe the motion, the flutter of his eyelids.

I'm reading his neck like it's a map. The four deep lines across it are rivers flowing east to west, with a network of shallow tributaries branching off to the north and south. His Adam's apple is a tall, rounded mountain in the valley between those two stretchy muscles that hold up his head. The hollow part just above his collarbone is a canyon, the little creases are trails. *Jamesland*, I think. I once traveled every inch of this country. Now I'm tracing my finger along one of its deepest rivers, following its path over rough terrain. His lips are dry and peeling. The pink moles on the top of his head have gotten meatier. His whittled-down legs stick out from under the quilt. He changed so quietly. Is it strange that I still find him beautiful? Even after all these years, there's so much left of him.

I've been numb for so long that when feeling finally comes I almost don't recognize it. Warmth. Skin. Feeling shoots through me, and it's like the jolt, like the boom, like victory. My body electric for the first time in forever. Alive. I grab James's face with both hands to hold it again, to pull it to me, to wake him, to tell him. His scruff is scratchy brittle fur. I kiss his lips, his cheeks, his hairy ears, the mountain and the canyon. His same sweet smokiness fills my lungs. *It's Caleb*, I say. *I'm here.* I'm shouting as loud as I can, my voice echoing off the bare walls. My teeth vibrate. I'm sweating! He goes on sleeping. Snoring like an old man. *Get up!* I say. Somehow I know that his dream is ending and that he'll wake into this new one of mine. I climb on top of him. I don't care that I'm crushing him. He's fleshy enough to bear my weight. I pull up his shirt—my shirt, our shirt—and lay my head on his bare chest, nuzzling into that patch of soft white hair, kissing it, breathing it in. We rise and fall together. My body with his body. His heartbeat is like distant thunder. It crackles and strikes, crackles and strikes again. I listen as it moves farther and farther off, like a storm passing to the next town.

ACKNOWLEDGMENTS

I am very grateful to the National Endowment for the Arts, Key West Literary Seminar, and Brandeis University for providing crucial financial support and residency opportunities during the writing of *Last Seen*.

Janet Silver and Patrick Nolan expertly shaped the novel from its earliest iterations, ensured that it found a good home, and, trickiest of all, managed my numerous anxieties throughout the process. Thank you for being such fierce, ardent, and savvy advocates.

Special thanks to Andrea Schulz and Brian Tart for welcoming me back to Viking. I'm honored to be on your illustrious list of authors.

Emma Dollar made each page of this book better with her sharp attention to the micro and the macro; she assisted the publication process at every stage with alacrity and preternatural wisdom.

The first-rate copyediting team of Katie Hurley and Chandra Wohleber, along with eagle-eyed proofreaders Logan Hill and Ryan Richardson, gave the manuscript a thorough and sparkling glow-up.

A novelist is lost without smart, thorough, and honest readers to offer insightful feedback on full-length early drafts. Lucky for me, Chip Cheek, Stacey D'Erasmo, Sonya Larson, Alex Marzano-Lesnevich, Stephen McCauley, Celeste Ng, and Whitney Scharer spent countless hours with multiple versions of *Last Seen* and improved it immeasurably. Jennifer De Leon, Calvin Hennick, Adam Stumacher, and Grace Talusan workshopped chapters along the way and made excellent suggestions. I'm forever indebted to you all.

Justin Surrett enthusiastically answered all my bro-ey questions, choreographed and proofed the sick moves in Matt's final scene, and, along with Travis Frederick, Tej Menon, and Andrew Castellucci, spent an afternoon in Ann Arbor schooling me on the mindset of the wrestler. Over the course of her semester at Colby, Angela Fernandez compiled and annotated an extensive file of Smiley Face material; thank you, Debra Spark, for introducing us. Defense attorney Walter Lesnevich provided sage legal counsel on a number of topics, including the legal ramifications of Tessa's and Kenneth's actions. Carolyn Hohl kindly gave me a crash course in Latin—and fixed my errors—at the eleventh hour. In sundry matters of millennial dialogue, psychiatry, and life in the Twin Cities, respectively, I turned to Hallie Kamosky, AJ Pesaro, Jennifer McLean, and Parker Ousley.

I wrote *Last Seen* almost entirely in coffee shops in Provincetown, Boston, and Key West. A big shout-out to the owners and baristas at Kohi, Joe Coffee, Pavement at Symphony, and Cuban Coffee Queen—especially Diana, Glenn, Mark, and Caden—for tolerating my long stays and for providing patronage in the form of free cappuccinos and pastries.

The character of Derrick was inspired in part by Malone in the novel *Dancer from the Dance* by the great Andrew Holleran. Any resemblance between the two is an intentional homage.

Writing this novel was a refuge during a challenging period of my life, and I am especially grateful for the various pep talks, opportunities, literary commiserations, and enormously kind favors big and small from Debra Allbery, Miriam Altshuler, Amanda Baker, Jenna Blum, Lisa Borders, Liz Braun, Gregory Burns, Evan Calbi, Christopher Dufault, Miciah Bay Gault, Jennifer Grotz, Kate Hohl, Jessica Keener, Aaron Lecklider, Rebekah Lengel, Lisa Leone, Margot Livesey, Clint Morris, Alix Ohlin, Peter Orner, Anna Rimoch, Katrin Schumann, Chuck Selvaggio, Barbara Shapiro, Preety Sidhu, Rose Smith, Justin Smotherman, Laura van den Berg, and Noah Whitford, among many others already mentioned above.

Michael Borum, my patient and loving partner of twenty-nine years, holds my hand through every joy and sorrow, and makes all the best things possible. *Te amabo in aeternum . . .*